Also by Ann Alexandra

Secret Lives

The Romance they never expected...
  The Love that binds their souls...
  The Danger that threatens to destroy
  them both…

"An unputdownable romantic thriller! Highly recommended and a Red Ribbon Winner!" 2015 Wishing Shelf Book Awards*

Second Place Winner! *2015 Book Buyers Best Award*

"Outstanding Novel" and Fourth Place Winner! *2015 People's Choice Award*

Hidden Truths by Ann Alexandra

For Mom and Dad

Who Worked So Hard So That I Could Have Wings to Fly

In Loving Memory

I0546464

Acknowledgements

I want to thank my wonderful beta readers—Rosemary Butcher and Beverly Norwood—for their generous consideration in taking the time to read *Hidden Truths* in advance of publication, and for providing me with their honest feedback and invaluable support.

Chapter 1

Her whole body turned to ice. Her muscles went rigid, as if frozen in time. The images that shaped her world started fading into the amorphous clouds of a new dimension, where everything swirled in a gray and silent mass. She could have heard the proverbial 'pin' drop as she stared at the photographs in her hand. Her eyes strained to focus on what she was looking at, but the shock of the images numbed her senses and blurred her vision.

These can't be real, she thought, as she slowly slipped one photo behind the next. These...she wouldn't do that...she wouldn't...she's not like that...she's not...she's just not. "She's not," she asserted, unaware she had spoken out loud.

"What? She's not what?" the man standing before her asked, noncommittally.

"Huh?" she looked up suddenly, eyes wide, brows raised, as if startled out of a reverie, and surprised to find someone standing there. His narrowed eyes focused intensely on her face, so that he could read the slightest alteration in her expression.

"You said 'she's not'. 'She's not'...what?" the man repeated.

Half mumbling to herself as she looked down again at the photos in her hand, Elaine replied, "She's not....she wouldn't...cheat on her husband." And then she lifted her head again, looked the man straight in the eyes, and said with more conviction, "She's *not* having an affair...with *anyone*...let alone multiple men. Especially, not with *these* men!"

Elaine shoved the photos back into the man's hand, placed her hands on her hips, and faced him squarely, her own eyes narrowing with determination. "Look, I don't know who manufactured these pictures, but you can be sure," she declared, her voice firm and steady now, "that they are not genuine. Representative Blanchard is very much in love with her husband. She has a wonderful and happy marriage. Obviously, someone is trying to sabotage her run for the U.S. Senate," she declared emphatically.

And before he could comment she added, with more force as she pummeled his lapel with her right forefinger, "Look, if you publish these photos with the election just ten days away, it won't matter that they're phony, because just the allegation will destroy her election chances. The sensationalism of the accusation will be all that matters, and you know that. Everybody knows that!

"The fact that she's running eleven points ahead of her opponent right now won't matter come election day," Elaine elaborated, with a tinge of anger, as she returned her hands firmly to her hips. "This kind of damage can't be undone—not ten weeks before an election, let alone ten days. The public tends to go with the allegations rather than the truth, especially when—and probably because—it's the allegations that get reported over and over again. Just try finding anyone who followed up with a report that allegations or rumors were, in fact, false. If you're lucky, you might find a retraction on the obituary page, for all the good that's going to do," she shrugged, dropping her hands lifelessly by her sides before she flung them in the air with, "And if a retraction is—by some unheard of miracle—actually reported at all, it'll probably be *after* the voting is over, rather than *before*!"

As Elaine began to breathe more evenly now, she added, in a steadier voice, "Obviously, Billingsley is desperate, and he's put someone up to this. He's tried a few dirty tricks this election—but I must say, this is really the dirtiest!" And then she eyeballed the man point blank again, and demanded, "So, are you going to be Billingsley's *patsy*? Are you going to spread his lies, so you can help throw the election his way? Or are you going to report the *truth*?"

"And just what is the truth, Ms. Kent?" the man eyeballed Elaine right back, with a single raised eyebrow challenging her. He folded his arms across his chest, leaving the photos dangling from one hand. As he watched her intently, wondering how she would tackle this threat to her boss, he found himself looking into the darkest brown eyes he had ever seen. Hmmm, he thought as he stared, and noted: light brown, almost sandy, hair, and dark brown eyes. What an unusual combination... And all those short curls bouncing around her face!

As she continued to stare boldly back at him, eyeball to eyeball, Elaine slowly became aware of an unexpected wave of heat, pushing its way from deep inside her, to the surface of her skin, in its manic search for a way to escape her body. Oh, goodness, she thought, I can't possibly be having hot flashes—I'm decades away from menopause. And then the realization struck her, as she caught the flicker of amusement behind those twinkling midnight blue eyes that were watching her. He was mocking her, she thought, as indignation welled up inside her breast, forcing her body to straighten its stance. Why that little...who the hell does he think he is? Coming in here with these photos, and flinging around accusations! Well, she'll put him in his place!

Fortunately, giving vent to her anger, even if only to herself, cooled her off enough to realize, of course, that he wasn't flinging around accusations. He had asked to see her specifically, and then he showed her the photos—clearly looking for an explanation, or at least for her boss's explanation. It did seem like he was trying to be fair by giving the Congresswoman a chance to tell her side of the story before he published the photos.

But how could anyone explain these photos? They appeared to show her boss in sexual encounters with three of the most despicable—at least in Elaine's opinion—lobbyists in Washington, D.C. But Elaine knew, deep down in her gut, that her boss would not have an affair with anyone, let alone some of the very lobbyists she's fought so hard against during her eight years in the U.S. House of Representatives.

Elaine had grown up living down the street from the Blanchards. She had known them all of her life, well before Kate Blanchard had run for her first political office. Elaine knew that Representative Blanchard was a hard-working elected official who understood, only too well, the political shenanigans that dominated elections today, and how deadly even the slightest hint of inappropriate or unconventional behavior could be to a candidate's electoral chances. It seemed to Elaine that the very wealthy could get away with all kinds of chicanery, but regular folks were still being held to a more traditional standard. This may be the 21st century, but the electorate was generally still in the Victorian age when it came to judging most of their elected officials, Elaine believed. She was convinced that her boss would never do anything stupid that would destroy her political career, or her chances for higher office, let alone have an affair that could shatter her marriage. No candidate in their right mind would take any risk that might lead to campaign-ending rumors, especially just days before a big election.

Elaine was well aware, however, that there were unscrupulous campaigners willing to do anything to derail a political opponent; all too often, the truth was obscured by the most blatant of lies. And the sensationalism generated by false accusations was more "newsworthy" than finding and reporting the truth.

Elaine was roused from her thoughts by the sound of a man clearing his throat. She squared her shoulders and faced the man, and in as formal and official a voice as she could muster under the circumstances, she suggested, "Look, give those photos back to me, and I will prove to you they are phony. Meanwhile, if you stick around for a half hour, I can guarantee you an audience with Representative Blanchard, and you can hear it directly from her, that these pictures have been created, rather than taken. Honestly, I'm surprised you would just accept such garbage without having them checked yourself," she chuckled under her breath at what she considered his obvious lack of experience.

But the man smiled enigmatically at Elaine, and replied, "But that's why I'm here, Ms. Kent. I did have an expert look at the photos before coming here—and he declared them to be genuine."

Chapter 2

Elaine stood in front of him with eyes that nearly bulged from shock, and with her mouth agape, unable to utter a sound, as if the air had been sucked out of her lungs. She stared at the man like he was a raving lunatic from another planet. Genuine? The photos were genuine? He was standing there telling her that the photos were genuine? That's ludicrous! This must be some sort of trick, her mind reasoned. Those photos couldn't possibly be genuine! Maybe he was in on the ruse! Maybe he had even manufactured the photos himself! Maybe he was just looking to make a name for himself! Maybe he...who *was* he, anyway?

And with that question, Elaine finally regained some presence of mind, enough at least to inquire, "Who *are* you, and why are you doing this?"

"My name is Jack Amory," he replied, rather blandly, "and I'm a reporter for a blog that covers legislative and political issues concerning Congress. The blog is called *TheSeeker.com*. Perhaps you've heard of it?" he raised his brows ever so slightly, waiting just a moment for some sign of recognition. When none came, he added, "And these photos are a *very hot* political issue, Ms. Kent."

"A blog? You write for a *blog*?" Elaine queried in disbelief, her eyes wide and round with amazement.

"That's right. A blog. Is that a problem?"

"You mean you are *not* from any main stream media? Or even underground, or off beat, newspapers? Just a *blog*?" Elaine was trying to grasp the notion that her boss's Senate race could be derailed by something as inconsequential as a *blog,* but she struggled with the idea. Who reads political *blogs*, she wondered. But she knew that, regardless of the source publicizing the photos, the photos would produce a potent political scandal that would quickly be picked up by the main stream media.

"You shouldn't belittle blogs, Ms. Kent," Amory stated, with a touch of resentment infiltrating his words. "Remember, it was a blog that blew the lid off of a former

President's peccadillos," Jack Amory looked meaningfully at her, as his eyes locked on her gaze with a penetrating stare.

"Look, I'm here to get your boss's response to these photos," he continued, with a steady, even voice. "If you would rather I report them, and then say your boss had no comment, I can do that, Ms. Kent, but it wouldn't look good for her."

"You mean it won't look good for *you* if you report a story and can't get the victim to comment on it!" Elaine countered, rather heatedly, as she tried to pull her glance away from his mesmerizing eyes. What's the matter with me, she wondered, as she literally shook herself to break away from his gaze. And when she finally got control of her senses, she added, "Look, you come here with phony photos that you say are genuine, and you want my boss to comment on what you are going to report as genuine?"

"No, I'm here to give your boss a chance to deny these liaisons ever occurred, if that's what she can do," Jack patiently replied.

His audacity made her pulse race. "But you just said you believe the photos are genuine! When were you going to mention that little tidbit? Huh? Are you setting yourself up to write a story where you report that Representative Blanchard denies these liaisons, and then you spring your so-called 'evidence' that the photos are genuine, making a liar out of her? Wow!" Elaine huffed in anger. "That's a pretty clever ruse, isn't it? What a sensational headline— 'Congresswoman Seeking Senate Seat *Lies* About Adulterous Liaisons'! That would make your blog a household name across the country, wouldn't it?!" Elaine hissed at him, hands on her hips again.

Jack blanched at the insinuation, anger beginning to boil in the depths of his blue eyes, whose dark foreboding foretold the coming storm. In a voice seething with heat, and spitting out every word individually, he countered, speaking through his teeth, "Ms...Kent, ..you.. can..either..."

"But breaking a story," Elaine angrily and forcefully interrupted, the decibel level of her voice rising, "that supposedly 'catches' a member of Congress in a blatant lie, is an even bigger story than just a story about any sexual liaisons, isn't it, Mr. Amory? Such a story, and the resulting notoriety it would engender for your blog, is bound to get you offers—*lucrative* offers—from several of the main stream media outlets—isn't it...*Mr. Amory*?" Elaine practically shouted at him, resentment at such manipulation fueling her anger.

The storm that was brewing in the back of Amory's dark blue eyes was raging now. Had he been stupid to come and give the Congresswoman a chance to explain away the photos? He had had them checked, yes, and they were declared genuine, by one of the best local experts on photo manipulation. But knowing Representative Blanchard's spotless, and stalwart, reputation, left him with some misgivings. And receiving the photos anonymously in the mail also kept nagging at his conscience, and made him question the motives of the sender—whoever that might be.

Ms. Kent could very well be right, that someone might be trying to use him as a patsy to kill Blanchard's campaign. He almost wished there were, indeed, some plausible explanation. But then, how can you explain away even one, let alone multiple, sexual encounters with men that were not her husband? Even worse, these were all lobbyists whose agendas Blanchard had vehemently opposed—at least in public—as destructive of both the nation's long term interests, and the welfare of the American people, in general. It wasn't just a sexual scandal that was being represented in these photos—it was a full-blown attack on Blanchard's integrity and credibility. She wouldn't just lose her race for the Senate—her political career would be so shredded that she could never run for any elective office again. That understanding had sent alarm bells whistling through his head from the first. Whoever sent these to him was going straight for the jugular. So he had to have his facts solidly nailed down.

If he just ignored the photos, and did not report on them, he was sure the pictures would surface through another outlet. And he had no idea how long "Anonymous" would wait before sending the photos to someone else for publication. So he had to find out what was going on, and as quickly as possible, or there might indeed be a destructive scandal that shredded the reputation and career of a dedicated, and popular, public servant who truly looked out for the public interest. And he was only too keenly aware of the powerful political enemies that Representative Blanchard had collected during her years in office.

Jack realized that Elaine Kent's concerns were normal —he had them himself. That calmed him down enough to be able to confess, "I'm sorry, Ms. Kent. I realize how this looks, but you're on the wrong track. Let me explain," he almost pleaded.

Elaine looked askance at him, but noted his changed manner, so she conceded, but with skepticism, "Go ahead. I'm listening," as she folded her arms across her chest.

"Look, I have enormous respect for Representative Blanchard. Whoever sent these photos to me wants to destroy her career as a public servant, permanently—no prisoners taken. If I wait for too long, then I'm sure someone else will find the photos in his or her mailbox, just like I did. I doubt someone else will be as concerned, or as scrupulous, as I'm trying to be, and will just throw them out there to gain some notoriety for themselves, the hell with what the photos will do —fairly or unfairly—to Blanchard's career, and the coming election.

"I had a highly respected expert on photo manipulation examine these, and he told me they were genuine. I'm a skeptical guy, so I want to nail down every possible glitch, to make sure lies are not used to turn an election. You see," and here he loosened his stance enough to display some exasperation, "I do not want to be a tool of some lie master, or puppeteer. I'm also being selfish—I do *not* want the kind of notoriety that will ensue if I publicize these photos and they are subsequently found, in fact, to be fakes. I do not, in other words, want to make a fool of myself!" he finished as he let out a huge sigh, spreading his hands wide to emphasize his exasperation, as well as his sincerity.

"So, Ms. Kent," he continued, "are you going to convince me how these photos are not real, as you insist? Or are you just going to try to stonewall me with arguments and shouts?" and his posture relaxed somewhat as he waited for her reply.

She stood there scouring his face for even the slightest indication, or hint, of deceitfulness or double-dealing. She searched the depths of his eyes, and the sharp line of wrinkles on his face, and the way he looked unflinchingly straight at her without any gesture of discomfort. Finally, she admitted to herself that she couldn't find any suggestion of duplicity. He sensed her body release some of her tension as she replied, and he knew she believed what he had told her, even if she still hated him for the pandora's box he had opened. But he found some cheer in remembering that when Pandora opened her box to let all those human ills escape, 'hope' still remained in the bottom of the box.

"Mr. Amory. You may have had what you consider to be a highly respected analyst examine these photos," Elaine replied evenly, "but I *personally* know the best in the industry. And I will have him look at these, and tell us what is really going on. In other words, I am going to take pity on your *naivete'* and *save your neck*!" she said, as she jabbed her finger at the knot in his tie to emphasize each point. "I am going to overlook your stupidity (jab), your inability to assess what's really going on around you (jab), and your obvious helplessness (big jab)! I'm going to help you in your quest to get to the bottom of this attack. And if you wait here, or return here in exactly thirty minutes, I will give you the *privilege* of speaking with Representative Blanchard herself, directly, one on one, to get her response." And with that, Elaine turned into Blanchard's inner office. Honestly, she harrumphed to herself, how could *anyone* be so blind?

He wasn't going to let her walk away with the last word. He wasn't stupid. He wasn't naive. And he wasn't helpless! She should be grateful, he told himself with passion, that he was fair enough, and objective enough, to be giving her boss an opportunity to enlighten him before the pictures got published. Someone—*any*one—else would likely just have gone with the pictures without even checking since, as she pointed out, the media were hooked on sensationalism. What they cared about was the buzz a story created, and the viewership/readership and ratings they got because of it—and how increased audience levels translated into increased advertising dollars. "Truth" was, all too often, a nonentity, he acknowledged—having little to do with this kind of attack.

So he followed her into Blanchard's inner office, and was about to grab her arm to turn her around to face him, so he could tell her, in no uncertain terms, how wrong she was, when a piercing, screeching sound rang through their ears. When they both ran back out of Blanchard's office, it stopped.

"What on earth...?" Elaine cried, feeling a little shell-shocked, the screech still ringing in her ears.

"Sounded like someone was trying to break our ear drums!" Jack responded, feeling somewhat dazed himself.

"But what could it be? What could have caused that horrible sound?" Elaine asked, as she gingerly approached the doorway again to the Congresswoman's private office.

Playing the gallant, Jack put his hands on her shoulders to draw her back, saying, "Here, let me go in first, and see what I can find."

To her surprise, Elaine decided not to object. But just as Jack stepped inside the doorway, and started walking into the room, the screeching returned, so he quickly backed out again to where Elaine was standing.

"It's you!" Elaine cried, her voice rising in astonishment.

"What do you mean, it's me?" Jack asked, eyes wide with questioning.

"Well, think a minute. I was in the room already, but it only started screeching when you entered. And now, again, when you entered the room, it started screeching again!" Elaine finished with a flourish, pleased with her observations.

And then, as if the sun were shining through after a raging thunderstorm, Jack's eyes lit up. He reached toward his back pocket, and removed what turned out to be a radio frequency scanner that could pick up the Capitol Police radio communications. You never know what political scoops you might discover, he had reasoned, just from following the Capital Police around. He placed it on Elaine's desk in the outer office where they were standing. Then he slowly stepped back into Blanchard's inner office, one step at a time, placing one foot carefully, and slowly, after the other.

Jack was about ten feet into the office when he called out, a bit victoriously, "No screeching!" He quickly returned to where Elaine was waiting, retrieved his radio frequency scanner, and then again, slowly entered the inner office. He had barely gotten clear of the door when the screeching started again, and he retreated, running.

"Well," he reported to Elaine with a bright smile, "that's it!"

"What's 'it', exactly?!" she asked exasperatedly, returning her hands to her hips, staring at the object in Jack's hand. Then, in an unexpected moment of self-awareness, Elaine marveled at the discovery that she had been going back and forth, from crossed arms to hands-on-hips, back to crossed arms, etc. Well, that's a first, she remarked to herself. But not surprising, she noted, given the hornet's nest this guy has been throwing at us this morning. And she filed the realization away, in a mental drawer, to think about later.

"That, of course," Jack pointed to his scanner, in answer to her question. "I carry a scanner around to keep tabs on what the Capitol Police may get called on to deal with. It's picking up an electronic signal of some kind, and the likeliest culprit in here is an electronic bug!" he seemed almost delighted.

"A bug?" Elaine was incredulous. "As in—spying? As in, someone was listening in on whatever we were saying in that room?" and her eyes got big and round again, this time with astonishment.

"Unless you harbor some electronic snooping devices of your own in here?" he queried cavalierly, with another raised eyebrow.

"Of course we don't!" Elaine nearly shouted. She went marching into the office, and started looking up and down and under and everywhere, moving this and that, in a desperate attempt to discover if he was right.

But it was Jack who found it, almost instantly, as he sauntered into the room, stopped for a moment to look around, and then walked directly to the coffee table in the middle of a conversational grouping of leather chairs and sofas. He lifted the table at an angle, and pointed victoriously to a tiny round metal object that was clinging to the underside of the table.

"No! Don't touch it!" Elaine hissed through her teeth, as Jack moved to pull the metal object away from its parasitic perch under the coffee table. She put a single finger up to her lips to silence him, grabbed his arm, and pulled him out of Blanchard's office. "Maybe there are fingerprints on it," she whispered up at him, when she thought they were out of reach of the bug.

"Who would be stupid enough to leave fingerprints on a bug?" he queried softly, leaning closer to her face, and feeling like he could drown in those soft, almost-black, pools that were her eyes. "I mean, if anyone is sophisticated enough to *plant* the bug, surely they are clever enough not to leave any fingerprints!" he exclaimed in a stage whisper, as he again headed for the office, and toward where the bug was still alive and well, and clinging to the underside of the coffee table.

"No, *don't*!" Elaine hissed again, grabbing the tail of his jacket, and dragging him back out towards her. "You're making a rash assumption! We don't know how clever this person is, or isn't." And then it struck her. "By the way, how did you know just where to find it?" she whispered, looking up at him amazed, her eyes bold now, not just with questioning, but with challenge.

"Common sense, Ms. Kent," he replied, a little smugly. "Where's the best vantage point to hear the full scope of a conversation? The center of a conversational group. Hence, the coffee table!" he finished, with a grand gesture of his arm, as he swung it to point toward the table in question. "And," he continued, "this coffee table is barely a few feet from her desk—close enough to pick up her end of a telephone conversation!" As he again headed inside the office to extract the bug, Elaine again cried, in what she thought was a good imitation of a stage whisper, "*No!*"

"Ms. Kent," Jack returned, and this time he was the one placing hands on hips, in frustration, to emphasize his point, as he stared directly into her wide and compelling eyes, "someone has sent compromising photos of your boss to a

15

political reporter, to get them released to the public. They may be phony, I grant you, though I have yet to see the proof of that," he emphasized, keeping his voice low. "And now we learn that someone has planted a bug in your boss's office. Someone is going to a lot of trouble to cause, well, *Trouble*! Whatever makes you think they are careless enough, or silly enough, to leave prints?" he finished, more than a little exasperated himself.

"Just my instincts, that's all. We don't *know* there are no prints on it. So let's just respect the possibility that there could be—can't we do that? Is that such a big deal?" and she looked up at him with a soft, almost pleading, appeal.

So, she's trying to play the innocent, Jack mused, as he looked down into those dark watery pools that seemed to have no bottom. A man could lose himself in the depths of those eyes, he found himself thinking. He could feel his resolve dissipating, as the sensation that he was spiraling down a whirlpool started to creep through his veins. Uh-oh, you fool, he jolted himself back to reality, just shake yourself loose, and focus on the problem at hand.

"And just how do you propose to get it unstuck from under the table, then?" he finally asked, with a single raised brow over his left eye.

How does he do that, Elaine wondered. Not just lifting one brow, but how he uses it to express some kind of sardonic criticism. And then she realized she was just standing there, staring at him. And from the tiny crinkles that she noticed forming around the outside corners of his eyes, he was obviously finding her fascination humorous.

She turned abruptly toward her desk, and pulled her handbag out of her lower desk draw. She opened it, pulled out a small leather clutch, and drew something long and shiny out of it. Holding it up, she turned and replied to Amory's question, "With this," she said, as she held up a slender steel finger file. "And we are going to put it in this tissue," she added, as she grabbed one from the box on top of her desk.

She stepped quietly into Blanchard's office, and extracted the bug from its hiding place. She returned triumphantly, and held it up for Amory's inspection, without saying a word. He just as silently removed it from her hand, still holding it in the tissue, and examined it. Then he deftly used the file to disable the device, and returned it to her, saying, "Ok, it's dead."

As she folded the tissue around the device, her eyes suddenly opened large again. She turned to him quickly, asking a bit breathlessly, "If the office is bugged, do you think her home here in the District is bugged, too?"

"Hhmmm. Good question. It's very possible," he noted, rubbing his chin with his hand, then adding, "but not necessarily guaranteed. How likely is it that people who have access to her office here, also have access to her home? I mean, don't lots of people visit here in her office, who might never see the inside of her home?"

"Well, yes, of course. But hadn't we better check her home, too?" And then she asked, as if to herself, "And how do we do that without involving the police?"

"Now that's the important question. What about the police?"

"If we call the Capitol Police now, then it won't be long before this gets out. I mean, even you have a scanner to listen to their calls. If some enterprising reporter," and here she narrowed her eyes as she looked pointedly at Jack, "hears the Capitol Police have been called to a Representative's office, they're bound to pick up on her name, and make a link to a big election race. They'll come running over here to find out what's going on, to see whether there's a story in it, or not. And if any reporter sees you in here, and has *any* idea who you are—as impossible as that may seam—then he, or she, is going to stick like glue until he, or she, finds out what's up. And then whoever sent those photos to you will have achieved their objective."

"But I could just be another skulking reporter," he grinned at her, innocently.

"Yeah, right, with you in here talking to the police—and you would have to, to explain this—no one will believe you just happened to arrive before anyone else. After all, anyone else would have to stay outside the door. No, we can't bring the police in on this yet," Elaine finished.

"Well, you could bring me to her house, and I could walk around with my scanner and see what we hear?" he offered. And for a fleeting moment he felt excited at the prospect of working *with* her to discover the answer to this mystery.

"Oh, goodness, *No!*" Elaine practically screamed. And Jack's fleeting moment of excitement gave up the ghost.

"And why not?" Jack asked, tensing up again, having taken personal offense at her instant sharp rejection. "After all, I'm here in her office now. What's the difference?"

"Really, are you so very dense?" Elaine queried, with exasperation. "If her office is bugged, and if someone is trying to peddle these horrible photos, maybe her home is under surveillance, too, not just bugged. Did that not occur to you?"

"Well," he conceded, rubbing his chin, "I see your point. Though it's not necessarily true. The likelihood is that whoever sent me these photos, also planted the bug. And so, if anyone is watching her home, it's probably for these same folks, perhaps looking for anything else that could be used against her." He paused a moment, and then he admitted, "It is likely, though, that if they saw me at her home, and I hadn't published the photos yet, they may write me off as a turncoat, and decide to shop these photos with someone else, pronto."

"Well," Elaine exclaimed with mock surprise, her eyes full of wonder, "you *are* capable, after all, of putting two and two together, and coming up with the right answer. Who would have thought?" and she drove the barb home with a chuckle.

Jack winced, feeling like he had just stepped into an ice cold shower. He turned towards the main doorway, then, to exit the office suite.

"My, but you have thin skin, Mr. Blogger!" Elaine laughed at his back, as she followed him to the door, arms crossed again, but this time in humor. "I would have thought that reporters would outfit themselves with the toughest outside casings available!" she mocked.

He stopped dead in his retreat, and turned sharply to face her squarely. His movement was so abrupt that she plowed right into him. He grabbed hold of her to push her away, but he kept a strong, vice-like grip on both of her arms. The muscles in his jaw tightened, as he stared directly into her cavernous eyes, and he spit out at her, "I am generally an easy going fellow, Ms. Kent, but even I have my limits!

"I have gone out of my way to investigate this matter fairly, and yet you have given me little beyond verbal denials, except to throw sarcastic and belittling barbs my way since I arrived," he hissed between clenched teeth. "You may not think much of blogging, Ms. Kent, but I am my own boss, and my own man. No one tells me what to write about, how to write about it, or when to write about it. Nobody owns me—I have no puppet strings attached to my pen. I'm not beholden to anyone for income. And I owe nothing to anyone. Now," he said conclusively, as the tension in his shoulders relaxed a little, while he retained his grip on hers, "I will return, as you suggested, in thirty minutes, for a one-on-one with Representative Blanchard. I hope you can keep your promises," he commented pointedly, as he abruptly dropped his hold on Elaine's arms, and walked out the door.

Chapter 3

Representative Blanchard leaned back in her leather chair and looked at him blandly, her muscles completely relaxed, as she asked, "Did you bother to ask your computer photo expert if the bodies and faces of the three 'gentlemen'," and she grimaced as she characterized them as such, "in these photos were real? If their photos are the primary original photo, and not just pasted heads or such, then they are the ones engaging in fraud, Mr. Amory. Though I admit that, even if they are pasted in, that would not necessarily exonerate them. They could still be the perpetrators."

They were in Blanchard's private office, with Kate Blanchard sitting behind her desk, while Elaine stood, leaning against a windowsill, with her back toward the window. With the light coming from behind her, Jack could not clearly read the expression on her face. He wasn't sure why this bothered him, but it did. Jack, himself, was in the hot seat, right in front of Blanchard's desk, directly opposite her, facing her squarely. The question raised the hairs on the back of his neck.

"Isn't the question whether *your* inclusion in these photos was added, or pasted in? I mean, if you were not pasted in, or your head not pasted onto the woman's body, then the photos must be genuine," Jack concluded, a little lamely, as Blanchard's point began to sink in. "Presumably, these are not pictures of you and your husband that have been doctored to look like you and another man."

"Oh, Mr. Amory, you are so naive. How do you survive in this rapacious political environment that we have today?" and she smiled innocently, as he clearly flinched at being called naive. "Or perhaps this little endeavor is an indication that you are not surviving well at all?" Pause. "I am telling you, unequivocally, that these photos are not genuine. They could not be. I am not sleeping with anyone except my husband. So, if I am telling the truth—and," she emphasized by leaning forward, "I assure you that I am—then how did whoever took these photos get pictures of three men I am supposed to be having liaisons with, and why these three men in particular? Hhmmmm?

"I mean, after all, the men are in compromising positions with *some*one, wouldn't you say? Perhaps they were all posing with a dummy, to hold a place for me to be added later? After all, the only part that is clearly recognizable as me is the woman's head, which doesn't seem to change from one photo to another, except in the angle of her head. How unrealistic is that? Furthermore, she's a bit hazy, wouldn't you say? Anyone could have cropped a head shot of me from one of many campaign photos, or from the thousands of articles written about me. It would be especially easy if they cropped a photo from an online article—like one in a blog," and she looked at Jack meaningfully.

"At any rate, if I am telling the truth," she continued, "then I ask you again, how did whoever sent you these photos get compromising pictures of each of these three gentlemen? If the men are genuinely part of the photo, then they must be behind this attempt to destroy my campaign. How could anyone else get such photos of them to use?" And she lifted a single eyebrow quizzically.

This time it was Jack on the receiving end of the single raised brow. He had been using that trick all of his life, even as a kid, to throw other people off their comfort zone. It said, or could say, so many different things. A single raised eyebrow was like a dare, or a punch in the face, about something. And now he was the one being walloped.

As he sat there facing her, wondering how to respond, Blanchard pushed her point, "So I ask again, are the photos of the men part of the original photos, or were they, too, photo-shopped in, like I have been?

"If the photos of the men are original, and not photo-shopped," she continued, not giving him a chance to reply, "how could a photographer get compromising photos of these three men, without their cooperation? These photos appear to be taken from *inside* a bedroom rather than through a window. How could someone hide inside a room—and a bedroom at that—and take these photos, and yet, not be seen?"

Jack realized the question was rhetorical, so he didn't even try to answer. Blanchard obviously had lots to say, so he just let her speak, while he listened very carefully, as her implications of his incompetence spread slowly through him with each word, like the spreading ringlets of waves around a stone dropped into a pond. And she kept hurling the stones.

"Suppose that whoever took these photos had gotten one photo that they could pass off as me, why would they have pursued more liaisons? One allegation of infidelity is enough to ruin my campaign. And why with these three men, in particular? What's the expression? Were they trying to beat a dead horse—just to make sure my campaign could not be salvaged? I am, after all, notorious for opposing all three of these lobbyists' legislative agenda. Just the allegation of a sexual scandal, with anyone, could ruin this election for me, but to be so duplicitous as to present one public image while pursuing a contrary path behind the scenes, would be the end of my political career. Period. There could be no resurrection from such condemnation."

And then, as if to rub salt in Jack's wounds, as a heat wave made his skin start to burn, she added, "And take a closer look at the scene—or, rather, the lack of one. You can't possibly tell where these photos were taken. Is it a home? Or a hotel? Which hotel? There are no extraneous identifying objects—plain white sheets, neutral blanket, no distinctive headboard on the bed, no view of any bedside tables or lamps. Where was the lighting coming from? The lighting looks like a photographer's dream, wouldn't you say?

"Where *were* these photos taken? Do you know?" she asked with innocence. Jack could feel himself sinking into the padding of his chair, as if he were being scolded by the school Principal.

"Did you even wonder?" Blanchard was asking. "The setting is so—noncommittal, it could be anywhere. I mean, you can't even tell if it's at a luxury hotel, or a sleazy motel. It certainly looks like these photos could all have been taken in the same location—and I assure you it's not my home, here or back in my home state. You are welcome to come check out my Capitol Hill home for yourself."

And turning back to the photos, Blanchard added thoughtfully, "There really is scarcely any difference in the setting. Though that alone would not necessarily be telling."

Then looking back at Jack, she leaned forward to bore down on him with, "Do you really think that I would be so stupid as to hold trysts with multiple different men, let alone in the same location? Really?" She held her pose firmly as she looked straight at him, unblinking, with one raised brow.

Jack felt the warmth of embarrassment spread up his neck and into his cheeks. Blanchard had some really good questions—and why hadn't he noticed these points, and checked them out himself? Why didn't he, or the computer expert he consulted, think of these questions? And why didn't he get the answers *before* he presented the photos for Blanchard's reaction? He had just handed the photos over to a pal who was a very reputable computer expert, and asked him if they were genuine, and his pal had said they were. What more should—or could—he have done?

"I ask you again, Mr. Amory. Is it possible," the Congresswoman continued, as if she were instructing a class, "that all three of these men are involved in a *conspiracy,* using fraudulent photos to game an election? If I am telling you the truth, as I again assure you I am, and these pictures are contrived, it would seem that these three men, at least, are in cahoots. And, while they clearly would benefit from my loss— I would no longer be a thorn in their sides—my opponent also stands to gain, by winning the Senate election. He's made it clear he would give the interests of these men a green light in terms of supporting their legislative agenda to the hilt, no matter who gets hurt by it. So, not only these men gain if I lose this election, but my opponent stands to win a Senate seat, and all the perks associated with the position, if these manufactured—and I emphasize the word 'manufactured'— photos see the light of day before we can prove they are, indeed, not genuine. Do you get my drift, Mr. Amory?" And there went that eyebrow again with the question.

He did, indeed, get her drift.

She wanted him to give her some time to have her own experts examine the photos. It was a reasonable request. Especially since he didn't want to be associated with a fabricated attack on a reputable member of Congress. After all, his own reputation and credibility were at stake, as well. He just hadn't expected things to turn out this way since he had gone to the trouble to have the photos verified. Had he been a little too quick to accept his pal's conclusion that the photos were real? Possibly. He should have asked his friend more about why he believed them to be real, but he had been in a hurry. He should have examined the photos closely himself for these kinds of issues. He should have asked his expert the questions that Blanchard was now asking him.

But this raised the question of how did his pal report that the photos were, indeed, genuine if they weren't? Who was telling him the truth? Could Blanchard just be trying to buy time to figure out some way to salvage the election in the face of these photos? With the election a mere ten days away, was there any way that the impact of such damning pictures could be nullified if they did turn out to be fake? Unlikely. The media would run with these pictures 24/7 until no other story could get through. Until the election was over, at least. Afterwards, especially if Blanchard lost, no one would care about her extramarital liaisons.

Clearly, he had more leg work to do before he, at least, could run with the story. But would Anonymous give him the time? And if not, would someone else be less scrupulous?

Chapter 4

"Diggie, *please*, I really need you to come to Washington right away to figure this out," Elaine pleaded. "You're the only one who can do this," she added, somewhat plaintively.

"Look, Sis, you know I'd do *almost* anything for you —*except* go to Washington. You know I hate the place!" Diggie whined.

"I know. And I wouldn't ask you if it weren't really critical to Kate Blanchard's Senate campaign."

"Can't you just send me the photos to look at here? I mean, all my equipment is here," he wheedled. "I need my equipment!"

"Come on, Diggie! You know that all you need is a computer, and you can access all your source and analysis tools from that. That's how you set yourself up—so you can be completely mobile. You have to be able to do your job from anywhere. And we've got lots of computers here. Or, if you want, you can just bring your own laptop with you. So what's the big deal?"

"Why do I have to be there, though? All those phony people. All those lies. All those dirty tricks. Besides, the election is here at home, not there!" he finished with a flourish, thinking this time he had her.

"Because, Diggie, it looks like the culprits are here. There's something fishy going on, and I would bet my instincts it has to do with more than just this Senate election. It's not going to be easy to ferret out who the culprits are, or what the real objective is. I need you here for whatever comes up, so we can deal with it right on the spot, so to speak. It's only for ten days. If we don't figure this out before the election, or sooner, really, before someone falls for these photos and prints them, then it won't matter. Whoever is behind this will have won. Period. Whatever their ultimate objective really is."

"But, Sis...,"

"But, Diggie...," Elaine interrupted.

"No. You know I hate to say 'no' to you, but this is one of those times. No. Just email the photos to me, and I'll see what I can figure out."

Elaine decided it was time to pull out all the stops. "Caroline Blanchard is here. She's back from her summer overseas, and is doing an unpaid internship in her mom's office."

Silence.

"Diggie?"

And, in a distant and somber voice, Elaine heard, "That's hitting below the belt, Ellie. That's not fair. That's not like you."

"I'm sorry, Diggie, I really am. But I'm that desperate to have your help in this," Elaine replied. "Look, this is big, and there's no telling what will follow. And even if we figure this out and thwart this attempt, there's no telling what else whoever did this will come up with. It's not just the photos, Diggie. Someone bugged Blanchard's inner office on the Hill, and I need you to check her home for bugs, too. We don't want to bring the police in on this yet until we have a better idea of what, or who, we are dealing with. This is very serious, Diggie. Someone is really trying to deep-six Caroline's mother's career," Elaine pressured him in the one way that could reach him. "I need you here, on the spot, to help us. I'm sorry, Diggie," Elaine finished, a little lamely.

The proverbial pregnant pause was followed by a quiet, "I'll be on the next flight, Elaine," and then the phone clicked off at the other end.

Elaine was relieved. But she knew she was in big trouble. The fact that Diggie had called her "Elaine" and not "Ellie" or "Sis" was a warning of storm clouds coming. Poor Diggie, she thought. I really did hit below the belt. But...he's so brilliant, and he's the only computer genius I can trust, she reasoned. Nevertheless, knowing that didn't alleviate her feelings of guilt and compassion. Diggie had been in love with Caroline Blanchard since they were in the third grade together.

Chapter 5

She didn't notice him approach because she was so focused on what she was watching, waiting for something to happen, or someone to arrive or emerge. Any movement at all. Anything. She'd been parked for some time now, just a few doors down from Kevin Lowell's house in the District; he was one of the lobbyists in the photos Jack Amory had shown her that morning. How long she'd been parked there, she wasn't sure. The sun had been setting when she arrived, and now the sky was pitch black. There wasn't even a moon tonight. And no stars were visible above the city's lights. A cloud cover must have moved in, she thought. And just what she expected to achieve, she couldn't say. She had just had some crazy impulse that if she could watch at least one of the lobbyists for a while, some clue about what was going on would surface.

But nothing was happening. It had been quiet the whole time she'd been parked there. Lights were on in the house, but she couldn't discern any movement inside. She was almost ready to give up and go home. She was so tired. And then...

The unexpected sound of a 'tap tap tap' on her car window made her jump so suddenly that she crashed her head against the inside roof of her car. It was all she could do to keep from screaming at the unexpected interruption. But when she saw who it was, her fright quickly turned to anger. She energetically swung her left hand back and forth to waive him away so she could concentrate on her task. When the 'tap tap tap' continued unabated, and started getting louder, she shrugged with exasperation, swearing under her breath as she opened her driver's side window barely an inch.

"What the hell are you doing here?! Go *away*!" she hissed at him, in her best impression of a stage whisper.

"I've brought provisions," he smiled expectantly, as he held up a large paper bag from Billie's Gourmet Burgers.

"What...? Get *out* of here! Can't you see I'm busy?" she hissed again.

"Actually," he kept smiling, "what I see is you sitting here doing absolutely nothing! And for at least the last two hours. Now," and his smile broadened ever so invitingly, "I've brought sustenance for both of us. I, too, have been sitting here watching since before you arrived—except, of course, when I bounced down to the Billie's Gourmet Burgers around the corner."

"You've been *what*?!" and Elaine could barely retain her stage whisper, so flabbergasted was she to learn he had been watching her since she arrived. That means, her mind raced to grasp the import of this information, that he was here even before her! How come I didn't notice him? she asked herself. And then she voiced that question out loud.

"That's because I'm better at stakeouts than you are," he smiled sweetly at her, certain that this kind of comment would grate on her nerves. "C'mon," he continued, "can't we at least enjoy each other's company while we both stake out this guy's house? I mean, at least it wouldn't be so utterly boring! We could even get to know each other a little better," and his broad inviting smile, as much as his words, were indeed beginning to grate on Elaine's nerves.

"Look, Mr. Amory," she replied, with what she thought was an equally smarmy smile, "I'm not interested in getting to know you any better. As a matter of fact, I wish I didn't know you at all. Since we met this morning, I've known nothing but grief and concern because of those *phony* photos you brought with you. So get lost, or do whatever it is you do, so that I can figure out what is really going on—and maybe, save an election!" she hissed with finality.

But Jack Amory wasn't buying. "Look, Elaine, unlock the door and let me in. It's really not safe to be sitting out here at this hour alone. Who knows who might come by and try to take advantage of the situation."

"You are *so right*, Mr. Amory," and Elaine looked meaningfully at him, staring straight into his eyes. Damn! she thought. What is it about those eyes? Those soulful deep blue eyes against his midnight black hair? In the soft glare from the street light, she could have sworn his eyes were mocking her —or worse, reading her thoughts this very minute. And then it hit her—he had called her 'Elaine'. "And what do you mean by addressing me so familiarly!" she almost spoke out loud, forgetting she was trying to be discreet.

"Well, I just thought that as long as we were going to spend the evening together, we might as well be on a first name basis. Mine is 'Jack', by the way, in case you've forgotten," he elaborated, with exaggerated sweetness, and an ear-to-ear grin. And then, more seriously, "Look, we might as well pool our resources if we are going to figure out what is going on. I don't like being used—if that's what's happening —and I especially don't like the idea that someone, or someones, think that I *can* be used. Now, you want to protect your boss from an election scam, if that's what this is, that threatens her success. The answers for both of us are the same, so it just makes sense to work together to discover whatever is going on. And if it's anything nefarious, maybe we can derail it before it achieves it's objective." This time he looked her straight in the eyes, too, and the power of his logic—and the idea that he was really trying to discover the truth as well—hit her right in the gut...a gut that had been telling her for some time with lots of unpleasant growls, that maybe she was hungry.

When he heard the car doors unlock, he quickly ran around to the passenger side and jumped in, being careful to minimize the sound of the click when he closed his door.

"Ah, now this is much better, isn't it, Elaine? Actually, it's quite cozy in here," he noted, as he tried to move his seat back as far as it went so his knees wouldn't be pushing up against his chin or the dashboard.

"Oh, what's the matter, '*Jack*'," and she accented his name, as her voice dripped with sarcasm, "is it a little *too* cozy? Why," and she feigned offense as she placed her hand demonstratively against her chest, directing her gaze innocently upward, "I'm so sorry you are finding my nearness such a disillusion!"

"Oh, it's not your 'nearness' that I have problems with. Actually, I kind of like it, as you can see," he stated as he leaned a little closer to her, and reached his arm around the back of her seat—close enough that she could feel the heat emanating from his body, and he could smell the fragrance of her shampoo. And then he added in a soft, caressing voice close to her ear, "It's just that I'm such a tall, strapping fellow, that small economy-size cars don't accommodate my height very well. Actually, they don't accommodate it at all!" he finished rather bluntly, as he leaned back in his seat.

"Well, you know there is a solution to the problem, don't you?" she queried sweetly.

"My car?" he asked innocently.

"*No!*" she hissed. "You can just get out of this car, and go on your merry way, and leave me to my task at hand!"

"I thought we got passed that issue, Elaine."

That's when Elaine just harrumphed in frustration, leaned forward, and put her hands up to her face, resting the backs of her hands on her steering wheel.

"So—which do you prefer?" Jack inquired, as he started taking food out of the bag, ignoring her display of frustration, "the double cheeseburger or the triple cheeseburger?" and he held up one in each hand, waiting for her to choose.

Elaine looked at him with complete and utter amazement—and then she just burst out laughing. He seemed so sincerely intent on her choosing! As she tried to get a grip on herself, she reached out and grabbed one of the burgers, and opened the wrapping. As she bit into it, she let out a very contented sigh. She hadn't realized how hungry she was, having come to the stakeout straight from her office. She had come on an impulse, hoping to glean something about what was going on, but not expecting to sit there for so many hours without learning anything. She was frantic to prevent this scam from turning her boss's campaign into a professional—and personal—nightmare. Not only would the election be lost, but who knows what might happen to her marriage. Was it strong enough to withstand such horrible lies?

"I take that as an apology. You're welcome, by the way!" Jack finished with a flourish, in response to Elaine's sigh. He moved away just in time, though, to prevent her from wiping his face with her burger.

30

"Come, come, now," he sighed, straightening up. "I've got fries—and fries—so which 'vegetable' would you prefer?" he continued, as if nothing had happened.

"Oh, just give me the fries," she relented, as she grabbed one of the holders and sat back in her seat, rather contentedly, to fill the gaping chasm that her stomach had become.

As he passed out the sodas, Jack knew instinctively that he had won this round, and so he, too, sat back, to the extent that he could.

They sat there munching in convivial silence for a few moments, the only noise coming from the crackling of the papers and the bag that the food had come in. If anyone had been watching, the pair would have looked like old friends—or lovers—sharing some quiet time together.

"By the way," Elaine queried as she munched on her burger, "you came by the office today, and it's a Saturday. How did you know anyone would be there?"

"Well, I *am* a political reporter. Remember? I knew that the House was in special session today to get some key votes done before the election, so they could all go home and campaign. It made sense that Blanchard would be in town instead of home campaigning, because a few of these votes are on controversial issues that are near and dear to her heart, *and* her district. How could she be running about campaigning, asking people across the state to let her represent them, if she missed critical votes on some key issues that were important to her current constituents, just to further her own career?"

"You're right, of course, it would not look good. But that doesn't stop some politicians."

"True. But Kate Blanchard isn't just any politician. Is she?" he queried, innocently.

"No. She isn't," Elaine replied in a small voice. She couldn't figure this guy out. Where was he coming from, she wondered.

When they had finished their burgers, and were munching slowly on the remaining fries, Elaine began again with "You know,...?"

"No. What do I know?" Jack interrupted, trying to be funny.

"If you would just keep your mouth shut, I would tell you what you know," Elaine smartly replied. But her voice held no challenge or animosity. Jack recognized that he was feeling unexpectedly light, though why he suddenly felt that way puzzled him.

"As I was saying,..." Elaine continued

"Well I'll be damned," Jack suddenly whispered under his breath.

"Will you let me finish what...."

"Look, Elaine. Look who's going into Lowell's house," Jack said with amazement, as he surreptitiously started snapping photos with his iPhone, making sure not to use the flash.

Elaine leaned forward and peered through the windshield, and asked slowly, "Who is he? I've never seen him before."

"That's Craig Bittiford. You know what this means, don't you?"

"I haven't the slightest idea what this means. Who *is* he?"

"He's my geek pal," Jack noted, slowly. "He's the guy I had check the photos to tell me if they were genuine, or not," and Jack's amazement hung in the air as he put his iPhone away.

Elaine sat there with her mouth open, not a sound coming out.

"Yeah," Jack acknowledged in a quiet voice, "it leaves me speechless, too."

"But...what could he possibly be doing here? Does he know Kevin Lowell?"

"I have no idea. I wouldn't have thought so. But by now, you know about Hill culture: it's always a surprise when you learn who knows whom—and who may be working with whomever!" Jack answered lightly. "Seriously, though, just because he is here doesn't mean he knows Lowell. And, even if he does know Lowell, just because he's here doesn't mean it has anything at all to do with the photos." Jack was trying to convince himself, it seemed, more than Elaine.

"But he's at Lowell's *home!* Strangers don't go to people's homes! It's a Saturday night, for goodness sake! And so close upon the heels of the emergence of these photos!" Elaine countered, a bit excitedly.

"So, they may know each other," Jack tried explaining, more to himself than Elaine, "but that would be all the more reason to believe his being here has *nothing* to do with the photos."

"Oh, ho, Mr. Amory!" Elaine exclaimed. "You obviously don't know the first principal of crime detection!"

"Oh, and *you* do, Ms. Kent!" Jack chided back.

"Well, when you've read as many murder mysteries as I have, you know that there is no such thing as a 'coincidence'!"

Chapter 6

"So, the person whom *you* trusted to validate these photos just walked into Kevin Lowell's house," Elaine observed, turning to look directly at Jack.

"That's what I said," Jack replied carefully, not knowing what to make of this turn of events.

"Are you sure you're not all in cahoots with each other?" Elaine queried evenly, while she stared at him with narrowed eyes, trying desperately to copy his trick of lifting just one brow, but failing.

"Are you crazy?!" Jack retorted, as he turned to face her potent stare. "What on earth would I be doing sitting here with you if I were in on it! I came to you, remember, to try to get at the truth!"

"The truth? What *is* the truth, Mr. Amory?" she beseeched him.

"Oh, this is ridiculous! You *are* crazy, you know that?" As he opened the car door to exit, he added, "I'm going. I'll call on Craig later, and ask him what this is all about. He lives on Capitol Hill, and, like me, he works out of his home. Want to meet me there later?" And he was surprised to realize he was hoping she would agree.

"No, I have to pick someone up at the airport," Elaine replied, then added, "How do I know you are going to confront him rather than conspire with him—sort of fill him in on what we know, like the fact that we found his bug?"

"You don't know he planted the bug," Jack said, a little testily. "And besides, I just invited you to come along. When you stop jumping to conclusions, and actually think about what's going on, maybe you'll see things more clearly."

"Well, I'll be picking up some help that I can *really* rely on. Maybe that will help me see things more clearly!" Elaine countered, as she angrily turned the key to start her car engine.

"Male or female?" Jack asked, and the words were out of his mouth before he could stop them. Why did he want to know? What did he care if there were some guy out there that she 'really' trusted? Did it matter? He knew she didn't trust him, but he had thought he was making some headway during their stakeout. But if not, so what?

"Male, *of course*," Elaine emphasized, much to her own surprise.

"Fine," Jack responded rather tersely, as he finally got out of Elaine's car. As he stood there with his right arm leaning on the open door, he added, "How is this 'male' going to help with our investigation?"

"He's going to prove that your photos have been manufactured!" Elaine answered with smug satisfaction. Then she added, as he moved to close her car door, "Come by the office tomorrow around ten, and I'll show you that you are all wet." And then she harrumphed, as she suddenly caught his reference to 'our' investigation.

Jack had to resist slamming the door, but it wasn't easy. It took all the self control he could muster.

Chapter 7

"Diggie, I hate to put you to work right away, but there's just no time to lose. I don't know how long we have before someone actually publishes those photos," Elaine was explaining, as they drove from Dulles Airport straight to Representative Blanchard's home on Capitol Hill.

"That's Ok, Sis. I understand, only too well," Diggie replied.

"Then you've forgiven me?" Elaine asked quietly, as she noted he had called her "Sis", instead of Elaine.

"You know I can't stay mad at you for long," he said with a wry smile. "And I know how devastating this attempt to smear Mrs. Blanchard will be for her campaign. Somebody must be in a pretty nasty panic to play at this game. But, Ellie," and here Diggie sounded a bit morose, "I took a cursory look at the photos you emailed, and if they are composed, it was done by an expert."

"Diggie!" Elaine cried out in shock. "You don't think they're actually real, do you?"

"I didn't say that, Ellie. I just said they were done by an expert at photo manipulation, so it's not going to be a simple matter to figure out how they were created."

"Oh," and Elaine relaxed back in the driver's seat. "Well, if anyone can do it, Diggie, you can. No one else can match you for your technical skills, *or* your perseverance," she tried to boost his spirits. But she knew his dampened demeanor was more about encountering Caroline Blanchard than worrying about how to figure out how the photos were constructed.

"By the way," she added, "we're heading straight to Kate's house, so you can check it for electronic bugs. I told you we found one in her office. Luckily it was only one, but it was right in her private office. We have no idea how long it was there."

"Any idea who put it there?"

"No, but if there are any bugs in her house, then it must be someone close to her, because it would have to be someone who has access to her Hill office *and* her home. Any visitor could have put it in her office. But not just anyone has access to her home. She doesn't usually hold business meetings at home like so many do, but there is always the occasional exception. She tries to keep home as someplace she can decompress, so to speak. It's her private sanctuary. Her business meetings with people who are not on her staff are generally scheduled for her Hill office."

"Wow," and Diggie whistled low. "That would be pretty awful if someone close to her is out to ruin her election."

"That would, indeed," and Elaine tried to shake off the shivers that rippled through her at the thought. It would devastate her, Elaine thought. Kate Blanchard put great store in the strong friendships that she built. The discovery that she had misjudged someone, and trusted someone who did not warrant that trust, would be disappointing, to say the least. "Well, let's not worry about that until we figure out if there's anything to worry about!" Elaine tried to brighten up, and lighten both of their moods.

As they pulled up in front of a town house on Capitol Hill, another car was parking across the street. Oh, no! Elaine moaned to herself, as she recognized the figure emerging from the car. Not Amory! Not again!

"What did you say?" Diggie inquired.

"Huh? Oh, it's just that blogger who brought the pictures to us this morning. Honestly, I feel like he has been dogging me all day!" she finished, exasperatedly, as she and Diggie emerged from her car.

To Jack, as he approached her, she hurled, "What are you doing here? I thought I told you that it wasn't a good idea for you to be seen here? What if the house is being watched by whoever bugged her office?"

"Well, I couldn't sit by and let you and your *expert*," and he nodded toward Diggie, "have all the fun, now, could I?" and his smile implied that a halo hovered over his head.

"Hey, weren't you supposed to be going to confront your 'pal'? The one who told you the photos were genuine?"

"I actually hung around Lowell's house for a while longer, waiting for Craig to emerge. When he did, I tried to

37

follow him, expecting he was going home from there. But he didn't head straight home, and I lost him on Constitution Avenue. So I just went to his house, assuming he would eventually show up there. After all, he didn't look like he was dressed for a night on the town. But I waited outside his house for a while—a long while, but nobody showed up. So....here I am!" Jack finished, with open arms.

"It's a Saturday night. Don't you have a date, or something?" Elaine blurted out without thinking. Then she mentally kicked herself as soon as the words escaped her.

"Inquiring about my personal life, Ms. Kent?" and the thought made him feel a little giddy inside. "Why, we've just met today. Don't you think we should wait an 'appropriate' period before we get personal? After all, we are in an antagonistic situation here, remember," he demurred. But the crinkling around his eyes made it clear he was having some fun at her expense. Or, maybe it was the strange male standing there, so close beside her and staring directly at him, that inexplicably rattled Jack, just a little bit. Jack sensed his presence more than he actually saw the man in the shrouded darkness.

Elaine was at a loss for words. All she could do was stand there. It was Diggie who finally broke the spell with, "This friend of yours who checked out the photos...what's his name?"

The strong male voice forced Jack to finally move his gaze from Elaine to Diggie, and he stared for a moment as the image registered. Diggie was poised there in jeans, collared shirt open at the neck, and a bulky wool pullover sweater. Very preppy, Jack thought. And then it struck him...very *young* as well. Why this gave his spirits a lift, he couldn't tell, but it did. He stretched out his hand, and remarked, "Hello, I'm Jack Amory. And you are?"

"I'm Gregory Bosworth Kent, Mr. Amory," Diggie replied, in a firm, officious voice that belied his youth, as he extended his hand in return. "I understand you have some compromising photos. So, who did you get them from, and who told you they are genuine? What kind of analyses did the technician do to make that determination? And what was the technology capability he used?" Diggie was pointed in his response. There was no room for excess paraphernalia, or loose change, when you were an expert in computer sciences, especially when you specialized in the detection of illegal computer operations.

Jack was only slightly taken aback by Diggie's abruptness, because his attention was caught by Diggie's last name: Kent. A relative to Elaine Kent? he wondered. He wasn't sure why, but it made him feel a little more kindly toward Mr. Gregory Bosworth Kent.

"His name is Craig Bittiford, and he's a leading expert in the detection of photo manipulation," Jack told Diggie. "To be honest, I'm not sure what technology he used, or what kinds of analyses he performed. He's a friend of mine— someone I've known for many years, so I am inclined to trust his work without feeling I need to probe into his techniques." And here, Jack paused. He might as well mention it, because Elaine already knew from their stakeout.

"There is one thing, though," Jack was adding. "Elaine and I saw Craig visiting the home tonight of one of the men in the photos." He had deliberately referred to Elaine familiarly, he realized. It seemed to imply more intimacy than he really shared with her. Why would he do that, he was thinking, as he stood there? Was he brandishing a little testosterone? It wasn't his style, so it surprised him to even be thinking of the possibility. Jack had never had any trouble appealing to women, so he never had to compete for a woman's attention. Why would he do that now? Why would he feel the need? Especially if Gregory Kent was, in fact, a relative, as it seemed? He couldn't be her *husband*—he was way too young! Wasn't he? And besides, Jack acknowledged, much to his own amazement, he had actually checked out her 'ring finger' while they shared their stakeout earlier, and found no wedding band.

Elaine broke through Jack's thoughts with, "We might as well all go inside, instead of standing out here in the open. We're not going to resolve anything out here."

"What if there are bugs inside?" Jack queried.

"Don't worry," Diggie cut in, "I'm going to do a sweep before any of us says a word." And with that, Diggie headed toward the front door. He was about to knock, when the door suddenly swung open.

"Diggie!" exclaimed Caroline Blanchard excitedly, as she threw her arms around his shoulders in the doorway, and gave him a generous hug. "No one told me you were coming! It's so good to see you! Wait 'till I tell you all about my summer abroad! You won't believe all the places I've been or all the stuff I learned! Come on in!" Caroline finished, as she stepped aside so he could enter. "You guys can come in, too," she laughed, as she noticed Elaine and Jack watching the episode, each with their own thoughts. Standing in the background, inside the foyer, was a dashing young man who, at that moment, looked a little disgruntled. It appeared to Elaine and Jack that the young man and Caroline had been on their way out.

Apparently, Diggie thought the same as he offered, "If you're going out, Caroline, we can catch up later. Actually, I have some work to do for Sis that's really time critical, so feel free to do whatever you were planning to do. We'll catch up when you get back," he concluded.

Caroline, familiar with Diggie's diffidence, replied, "No way, Diggie! I know you! If I don't catch you when I see you, who knows when I'll be able to get your attention. Especially if you're here to work, and not just to visit!" Caroline commanded. "You're always so engrossed in your computers these days. Spencer and I were just going out for the sake of getting out, so it's nothing important. It's not like we'll be missing some critical event, or anything!" While Caroline smiled brightly as she spoke these words, Spencer Ainsworth grimaced behind her.

"But Caroline," Spencer seemed to whine, "Mallory and Drake will be expecting us to be there."

"Oh, fiddlesticks, Spencer! I'm sure they will do just fine without us, or at least without me. But if you are so concerned, why don't you just go on ahead, and comfort them?" Caroline asked innocently, querying him with wide open eyes that were as green as a field of grass. "Obviously,

40

we're going to be very busy here for a while—we're old friends, you see, and we have a lot of catching up to do."

And then Caroline laughed again as if at a joke, as she realized she had made no introductions. "Oh, I'm so sorry, folks! Spencer, these are old friends of mine. This is Diggie Kent. We were in school together since the third grade! But he's a genius, so he just raced through college *and* graduate school, while I graduate from college next June." Then turning to Elaine, she noted, "This is my mom's Chief of Staff, Elaine. She's Diggie's sister..,.and…uhmmm..?"

As Caroline looked questioningly at Jack, Elaine piped up quickly, perhaps a little too quickly, with, "This is a friend of mine, Caroline. Umm, we just picked up Diggie from the airport, and he has a lot to do. Umm, he's making some upgrades to your mom's computer connections with her office, so maybe we'd best be getting started, right?"

Caroline was no dummy. She turned deliberately and said, "Spencer, you get going, and meet up with Mallory and Drake, and if I can, I'll catch up with you in a bit. You'd just be bored with our 'hellos', and inside jokes, so you go on now!" Then she pushed him out the door and, as she hollered after him "I'll see you later!" she closed the door firmly behind him.

And then she turned, with a mischievous smile curling at the edge of her lips, and with her eyes pointedly on Jack, addressed her question to Elaine.

"So, Elaine, you have a 'friend'? When did this happen?" and then she slowly turned her questioning glance towards Elaine, with wide open eyes full of false, even mocking, innocence.

"Caroline," Elaine cautioned her, "we really do have a lot to do, so we'd best get started." And then she conceded one thing, "By the way, thanks for getting rid of the tad pole. Did you say his name was Spencer?"

"Yes, Spencer Ainsworth. Why?" But she wasn't distracted by Elaine's redirection of the conversation. "Are you going to tell us *your* friend's name?"

"He's not my friend, Caroline. This is Jack Amory. He's the blogger who brought me the compromising photos of your mother, which he claims are genuine." Diggie pinched his sister's arm as the words escaped her, but he was too late to stop the announcement. Elaine winced, remembering that they needed to sweep the house for bugs.

Teasing chumminess turned into blazing fire. The speed and intensity of the transformation caught Jack a little off guard. Caroline swung around to confront him square in the face, and with hands on her hips, spit out her words with a rattlesnake's venom.

"Oh, so *you* are the bastard who's trying to slander my mom! Who the hell do you think you are, huh? Why are you trying to kill her election, huh? Are you working for those despicable men in the photos? Huh? Huh?"

Diggie grabbed her shoulders from behind, then put one hand over her mouth, while he whispered in her ear, "Shshshsh! We came to sweep the house for bugs! Don't say another word until we know!" And then he let her go.

Caroline didn't say another word, but she glared at Jack with such menace that he winced, as if he'd been struck by a powerful blow from a heavy object.

Diggie put his finger to his lips, motioning for all to be silent, and then started them on their journey through the house as he pulled out of his pocket, and turned on, an electronic bug detector. It was state-of-the-art, with the ability to detect wireless audio listening devices, wireless cameras, wi-fi signals, and other kinds of radio frequency transmitters. Hopefully, if there were any bugs, they were far enough away from the entrance that the bugs wouldn't have picked up their doorway conversation, at least not clearly enough to make out the words. He kept his fingers crossed as they started their way through the rooms.

It was a beautifully appointed row house on Capitol Hill, with tasteful, colonial styled furnishings in burgundies, navy blue, and rich green, that invited the visitor to make themselves at home. Anyone watching their progression from room to room, however, might have found their stealthy sojourn something to laugh at. They moved in a line, with Diggie at the front, holding out his detector, his arm waving around as if gesturing to all of the decor as he gave them a tour. Only he wasn't saying a word. And the stealthy nature of their inspection caused his followers to tip-toe, while everyone looked right and left, and up and down. It could have been a scene out of a Scooby Doo cartoon!

"Uh-oh," Diggie whispered as he held up his hand to signal everyone to stop in their tracks. The signal panel on his detector was indicating that a listening device was nearby, and as he moved in the direction indicated, he led them to the kitchen, and specifically to the kitchen table.

"Oh, my God!" Caroline let out in a loud whisper.

"Shshsh!" Diggie warned again for everyone to be quiet. He searched around, then under, the table, and grabbing a hanky from his pants pocket, he pulled the bug off from the underside of the table, and held it up for all to see, as he disabled the audio listening device.

"Well,..." Elaine started to say, but Diggie silenced her quickly, and then continued on their exploration of the house. He knew only too well that if one bug had been planted, there could be others. They needed to go through every room. The others instinctively understood, and fell into line again behind Diggie.

They found only one bug in the kitchen, but they found another in the living room, and even more intimately, in the Congresswoman's home office. Curiously enough, they did not find one in the master bedroom, or any other room on the second and third floors.

"What does that tell you?" Elaine asked Diggie.

"Well, it's obvious it's someone who had access only to the first floor, and not the floors where the bedrooms were located. I think that's good. But then, if only family and friends frequent the house, then that's pretty depressing. Caroline, have there been any workmen or service representatives, like a cable guy or someone, coming to the house, say, in the past month?"

Caroline thought for a moment, then replied, "No, I don't think so, Diggie. Of course, I'm interning in mom's office so I'm on the Hill during the day, but I'm pretty sure there have been no instances of repairs or service calls needed for anything in the house."

"Can you name all the folks who might have been here in the past month or so?"

"Well," Caroline thought again, "Mom and Dad, of course. And me. I got back from England about eight weeks ago and came straight here. And, let's see, my aunt and uncle and their four kids visited two weeks ago,...and they were running all over the house!" she recalled, as a remembering smile flitted across her face.

"Who else? Did either your mother or father bring home any strangers...or friends, for that matter?" Diggie pursued.

"Well, of course, Elaine has been in and out frequently after work, just to keep tabs on coordination of mom's legislative work and her campaign. You know mom can't conduct campaign business in her Hill office. And Elaine can't do anything in relation to mom's campaign during her official working hours on the Hill. So she often stops by the house on her way home, to make some calls to campaign headquarters back home, and make sure there are no conflicts, or anything, especially between mom's legislative calendar and her campaign commitments."

"But I haven't brought anyone with me on any of those occasions, Diggie," Elaine added.

"What about your friend, Caroline?" Diggie inquired, though he wasn't sure he wanted to hear the answer. "Spencer has been in the house, obviously. Has anyone else?"

"Well, that's right. Spencer has been here several times over the last two weeks. But you can't think he would do something like that, could you? I mean, he had never even met mom before two weeks ago. Why, I only met him a month ago when the intern program started. He's an intern on the Hill, too, working for another Congressman. The program administrators get all the new interns together for an orientation, and some socializing after hours. That's how I met Spencer."

"Have you brought any of the other interns home as well?"

"Well, no. Spencer invited me out and, being the gracious southern gentleman that he is, he actually came here to pick me up that first date...and several times since. I never gave it a second thought," she finished a little lamely, as grave possibilities started forming in her mind.

After a moment, she added, "He's been in the Hill office, too. I brought him by one day to show him around before we headed out to lunch."

"Did he go inside her private office?" this time it was Jack asking.

"Actually, yes," Elaine recalled. "I remember him remarking about wanting to compare a woman legislator's office with that of the man that he was working for. Really, I thought it was kind of a sexist remark, but I didn't pay much attention to it. I kind of sloughed it off. After a while you just tune out the typical disparaging references to women that you may hear."

"So, he had access to her office on the Hill. He had access to the house," Jack tallied. "Does he roam around the house, too, Caroline, or does he just stay in the doorway when he comes to pick you up?"

"No...I mean, he doesn't just stand in the entrance hall. I actually gave him a tour of the first floor," and here she paused, then said in a small voice, "including mom's office." Confusion spread over her face. "But, I mean, why would he do something like that? What could it possibly matter to him? He's an intern, like me. This is his first trip to Washington, D.C. What would motivate him to be involved in doing something like that? Why could he possibly care about mom's election? He doesn't even come from our home state!" she finished, a little shrilly.

It was Jack who spoke first. "We don't know it was him, Caroline, but it's a strong possibility. As to why, we won't know that without discussing it with him. Which, I might say, I don't think we should do just yet."

"Why not?" Caroline and Elaine burst in together.

"Because, if he did plant the bugs, then talking with him about it would tip off the perpetrators that we might be close to discovering them. I'm convinced the people listening in on the other end of those bugs are the same ones responsible for these photos."

"Oh! So you admit the photos aren't real!" Elaine nearly shouted.

"No. I don't—yet. But these bugs, in Blanchard's Hill office, *and* her home, make it look like they could be phony. But, there's still the issue of my pal saying they were genuine."

"Ah, what was he doing visiting Lowell? That should prove that he was lying to you," Elaine reasoned.

"I admit, it could. But it's all circumstantial at the moment. Why would he lie to me about it? Why wouldn't he tell *me* they were fakes, if indeed they are? We go back a long way. If he saw that they were manufactured, why would he be trying to compromise Blanchard's campaign, and her entire political career, by telling me they were genuine photos? I can't see how, or why, he would care!" Jack concluded, his face enveloped with these puzzling questions, and a dawning sense of betrayal. If the photos aren't real, but his pal let him go ahead and publish them as genuine, Jack's own reputation could be ruined, or at least compromised. Why would Craig do something that would destroy him? And why wouldn't he tell Jack the truth to protect him?

Seeing Jack's distress, Elaine quietly noted that "we need more information—about Spencer, *and* about your friend. And more, we need Diggie to examine the photos thoroughly, and tell us what we are dealing with. Until then, we can't come to any definite conclusions. So, we shouldn't be making any accusations, yet, either. I agree with Jack, that we shouldn't say anything to Spencer, or to this Craig guy, until we know more."

Jack looked at Elaine, with gratitude flooding his face. He felt the compassion of her gesture, as well as the wisdom of it. And it filled him with a strange new warmth. They were in this together. They would solve this mystery together.

Chapter 8

Elaine rolled over as she reached for the phone that was ringing on the nightstand beside her bed. Who would be calling so early in the morning? she asked herself. And on a Sunday morning, at that.

And then she remembered. The photos. It must be something about the photos. She hadn't gotten home until after two in the morning. What a day it had been! So she shook her head, as she answered the phone, to rid herself of the cobwebs that had enveloped her brain in her sleep.

"Hello?" she inquired, trying to sound bright and cheery.

It didn't work. But when she heard the voice on the other end, that did shake her out of her sleepiness. "Well, aren't you the sleeping beauty!" she heard the voice remark.

"Jimminy Cricket, Amory!" Elaine exclaimed in exasperation. "What on earth are you calling for so early? Didn't we just say 'goodnight' a few hours ago?"

"Well, when I say goodnight to a lady, I usually like to say 'good morning', too," Jack crooned through the phone.

"Really?" she said, with more than a little sarcasm. "Well, that's something you'll never get to do with me!"

"But I'm doing it right now," he exclaimed, with innocent surprise. "And besides, I'm a lot taller than Jimminy Cricket. It should be easy for you to tell us apart."

"Oh, for crying out loud, Amory! What do you want?!"

"Well, I seldom cry. And never out loud. And what did I do to cause you to call me by my last name only? I thought we made a lot of progress yesterday. You're 'Elaine', and I'm 'Jack'." He knew he was annoying her, but he did it deliberately. Why? He wasn't sure. But he liked pulling her chain. She was such an easy target. Maybe she doesn't have much fun, he speculated. Maybe it would be entertaining to try to fix that. Or maybe he was just bored from the four hours he had just spent on his latest stakeout—alone.

"Look, Amory. Get to the point! Why are you calling?"

"I thought you might like to know something," he stalled.

"Well, what is it?! Do I have to pull it out of you one word at a time?"

"No. But while you've been getting your beauty sleep, I've..."

"Beauty sleep?!!" Elaine nearly yelled, her voice rising at least an octave, and resenting the implications. "I didn't get home until after 2—in the *morning,* as you well know—and you call a few hours of sleep 'beauty sleep'?"

"A 'few hours'?" he asked, and she could just see his single raised eyebrow as pointedly as if he had been standing in front of her, right there in her bedroom. "Have you checked your alarm clock lately? Or don't you have one? I'll put it on my list of things to do, to get you one." It was almost an intimate remark.

"If you don't tell me why you called I'm going to hang up! You've got three seconds, and counting!"

"Is that on 'three', or is it after the 'three' that you will hang up?"

She slammed down the phone. It was a landline phone, so it made a satisfying crashing, ringing noise as she flung it into it's holder.

Ten seconds later her phone rang again.

She thought of not answering, but she had become concerned about what he thought she should know, so she relented, and picked up the phone, but she didn't say a word as she held it to her ear.

"I know you're there," Jack's voice crooned, "so listen to this: Craig is not answering his cell phone, so I've been staked out at Craig's house since 6 am. No Craig. He wasn't there when I arrived, and he hasn't come home yet. That's four hours,... in case you don't have a clock," he finished mischievously. He had to admit, teasing her was definitely fun.

Elaine was dumbfounded. She must have been exhausted to have slept in so late. But even more, where was Craig? He hadn't come home the night before, and he wasn't there this morning.

48

At last she spoke. "Maybe he got home after you left last night? And then went out before you got there?" she queried.

"Oh, thank you for still speaking to me. I was beginning to wonder."

"Oh, shut up!"

"Ok." And he hung up.

No! she thought. And she jumped out of bed, frantically looking for her purse where she had put his card with his phone number on it. When she found it, she heaved a sigh of relief, and dialed.

"Jack Amory's line. He's unavailable at the moment. If you care to leave a message...."

Elaine could only laugh this time—so that she wouldn't cry. She was so upset by the photos, and then the bugs, and then just the whole mystery of it all, worrying about how to prevent a disaster that her boss didn't deserve. And then she had been so frustrated by Jack's verbal sparring, that the only emotion she seemed to have left was to giggle and giggle and giggle—because she could tell it was his voice, live on the other end, and not really a recording.

How can he stay so light when it feels like the whole world is coming crashing down? Granted, he brought the tornado into her world with those photos. But his career is at risk as well. If he makes the wrong judgment, he could lose what he's built up, and worked for. It's clear he values his integrity, or he wouldn't care if he published the photos and they were later identified as bogus. He wants to make the right choice. He wants to find out the truth. Of that she was convinced. Otherwise he would have just published the photos already, and been reaping the glare of the spotlight, regardless of the consequences to her boss. And he's clearly upset about the possibility that his longtime friend may have lied to him when so much was at stake for his career. This can't be easy for Jack either, she realized.

"I'm glad you can still see the humor in all of this," Jack was saying on the other end of the phone. "After four hours of staring at Craig's house, desperately struggling to stay awake, I don't have quite so much tolerance left in me to

49

laugh at this. Granted, this could all be someone's sick joke, but I'm not laughing," he moaned, trying to engender some sympathy from her for his lonely, four-hour vigil.

Elaine calmed down at this, at least enough to ask, "Have you had any breakfast?"

Jack perked up immediately. "No, I haven't. Have you any suggestions?"

"As a matter of fact, I do," Elaine replied, with a smile in her voice.

"I'm all yours," he said brightly, suddenly fully alert.

Elaine chuckled at his readiness, and then said, "Meet me in thirty minutes at Bullfeathers. After we eat, we can go to Kate's house, and see what Diggie has figured out."

"I'm on my way," he jumped at the suggestion. And then, "Will he have learned anything so quickly? I mean, when we left that house last night—or, rather, early this morning— he was still trying to get set up."

"Diggie stayed there to do just that. I'm sure he's working away already, and has been for quite some time. He's very determined when he has a job to do. That's where he got the nickname 'Diggie'—he sticks to a project until he's done, and finds the answers to his questions. He's really incredible."

"You're not just saying that because he's your brother, are you?"

"No!" and she laughed again. "And since it's Caroline's mom that's in jeopardy, he's going to stick to his task until he has the answers we all need. Especially with Caroline there for company!"

"Umm, I take it something is going on between him and Caroline," it was a statement more than a question.

"How did you pick up on that?" she asked, with feigned surprise.

"Oh, that's my little secret!" he teased her.

"Well, just don't make any wisecracks about it in front of either one of them. You'll be sorry if you do!"

"I'm as silent as the snow," Jack responded. "I'll see you at Bullfeathers in half an hour."

Chapter 9

She leaned back in her chair, and folded her arms across her chest, as she watched him scarf up the last of his eggs benedict, with sausage and home fries. Well, he certainly has a healthy appetite, she mused to herself.

"I certainly do!" Jack cut into her revery.

"What?" Elaine jumped, startled by his interruption of her thoughts.

"Have a hearty appetite!" he replied. "That's what you were thinking, weren't you?"

"Wha...I mean...," Elaine stumbled, surprised that someone could read her so clearly.

"That's ok!" he laughed. "I really am a good reporter, you know. It's because I can read people, and read between the lines. I'm also especially good at reading subtext and facial expressions!"

"Subtext?" Elaine asked, never having heard the concept before.

"Yes, what people are *not* saying, but want to say, more than what they are actually telling you," Jack explained. "The point they are really trying to make, or the message they are trying to stealthily convey, without actually verbalizing it directly."

"Since you brought up the subject...," Elaine leaned forward, placing her elbows on the table, and her chin in her hands.

"Yes?" and up went both of Jack's eyebrows this time. As he mimicked her position, they came almost eyeball to eyeball across the small table.

Elaine felt an electric jolt surge through her body. Startled by her reaction, she struggled to suppress any sign that she had felt such turbulence. He was so close. And he was looking her directly in the eyes, and he didn't flinch a speck. Was he challenging her? To do what? Or to see what?

And then she recognized a look of self-satisfaction slowly spreading across his face, finally reaching his eyes, which now seemed to be mocking her, again.

Before she could return to the question she had wanted to ask, Jack jumped in with another disarming comment. "You have such intensity in your eyes, Ms. Kent." When he followed that observation with the question "Do you ever have any fun?" Elaine's eyes grew big and round, as she quickly pulled her elbows off the table, and leaned back again in her chair. But she didn't fool Jack. He could tell he had shaken Elaine's composure, by the visible deepening of her beautiful dark eyes. And the slight flush that spread across her cheeks. And he finally acknowledged, to himself at least, that he could probably sink into those deep pools of liquid and never want to swim to safety.

Leaning back in her chair gave Elaine a few seconds to regain enough of her composure to quickly shoot back with some heat, "I have *lots* of fun, Mr. Amory! But you will never know how! But I will admit that since I met you, I haven't had any fun at all! I think we should get to Kate's house, and see what, if anything, my brother has figured out." And with that, she rose and left him to pay the entire bill.

Chapter 10

They walked from Bullfeathers, which was just a block down First Street, SE, behind the Cannon House Office Building, to Kate Blanchard's Capitol Hill home on A Street, NE. As they approached the front door, Elaine pulled out her own key and let the two of them in. They heard voices coming from the living room, so they headed in that direction. Diggie was perched on the sofa, with his laptop on the coffee table. His hands were racing across the keyboard as Caroline, sitting next to him on the sofa, and resting her right hand on his left shoulder, was pointing to this and that on the screen, saying "Try here..OK try that...and...Oh! Hi, guys!" Caroline exclaimed, as she looked up, and saw Elaine and Jack standing in the archway watching the two of them fly around cyberspace.

Caroline quickly removed her hand from Diggie's shoulder and placed it in her lap, with her other hand. She sat up a little straighter, as she fidgeted in her seat to put some physical distance between herself and Diggie on the sofa, but she couldn't hide her pride in Diggie's success as she exclaimed excitedly, "Diggie's amazing! You won't believe what he's discovered! I don't think anyone else could have figured it out!"

"Figured out what?!" Elaine and Jack asked simultaneously, as they entered the living room. Jack crossed his arms and looked deliberately at Diggie, while Elaine put her hands on her hips expectantly.

"You tell them, Diggie! You did it!" Caroline patted Diggie on the shoulder, and Elaine could hear the pride in her voice.

"I couldn't have done it without your help, Caroline," Diggie said, as he stole a quick glance at Caroline to acknowledge her contribution. He could feel the flush of pride from Caroline's recognition, as heightened color rose to his face and gave his cheeks a warm reddish glow. When he could stand to move his gaze from Caroline, finally, to Elaine and Jack, he explained, "Caroline has much more precise visual comprehension than I do," and he turned again to acknowledge Caroline, admiration pouring out of his glance. Caroline smiled back her 'thank you', clearly as enamored as Diggie. What Elaine could never understand was why neither of them had yet been able to bring their mutual attraction to fruition. It was clear to any observer that they were besotted with each other—in spite of the fact that they had known each other most of their young lives. It must be nice, Elaine sighed to herself, to feel that way about someone, and more so, to have that feeling returned.

Without missing a beat, however, Elaine and Jack slowly turned their heads toward each other, just far enough to make eye contact, then silently nodded their heads sidewise toward the pair on the sofa, and smiled. And then they both bombarded the pair with questions.

"So, what *did* you find?" came from Jack, while Elaine piped up excitedly with, "Are they phony, Diggie?! Did you figure out how they did it?!"

"Wait a minute! Slow down! Stop talking at once! I can't understand either one of you," Diggie quieted them, with one hand raised, as if in self-defense.

Elaine was first out of the gate. Trying very hard to speak evenly and carefully, she inquired, "Ok, Diggie. In English, please. What did you discover?"

"They're phony!" Diggie shouted with glee, throwing both of his hands in the air. Caroline's face broke into the broadest grin imaginable, as she bounced up and down on the sofa, clapping her hands with excitement.

"I told you so!" Elaine practically screamed at Jack; as she turned toward him to brandish her success, her own face lit up with a huge grin. "Ok," she turned back to Diggie, not giving Jack a chance to comment, "tell us how you know, and you can stray from English, if you need, but just a little bit!" Elaine instructed, unable to hold back her happiness.

Jack remained silent, arms across his chest, trying to understand everything that was going on, and wondering why, in hell, his friend had lied to him, if, in fact, he *had* lied. Jack stood very still, gazing down at the couple on the sofa, the blue of his eyes clouding as he waited for the explanation of how the photos had been manufactured.

"Well," Diggie started, "you know how photos are made up of pixels," he stated, more than asked. "Well, one way to determine if a photo is manufactured is to identify whether different parts of the photo have different pixel compositions."

"Nobody trying to pull this kind of thing off today," Jack interrupted, "would be inexperienced enough, or careless enough, to make a mistake like that. It's too easy to detect. Even I understand that kind of trickery!"

"You're right, generally," Diggie conceded. "But our inventor here thought he—or she—had been clever enough to hide the discrepancy so that it couldn't be discovered through the typical, rather shallow, exams that most analysts use, especially if they are under a deadline," and Diggie looked pointedly at Jack, as if to emphasize the hurried—and harried—nature of journalism.

"Go on," Jack's eyes narrowed, while his arms remained firmly folded across his chest, tension tightening the muscles in his jaw.

"Well, in a case like this, if the photo is manufactured, then the perpetrators might have used a photo of Mrs. Blanchard that was not of their making. That's what they did." And as he said that, he pulled up, in a separate window on the computer screen, a news photo of Kate Blanchard looking up at something, and pointing. "See the angle of her head, the way she's leaning back looking up? That angle made this a perfect photo for portraying her as if she were lying down, looking up at someone," Diggie explained. "The image, and the pixel count, in this photo are a perfect match for the original image of her head in the photos," he stated.

There was a moment of expectant silence from Jack, who was clearly waiting for more explanation. "This is a photo of Blanchard at an air show held at the Manassas Regional Airport in Virginia, six years ago," Diggie added. "She's looking up, and pointing at one of the planes in the airborne demonstrations. Maybe whoever did this thought the photo was too old to be identified," Diggie muttered, almost to himself.

"So," Jack broke his silence, "this is the picture they cropped to get her head?" And as Diggie and Caroline eagerly nodded, Jack continued, "That can't be your only evidence, can it? How can you tell that the pixel count in that six-year old photo is the same as the pixel count for her head in these new photos? Or that her head, alone, was *added* to these photos? I mean, what's to say these aren't just two very similar photos, given that in both cases she is looking up at *some*thing, or someone?

"That's just the start," Diggie informed them. And then, taking a deep breath, he further explained, "To make the composite, they used a digital camera that had the same pixel count as the photo they cropped—which is probably why they didn't bother to get their own photo of her with their own camera—but they couldn't match the texture exactly because the original photo of Kate Blanchard was actually taken with 35mm film, and the photo used to portray the rest of the image was taken with a digital camera. The differences are microscopic—but a powerful enough computer can see them!

"The interesting thing, though," Diggie continued, "is that a digital camera that can match the quality of a 35mm camera is still quite expensive, in case that helps you narrow the field of perpetrators," and he smiled up at them. "You can't buy one with chump change!"

"But did they use the same cropped photo of Kate in each of the three fakes?" Elaine asked.

"Yeah, Sis, they did. But they angled it just a little differently in each photo, and posed the men to fit the angle of her head. They also used creative retouching to alter the light that reflects off her hair, just a little each time, and to try to change the outline of her head in each photo so that it didn't easily look like it was the same one. That way there would appear to be enough differences between the three photos that, to the casual eye and to the shallow analyst, they would not appear to be the same photo of her. Why," Diggie wandered out loud, though he seemed to be talking to himself, "they would go to all this trouble and not use 3 different photos, I can't understand."

"That still doesn't explain why they thought they could get away with it," Jack cut in sharply, unable to compute his friend's deception.

"If you let me finish, Mr. Amory, I will show you," and with that, Diggie called up one of the photo composites on his computer. "Look, here's the finished product, and if you do a standard scan for different pixels, it looks clean—like there's no discrepancy at all throughout the photos."

And Caroline just couldn't hold it in any longer. Bouncing up and down in place on the sofa, she exclaimed, "Diggie discovered that they had layered the final photo so many times, after flattening the original composite, that it hides the pixel inconsistencies from standard scans!"

"Ok, we need to go back to English, here, folks," Elaine noted somberly.

"It's simple, Sis," Diggie replied. "They digitized the photo of Blanchard. Then they flattened the composite file, and they kept taking photos, over and over, of each of the finished products, so many times that the pixel differences would be nearly impossible to detect!" Diggie finished with a flourish. "You need a really powerful computer to detect it. I linked into the super duper computer at my alma mater, where I also teach occasionally, which I can access for my work whenever I want," and he stopped at that comment so as not to compromise what he does, especially in front of someone who was still, really, a stranger.

"They probably analyzed each copy of the photo, until they had one that didn't indicate any pixel differences on standard equipment!" Caroline chimed in.

"Can you tell how many copies they made to get to this final one, Diggie?" Elaine asked. She was wondering how this would play out in the media. How will Representative Blanchard be able to prove the photos aren't genuine using Diggie's analysis, if typical scanners come up with nothing wrong? Would the explanation be too complicated, or esoteric, for the press? If the explanation weren't simple enough for today's thirty-second media stories, would it be possible for people to raise enough questions about Diggie's findings to prevent the unequivocal resolution of the issues, if the photos ever saw the light of day? For even in this moment of relief, and glee, with the proof that the photos were, indeed, phony, Elaine strongly believed that whoever was behind this smear attempt would be able to achieve their goal just by releasing the photos. It was, after all, just nine days until the election.

"I believe it took nineteen copies—that is, we are looking at the nineteenth version of the photos."

"You *believe?*" Elaine's eyes widened as she looked at her kid brother, and her voice was barely a whisper. "You don't *know*, Diggie?"

"Well, their follow-on photos of the original composite used the next lowest pixel count, presumably to blur the minuscule differences in the original composite. A higher pixel count would have made it easier to pick up the different pixel counts, but you would still have to have been looking for it, if you were going to go deep enough to find the original fake," Diggie finished.

Elaine turned to Jack, and in spite of Diggie's "believe", her voice held a triumphant note as she stated what she considered the obvious, "Well, Mr. Amory, there you have it! They're phony! P-H-O-N-Y, Phony! So you can forget your scandal-mongering! This case is Closed!" she finished with a flourish.

"Not quite so, Sis, I'm afraid," Diggie commented, with what sounded like a small, almost fearful, voice.

Caught off guard, Elaine quickly turned to look squarely at her brother, and suddenly she felt the hairs on the back of her neck stand up. "What do you mean 'not quite'? What more *is* there, Diggie? What more *could* there be? You said they were phony, right?"

"Well, yes, they aren't real," and you could hear Elaine breathe out a sigh of relief, as her shoulders sank to their natural level—all too soon, it turned out, as Diggie continued, "But, Sis, there's—well, there's another anomaly," Diggie added, in that same small voice.

"What *anomaly*?!" Elaine nearly shouted in exasperation.

"Well—it's like this," Diggie hedged.

"Oh, for goodness sake, Diggie! Spit it out!" Elaine ordered, as she felt the chill of the room reaching her bones.

"Well, it's not just Kate Blanchard's head that's been added. The heads of the men in the photos are also additions! That is, they, too, have been photo-shopped into the pictures."

Chapter 11

Elaine stood very still, not understanding what she had heard, the numbness slowly seeping down from her brain and into her body. She tried to open her mouth and speak, but no sound came out, probably because she could not think of what to say, or ask. She felt a hand on her elbow directing her toward a cushioned chair opposite the sofa in which Diggie and Caroline were ensconced. She let Jack achieve his objective, as she plopped down into the soft seat, her rear end sinking close to the floor, while her knees were pushed up toward her chin. Her arms lay limply in her lap, as if she didn't have a single bone in them.

"Ok," Elaine said slowly out loud after a moment, though her voice sounded, even to her, very far away. "I'm trying to get my brain to process this, but it boggles my mind. The obvious conclusion is, if the photos aren't genuine, as they clearly aren't, then these three lobbyists had to be in on it, and together. They have to be the ones who conjured up this nightmare. They are the ones who will gain tremendously if Kate Blanchard loses her bid for the Senate. They would eliminate a major opponent from Congress. And everyone knows Billingsley will just be a patsy for the policies each of them pursues. Billingsley may, or may not, be in cahoots with them. But if their presence in the photos was also photo-shopped in, did they do that deliberately—or could it possibly mean that they are *not* the source of this effort to destroy her candidacy? And if not *them,* then *who?*"

Elaine looked up at Jack with eyes that were full of wonder and questioning... and disbelief that they could be in the quandary they were facing. And then she noted, full of astonishment, "I know Kate's main issue with you was whether the men were real or not, but, honestly, I don't think any of us ever thought they weren't real! It never occurred to us they were *not* the ones behind this."

Jack's mind was working furiously to sort out this incredible finding. In spite of Blanchard's focus on the genuineness of the photos of the men, he, too, really thought they would be the ones behind this if the photos were, indeed, phony, as he now accepted them to be. It was easy to figure out the political motivation if one, or more, of these three lobbyists were responsible. But what political motivations could generate such a really vicious attack, if they were not the ones setting off this scandal? Billingsley was running a dirty campaign, but no one credited him, or his backers, with this kind of skillful plotting. Not on his own, at least. But maybe they were being too quick to write him off as a possibility.

"It could still be a conspiracy by these lobbyists," Jack offered, rubbing his chin in concentrated thought. "I don't know if they would have done this on their own, or in cahoots with Billingsley. You are so right that anyone with any political savvy knows Billingsley's a patsy for the kinds of policies and programs those guys push. But Billingsley needs to be able to deny participation in such a scandal, and he has to be believable."

"When we report that the photos are not genuine, after all," Caroline interjected, "that will mean also revealing that the images of the lobbyists are photo-shopped in as well, won't it? That would exonerate them, in the public eye, at least, of any wrong-doing. No one would believe they were actually behind the leaking of photos in which their own images were faked. Mom would lose the election, and they would be free of any blame! It's as if they found a way to have their cake and eat it, too!" Caroline wanted to cry in frustration.

Jack stood there trying to focus his thoughts, as everyone stared at him expectantly, waiting for him to analyze the context, and come up with a clever political motive and perpetrator. "You're right, Caroline. They could have deliberately faked their own images, as well," he spoke slowly, and quietly, "to be able to argue credibly, though not truthfully, that they were not to blame for the scandal. When asked if they were involved in an affair with Blanchard, all they have to say is 'no comment', or even something as coarse as 'don't be ridiculous!'. They would not be lying by confirming an affair that never happened, but they would not be denying the alleged affair either. The media would interpret that non-denial as validation of the affairs, and that's the message that would run through the media, for at least a few days."

"Now that's really clever, but could any of those three men actually be *that* clever?!" Elaine chuckled, as she tried to interject a moment of humor to cut through the tension.

"Never underestimate an opponent, Ms. Kent," Jack warned darkly, tilting his head to one side to look down at her, both of his brows raised in blunt warning. "All three of those men are, very much, clever enough to construct precisely that kind of scenario."

It was a sobering thought. After some consideration Elaine admitted, "Ok. We know the photos are not genuine. And the election is only nine days away. I mean,...."

"Yes, just what *do* you mean, Ms. Kent?" it was Jack's turn to try to lighten the atmosphere, by teasing Elaine about her habit of repeating favorite expressions.

But when all he did was make her turn a silent, scornful look at him, he continued, in a more business-like manner, "You are right. With the election 9 days away, by the time the truth gets reported, if ever, the reports would either come *after* the election, or so close to the election that the revelation would get lost in the chatter about the scandal. And again, as you pointed out yesterday, the scandal is the news, and it's all that the news cycle cares about."

After a moment of silence, in which everyone seemed lost in their own nightmarish thoughts, Jack added, rubbing his chin again, "My guess is that they will, in fact, give a non-denial to the alleged affair, if the photos ever go public. Even, ironically, if they've had nothing to do with the creation and distribution of the photos."

Elaine mentally cataloged the chin-rubbing gesture, along with the raised eyebrows, as peculiarly Jack's. Opening her mouth to comment, she suddenly closed her jaw tight at the realization that her mind seemed more interested in logging Jack's personal habits, than in the problem at hand. How can my mind be focusing on anything but the photos at a time like this?

"Look at it this way," Jack continued, when no one commented, "since the affairs are *not* real, they can deny the affairs and be telling the truth. And if they are really not involved, they *should,* ethically, make a true denial, not muddy the waters by simply refusing to comment. That way, they wouldn't get blamed for playing politics in a really nasty way. Any denial from them won't prevent the photos from doing their damage, because everyone can deny affairs all they want, but the photos are there for everyone to see...especially if they are initially credited as real.

"But I can't vouch for the ethics of any of those guys. If they go for the non-denial comment, then all bets are off. They would be implying they did have affairs, but never actually saying they did. That would inflame the scandal. And they would benefit then, from any negative impact on Blanchard's campaign, even if they are not the perpetrators," he observed.

"That's what will make Blanchard's defense difficult," he added, "because the technical explanation of why the photos are phony is a bit complex—the validity of that defense could be debated, but remain unresolved, all the way up to election day."

"By the time Kate ever got exonerated in the media, if she ever did, she would probably already have lost the election," Elaine softly noted. "Still," she added, looking up at Jack, "it does seem rather elaborate—and you know those three don't normally work together in their legislative agendas, so why would they be willing to collaborate on something as risky, and nefarious, as this?"

"It sounds elaborate," Jack noted, "but think of the amazing success Blanchard has had in her opposition to their legislative agendas. We're talking hundreds of millions, even billions, of dollars involved, when you look at their combined interests over the years. You shouldn't be surprised to learn they would go to extremes if they could de-rail her election, and, even better, permanently destroy her career—and still come up smelling like roses."

"You're right about that," Elaine conceded, "but it still..."

"My question," Diggie chimed in, "is, *who* is the technician who created these photos, and who did they do it for? Even if these lobbyists are behind this, they didn't actually create the photos themselves. And who will media outlets go to for verification? You went to a computer technician you consider reliable and talented, and I can say that he has a very good reputation in the industry, yet he was wrong!"

Everyone looked at Diggie as if he had struck gold, asking the most critically important questions. Determining who had, in fact, actually constructed the photos, and as soon as possible, was probably the best way the scandal could be deflated quickly enough to prevent permanent damage in the election if the photos ever go public.

"I mean, who has the skill to have created phony pictures so cleverly that the photos could survive typical media scrutiny, at least for long enough to impact the election?" Diggie pursued his query.

"It's your field, Diggie," Elaine countered, "you tell us who you know, or think, is capable of creating photos that could evade typical detection techniques. There can't be that many, and I would think they are folks who would be known in the industry, wouldn't you?"

"Well," Diggie sighed, looking down at the floor for a moment, then examining his finger nails, and then directly meeting Jack's eyes, "your friend who declared these photos genuine, Craig Bittiford, is a distinct possibility. He's very talented. But then, if he didn't create them, and he simply used the basic shallow analytical techniques to examine them, he could have been fooled. I mean, when he told you the photos were genuine, he may really have believed they were.

"But, locally, he's one of two or three that I can think of with the skills and knowledge to come up with this kind of construction. So I can't imagine he would have done a shallow examination," Diggie continued. "Of course, it could also be someone from out of town. I can give you the names of a few. But it's a dicey effort. In spite of the skill of the technician, there is still the risk the falsification of the photos would be discovered at some point, and then the technician's reputation in the industry would go down the drain as far as legitimate work goes—not to mention the downside of any possible criminal charges. The only people who would patronize someone discovered to have done something like that, are people who want to develop deliberately deceitful advertising campaigns, for whatever. Not that there wouldn't be a lot of money in that..."

"So maybe there is no downside to being discovered to have manufactured such photos?" Elaine wondered. "After all, the public can, at times, have a very short memory—here today, gone tomorrow!"

"What's clear is we really need to get the listening devices checked for finger prints, to see if they provide any clues," Diggie interjected.

"Yes, I agree," Elaine nodded. "It's even more important now to know exactly what is going on, and who is involved, so we can know how to respond if anyone goes public with these photos. But how do we get those devices checked for prints, and get any prints identified, without involving any police? I mean, I don't think we should be going to the police yet with this—we don't know if we need to file a complaint about the bugs, or if we should let this lie low, and hope it just disappears. If news of the bugs becomes public, and we don't know who planted them, some people might accuse Kate of a stunt to solidify her election," Elaine noted. "If you don't publish the photos, Jack, maybe no one else will either?" she looked at him expectantly, hoping for a miracle.

"I don't want to be the party poop, but you know this isn't going to disappear, Elaine," Jack stated with conviction. "If I don't go public with these photos—and soon—I'm certain they will be sent to someone else to publicize. Whoever is behind this went to a lot of trouble to produce those photos. The question is, how long will "Anonymous" wait for me to publish them, before sending them to another outlet? And if discovering that the photos are not genuine is as difficult as Diggie implies, whoever else gets them is going to believe they are real—even if they have them checked out, it seems, like I did," Jack added, sounding a little deflated. "I'm not sure there is anyone else around here with the skill to figure out what Diggie and Caroline have discovered, or who cares enough about the truth to dig deeply enough for it."

"And even if there *are* any fingerprints on the listening devices," Elaine continued, as if no one else had spoken, "what if they don't belong to any of the lobbyists?! I mean, I doubt very much any of them have been in Kate's private office, let alone her home," she finished, emphatically.

"What I need to know," Jack posed, "is, should I pre-empt any, almost certain, publication by another outlet, or do you want to wait until they get published by someone else, and then react?"

"I'm not sure we can make that decision," Elaine noted. "I think we need to lay all this out for Kate, and see how she wants to proceed. I'm sure her campaign manager will want to have some input on this, too."

And at that point, Caroline chimed in with, "Mom's on the Hill already. The House started up really early this morning, I guess in the hopes of clearing the legislative agenda some time today, so everyone can go home and campaign."

"Do you have any idea, Amory, how long before whoever sent the photos to you will wait before shopping them elsewhere?" Diggie asked.

"Your guess is as good as mine," Jack replied, "since I have no idea who sent them to me. And now I'm really curious as to 'why me'. I got these in my regular mail on Friday afternoon. They came to my home address, which, however, is also my business address. I had my friend check them out Friday evening, and I showed up at Blanchard's office first thing Saturday morning. It seems very likely that whoever sent them knows Congress is still in session, and I'm sure that person also has a very keen political sense. Whoever it is won't wait too long—there needs to be time to blanket the airwaves and wires with the release of the story before election day. So, at this point, I would say that the perpetrators need public release of the photos to occur sooner rather than later."

"You know," Elaine added thoughtfully, "that question of 'why you' is curious. I mean, you would think those kinds of photos would have been released back home, where the election is, rather than here in Washington. Why do you suppose they were released here?"

"Maybe if we can find out who sent them, we might be able to figure that out. I don't think we have enough information to answer that yet," Jack replied.

"Honestly, my head is beginning to ache! I'm not sure I can think clearly any more," Elaine exclaimed in response, raising both hands to hold her head, as if that could stop the pain that was now hammering at her brain.

At that pronouncement, though, and without skipping a beat, Jack was suddenly on his feet and grabbing Elaine's hand. "I have just the remedy for that, my dear," Jack interjected, as he pulled her up from her chair and started leading her out of Kate Blanchard's home.

"Wait a minute! What are you doing?" Elaine protested, as she resisted his pull.

"I'm going to clear your head for you! So we can figure out what our next steps should be!" Jack explained, with a mischievous twinkle in his eye that made Elaine's breath catch in her throat when she caught site of it. "C'mon, grab your coat!"

"No! We have to figure out what to do about this *now*! We need to set up a meeting, as soon as we can get Kate hooked up for a videoconference with her campaign manager," and she tried to pull away from his grip.

"Look, there is too much to grapple with on too little sleep—for both of us. And I have just the remedy. We are going to a place where the stars can fill our eyes with wonder, and give our brains a rest, by making us think of something completely unrelated, if only briefly!"

"But there's no time!" Elaine protested.

"Oh, yes there is! It's more important than ever to give your mind a break when it's full of stuff that does't make sense. You'll be surprised how your mind can sort confusing things out when you are relaxing and concentrating on something else entirely!" Jack beamed.

They were actually out the door by now, as Jack tossed Elaine's coat to her. When she looked up at Jack's smiling face, so thoroughly pleased with himself, and so confident he was right, she couldn't find a reason to disagree with him. So she quickly donned her coat, and let him escort her down the street.

"Ok, Mr. Therapist, where are we going for this stellar distraction?" Elaine asked. "And how long will it take?!" she looked up at him threateningly, but no longer trying to pull him in another direction.

"You'll see!" he replied, completely unperturbed. "I hope you don't mind a bit of a walk. We're only about a half mile away," and he looked down at her with a challenge in his eyes.

"Oh, you think I can't walk a half mile, Mr. Amory?" she asked, with her nose in the air. "Well, I'll have you know I can do six miles on a recumbent bike—in less than thirty minutes! And I often go for a three-mile walk through the neighborhood, just for the exercise," Elaine noted, with her chin a little raised, "that is, when I get the chance," she added, her voice trailing off.

"Ah! The operative phrase—'when I get the chance'! And just when is that, Elaine? Just how often *do* you 'get the chance'?" As he looked down at Elaine, waiting for her answer, she just kept her glance straight in front of her.

Chapter 12

"Just what do you mean?" Elaine finally challenged him, as they carefully stepped over the uneven bricks in the sidewalk.

"I mean exactly what I said—how often do you get the chance to do something that has nothing to do with work?" Jack replied, matter-of-factly.

"No, you're really asking me if I'm a workaholic, or if I know how to play."

"If you say so," Jack conceded. After walking about half a block in silence, he repeated, "So—*are* you a workaholic, or do you also know how to play?" and he looked directly at her as they headed west on A Street, NE, towards the Library of Congress.

"I don't think that's any of your business!" Elaine exclaimed, the decibel level of her voice rising. "I mean, I've only known you for a little more than 24 hours, and in an adversarial business context, so what business is it of yours whether I am a workaholic or not?! And why would you care?!"

"Well, you are correct about the chronological length of our acquaintance," Jack chimed back, ignoring her heightened energy, "but you are so wrong about the quality of our relationship! We may have met just yesterday, but think back, Elaine, we've spent nearly all of those hours together! Why, that's more time in a single day than married couples typically spend with each other!" he finished with a flourish.

Elaine was caught off guard by this revelation, as her mind tried to process the truth of Jack's observation. Why was she being so prickly? Was it because he was hitting a little closer to home than she liked? It unnerved her when someone else made observations—especially accurate observations— about her life, or personality. And Jack seemed bent on unlocking the door to her hidden world. Why should it bother her? She had always defined her "private space" herself, and carefully regulated who was allowed to cross the moat. No one entered through that locked gate without her permission. No one was allowed to push their way into her world. *No one* invaded. Period.

"Aha! You see, even you are left speechless by the intimacy of what we have shared!" Jack pushed his point home. And he marveled a little, as he acknowledged to himself, that the past 24-plus hours not only had sped by, but had actually been fun, in spite of the seriousness of the situation they were dealing with. But my professional career is on the line here, he reminded himself, so why do I feel like I'm having a good time?

Elaine gave him a sidelong glance through her lush lashes before she spoke. Then she interrupted his self-examination to bring him back to the "here and now" with a slightly curt, "Is this going to take very long, Mr. Amory?" She couldn't argue with the validity of his comment on the past day, and she wasn't inclined, at the moment, to examine her own feelings about those hours. So she decided to deflect the conversation.

"Elaine, Elaine, no more 'Mr.'—Please! We are becoming such good friends!"

"Friends? Friends? Oh, I don't think so, *Mr*. Amory," Elaine chimed back.

Since it didn't look like he was going to win this line of chatter, Jack decided to answer her question. "I promise you, it won't take more than an hour. Look," as he pointed to the Smithsonian Institution's Air and Space Museum on the National Mall, which they were approaching, "we're almost there!" And in spite of the moment, there was a sense of excitement in his voice. He loved the Smithsonian Museums, and especially the Air and Space.

"We're going to the Air and Space Museum?" and there was a sense of breathlessness in Elaine's voice, as her own eyes widened with a dawning glee.

"Yup!" Jack answered. Then, more seriously, noticing the lift in Elaine's voice, he asked, "Does that interest you?"

"What are we going to do there?" she replied lightly, trying to make the question impersonal.

"Well, I promised you the stars for a diversion, and so it shall be. We'll head to the Planetarium—the shows are only

70

about 25 minutes long, and they start a new one about every half hour," and he checked his watch, "and we have 8 minutes to get in there before the next one starts. So if I am going to keep my promise to have you back at Blanchard's house in an hour, we'd better skip," and he gently tugged on her hand, which he had never let go of once they had left Blanchard's house, as he picked up their pace. He shot her a side remark, "I'm not sure which show is up, but they have one that's all about the current lineup of the stars in the sky. I did promise you the stars!"

"Well, I'm glad this was your idea, because in our hasty departure from the house, I left my wallet there! So this really is your treat!" and Elaine beamed up at him playfully. Somewhat to his own surprise, Jack realized that he didn't mind playing the gallant with Elaine Kent.

Elaine, too, loved the Air and Space Museum, but she couldn't remember the last time she had been there. She loved the IMAX theater and the Planetarium, but the only visits she could recollect had occurred many, many years ago, when she had first arrived in D.C. for Kate Blanchard's freshman year in Congress. Can it really be that long ago? Elaine asked herself. It didn't seem possible, but she racked her brain for a more recent recollection, and could not come up with one.

It made her wonder, for the first time, what her life consisted of after so many years in the nation's capitol. She loved her work, and so she gave her heart and soul to her responsibilities. But was her commitment to Kate Blanchard leaving her with no time to live a life of her own beyond the office? Did she ever really actually leave "the office" since she had become Blanchard's Chief of Staff, or did she just carry her work around with her wherever she went? It was a common occurrence among those who worked on the Hill.

In spite of all of her responsibilities as a member of Congress, and spending time in both D.C. and her home district, Kate Blanchard managed to keep her family at the center of her life. It took lots of effort, but she *made* it work. Had Elaine lost sight of herself as someone with a life to live outside of work? Had she become defined only by her job? She remembered her comment to Jack about 'when I have the time', and he had picked up on it right away. HHhhmmmmm, she thought. Maybe I need to think about that a little more.

They had arrived at the ticket booth inside the museum, when Elaine heard a grumble of "Oh, no!" from Jack, with a hint of pending doom in his voice.

"What's the matter?"

"Well, I promised you the stars, but the next show is 'To Space and Back'. I'm not..."

"Oh, that's wonderful!" Elaine interrupted. "I love Space. I even considered becoming an Astronomer once, when I was a teenager! When I was eleven years old, my parents decided to put fresh paint and new wallpaper in my bedroom, and they let me pick the wallpaper. It came down to a pretty feminine pink paper with a design of French poodles and boudoirs, on the one hand, or a bluish speckled paper with abstract images of different kinds of spacecraft—or so the images appeared to me. It wasn't a simple choice. It was as if two parts of my personality were competing with each other. But I ended up choosing the space design!" Elaine finished, without realizing that she was sharing something so personal with this stranger. She had just blurted it out. It just seemed so natural to tell him something like that. And yet, she couldn't remember telling anyone else that story—ever. It was so very personal. "Besides," she added aloud, "you can't travel through space without seeing a lot of stars!"

"Whew! Well, that's good, then," Jack noted with relief, after being momentarily thrown off guard by Elaine's unexpected outburst of information—personal information, at that. "Next time, then, we can come and learn about the stars in the winter sky!" And he took Elaine's hand, tucked it into the elbow of his bent arm, and led her into the Planetarium.

Neither one acknowledged the 'next time' reference, but their entrance into the theater was particularly light-footed for both.

Chapter 13

They had spent the last half hour sitting shoulder to shoulder, their bodies sunken down into the seating inside the Planetarium, with their heads resting on the chair backs so they could look up at the dome, and see 'the sky', as it came alive with the images of space. It was quite dark, of course, and Elaine found herself captivated by the notion of floating through space to places and experiences far beyond her imagination. She had always loved the sensation of floating—it was why she had a life-long fascination with ice skating, and why waltzing, particularly to a Strauss waltz, filled her with the sensation of romance.

As she sat gazing up at the "sky", eagerly anticipating being carried to another universe, she realized that part of the pleasure of the moment came from sharing the experience with this unusual man. For she had to admit to herself, as she sat so close to him in the darkened theater, that he was definitely not a run-of-the-mill reporter. He seemed to be an oxymoron, a journalist who might actually have some ethics. He had been handed, free and clear, out of the blue, a gift that would have given him, and his political blog, household recognition across the country. Mainstream news outlets would have been inundating him with requests for interviews, and pouring over past issues of his blog, looking for some erudite intelligence that might be hidden there, and hoping to discover untold secrets they could then be the first to publicize. It didn't matter if the photos were ultimately revealed as phony, because the sensational revelation is what would have made him famous. His future would have been guaranteed, whatever the validity of the photos. It would have been so easy.

But he had not taken the easy road. Instead, he had actually tried to get at the truth. Doggedly so. He could have taken his friend's certification that the photos were valid and run with his story. And if they were shown to be phony later, he would have been exonerated from the epithet of "poor journalism" because he had taken the trouble to have the photos validated, and was given such validation by a highly reputable expert.

And yet, Elaine marveled, in his independent judgment, he suspected there was something not quite right. Representative Blanchard had an exceptional reputation for straightforwardness and candor, and for serving the public interest. She had a history of legislative actions, and public policy positions, that belied the message those photos were sending, that she was literally and figuratively 'in bed' with these lobbyists. Knowing her political reputation, Jack had sensed the possibility that something wasn't kosher, in spite of the validation his friend had given him. So he took the time—when time was at a premium if he was to cash in on this gift—he took the time to get the true story, so that he didn't unfairly ruin someone else's career, and perhaps aid and abet the election of someone who might not deserve that help.

He was a professional, Elaine had to admit. And he was honorable in his profession. And she admired that—a lot. In today's media world, he was an exception. And that made him special. Definitely special, she concluded. Why that gave her spirits a bit of a lift, she told herself, was because his fairness was helping to protect her boss from an obviously scurrilous attack.

" 'Don't let's ask for the moon...we have the stars' , or something like that."

"Huh?...wha...what?" Elaine was jolted from her revery. "Were you saying something?"

"Oh, just trying to bring you back to earth, my lady," Jack replied. They were still slunk in their seats as the mesmerizing journey into space came to its end. He turned toward her, so that he could lock his eyes on hers as the dim lighting returned. As she angled her glance at him to reply to his comment, her breath caught in her throat by two beautiful blue eyes that seemed to be dancing with mirth. They held her glance, as she sat there momentarily transfixed, her mouth open, but with no sound emanating from within. His face was so close to hers that she felt like his eyes had tentacles that were reaching deep into her soul, perhaps unlocking truths that were hidden even to her.

She tried to shake off the hold of his gaze. "What...what did you say?" she whispered.

"I was quoting from an old movie," he whispered back, leaning closer, his gaze unrelenting. "One of my favorites—'*Now Voyager*'. The ending is probably one of the most sexually tense scenes on film—and yet they never even touch," he finished quietly, in awe of the emotional power of that closing scene.

"Oh, I know the film you mean!" Elaine was trying to wade through the thick and heavy atmosphere, to where she might breathe more easily. "Bette Davis and Paul Henreid share a forbidden love," she related.

"Exactly!" Jack was both surprised, and delighted, that she knew the film. "And at the end, though they know they cannot consummate their love, they accept the shared raising of his neglected younger daughter as enough—'We have the stars' Bette Davis says to Henreid. And then he lights two cigarettes and gives one to her, and the camera pans to the stars in the night sky outside the open window they're standing in front of. It's some of the most powerful emotional storytelling on film!"

Elaine sat there transfixed, just staring up at him. Then without even a hint of sarcasm, she noted, "You know, for a man, you have surprising hidden tastes, Mr. Amory."

"And just what would those be, Ms. Kent?" giving like for like, without ever lifting his gaze from her.

But she broke the spell—and lost a moment of truth—with a cavalier reply, as she unexpectedly rose out of her seat, "Well, if and when I ever figure that out, I'll let you know."

"What? Are you afraid to admit it?" Jack asked in a low voice, looking up at Elaine from his seat.

"Admit what?" she asked, looking back at him just sitting there.

"That there is sexual tension between us, just like the sexual tension at the end of '*Now Voyager*'." And then he rose slowly from his seat, giving Elaine enough time for his words to sink in.

"Sexual...*what*?! Don't be ridiculous!" and the pitch of Elaine's voice was just a bit shrill. "We don't even *know* each other! We just met yesterday morning, for cryin' out loud! And not in a friendly encounter, either!" she finished, with some exasperation, looking away from him as she started to move out of the row of theater seats and toward the exit.

"Oh, come now, Elaine," and Jack kept his voice low as he followed her, "you know, as well as I do, that it has nothing to do with how long you know someone. It has to do with the electricity that flies between two people. When it's there, it's there, even between complete strangers. But you know it's there."

"You're *crazy*, Jack Amory!" Elaine cried in a loud stage whisper, soundly rejecting the whole notion of being attracted to him in any way.

But what *was* that prickly sensation that had sent shivers through her whole body as she sat so close to him in the dark? And why does she feel the need to hide, or suppress, the fact that she understood, only too well, that he was right. Why did she want to keep the truth hidden?

Chapter 14

"So, what are your thoughts on the road ahead?" Jack asked.

They were turning the corner towards the rear of the Library of Congress' main building, as they headed east from the Capitol, back down A Street NE, all notions of a shared sexual tension being left to steam on the back burner, under a low, simmering flame that each thought they could ignore, at least for the time being. They were not holding hands, as they had on the way to the museum barely a half hour earlier, but there was a quiet, thought-filled, intimacy between them as they considered how best to prevent an election disaster.

"Well," Elaine mused out loud, "first we have to inform Kate of Diggie's results. She needs to consult with her husband, and her campaign manager, about the best way to deal with this." Elaine looked up at Jack walking beside her, but he seemed more focused on the ground than the way ahead. "Of course, we cannot decide how you should proceed," she continued. "That's up to you. You are, after all," she conceded, with a slight smile that was more friendly than hostile, "an independent journalist. What you publish in your blog is your decision, as is what you choose not to write about."

"Now, you don't think I'm going to write the story that the anonymous sender of these photos wants me to write, do you?" Jack asked, with disbelief permeating his voice.

"No, of course not," Elaine conceded. "And don't think that I haven't noticed the 'we' in your earlier pronouncements about how best to proceed. You really have been open-minded and fair," she conceded, as she gave him a side-long glance through her lashes that, while veiled, was, again, more friendly than hostile. "No, the game would seem to have changed," she continued. "For you, it's basically a question of to publish or not, and if so, what you would say about it—that is, deciding what your story line will be.

"And you are right," she continued, "that soon enough someone else will receive the photos, and publish them if you don't. And they will publish, with the belief that they are

77

genuine, as you have noted, and with the message that the anonymous sender wants. Representative Blanchard needs to figure out how she will respond to the trumped up scandal—or whether she wants to make a preventive strike, and go public with the attempt. Though a preemptive strike has its pitfalls, too."

"Wait a minute!" Jack's face was turning red, as the heat began rising from somewhere deep in his gut. "It's not just a simple question for me of 'to publish or not to publish'. Or probably, more aptly described as 'to perish or not to perish'. I want to know who sent those pictures to me—who was trying to use me as a patsy to influence the outcome of an election! A major election!

"Look, someone thought I was really stupid, stupid enough to be completely fooled," he noted. Elaine's glance was filled with empathy, remembering it was his friend who had told him the photos were genuine. "Who is it who is willing to destroy my professional reputation as a journalist, without so much as a care in the world, as long as he ruined Blanchard's election chances?! I want to know who that is! And I plan to devote my time, between now and the election, to finding out!" Jack promised. "Actually," he added, putting his journalist's hat on, "it could make a good post-election story. Or even the story line for a novel!"

"Are you planning to try for a Pulitzer, Mr. Blog Man?" Elaine queried lightly, with a half smile.

"Well, you never know what talent you might have if you don't try!" he responded in tone. "After all, you *did* say that I had hidden talents!" and he smiled warmly as he looked down at her.

They were just a block from the Blanchard home now, and as they approached, they saw Spencer Ainsworth leaving, and not looking too happy. Caroline was in the process of closing the door when she caught sight of them.

"Hello!" she hollered, waving her arm.

"Hello!" Elaine shouted back, waving as well.

But it was Jack who asked the obvious question when they reached the entrance. "So, why was Ainsworth so angry?"

"Was he?" Caroline asked, a little too innocently, her eyes big and round, answering Jack's inquiry with a bold look back at him.

"You know he was, Caroline. May I call you Caroline?" Jack shot back.

"Yes, of course you may, since you are obviously now a *friend* of Elaine's!" and she smiled mischievously.

"And?" Jack coached, ignoring her insinuation, as did Elaine.

"And—yes—I guess he *was* a little angry. He wanted to know why I didn't show up last night, and I told him I had no obligation to show up! After all, we have guests from out of town," and she nodded towards the inside of the house, presumably referring to Diggie, who had not left the house since he and Elaine had arrived the evening before.

"Ah!" Jack exclaimed. "You are an independent little minx, is that it?"

"No!" Caroline retorted, then caught herself. "Well, *yes*, as a matter of fact, I am! I met Spencer only a month ago! He doesn't own me! We've just been hanging out with other interns, sharing a common experience, so to speak! Besides, he planted those bugs in Mom's office, and here in the house, didn't he?!" she finished vehemently, crossing her arms in front of her to emphasize her point.

"Well, it's definitely possible," Jack said, "but we don't know for sure yet that that is the case. It could have been someone else. But he seems to be the best candidate so far, based on opportunity. Can you think of any reason *why* he would do something like that?"

"Not really," Caroline answered slowly, after a moment's pause. "But then, I can't think of who else it might have been either," she finished, a little triumphantly.

"Well, the more important question at the moment," Elaine interjected, as she and Jack entered the house, "is how are we going to proceed from here, given what we know, and what we don't know?"

Chapter 15

They were seated in a semicircle around one side of the coffee table in Kate Blanchard's living room. The Congresswoman was in the middle, on a long sofa, with Elaine on her left. Her husband, David, and then Diggie, were on her right. Jack sat on a wing chair beside Elaine, while Caroline, sitting on a dining room chair next to Diggie, was adjusting her chair by moving it as close beside Diggie as was physically possible to get, ostensibly, she noted, to make sure the computer's camera included her in the viewing range. Picking up on that, Jack gently moved his chair closer to Elaine, "so that they could all be picked up by the computer's camera," Jack explained to Elaine. Elaine raised her eyebrows to question his motive, but she didn't challenge his explanation, or objective.

Diggie's laptop computer was open on the coffee table, and facing them, as he made the connections to campaign headquarters back home for a live chat with Blanchard's campaign manager, Krystal Kincaid. As introduction, Elaine had explained earlier to Jack that, although this was Krystal's first election for Representative Blanchard, she came with excellent credits. Krystal had spearheaded an open Congressional race in the neighboring district two years earlier, and her candidate had won—not handily, but he had won. It had been an open seat, vacated by a Congressman who had served for forty years, but decided not to run for re-election. So it was a hard-fought, and hard-won, victory, that had demonstrated tremendous organizational skills on the part of Ms. Kincaid. When Kate Blanchard was looking for someone to manage her Senate campaign, she had immediately approached the "wonder girl" of the Sixth District's race.

"Oh, hey! I can see you all! Hi!" hailed Krystal, waving her arm. "How's it going there?! Are they ever going to adjourn, or at least recess, so you can come back here and do some campaigning, Kate? We really could use your physical presence here! Lots of opportunities to give speeches and shake hands, you know!"

"Hi, Krystal," it was the Congresswoman. "I think we're going to be here for a few more days, unfortunately. There's a lot of negotiating and bargaining going on just now, trying to get some major bills passed before adjourning. You know all of the hard bargaining occurs when the pressure of adjournment is staring us in the eyes! And no one really wants to come back after the election as a lame duck Congress."

"I can understand that, but all the House members, and one third of the Senate, are up for election, so you'd think more of them would want to be done with everything before it's too late to campaign!"

"I hear you, Krystal. I'm hoping we'll be done by Tuesday, or at the latest, Wednesday."

"Great! I'll start scheduling events for after Wednesday, and if you get home sooner, I'm sure there will be lots of activities still available, even at the last minute. As it is, there are only 5 full campaign days after Wednesday!"

"Thanks, Krystal. That sounds like a plan. But that's not why we wanted to chat with you folks today."

"I was wondering what was up—especially since you asked that Tony and Troy be here for this."

Kate Blanchard wasn't sure how to break the news to her campaign manager, press agent, and pollster. "Well, we have a situation going on here that could potentially blow up the election," she opened, "maybe even turn it around, in spite of our current lead in the polls."

"What could possibly do that, Kate?" Krystal asked in a small voice filled with disbelief. Kate Blanchard was a shoe-in in this race. And this election would be Krystal's crowning achievement. Winning this Senate race, just two years after her hard-won success in a House race, would give her national visibility that could translate into a powerful and lucrative role in the Presidential race two years hence. And success in that role could lead to a prominent position in the national party committee's headquarters, or even in the White House. Kate Blanchard's win this year was the key to Krystal's future, as well.

"Let me introduce to all of you a couple of people here that you may not know," Blanchard continued. "You all know my husband, David," and he returned the smile she gave him, "and, of course, you know Elaine," who nodded at the introduction. "Beside David is Gregory Kent, Elaine's brother, and a downright brilliant computer specialist, and beside him is my daughter Caroline. To Elaine's left is Jack Amory. Jack writes his own political blog that extensively covers the ins and outs of Hill activities and legislative affairs.

"We needed to meet with you to discuss a very serious attack on my election campaign. Jack received anonymously in the mail on Friday, three photographs showing me, literally, in bed with three lobbyists—and not just any lobbyists, but those pursuing programs and corporate handouts that I have fought against since I first arrived on Capitol Hill as a Freshman—opposition that has garnered us a bit of notoriety!"

There was complete silence on the other end of the video stream. No one moved a speck, and no one seemed to be breathing. As they waited for the next shoe to fall, they could have been mistaken for some of the many marble statues that dot the city.

"Now, very much to his credit," Kate Blanchard continued, "he has not published those photos. He had a highly reputable computer specialist examine the photos, and that expert declared them legitimate. Then he came to me for my response, and that made it possible for Elaine's brother to review them. Gregory did a more sophisticated examination, and found that the photos were very cleverly manufactured."

You could hear the sighs of relief, almost in unison, as the campaign leaders once again felt it safe to let out a breath.

"But this isn't as simple an issue as we thought. The photos are very puzzling. Not only was my face photo-shopped in, but the faces of the three lobbyists were *also* photo-shopped in."

Chaos seemed to break out at the campaign headquarters, as if a sheet of glass had just been shattered. Each of the three recipients of this news started talking at once.

"I don't understand, Kate! Who would *do* something like that?!" screeched Krystal. "What on earth is going on there?" came from Tony Esperanza, the Press Agent for the

Senate race. And Troy, the pollster, chimed in with "Oh, good grief, this could be explosive!"

"Hold on now!" Kate regained control of the discussion. "We don't know who is behind it yet. The question we are dealing with is what to do now? Mr. Amory accepts that these are phony photos, but none of us can figure out who might be behind it since the lobbyists' faces are also photo-shopped in."

"Who are the lobbyists in the pictures?" Krystal asked.

"You can probably guess—Kevin Lowell, Barker Phillips, and Arthur Cantrell!"

"Oh. My. God." Krystal moaned.

"Yes, my sentiments exactly," Kate rejoined.

"So, Mr. Amory. What are you going to do?" Krystal posed her curt question to Jack.

"Well, obviously, I'm not going to do what whoever sent the photos wants me to do—which is print them, which would imply, at least, that they are legitimate. I don't publish fake news. And I don't like the idea that someone is trying to use me as a tool for their own ends. I think what we are all trying to figure out here is, how to preempt the release of the photos. If I don't publish them, then the photos will probably be sent to someone else to write up, who may very well get the same kind of validation I got. That may be good enough for someone else, so it's highly probable that the photos will get publicly released, thereby achieving the sender's objective—to besmirch Representative Blanchard shortly before the election, so that she loses her Senate race. At this point, there may be too little press time to get the initial stories fully, and publicly, corrected before folks go to the ballot box."

Then Tony, the Press Agent, chimed in, "But if you don't publish them, why do you think it's a guarantee that someone else will? Maybe the best thing to do is nothing. By the time the sender figures out you are not going to publish the photos, it could be too late to gain any ground by sending them to someone else."

"Because it's already been a little more than 48 hours since I received the photos. That's more than enough time for me to have them checked. Whoever sent them understands that I would need a little time for that. But that person also knows that these photos are a hot story that would gain the publisher quite a bit of notoriety, whether the photos are genuine or not, so whoever is going to publicize them will want to get them out and about as quickly as possible. They are no good, for the sender *or* the publisher, *after* the election. Post-election publication could discredit Representative Blanchard, but by then the election would be a *fait accompli.* Based on Blanchard's current voter support, she would be the Senator-elect. It's a lot more difficult to undo the results of an election, than it is to prevent the undesired outcome. So, if I don't publish them within, say, another day, whoever sent them may conclude that I am not going to publish them—for whatever reason—or the sender may simply decide he or she gave me enough time and doesn't want to wait any longer. The upshot will be the same—the photos will likely be sent to someone else."

A heavy silence hung on both ends of the videoconference as everyone digested the situation, each hunting for that proverbial "light" at the end of a very dark tunnel.

It was Elaine who focused the group on the critical decision.

"Look, our starting place is: Do we present our own exposure of the photos, in an effort to pre-empt revelation—and accusation—by another source, or do we sit tight, hope against hope that the photos will not surface, but be prepared to respond if, and probably when," Elaine nodded at Jack, "the photos do show up in the public domain?"

"If we take a pre-emptive shot, and expose the photos and the fraud," it was Press Agent Tony, "then part of the outcry is probably going to include questions from some of our opponents asking why *we* exposed the fraud rather than just keeping quiet, especially since we cannot offer an explanation of their source. They will allude that, maybe the hoax is all ours, in order to disparage our opponent through innuendo, and really put a lock on the election result. That could backfire on us, and create a sympathy vote for Billingsley."

"You've hit on a critical point, Tony," Elaine acknowledged. "Just because the men in the photos are also photo-shopped in, doesn't mean they didn't create the fakes deliberately. We can't assume it was Billingsley, only Billingsley, or that Billingsley even knew about it."

"From a reporter's perspective," Jack chimed in, "part of the difficulty in fighting back—whether by pre-emption, or in response—is that the technical explanation of how the photos were constructed is difficult to describe simply, or in layman's terms. And you know how teflon-coated the media are when it comes to anything more complicated than one-plus-one equals two!"

"What do you mean?" Krystal asked.

"Whoever built these photos," Diggie contributed, "was very savvy technically, and the process used to build the photos, to make them pass muster by most analysts, is complicated. I'm sure you know only too well, Ms. Kincaid, how media coverage glosses over anything too technical, as Jack mentioned. Presenting a defense will not be easy to communicate—or, at least, will not be easy for the media to describe. And then, any *good* reporter," and here Diggie looked meaningfully at Jack, who winced in acknowledgement, "will want to test out the process, and that will be very difficult to do. There aren't many computer experts with the skill and sophisticated computer resources to figure out how the photos were actually created."

"And *that* will leave lots of room for media reports that talk about 'unclear' explanations that 'can't be easily proven', etc. etc.," Jack added. "And that means there could, even would, be lots of clouds hanging over the election, in spite of Representative Blanchard's proof that the photos are not genuine. No post-election vindication can change the results of an election, once it's over."

It would be an understatement to say that the general atmosphere on both sides of the videoconference was dominated by a growing sense of gloom and doom.

Chapter 16

It was 7:00 Sunday evening, and he was wondering where the other two were. He was sitting at a table at the Capitol Grille restaurant on the corner of Sixth and Penn, NW. The Grille was a place where they could all hide in public, so to speak. There, they would be just three more Capitol Hill players, among so many, sharing a meal, and strategizing about how to achieve their legislative goals. It was better than trying to meet secretly, where their gathering might, oddly enough, be more noticeable. At the Grille, a public meeting might hardly go remarked upon, especially during this time of scrambling on the Hill to clear the legislative agenda so everyone could go home. Or so Kevin Lowell hoped.

Finally one, then the other, walked through the door. Lowell raised an arm to wave them over to his table.

"So," Arthur Cantrell asked, as he and Barker Phillips sat down, "to what do we owe the pleasure of this invitation, Kevin?"

"Well, my friends, we have had an amazing piece of luck fall into our laps!" Kevin said excitedly, but in a low voice.

"Oh, yeah?" Phillips was skeptical. "What could that possibly be? Have you finally gotten your friend to kill that bill that I was able to get held up in Committee?"

"No, sorry," Lowell replied. "There is still the likelihood that the Committee will report it out before adjournment. No, it's something else. Nothing to do with this legislative cycle, but it could be wonderful for all future legislative cycles!" he beamed mysteriously.

"Well, are you going to share this tidbit of luck with us, or are you going to make us play guessing games?" Cantrell asked, showing signs of impatience. He had a lot of ground to cover before the House and Senate reconvened the next day.

Lowell leaned closer to them across the table, and whispered, "I have become aware of a pending scandal that could completely derail Kate Blanchard's Senate race!" Then he told them about the photos that allege Blanchard was having affairs, not only with multiple men, but with *each of them.*

Cantrell and Phillips were momentarily speechless. Cantrell recouped his senses first, as he slowly asked, "How can that be? Where would anyone get such photos? I, for one, am not having, and have not had, an affair with Kate Blanchard. My God, she hates the sight of me!"

"None of us are having affairs with her," Lowell commented, "at least I don't think we are," and he looked directly at Phillips.

"Well, *I'm* not having an affair with her!" Phillips nearly shouted.

"Please, keep your voice down," Lowell remonstrated, gesturing with his hand to calm Phillips.

"So what's going on, Kevin? Did you summon us just to tell us about it? Or are you scheming something?" Cantrell queried.

They tried to pretend they were having a casual meal, as salads came for Lowell and Cantrell, and a cup of soup for Phillips, while they discussed legislative activities at the Capitol. But their conversation was much more intense and focused. How could they capitalize on this opportunity, but without becoming the demons? If they were blamed for such interference in a federal election, especially once it became known on the Hill, at least, that the photos were really phony, members of Congress might be skeptical about trusting them as lobbyists for fear of generating a similar interference in their own re-election bids if they did not vote the way these lobbyists desired. They discovered that finding a way to benefit from this pending scandal, without getting blamed, was a tricky proposition since they were the men in the photos, and their antipathy towards Kate Blanchard was well-known.

But it was Cantrell who asked the obvious. "Is it possible, Kevin, that *you* are the creator of those photos?"

"Who, me?" Lowell replied, with surprise. "Why would you think it was me? I had nothing to do with it. I just have the good fortune of finding out about it."

"And just how did you do that?" Phillips asked.

"That is not important," Lowell deflected the question. "What's important is how can we benefit from this caper without getting our heads chopped off?"

Chapter 17

"Are you coming, Diggie?" Elaine called from the front door of Kate Blanchard's home. Diggie had agreed to stay in D.C. for awhile so he could be available in case the photo issue goes public, so he would be staying with his sister at her home. But, apparently, he wasn't ready to give up Caroline's company for the evening.

"Um, I'm going to stay here for awhile, if you don't mind, Sis. I want to hear about Caroline's European adventure!"

"Oh, ok, no problem. I'll leave you the car, then, since it will probably be dark when you head home."

"You don't have to. I can walk. It's not that far, and I know the way."

"Oh, I can drop him off, Elaine!" Caroline piped in.

"It's ok. I was planning to make a stop at Eastern Market to get some groceries, so I can just hop on the Metro. There's enough time yet before they close today. I'll see you later, Diggie!" and Elaine quickly headed out the door, leaving her car keys for Diggie, and chuckling to herself. Honestly, she thought, they are both enchanted with each other. Why is it so difficult for them to admit that to each other?

"Can I give you a lift to the Market, Elaine?" Jack invited, as he followed Elaine out the door. "If you are going for groceries, you will need a chariot to bring them home in, or you'll be pretty restricted in what you can buy," he encouraged, hoping for a positive response. He had spent most of the last 36 hours, or so, in her company, and the thought of going home alone for the rest of the evening made him realize he was reluctant to part company with her just yet. After all, he justified to himself, her company was better than no company. And they seemed to get along pretty easily, once they got past the confrontation over the photos. He had to admit to himself, that he really enjoyed sharing the adventure to the Planetarium with her.

To her surprise, Elaine's unrestrained reaction was pleasure at the idea, but she didn't want to take him out of his way, especially if he had a long drive home. Traffic heading out of the District to either Virginia or Maryland, she reminded him, was usually pretty heavy, whatever day of the week, or time of the day.

"I don't want to keep you in the District longer than necessary. I would hate for you to end up spending hours trying to get home."

"Oh, that's not a problem at all. I live just a few blocks from here. And truth be told, it wouldn't hurt to pick up some groceries myself! The cupboard's running a bit bare," he noted, with a grin.

"Well, in that case, drive on, James!" Elaine replied, a little too eagerly, she later thought.

"Uh...*Jack*...please!" he remonstrated.

"I know. I was only teasing. You've offered to play chauffeur, so I thought I'd try on the role of grand dame! I guess I didn't do it so well!" Elaine laughed.

"Oh, I doubt there is anything you don't do well, Ms. Kent," Jack stated, rather enigmatically. Instinct warned Elaine not to ask what he meant.

As they strolled over to Jack's car, and got in, Jack asked Elaine if she was satisfied with the decision the group had made about how to proceed.

"I think the question is, are *you* satisfied? You've just been robbed of a story that would have given you, and your blog, household recognition across the country—or at least across one of the fifty states, as well as here in the District."

"As I explained yesterday, Elaine, I don't want notoriety based on a false story. I don't want to be spreading lies, let alone lies that could have a critical impact on the outcome of an election. It may sound corny to you, but I believe in the democratic system we have. It's really pretty marvelous, when you think of it. With economic power, and money, so highly concentrated in this country today, the only real decision-making opportunity for the citizenry, in general, to affect the direction of the country, is the vote. When it becomes possible to truly buy an election, then we'll be in trouble, because then it will be all over for the rest of us. When lies about candidates become the deciding factor in an election, that comes close to making it possible to buy an

90

election, because it's money that instigates and promotes the lies on a big scale. I don't know. Maybe it's already too late! Sorry," Jack apologized for his lecture, "you hit a sore spot!"

"No need to apologize for those beliefs. I am in perfect empathy with you there. But here you are, an actor in the media, and isn't the media the problem? Why isn't there more integrity in the Fourth Estate?" and she shrugged her shoulders in exasperation before adding, "But it's my turn to apologize. In answer to your question, yes, I am satisfied that we all agreed to be silent about the photos, and wait for them to go public. I think we would have damaged ourselves if we made them public to pre-empt the attack, for the very reasons that Tony mentioned. And you know, we really don't know that Billilngsley is the perpetrator, or that those lobbyists are *not* involved, just because their pictures were also photo-shopped in. They could use that for a credible public denial of all culpability. Oh," she finished, with dejection, "there are just too many possible negative ramifications, no matter how you look at this!"

"Yes," Jack agreed, "we're sitting between the proverbial rock and a hard place! Well, isn't it all about 'location, location, location'?" and he smiled down at Elaine as they were stopped at a traffic light.

"Hhmmmm. Speaking of 'location', what do you think are our chances of finding a parking place within a reasonable walking distance of the Market?" Elaine wondered.

"Well, parking is one area where I have the 'luck of the Irish', as they say!" Jack replied, as he skillfully eased his car into a spot that seemed to magically open up right next to them, just a block from the market.

Amazed, Elaine shook her head in disbelief. "Then it's a good thing *you* were driving and not me, because if it were me behind the wheel, we'd probably end up ten blocks away, at least! And then, what would have been the point of taking a car, because we'd have had to carry our groceries for blocks anyway!" Elaine joked, as they emerged from Jack's vehicle.

As they strolled to, and through, the market, Elaine couldn't help observing to herself, how much fun it was to have company doing such mundane things as grocery shopping. It had also been a lot of fun going to the Planetarium with him, especially because, if it hadn't been for him, she probably would never have done that this afternoon. After all, it *was* Sunday. Realizing this, she resolved to make the effort, in the future, to create more space from her responsibilities as Chief of Staff to a member of Congress, to make more time for non-work related activities. It's as if I've forgotten how to play, she acknowledged to herself. It was so easy to let work, and maintaining a home, take over all of my time, she realized. She did what she had to do to fulfill her responsibilities and obligations at work, and to manage her household. Looking back, she suddenly saw how these duties had taken over her life, and she decided she really needed to change that—as soon as the election was over, that is.

"So, you said you live on Capitol Hill, not far from Kate Blanchard. Is blogging such a lucrative profession then?"

"Well, it suffices! I live about three blocks from Blanchard, in the Littleton Spite House."

"The Littleton Spite House?!" Elaine nearly shrieked, as she stopped in place and looked straight at him, eyes wide open with wonder.

Startled, Jack just nodded his head. She resumed activity as they both completed their purchases and headed back to his car, each laden with several bags full of things like fresh lettuce, carrots, cucumbers, tomatoes, etc. Interestingly, there wasn't a lot of difference in the purchases each had made, and that did not escape Jack's notice, at least.

"But how did you get to do that?" she asked, returning to the topic of his house, her voice full of awe. "I mean, I had inquired about it when I was looking to buy, and was told it had never left the family fold, and probably never would, in terms of ownership. Are you renting it, then?"

"No. I *own* it!" And for some reason, Jack felt quite pleased to be able to say that to her.

'*You* own it?! Oh, you are so lucky!"

"Why?"

"Well, it's such a neat fixture. I don't know, there's just something about Spite Houses that captivate me! I mean, they all have such curious origins that give them unique personalities. The Littleton Spite House, actually, is pretty wide for a Spite House. It's all of twelve feet, I think. There's a famous spite house in Old Town Alexandria that's only seven feet wide!"

"Actually, the Littleton Spite House is fourteen feet wide, which I admit is kind of wide for a spite house," Jack observed.

"Oh, I stand corrected," Elaine said, but without trace of apology. "Before I goof again, tell me how you come to own it."

"I inherited it from my grandfather, whose father was General Horatio Beauregard Littleton, the builder of the house. Originally, he owned the house that is next door, where he lived after the Civil War ended. The land between his primary home and the house next door, was open ground, and belonged to his house lot. But all kinds of traffic, even carriages and people on horseback, would cut through his land as a short cut whenever they felt like it. It really annoyed, even angered, him that people didn't seem to respect his property. And, of course, the noise from some of the traffic cutting through drove him crazy. So he decided to put a building up in the space. And, voila, we have the Littleton Spite House!" Jack finished with a flourish.

"What about his neighbor on the other side of the lot?"

"Well, he owned that house as well, which he let his nephew and his nephew's family live in for free, so they couldn't exactly complain, even if they had wanted to. But why would they?"

"Wow," Elaine said with some awe, "that's so interesting. Imagine. Here I am riding around with the owner of the Littleton Spite House," and she fell into a kind of dreamy silence.

"What makes it so appealing to you?" Jack was curious, after giving her a moment to reflect.

"Oh, I just love architecture. And I love looking at floor plans for homes—I don't know why. They just fascinate me. I'm always wanting to redesign them, though! Once upon a time, I actually considered becoming an architect."

"And why didn't you?"

Elaine thought back to her early college days, and eventually replied, "I guess it just seemed like too much of a solitary profession. I was afraid I wouldn't be happy spending so much of my time alone, drawing and designing buildings, calculating proportions and weights, etc. And I was afraid I would spend all my time designing what other people wanted, instead of what I would like to build."

"And yet here you are, building someone else's career, instead of your own," Jack observed quietly.

In the ensuing silence, Jack could have kicked himself. And he would have, if he hadn't been behind the wheel of a vehicle in motion. Had he overstepped her boundaries? Had he lost the connection they were building? He was surprised at how deflating that thought was.

Instead of shutting him out, though, Elaine was ruminating about what he had said. His observation seemed right on the mark. She had never really thought about it too much. She had barreled forth at what had been a great opportunity for a Political Science major—even a dream job—to work on Capitol Hill. In just four years, she had earned the position of Chief of Staff. For her, that was an accomplishment to be proud of.

But Jack was right that all of her work was to support the career of someone else. Her fate, her very job, was dependent on the success or failure of her boss. Yes, she had a "career path" of her own, through the ranks of Congressional staff. But it was a career in which she would remain in the background, supporting someone else's dreams and goals. And it was a career in which, for her at least, *who* she worked for was what mattered. She could not work for a legislator whose professional conduct and policy goals she did not also admire and believe in.

Elaine's silence made Jack start to feel restless. "Look, I'm sorry! If I've overstepped the bounds and..."

"No, no!" Elaine shot back, roused out of her reverie. "I was just thinking about what you said. Your observation was actually quite accurate. I just hadn't consciously thought about it very much, that's all, until you brought it out into the cold—literally!" and Elaine smiled up at him as she shivered a little, since Jack had forgotten to turn on the heat in the car on this cold October day, two days shy of Halloween.

Relief spread through him in waves. She wasn't angry with him! As he absorbed the warmth of her smile, he blurted out without thinking, "Would you like to come and see the Littleton Spite House? I will show you every nook and cranny of the edifice, and even offer you a homemade supper. I'm really a pretty good cook!" Luckily, driving forced him to keep his eyes mostly forward, so that if she declined the invitation, he could look like he was concentrating on the road. But to his immeasurable delight, Elaine did not decline —at least, not exactly.

"Oh, I would so love to see the inside of your house! But I wouldn't want you to go to the trouble of feeding me." And then she remembered Diggie, and it was her turn to feel deflated. "Besides, Diggie is staying with me, and he'll probably want to find some food in the house when he gets home."

"Really, Elaine," disbelief riddled through his tone, "do you think he's going to leave Caroline before he absolutely has to? And do you think she wants him to leave at all?"

"You have a point," she observed, thoughtfully.

"Look, if you go straight home now," he pushed his point, "you'll probably sit around all alone waiting for him to come home, and if you don't fall asleep before that, you'll just end up staying up until about midnight!"

Elaine thought about this, long enough to assuage any guilt she might have at leaving Diggie to arrive at an empty house, without a lot of food options. Jack was right again, it seemed. Hhmmm, he keeps making accurate observations, Elaine mused. I wonder if he can read my mind. But aloud, she replied, "Ok, I would like very much to see the Littleton Spite House," and for some reason she couldn't bring herself to refer to it as "your home". That made it all sound so personal, and why that spooked her, she wasn't sure. "But you really don't have to feed me."

"I know I don't *have* to. But I would very much *like* to."

Chapter 18

"Mmmmm, this is delicious!" Elaine exclaimed. They were sitting at a cozy table for two in an alcove off of Jack's kitchen. Candlelight at the table, and indirect lighting in the kitchen created a serene, and intimate, setting. "The tomato sauce really makes it," she complimented.

"Thank you," Jack was pleased. After touring the house, Jack had prepared a simple meal of stuffed peppers, smothered in tomato sauce. "It's my own version of spaghetti sauce, but it works for so many other dishes."

"But there's something different about it, something not quite typical?"

"You have sharp taste buds, Ms. Kent!" Jack exclaimed. "In addition to Oregano, I add a bit of ground cloves, and a bit of thyme. I stumbled on the combination playing around with some spices."

"It works beautifully!"

"So, Ms. Kent, you admit that I'm a pretty good cook?" and he leaned slightly across the table and challenged her, with a single raised eyebrow, to disavow his skill.

"All I will admit to is that I don't think I will have a tummy ache tonight!" Elaine countered, mischievously. What she also admitted, but only to herself, was that Jack could be a lot of fun, especially when he tried to get the better of her with some witty repartee.

As they shared the cleaning up, Jack decided to check on Craig. "It's late enough on a Sunday for there to be a good chance he's home, but not so late he'd be in bed," Jack explained.

"I'd like to go with you," Elaine said.

"He might not talk as freely with a stranger there, and especially one from Blanchard's office, Elaine. I've known him since college, and we often cross paths in our work, just like when I asked him to examine the photos. And this is going to be a rather touchy discussion. After all, he did validate phony photos. It's possible his technical skills are not as good as your brother's, and so he was fooled by the photos, but it's also possible he deliberately lied to me. I can't believe he

97

would, but I have to be open to the possibility. If that turns out to be the case, then the discussion will get pretty dicey. So it would be much better if you weren't there."

"I could wait in your car," and she couldn't hide her anxiety and eagerness. "I wouldn't mind. I want to know right away what you learn from him, if anything."

Jack thought for a moment, as he put the last clean dishes away. "He doesn't live far from here, though, if you'd like to wait here. Or I could drop you off, and then come by your place after I've seen him."

"Please, Jack?!" and she looked at him with pleading eyes.

He paused again, trying to resist her compelling glance, but finally said, "Ok. But you have to stay in the car."

As Jack pulled up near Craig's house, he turned to Elaine and reminded her to "stay in the car." She nodded her agreement, as he opened his door to exit the vehicle.

He walked slowly, almost heavily, up the front steps of another Capitol Hill stone front row house, and rang the bell. It bothered him to think, even for a moment, and as remote a possibility as it had to be, that Craig might have deliberately misled him. They were friends, not just acquaintances, and that means they should be able to trust each other. If Craig knowingly lied to him, he put Jack's professionalism and integrity on the line. He would have been setting Jack up for a horrific fall if Jack had published those pictures, only to have someone else discover they were not genuine. It was with a heavy heart that he rang the bell a second time.

He stood there a few moments more, but no one came to the door. He leaned back a little to peruse the windows, noting that there were no lights on. Craig could be in the back of the house, though, so he rang the front doorbell once again. But when no one answered this time, he came down the steps, and headed back to his car.

"No one home?" Elaine queried.

"Apparently not," was Jack's cryptic response.

"What's wrong?"

"I'm not sure. I expected him to be home. I've often stopped by on a Sunday evening, just to catch up. This is really weird. It seems like he hasn't been home since yesterday. Today's paper is still on his doorstep."

"Maybe he's just gone away for the weekend," Elaine suggested.

"Possibly. But I can't recall when he's ever done anything like that before."

"And does he check in with you about everything he does?" Elaine teased.

"No!" Jack laughed back. "I guess I'm just miffed, that when I really need to talk with him, I can't seem to reach him."

"Well, try again tomorrow morning, since he lives so close to you."

"Good idea, Ms. Kent. Now I know why you are in charge in Blanchard's office!" it was his turn to tease.

*****

She closed her front door gently with Jack's departure, after he helped carry in the groceries she had bought at Eastern Market. As she turned back toward the kitchen counter, where the food waited to be put away, she felt a strange silence that seemed to permeate the house. It was a new, unfamiliar but heavy quiet, that made her wonder if she could have entered someone else's house by mistake. She had never felt alone in her own home, even though she lived by herself. Her home was her sanctuary, her security blanket, where she could secretly revel in her successes, or hide to lick her wounds. So she was a little unsettled by this unexpected sense of quiet, by a new awareness that she was the only person in the house.

Jack had been right. It was a little after ten, and Diggie had not yet arrived. Even his suitcase must be still in her car, which she had left with him at Caroline Blanchard's. A surprising, but sharp, chill raced through her spine, but she suppressed it with the reminder that Diggie was nearby, and would eventually land on her doorstep. Be patient, she told herself.

Nevertheless, she couldn't help wonder why she was so conscious of being alone. It's true, she noted, that her life had suddenly been full of activity since yesterday morning. And she had spent most of that time in Jack's company. But could one person, who had been a complete stranger just a day and a half ago, invade your world so thoroughly as to make you feel lost when they exited the stage? It didn't make any sense to Elaine. Surely, she thought, it's just that the past 36 hours, or so, have been driven by adrenaline as they tried to deal with a game-changing political threat. That had to be it. Now that they were in a lull, a period of waiting, the pace had not only slowed, but come to a kind of stop. The next move was not up to them. Would someone else throw the photos into the public arena? They could only wait and see.

Chapter 19

"Miss Kent! Oh, Miss Kent!" cried a young girl, as she hurriedly approached Elaine from across the large hotel event hall, waving an envelope in one hand.

"Hi, Maggie," Elaine replied, turning to one of the students interning in Representative Blanchard's office for her fall college semester. "What can I do for you?"

"I brought that list of tonight's attendees that you asked for. The campaign headquarters emailed the final list just a few minutes ago. I printed out a copy for you." And then, her eyes turning toward the entrance to the hall, she anxiously added, "Have I missed anything—or anyone interesting yet?"

"Oh, great, Maggie. Thanks a lot," Elaine said in acknowledgement. She smiled warmly at the intern who was so eager to do a good job, and who was clearly experiencing an adrenalin rush at her first real "political" event. "No, nothing has happened yet, and the guests are just beginning to arrive.

"By the way, you look lovely in your cocktail dress!" Elaine added, making Maggie's face light up as she beamed with pride. "And thank you for being willing to contribute this extra time after hours."

"Oh, I wouldn't have missed this for the world, Miss Kent! Thank you for letting me be here."

As Elaine opened the envelope to peruse the list, she heard Maggie exclaim under her breath, albeit in a rather high pitch, "OMG!"

"What?" Elaine queried, turning her attention back to Maggie, and wondering what had caught the intern's attention. "OMG—what?" Elaine repeated.

"Oh!" Maggie was startled out of her concentration. "I'm sorry, Miss Kent. I didn't mean to say anything out loud," the embarrassed girl replied, her face turning a deeper shade of pink than her blush makeup.

"But, 'OMG' what, exactly?" Elaine repeated.

"Oh, I was just startled by that gorgeous guy who just walked through the doors—that's all, Miss Kent," Maggie finished a little lamely, her voice dropping several decibels as her shoulders slowly slouched.

Always one to appreciate a good looking guy, Elaine turned towards the entrance, and then she, too, exclaimed under her breath, but with a decidedly flatter voice, "Oh. My. God."

"He *is* adorable, isn't he, Miss Kent?!" Maggie sighed, energized by, but misinterpreting, Elaine's declaration. She wasn't prepared for Elaine's followup comment.

"Oh, no!" Elaine moaned, her hand automatically reaching for her face, as if to stifle an expression of horror in the hopes of keeping her face expressionless. "What's *he* doing here?"

"Do you know him, Miss Kent!? Do you?" Maggie inquired excitedly, looking like she was ready to jump up and down with joy if the answer were in the affirmative.

Instead of answering Maggie's query, however, Elaine ripped the attendee list out of the envelope and searched it doggedly, looking, it seemed, for a specific name.

"Well, honestly! Is he crazy showing up here?!" Elaine muttered to herself. She had confirmed he was not on the attendee list. That means he hasn't paid the $1000 cost for the event. After all, it *is* a fundraiser. Well! I'll just nip this party crashing in the bud right now, Elaine decided, as she walked, single-mindedly, in the direction of the interloper, leaving Maggie to stare, open-mouthed, at her departing back.

She intercepted the fellow as he was reaching for a glass of wine. She pointedly removed the glass from his hand before he'd had a chance to sample it, and returned it to the serving tray by the entrance.

"Just what do you think you are doing here?" Elaine whispered, in a low voice that she hoped only he could hear.

A little put off by the abruptness, and apparent hostility, of Elaine's question, the gentleman replied, somewhat sardonically, "I *was* just about to sample the wine being served tonight. Do you mind?" he asked, as he reached again for a glass.

Just as quickly, Elaine grabbed the glass from his hand again and replied, in explanation, "No *pay, no* play," she informed him, hoping that would make him leave.

"Oh, I see. Well, I *am* a guest here this evening, Ms. Kent."

"Oh, *really?*" Elaine countered, as she energetically flipped through the 3 pages of the attendee list. Making each page "snap" as if to attention, she noted somewhat acerbically, "Well, I don't seem to find your name on this list of supporters who paid the $1000 contribution to attend tonight's fundraiser —the operating word being 'fundraiser', *Mr.* Amory!" Elaine shot back at him.

"Oh, well, I'm not surprised," Jack replied rather glibly. "You know I can't really be a supporter, because you know that would raise questions about my journalistic objectivity and integrity," he pointed out, as he smiled sweetly back at her. "And you know how I feel about preserving my objectivity and integrity," he looked directly into her wide open eyes. As he held her glare with his eyes, he pulled a plastic coated name tag out of the righthand pocket of his jacket, and clipped it to the edge of his left lapel.

Elaine leaned closer, squinting her eyes a bit so that she could read the tag. It was a press badge from Blanchard's campaign office, which gave him free access to all campaign events that were open for general media coverage, including fundraisers. That included this particular one.

Elaine's mouth opened wide, as if she were about to protest, but not a sound emitted from her mouth. The brashness of his coming, the threat his presence posed, left Elaine breathless. She could only stand there in front of him, speechless, looking back up at him with her eyes opened wide and non-believing.

"I would think," Jack continued, ignoring her stare, and the obvious questioning in her eyes, "that as long as this event was open for media coverage, you would want to assure that the reporters were well fed and contented, so that they would write a positive story about your candidate. But if you don't want me consuming the victuals, I will be happy to remain the objective observer, though it's difficult to have a positive attitude when your stomach is not just growling, but howling," Jack finished with a flourish, as he aimed his wide, and innocent, stare back at Elaine's scowling face. "And besides," he added, "I fed you last night, so how can you object to feeding me tonight? Especially since you don't have to go to the trouble of cooking and cleaning up?"

"What are you doing here?!" she whispered forcefully again. In spite of the lovely evening the night before, Elaine recognized that he really could be exasperating. "Don't you realize how you are risking exposure of the photos if anyone sees you here?"

"What photos?" Jack looked at her, with what he hoped was a blank expression.

"Oh, *very* funny!" Elaine shot back.

"I'm so glad you think so. I used to do a stand up comedy skit back in the day, you know, but it didn't last very long, because, apparently, no one thought I was as funny as you seem to think I am right this minute—Ms. Kent," and he looked down at her with a mischievous twinkle in eyes that were shining bright, and vividly blue, at that moment.

Oh, Elaine thought. That amazing combination of blue eyes and black hair. Maggie is right, she admitted to herself. OMG.

Then he added in a low voice, as he leaned a little closer to her face, "Don't worry. The only other person who knows the photos are in play is the person who sent them to me—and, since there was no return address on the envelope, I rather doubt that person wants me to know who he or she is, so I don't think they will raise the issue," Jack explained. "Besides, whoever it is doesn't know yet that we, at least, have shelved the photos, and that whoever sent them is going to have to find another outlet."

"But he, or she, will figure that out soon enough," Elaine lamented, with a hint of defeatism in her voice. "Early enough to still use them to disrupt the campaign momentum."

"True. But as Blanchard said yesterday afternoon, we'll have to deal with that if, and when, it happens."

"You mean *when* it happens," Elaine clarified, the defeatism in her voice growing stronger. But she did like the sound of the "we".

"Yeah, I guess you are right there," Jack conceded.

And then the strains of music played by an eight-piece ensemble, as it started a new song, reached Jack's ear, and he recognized a familiar melody from one of his favorite movies. He looked down at Elaine's sober face, and without seeming to even think, he suddenly burst out with, "May I have this dance, Ms. Kent?" as he extended an open hand to her.

Elaine noticed his hand before the words registered, her mind so clouded with concerns about the photos. She looked at the extended hand, and then up at Jack's expectant face, his eyes smiling and encouraging. As she looked directly into those eyes that were so clear, and bright, that they seemed to drive away the clouds filling her thoughts, she asked quietly, "And what if the perpetrator is here, what will he, or she, think of us dancing? Maybe it will look like I'm trying to seduce you in order to keep you from publishing the photos?"

Jack returned her directness, and softly responded with his own question, as he leaned closer to eyes that seemed to draw him into a maelstrom, "And *are* you trying to seduce me, Elaine?"

It wasn't the topic of conversation she was expecting, so she stumbled verbally for a moment with "Huh? Uh, um..."

"Oh, come on, Elaine," Jack chided lightly, "let's just enjoy a dance. It's a great song. One of my favorite. The only thing anyone is going to wonder about is what great insider information I'm getting from you while we dance. Come on," and he took her hand, and led her to the area of the hall where hotel management had constructed a hardwood platform for dancing, in case anyone wanted to slide along to the music.

Elaine offered no resistance. She couldn't think of how to refuse without drawing attention to them both. Or, was it that she really didn't *want* to refuse him? Then Jack put his arm around her waist, and gently closed the space between them, so she relaxed, and let him lead her around the dance floor.

He was right, of course. There were lots of members of the press there tonight. And since this was an event all about the coming election, most of them were chasing after Kate Blanchard, or her campaign manager, Krystal Kincaid, who had flown in just a couple of hours earlier to network for the campaign at this important fundraiser. Elaine's job was running the Washington office, not the campaign, so she was drawing less attention than if the number one topic were some legislative issue coming up for a vote. No one was likely to notice her dancing with a political blogger, she ruefully admitted to herself—even if any other folks knew who he was, or that he was a journalist. She rather doubted anyone attending would know him. And she did notice the admiring glances of several women as the two moved around the dance floor, giving her own self esteem a bit of a boost.

As they glided to the music, Elaine discovered that she liked the feel of Jack's arm around her. How long has it been since a man has held me in his arms, she wondered. It's not Jack, in particular, that makes it feel good, she tried to convince herself, but just the feeling of being held by a man— *any* man. Has it really been that long since I've had that pleasure? Has it been so long, that I can't even remember when the last time *was*? The realization amazed her.

Could it be before I ever came to Washington, Elaine mused. That's just incredible! Can that mean I haven't had a single date since I got here? That can't be true, can it? Her mind raced through the many social events she participated in as part of the Washington staff of a member of Congress. When was the last time I had a date, just for fun, just for me? Always lots of people around, and lots of men, of course. Political Washington was still a man's world. At least the political power structure was. As Chief of Staff to a member of Congress, Elaine skirted the edge of that power structure. She was always meeting lots of new people in a work context, lots of receptions on the Hill, lots of food, and lots of chatting. But to her amazement, Elaine could not recall any personal social activity since she had come to the political capitol of the nation—except for yesterday afternoon at the museum, and last night. With Jack Amory.

Then, of course, she noted that this political fundraiser wasn't a personal social event either. Just another one of hundreds of work events, conducted in a seemingly social context. So why was her mind focusing on the personal? Is that the effect Jack Amory has on me?

And then Elaine froze. Right in the middle of the dance floor. Luckily, there were enough other people dancing by then that her abrupt stop might not have caught anyone's attention. Almost as quickly as she had stopped their progress, she started them moving again, only now she was aggressively leading Jack away from the entrance.

"Hey, ummm, aren't I supposed to be leading?" Jack joked.

"Come on! We have to move into the crowd, and then you are going to go somewhere else in the hall. *Any*where else, but *away* from me!" Elaine hissed in his ear. To anyone else, it might have looked like she was sharing a secret with him. Or maybe she was agreeing to an assignation later in the evening.

"Wait a minute! I thought we were doing pretty well out there!" Jack noted, as Elaine tried to guide him towards the food table, where there was a large crowd.

"Did you see who just walked in here?!" Elaine asked.

Chapter 20

"No. Who?" Jack queried, as he changed their directions on the dance floor until he could unobtrusively peruse the main entrance into the hall.

"Kevin Lowell! Who do you think?!" Elaine hissed, again looking to others like she was whispering sweet nothings in his ear. To do so, of course, meant that she had to close the distance between them until her lips were within millimeters of his right ear.

Distracted by the moist warmth that enveloped his ear lobe, Jack's composure was shaken enough that he stepped on Elaine's foot. And there ensued one of those keystone cops routines where they both screeched, and jumped up and down a moment, before regaining their equilibrium. Fortunately, the scene consumed only seconds of time, so no one paid very much attention to it, including the new arrival.

When Jack regrouped enough to reply sensibly, he told Elaine, "Well, I really didn't know *who* you could have meant, but it was obviously someone who upsets you a whole lot."

They were still sliding across the dance floor, when Elaine unexpectedly remarked, as she lifted her head to look up at him, "You know, you are a really good dancer. You kept cool, and kept going as if nothing had happened. That's pretty impressive."

But it wasn't a pair of admiring eyes that Jack gazed back down at. Instead, he saw an expression of matter-of-fact surprise, and, no, that's not a contradiction in terms. Rather than beam from the pleasure of a compliment, Jack scrunched his nose with a bit of irritation. It seemed that she just couldn't give him any real credit. Maybe that was part of a wall she built to keep people out emotionally. What must he do to get her to trust him enough to show him where the gateway through that wall was? But, then, why did he care if she did, or didn't, let him "in"? They met because of an expediency. And once that expediency was over, so would their relationship be over. That thought filled Jack with unease. Why, exactly, he wasn't ready to admit to himself—let alone to Elaine.

And then another sudden gasp escaped Elaine in the middle of the dance floor.

"What is it this time?" Jack asked, with some irritation.

"This...this is just too incredible! Move us around again to where you can see the main entrance."

It was Jack's turn to almost gasp. "What in...?"

"Yeah, that's how I feel," Elaine agreed. "What on earth is Barker Phillips doing at a fundraiser for Kate Blanchard? Even on his own, this would be shocking, but in addition to Kevin Lowell, this is just flabbergasting!"

"Has either one ever attended one of her fundraisers before?" Jack, the journalist, asked.

"No! Of course not! That's just it! Never! They wouldn't! They have to hate her...she's been an obstacle to their most cherished objectives!" Although Elaine was highly annoyed, she kept her voice low so that others couldn't hear what she was saying to Jack. Which also meant they had to dance really really close. And while neither wanted to acknowledge the pleasure that brought, neither seemed in a hurry to end the intimacy of the dance.

"Could they have possibly gotten in without paying the thousand dollars?" Jack whispered back.

"No, certainly not!"

"I did."

"But you're a reporter! She holds only one Washington fundraiser, and the K-Street lobbyists know well enough by now that she won't accept their money. Anyone who has tried to attend in the past has gotten their money returned to them once it was discovered they were registered lobbyists. She doesn't accept money from registered lobbyists, whether they lobby for positions that she supports or opposes. Tomorrow, her campaign staff will check the names of the attendees against the list of registered lobbyists. That's been policy from the start when it comes to fundraising.

"So the question is," she continued, "why are they here tonight? Do you think it could possibly have something to do with the photos?"

109

"You say they should know their money will be returned to them?"

"Oh, yes, of course!"

"So they know they are not risking the cost of this event. Then they must be up to something. They wouldn't be here to support her, so they must have some other purpose in mind. They are definitely not altruists!" Jack observed.

When the song finished, Jack wanted to stay on the dance floor, but Elaine led him to the other side of the hall, where they could watch the two lobbyists without being observed. They tried to behave as normally as possible, munching on the food nearby, and trying not to stare at the two men.

Lowell and Phillips 'discovered' each other and started chatting. Then they both seemed to agree it was time to join the line of people waiting to shake hands with the Candidate. Elaine and Jack admired their cavalier manner.

"I wonder just what they've got up their sleeve," Elaine muttered, as she surreptitiously watched the two.

"It could be they genuinely prefer her to win this time!" Jack joked, a bit lamely.

"Oh, no," Elaine countered, taking his comment seriously. "*That* is an impossibility."

"Are you sure, Elaine?" This time Jack was being serious. "This is a Senate race, not a re-election bid for her congressional seat. And she's ahead eleven points in the polls, so most people expect her to win the seat. Maybe they are trying to ass-kiss her in the realization that they are going to have to deal with her, in the future, in an even more powerful role. Maybe, just maybe, they want to sort of start all over again, on a new footing?"

"Oh, no," again from Elaine. "Trust me. There is absolutely no possibility of that. No, they are up to something. I only wish I knew....," and in a whisper that reflected her incredulity, Elaine suddenly added, "No, no, this just can't be..."

Jack followed the direction of her glance, and recognized the lobbyist Arthur Cantrell as he entered the hall.

"Oh, now I'm sure there's something going on with them tonight," Elaine commented, as Cantrell casually strolled over to where Lowell and Phillips were in line to greet the Candidate. "Maybe they are scheming together to try to discredit Kate, by making people believe she is really in cahoots with them."

"I thought you said those three guys usually don't work together," Jack observed.

"Well, this is a big deal, this election. Kate will have so much more influence, and impact on legislation, as a Senator than she could ever have as a Representative."

They stood there, each in their own minds, trying to rationalize the presence of these three lobbyists, at this time, at a fundraiser for Kate Blanchard's Senate race. As politically astute as Jack and Elaine both were, this particular puzzle was not easy to solve.

"Are we sure they are not behind the photos?" Jack broke into her thoughts, as he remembered Craig's visit to Lowell on Saturday evening.

"We can't be sure of anything just yet, can we? Come on," Elaine tugged at Jack's sleeve, "let's meander over towards where Kate's receiving guests so we can listen in as they approach her. I can't imagine what they are going to say to her—or what her reaction will be when she sees, not just one, but all three of them here."

Chapter 21

"By the way," Elaine told Jack as they neared the spot where Kate Blanchard was greeting, and thanking, her guests who paid one thousand dollars to attend this fundraiser, "there were no fingerprints at all on any of the bugs—not the one from the office, nor on any from the house."

"When did you find this out?" Jack was a little perturbed he had not been 'in the loop'. "And *who* did the testing?"

"Diggie dropped them off last night with a friend of his who teaches forensics here at the University. His friend made it a class project for his Monday morning graduate class, to test the devices for fingerprints, or traces of any other telltale substances."

"That's just great! Now there are lots of people who know about what's going on! And lots more opportunities for a leak!"

"No. Calm down. Don't be ridiculous. They were told nothing about the source of the devices—only that they were being given an opportunity to practice some of what they've been studying, on a real life occurrence!"

"You're awfully mellow about this!"

"And you have no reason to be unnerved about it! Unless," and Elaine eyed him warily, "you are worried that someone else might scoop your story!"

"What story?!" Jack's face flushed at the insinuation. "There *is* no story. Remember? And why am I the one worried, instead of you?!" Elaine could see exasperation written all over his face. "Anyway, I'll drop off the photos and the envelope to you tomorrow. Maybe that professor can have one of his classes check those items for fingerprints—other than yours, mine, Kate Blanchard's, your brother's, and whoever else we know who touched them."

"I rather doubt there will be anyone else's prints on those, if there were none on the bugs. Whoever is doing this has been very careful. What's more confusing is, they did trace the serial numbers on the devices to an electronics store in Omaha, Nebraska!" Elaine explained. "But the devices were paid for with cash, so the store manager could not identify who bought them. The good news, if there is any such, is that they were sold just four weeks ago, so they could not have been active for very long."

"Good grief!" Jack exclaimed. Then, "You're right about one thing, though. This *has* been a carefully planned attack. I wonder how the perpetrator will respond when he, or she, finally figures out that I'm not publishing the photos, either in my regular edition, or in a special edition. I just hope we can handle whatever happens next."

There is that "we" again, Elaine grinned to herself. He shifted to the "we" so quickly. And it seemed so natural. Of course, she admitted to herself, he was protecting himself as much, if not more, than Kate Blanchard. Nevertheless, hearing Jack say "we" sent a wave of warmth through her whole being. And she liked that feeling very much. Yes, she liked it very much.

Chapter 22

As they came within hearing distance of Kate Blanchard's exchanges with supporters in the receiving line, Elaine and Jack tried to appear as if they were just casually standing nearby, but they did make sure they were not actually looking over Blanchard's shoulder. After waiting just a few moments, the three persons of interest reached the hand-shaking stage of the line.

Elaine noticed the slightest tightening of Kate Blanchard's jaw as she recognized the lobbyists. To her credit, Kate was able to maintain her equilibrium under the most stressful, and unexpected, of conditions.

"Well," Blanchard said, as she held out her hand to Lowell, who was first of the three to greet her, "to what do I owe this homage? It can't be to my support for your legislative programs, because we all know that has never happened."

"But you are a highly respected member of Congress, Mrs. Blanchard, and we have come to acknowledge that," said Lowell. "We are also aware of your eleven point lead in your bid for the vacant Senate seat in your home state, and we want you to know that, in spite of our past differences, we hope very much to be able to work with you in your new position."

"Well, I'm not in any new position yet. And I hope you have always been respectfully received by my Congressional staff, and myself, whenever you have presented your legislative positions?"

All three lobbyists were now collected around Kate and her campaign manager, who stood next to her in the receiving line.

"Oh, yes, Mrs. Blanchard," Cantrell responded. "I, certainly, have always felt I have been received, and listened to, courteously by your staff, as well as yourself."

"And I can reiterate that," echoed Phillips.

"Well, I'm pleased to hear that. And you can count on that respectful consideration continuing, should I have the honor of being elected to the Senate." And as they were all smiling and nodding, Blanchard posited, with a smile, "So I hope you will not consider it any disrespect if I return the money you paid to attend tonight's fundraiser?"

As they all started shaking their heads, and murmuring comments like, "Not at all", and "If you so wish...", she explained, "Because, as a rule, I do not accept campaign contributions from registered lobbyists—on either side of an issue. I would have thought that you were all already aware of that," she noted pointedly. But to make sure she was being clear, she added, "That way, my votes are truly independent, and based on my reasoned judgment of what I think is in the best interests of my constituents and the country. You understand, of course?"

"Of course," was the response, almost in unison, as a flash of light hit them all in the face. A news photographer, who aimed his camera straight at the group, got a great shot of the three lobbyists smiling agreeably at whatever Blanchard was saying.

"Are you guys and Representative Blanchard burying the hatchet here tonight?" the photographer asked, in hopes of a possible story.

"What hatchet? We've never been at war!" Lowell responded.

"But as you are well aware, Olson," Blanchard directed her remarks to the photographer, "I have not shared the same policy perspectives as these gentlemen." Blanchard was trying to assure the photographer that there was no alliance between her and these lobbyists, whatever the photo might give the appearance of.

Turning to her campaign manager, but still within hearing of the photographer, Blanchard instructed, "Krystal, these three gentlemen are welcome to enjoy the evening as long as they desire. But please, go now, and make sure that their contributions are refunded to them immediately."

"Yes, ma'am." Turning to the three men, Krystal smiled and added, "Please, come with me so I can take care of your refund." The three men smiled enigmatically, and followed Krystal to a small room being used as an administrative office for the event, at the other end of the hall.

As the lobbyists departed, Blanchard's attention remained focused on the many people who remained in the reception line, waiting to say hello to her. Elaine and Jack were left to themselves to wonder about what had just transpired.

"Ok. What do you make of that?" Elaine wondered out loud.

"You said none of those men have ever attended one of Blanchard's fundraisers before? Or contributed to her congressional campaigns?" Jack asked.

"That's correct. Didn't you hear Kate explain that she doesn't accept campaign contributions from registered lobbyists, like I told you? Even ones whose policies she supports?" Elaine replied, looking up at him with brows both raised and knit, as if to really ask "Are you deaf?" Then she asked, "Why?"

"Well, I can't shake the question of why they came tonight. It's hounding me. Why tonight? Why this election? And not any other election?"

"I suppose, if you asked them, they would say what we thought before, and what they told her—that they expect her to win the Senate race, and they want to be able to have a seat at the table, so to speak, when she is a United States Senator."

"But look at what happened. A photographer took a picture of all three with Blanchard. And everyone was smiling and happy—at least that's what the photo will show. No one will know what they were talking about. They could have been swearing at each other under those smiles, and they sort of were. I mean it was like a polite verbal war, with each side trying to get their point across. But the photo is of a happy, jolly group, where everyone *appears* to be getting along as well as peaches and cream."

"I'm not following you, Jack. What's the problem?"

"Suppose someone else releases those phony photos to the public. There will be denials from Blanchard's office and campaign headquarters, of course. Who knows what any of these guys will say. But amidst the 'he said/she said' media coverage, this photographer comes up with this happy, chummy photo of them all together—and it's dated *today*! It's as if it could be used to put the 'lie' to any disclaimers that come from Blanchard."

"Oh, my goodness! You're right!"

"Yeah! Exactly! It certainly can raise enough reasonable doubt about Blanchard's claims that the scandal photos are phony, to make it impossible to convince the public of the truth before the election!"

Chapter 23

She felt her stomach grumbling as she answered the ringing phone on her desk the next morning, and heard a distinctly masculine voice asking, "Have you checked your email inbox recently?"

"Jack!" Elaine exclaimed, a little more excitedly than she would have liked. Trying to get control of her manner, she added, "And to what do I owe this," and she hesitated before starting to say, "...p"

"Pleasure?" Jack interrupted.

"I was going to say interruption," Elaine finished, a little annoyed with herself.

"You were really going to say 'pleasure', but you just can't admit it to yourself, can you?"

"No, I was *not* going to say 'pleasure'! Now, just what do you want?" Elaine cut him off bluntly.

"Well, I noticed that Representative Blanchard recently—very recently—like, yesterday—subscribed to my political blog. Yes, my *blog,* which you once derisively called it. And I was wondering if you've read it yet?"

"Welllll..."

"Oh, come on, now! You know you have! And you *loved* it, didn't you?!" Jack pressed her.

"Honestly! You are so *exasperating*! You're ego seems to know no bounds!" Elaine teased, with only a hint of hostility. Because she *had* read it, and found it quite insightful, surprisingly so, as a matter of fact. But she didn't want *him* to know that. After all, she had mocked the whole concept of a political blog when she first met him. But, having read this week's edition, it did make her wonder about all the other inside political information and analysis she, that is, Representative Blanchard, had missed all these years.

"I seem to have left you speechless, Ms. Kent," Jack mocked.

"Not really," she collected herself. "Actually, I admit, your data collation and observations are quite impressive," Elaine conceded. "And the political analyses are of a quality that I felt Representative Blanchard would benefit from. You do offer a great understanding of political pressure points, you cover a broad scope of political perspectives, and you provide highly useful detail on the content and status of proposed legislation. And since you made this office aware of your blog, I have noticed references to your blog in various other information sources, so naturally it seemed a good idea to become a subscriber," Elaine explained, a little too energetically, as if she were trying to get through an admission of guilt as quickly as possible.

"I *knew* you would find my blog useful!" and Jack's voice betrayed more excitement from Elaine's approval than even he expected. "Does that mean you will treat me to lunch today—as an apology, of course, for your making fun of my work earlier?" And when she hesitated, he added, "Come on, Elaine, you owe me *that* much! Your disdain really hurt, you know," he plaintively admitted.

"I tell you what. It's Halloween tonight, have you forgotten?"

"Of course not! It's a night for ghouls and goblins and witches!" Jack laughed.

"And Fairies and Princesses!" Elaine laughed back.

"So, are you going to transform yourself from a witch to a princess?" and as soon as the words were out of his mouth, he knew he'd made a mistake.

"Well, if I'm a witch, Mr. Amory..." Elaine shot back, her defenses instantly aroused.

"Uh-oh! I didn't mean that the way it sounded!" Jack cut her off. "I was just..."

"Oh, I think you meant that exactly as it sounded!" but she was laughing again. Why was she so sensitive to his reference to her as a witch? He was obviously just bantering with her. Why did she care what he might think of her? Theirs was a relationship of necessity, generated by the threat to Blanchard's Senate race. When that threat was over, their interaction would also end.

"Look, I have a lot of work to do today. It looks like Congress will not adjourn tomorrow after all, and maybe not even before the election. There's a huge legislative calendar for tomorrow, at least, so I have meetings, etc. right through lunch. But if you come by my home tonight, I promise to fill you with treats, and maybe I'll even feed you some supper—if that interests you at all," she finished, her voice lowered and not as confident.

And when Jack replied that he would "be there in time to help give out candy, and I'll even bring my own!" Elaine suddenly felt much lighter in spirit, in spite of all the work she would have to do before she could leave the office that day. She loved giving out candy on Halloween, and had always put lighted pumpkins in her first floor windows, and several carved pumpkins on her front steps, to let kids know her home was welcoming. She even dressed up in a costume to greet the trick-or-treaters!

"That would be great!" and Elaine tried to sound a little less excited than she was feeling. "But I warn you, there will be around a hundred kids stopping by! Are you prepared for that?"

"Oh, I'm prepared, all right!" Jack replied. "I'll be by around 6 pm. See you then!"

"Ok! See you later!"

And if either could hear the other once they had each hung up their phones, they would have discovered that they were both humming softly as they went about the rest of their day's activities.

Chapter 24

Elaine opened the door, expecting to find Jack on her top step. Instead, two neighborhood kids stood there, pushing their empty pumpkin containers toward the opening door, demanding "treats" so that they wouldn't play any of their "tricks" on her. The sweet 3-year old girl, who lived next door, was emphatically threatening to "spread toilet paper *all 'round* your front yard if you don't give us any treats!" When Elaine opened the door wide to hand them some treats, the little girl suddenly screamed and started to run off without her bribe of candy. Fortunately, the girl's older brother was quick witted enough to catch his sister before she plummeted down the stone steps, as he explained to her that it was "just Miss Elaine pretending to be someone else". Dressed in black, with a large ugly fake nose pasted on her face, and a shiny black pointed hat about two feet tall on the top of her head, Elaine could easily understand why the little girl had been surprised, though she hadn't expected such a frightened reaction.

"Ok! Ok, Tina! Quiet down!" Elaine laughed. "It's just me, Elaine! Please keep your toilet paper to yourself! Here you go, the two of you!" and Elaine handed them candy from a box overflowing with a variety of chocolate bars, that had been sitting on a table inside the doorway.

"I'm *not* Tina!" the little girl insisted, once she was convinced the 'witch' would not zap her to infinity with a wand. "I'm a Good Fairy! Like in Cin'rella!" and to prove it, she threw a handful of 'fairy dust' in Elaine's face.

"I'm sorry! I'm sorry! Of course you're a fairy!" Elaine laughed, as she hurriedly tried to brush away the glitter that was sticking to her, and everywhere else that it landed. "And a very pretty fairy, too!" she added.

"There!" Tina exclaimed, beaming at Elaine's complement, as she hurled a second handful of glitter. "Now you will have good luck on Halloween!"

"Thank you, Good Fairy," Elaine solemnly replied, still brushing off glitter.

As the two trick-or-treaters descended Elaine's front steps, another trick-or-treater approached, dressed like a medieval knight, helmut covering much of his face, and standing more than six feet tall when he reached the top step. Elaine had remained in her doorway as the knight errant approached, marveling at the clever costuming, until it dawned on her that it was Jack, all dressed up for Halloween! How wonderful, she thought. He has a sense of fun!

"Ah! A witch," Jack stood there staring. "I was expecting to find a fair maiden, a princess, or a fairy, at this abode. I've come to rescue her from whatever she needs rescuing from!"

"In the past you were more likely to find a ghost answering my door, dear Knight," Elaine played along. "But a recent allusion to my being a witch..."

"I *didn't* call you a witch!" Jack shouted, with unexpected vehemence. Then it sank in that she had called him "dear" knight, dissipating all of his anger.

"Well, you alluded to my being witch-like, at least!" Elaine retorted. And in the face of Jack's speechlessness, she continued, "...so I thought I would search the darker reaches of my essence, and discover the witch in me. And, voila!"

"You *do* make a fetching witch—umm, except for that *huge*, monstrosity of a pimpled nose," and Jack's face, *and* his nose, curled up in a grimace to emphasize the repulsiveness of the crooked, bumpy appendage sticking rather far out from Elaine's face.

"Well, that is easily remedied," Elaine decided, as she unexpectedly ripped the attachment from her face, and tossed it aside. "After all, since you are..."

"Your Knight in shining armor?" Jack interposed, rather energetically.

"Ummmm, I will concede you are a knight," Elaine drawled, "though that's an optimistic assessment. But 'shining armor'? I don't think so!"

Jack spread his arms wide to shoulder height on each side, and announced, "Oh, fair...ummm, witch...you cut me to the quick!" Then he placed his right hand over his heart to emphasize the pain she had inflicted on him. "I am supposed to be the dashing defender of your fair maiden...ly...hood..."

Jack stammered, fearing he was putting his other foot in his mouth.

"What?! 'Maidenlyhood' !? Just what is *that* supposed to be?! Come on, Jack, you're a writer! You can do better than that! It's not even a real word!"

"But it's a real *concept*!" Jack retorted, in an effort to rescue himself from ignominy.

"Ok! Ok! You win! Come inside before we both scare off the rest of the neighborhood kids!"

Just as Elaine closed the door behind them, the doorbell rang, and the trick-or-treaters streamed by for the next hour or so. Elaine had to admit to herself, in the midst of handing out candy to ghosts and goblins, firemen and policemen, and she couldn't count how many Disney characters had climbed her steps that night, especially those dressed as Elsa from "*Frozen*", that having Jack there to share in the crazy mayhem that was Halloween, made this one really special. Not just any guy. But Jack. He shared so completely in the gaiety and fantasy that she had always loved about Halloween, that she found herself a little depressed by the thought of doing it all alone next year.

Somewhere in the back of her mind, that realization conjured up feelings of loneliness from deep within. Had those feelings been there all the time? Had she succeeded in keeping them buried in her mind, or her heart? The sensation of sharing so much unreserved madness had somehow unlocked a hidden treasure chest that released a flood of emotions she had scarcely been aware of.

Elaine was comfortable living alone and being on her own. She had not consciously thought she felt lonely. You can be alone, without being lonely, she reminded herself. But the contrast between this evening's delightful adventure, and her typical daily life was a wake-up call that entreated her to be more honest with herself, and face some hidden truths.

She watched Jack joking with a trick-or-treater, guessing what, or who the costumed figure was supposed to be, and she realized he had been having as much fun as she was. He had been true to his word, bringing with him a basket full of candy bars. And just as well, Elaine noted, because her own stash of about a hundred candy bars had not lasted very long. But while she was willing to acknowledge her joy from the evening, she was not willing to explore the cause of that joy just now. Instead, Elaine opted to pull a *"Scarlet O'Hara"* and postpone thinking about any of this until some indefinite time in the future.

"Either there's been an explosion of new residents with kids this past year, or there's been a rash of grown kids being born!" Elaine laughed, as she finally shut off the outside front light after no one had rung her doorbell for more than twenty minutes.

"The kids seemed to have as much fun because we were in costume, as they were having being dressed up themselves," Jack observed.

"I think you're right. At least I'm having as much fun being dressed in costume as the kids who were collecting all of that candy! Come on. I think I owe you supper!"

As they sat opposite each other at the kitchen table, finishing a double chocolate brownie full of walnuts and extra chocolate chips, topped with maple walnut ice cream and hot fudge sauce, the shriek of shattering glass crashed through their placid moment. Startled, Jack jumped up with "What was *that*?" as his head swiveled around and settled in the direction of the living room. When he turned his attention back to Elaine, he became nonplussed because she was just quietly sitting in her chair, staring at the table, her two hands locked into a fist resting in front of her on the beautiful walnut wood of the table top.

"Elaine," Jack spoke excitedly to her, "didn't you hear that racket?" Then he glanced back toward the living room, and then again turned to fully face her, wondering if she was playing a Halloween trick on him, and lightly queried, "Or am I possibly imagining things? Was that just a Halloween joke? Did you think you could actually spook me?" he finally chuckled.

"No," Elaine replied with resignation, as she slowly placed her hands on the table and pushed herself up from her chair, suddenly feeling very tired. "It's real," she added, exhaling noisily through her teeth. "I mean, the crashing sound is real. It's probably a vase I have on the fireplace mantel...it must have fallen over." And in a small voice, as if she were talking only to herself, she whispered, "I guess I knew it was too good to last."

"But...I thought Diggie was over Caroline Blanchard's house."

"He is."

"But...that would mean the vase fell over on it's own? How could...? No, wait a minute! What did you just mumble?"

"Mumble?" Elaine looked questioningly at Jack.

"Yeah, something about 'too good to last'." Is that a polite way of trying to tell me to get lost?" And here Jack's voice mellowed as he crooned, "After all we've been to each other? Now you want to get rid of me?"

"No! No! It's just that..."

"It's just....what?" he gently encouraged.

"It's just that...I think my house is haunted by a ghost," she blurted the words out in a flat voice as quickly as she could.

"A ghost?" Jack commented, disbelief spread across his face, his eyebrows flying high. "You're kidding, of course?"

"No. I'm not kidding." Elaine insisted. "She's generally been a benign ghost, though occasionally she lets go of her temper and throws things."

"Ummm, are you playing games with me? I mean, I know it's Halloween, and all..." Jack asked, skepticism ripe in his question.

"No. Really," Elaine was serious. "I believe her name is Emily. There was an Emily Waring living here during the Civil War. Her husband, Josiah Waring, was a Major in the Union Army. His unit had been encamped here in Washington, but it marched out of town in July of 1862, and he never returned. She never knew what happened to him. His unit returned, but he simply never did. No one could account for him—or his body. He may have died in battle, or been taken prisoner and died in captivity. Or he might just have taken off for a new life at some point. There was so much chaos and bloodshed, what with all kinds of battles being fought all through Virginia. Missing in action, presumed dead, was all she ever heard from the Army.

"Anyway, Emily lived out her years in this house, until she died in 1894. She never married again. I think she never moved, either, because she secretly hoped her husband would someday return. But he never did. I think she's still waiting for him to come home."

"Wow! That's a great story! You'd make a great fiction writer!"

"It's not just a story," Elaine persisted, "although I'm filling in some of the blanks." Then she added, "Let's go see what crashed."

Jack followed Elaine into the living room. Lying on the floor in front of the fireplace, as she had suspected, was a pool of lavender glass, some water splattered through it, and a few stems of chrysanthemums.

Jack was still unconvinced. "How do you know there's a ghost?" he asked, looking down at the carnage. "Couldn't you have just placed the vase a little too close to the edge of the mantel?"

"I used to think like that. I used to question myself. But, well," and here she looked askance at Jack, in anticipation of being laughed at, "you can hear her crying, or moaning, at times, and not just at night, either. Sometimes it sounds like she's pacing the floor, walking back and forth, as if she were expecting her husband to return any moment. And, occasionally, she throws things."

"Like what?" Jack was intrigued.

"Well, like this vase," and Elaine pointed to the mess on the floor, and then Elaine headed back to the kitchen to get a broom, and some paper towels, to clean up the mess.

When the last shards of glass had been carefully swept up, and everything tossed into the rubbish bin, they returned to the remains of their brownies, which were now sitting in a pool of melted ice cream.

As they sat down again at the table, Elaine picked up her story with, "She mostly throws dishes, though. I've actually put locks on certain cupboards in the kitchen, as you can see," and she gestured with her arm, "after several of her

126

throwing fits. The cupboards with the dishes and glasses. But I leave them unlocked during the day, so sometimes she still gets to break a few things!"

"You're serious, aren't you?" and Jack was fascinated, watching Elaine's animation rise as she talked about Emily.

"Yes, I am. Ghosts are nothing to joke about!" and then Elaine's voice became very soft.

"When I hear her crying, as if she's bemoaning her husband's absence, I am filled with the sensations of her pain and misery—and her loneliness—almost as powerfully as if those feelings were my own. Sometimes I feel like she's wrapped her hands around my heart, as if she can't bear to be alone one more second, and in those moments I am filled with her sense of despair and loss. And understanding her feelings in those moments truly breaks my heart," Elaine finished in a quiet voice.

"Maybe Emily feels like she has met a kindred spirit," Jack observed somberly.

"Well, whatever it is," and Elaine shuddered a little, "I've come to terms with sharing the house with her. I believe she's kind of accepted that I live here now, too, because she seems to cry, or moan, much less often than when I first moved in. And at times, I just sense that she likes having company. Sometimes, particularly when I've curled up with a book in front of the living room fireplace, the rocking chair across from my chair, will...rock. On its own." Elaine's voice had become very low again, as if her mind were puzzling over these events, still trying to understand the reality. "There's a framed photo of her husband on the little end table beside the rocker. I did not put it there, obviously. I tried to put it away in a draw once, and the next day it was right back on the end table. It really spooked me," Elaine recalled. "I've never tried to move it since."

"Wow. I don't know what to say." Jack was thoughtful for a moment, and then he added, "I'm not sure I would care to share my home with a ghost."

And then Elaine got an idea. "Hey! What if she thinks you're her husband, finally returned from the war? Or maybe she just doesn't want a strange man in *her* house. Maybe she broke the vase to scare you off. Or, maybe, she broke the vase out of disappointment that you *weren't* her husband come home." And Elaine thought about this for a moment before adding that "the first time she actually broke something was the first time Diggie came to visit."

"Speaking of visitors," Jack observed, trying to change the heaviness of the mood that was overtaking them, and to satisfy his own curiosity, "where *is* your brother tonight?"

"Oh," Elaine chuckled, "he's at Caroline's house right now, helping *her* give out candy! He was really angry with me when I forced him to come to Washington, but I think maybe this trip is finally breaking the ice between him and Caroline. He was actually singing in the shower this morning!"

Lucky him, Jack thought, as he wondered what it would feel like to be showering in the same house as Elaine. Maybe, even, in the very same bathroom. It sure would make him feel like singing. And a dreamy look suddenly crossed his face.

"And here I was, thinking you shooed him out of the house, so that *we* could be alone," Jack crooned, as he leaned closer to Elaine across the table, extending to her an invitation to greater intimacy.

Red flags exploded in Elaine's mind, much to her surprise. Instead of accepting his overture, she suddenly got skittish at the prospect of a genuinely romantic interlude, or any kind of deeper intimacy with him, so she deflected the invitation.

"Honestly," Elaine eyeballed Jack, "why is it that men think the world revolves around them? Huh? Why do you think you're God's gift to the world—not just to women—but to the world?"

For a moment, Jack just sat there, puzzled, sort of a little shell-shocked. His mind didn't make the switch as quickly as Elaine's did. Or maybe he just didn't want to make that switch just then. How did she jump from her brother singing in the shower, to men thinking the world revolves around them?! He was struggling to find the intellectual road map that showed the route she had traveled from one point to the other.

"Why," she continued, ignoring him, as if she were deep in thought, trying desperately to solve an incorrigible mystery of the universe, "why do men want all of the attention going one way—to them? Why can't they accept that there are other people in the world who expect—and deserve—to have some attention paid to *their* wants, and needs, and egos? Where do men get such *huge* and magnificent egos, anyway?" Unlike other male traits, she muttered to herself.

"Why," she asked aloud to the world, as if she were strolling down the street alone instead of sitting at her kitchen table, finishing supper with a perfectly delightful member of the male gender, who remained leaning a bit too close over the table, "why is it all about 'take' for men, and practically no 'give'? What's more, why don't they care what kind of pain, or how much misery, they fill someone else's life with, as long as they get all the goodies they want that their ego thinks they are entitled to?"

Her face had become a bit flushed. Emotions which she thought she had let go of, or at least buried long ago, were unexpectedly pushing their way to the surface of her mind, and, worse, out of her mouth. She was becoming confused. She didn't want to put Jack off. On the contrary, she had been warming to the idea, all day, that maybe they could have some fun together. So why did she go ballistic in response to his very friendly, and actually appealing, overture?

"But the world *does* revolve around men," Jack innocently explained.

"Whah...what?!" Elaine couldn't believe what she was hearing.

"I said, the world *does* revolve around men. It's not their fault if they have huge egos. The world confers that distinction on them!"

"Are you *crazy*?" Elaine could hardly believe what she was hearing. Maybe she had been too precipitate in thinking she wanted to spend more time with this man.

"No," Jack said firmly, defiantly even. He was upset with her effort to rebuff his overture. "I'm not saying it's right

—or that it's good—or that it *should* be that way. I'm just saying that that's the way it *is!"*

And then, "Ah!", and you could see the light bulb turning on in his mind by how brightly his eyes suddenly shone, "so, now we get to the real issue."

"The real...?" Elaine collected herself. "The real issue is the boundless self-interest men display, that is so voracious it can never be satisfied!" She could feel her cheeks burning bright red by now.

"Aha! I'm right!" Jack muttered under his breath. And, because he knew he was treading on egg shells, he added, even more quietly, "so that *is* the issue then, isn't it? That's why you've built up an impenetrable wall—no man is going to crumble that wall because you made it amazingly thick and strong. Probably not too long ago, I would guess, some guy really *really* disappointed you, to put it politely, and the only way you can prevent having ever to live through that searing pain again, is to keep all men out."

"Oh, I get it! You're just trying to prove that I have witch-like qualities, by bringing out the darker, more excitable, more shrewish, side of me, is that it?" Elaine's voice was bordering on shrill now.

"No, Elaine," Jack replied very, very softly, "I'm trying to reach the womanliness in you, the womanliness that I know is there. That part of you that you seem so determined to hide, or keep hidden." As he spoke, he slowly rose from his chair, and walked around to the other side of the table, and stopped beside her chair. He gently placed his hands on her shoulders, and encouraged her to stand up, as he continued, "because that's who I want to embrace." As he finished speaking, he lifted her chin so that she was looking up at him, with her face just inches away from his. Ever so slowly, he lowered his face to hers, so that he could fulfill a desire that had been building inside of him since he first walked into Representative Blanchard's office.

Chapter 25

Elaine couldn't move. Her feet felt glued to the floor. She wasn't even sure where she was anymore. Everything around her had become a foggy blur. The room was slowly starting to spin, knocking her off balance, and draining from her soul her will to resist him. She was mesmerized by the beautiful blue of his eyes in the soft light. Eyes that were bright, vivid, but at the same time, dark and fathomless. When she felt his lips finally reach hers, she found his embrace gentle, warm, and tender. He wasn't demanding, or insisting. No. He was asking her, inviting her, to partake in something loving—and, oh, so sweet.

He was a keen observer. Because he was correct about the wall she had built around her to keep everyone outside of her emotional range. No one was going to get close enough to establish an emotional connection with her ever again. She had learned the hard way, that emotional connections defy logic. Your heart overrules your head. And when that happens, you end up hurting. Really hurting. You find yourself thinking that you might as well be dead, because you just can't go on living with that excruciating pain. And then you become numb. That's when you bury your pain, and the memory of that pain, deep inside of you. And that's when you build that wall. So that no one else can ever again make you hurt so badly that you become an emotionless zombie. No one was ever going to make her experience that agony again. Only she could prevent it.

But here he was. This man was cracking through her best defense. He saw, and understood, the fear, but it didn't put him off. For some unknown reason, which she didn't yet understand, he was determined to create in her, again, that sense of longing that envelopes you when you are in love.

His embrace was dizzying. Inside her head, a voice was shouting, "Go away! Go away!" Yet her arms slowly reached around his neck, where her hands locked behind his shoulders, drawing him to her, and holding on to him as if for dear life. She was not just returning his embrace, she was clinging to him, as if he were her only anchor in a raging storm. A storm of conflict between her heart and her head.

He pulled away from her, just a little, and looked deeply, and longingly, into her soft brown eyes. He could feel the rhythmic beating of both of their hearts. He had kissed many women before in his life, but he had never felt this kind of connection with any of them. It was as if the threads of their lives were becoming woven together, intertwined, to form a single whole.

He wanted to bury his face in her hair, and smell the sweet fragrance of her shampoo. He wanted to bury his face in her neck, and taste the creamy smoothness of her skin. He wanted to lock her in an embrace for all time, and feel the warmth and comfort of coming home.

Suddenly she was a part of him, a part of his very soul. He had had inklings of this sense of connectedness from the moment he walked into her office last Saturday morning. Saturday? Has it been just four days since we first met? That's so unbelievable, he thought. Why does it feel like we have been a part of each other all of our lives? The thought that she could disappear in a moment made him suddenly feel like he would suffocate. She feels as much a part of my being as my breathing, he realized. The breath that fuels my life. And that discovery unexpectedly frightened him.

He had never been afraid of relationships before. And he'd always been able to walk away whenever it seemed that a relationship had played itself out. This was different. The thought of her going anywhere away from him left him feeling bereft. He was afraid that he might just wither away and die. What was going on here? Why now? Why with her?

Chapter 26

He clicked the "send" key, and off the emails went.

"Ok," he turned to look up at the person standing behind him, from where he sat in front of the computer, "it's done!"

"Oh, you incredible, wonderful man!" his companion responded, a grin spreading from ear to ear. "They thought they were so clever. But we've outfoxed them!" his friend gloated. "I love it when a plan comes together! I so wish I could be a fly on the wall when they discover what has happened!"

They were alone, and in the dark. She swiveled his chair so that he was completely facing her, and she gently sat in his lap as she slipped her arms around his neck. "And you know how success arouses me, sweetie," she cooed, as she lowered her face to his for an embrace. But he turned slightly to avoid her overture.

As she pulled away, eyes questioning, she asked, "What's the matter, honey? Aren't you as excited as I am that we've pulled this off?"

"Have we? Pulled it off, I mean?"

"Of course! Didn't you just say you succeeded?"

"Yeah, but..."

"But what?" she asked, sensing something unsettled him.

He sat there with one arm loosely around her waste and the other sitting languidly in her lap, but he was shaking his head, not sure he should admit his fears to her. "I don't know. I just...I'm just not sure we will really pull this off. I mean, they've figured out what we did."

"Darling, you know how the media will feast on the scandal rather than the resolution of the scandal. It's the scandal that's the news. The media will keep it alive as long as possible. That's what makes people watch in large numbers, letting them charge more and more for advertising, because of increased viewership. They won't want to close the story until they've gotten all they can out of it. And the 24-hour cable news stations will absolutely *feast* on a scandal."

"But they know! And that will squelch the scandal. And then where will we be?"

"But the media will never resolve the scandal! Pretty boy will get the credit, at first, and then the blame," she said as she rose from his lap, annoyed that he was dampening her sense of accomplishment.

He closed his laptop, and rose from his chair, still shaking his head.

"Look," she said softly, as she placed both her hands flat on his chest, "you aren't having second thoughts, are you, Sweetie?"

"Nnn...nnooo...I just...I mean...I'm not used to being in the center of a maelstrom!" he finished, exasperated by his own misgivings.

"No one is going to find out we are involved! We are the last people anyone would think of!"

"I just keep thinking of what's probably going to happen—what if I'm called on publicly to give my expert opinion? My career is at stake, now, too! What will I say? I guess, suddenly it just doesn't seem as simple as it did before..."

"You don't doubt yourself, or us, now, do you?" she asked, hesitantly, then added, to get confirmation, "You realize you can't do that, don't you? We can't go back now."

"But real people are going to be hurt..., including you and me, if anyone finds out!"

"Sweetie, this is politics. It's all about power, and who has it. Power begets power. We have it now, and this will get us even more!"

"Will it? I'm not sure power means all that much to me. I guess I'm just not so sure, anymore, about a lot of things," he murmured dejectedly.

"Come on. Let's go to your place, and you can discover just how much power you do have...especially over me," and she took his hand as she led him out the door.

Chapter 27

Elaine was still in her pajamas and slippers early the next morning, when she shuffled into her home office to check her email for any possible crises, before getting ready for work. She hated to arrive at work and be blindsided by even one fire that needed putting out immediately, let alone multiple ones. She preferred to have a "heads up" check at home, so she could work on solving any problems on her walk to the Cannon House Office Building, where Blanchard's congressional office was located. One of the great benefits of living on Capitol Hill was being able to walk to work. Elaine loved those quiet moments as she walked to and from her job.

She discovered she was humming to herself as she sat down in front of her computer. Hhmmmmm, she remembered, I've read that women hum, or sing, when they are sexually satisfied. I'm just sexually aroused, rather than satisfied, so why am I humming? Could it be because I now see the possibility of being sexually satisfied? She smiled to herself at the thought.

Jack Amory was really different. And sweet. Ssooooo sweet. The embrace they shared the evening before became their goodnight kiss—a definitely unexpected treat for Halloween, for both of them. I wonder how long I will have to wait for another such treat, Elaine mused out loud as she smiled at nothing, or no one, in particular.

It had been a very long time since Elaine had felt so smitten—since before she had arrived in Washington to work for then Freshman Representative Blanchard. She had shut out the memory, as a way of shutting off the pain. But it doesn't work that way—or rather, it isn't that easy to stop hurting emotionally. Intellectually, you can tell yourself you don't like the guy anymore, but the emotional side of your brain has a mind of its own. Elaine guessed that it was nearly two years before she had finally let go of her feelings for the guy who truly broke her heart, and still a little longer before she actually stopped thinking about him every hour of every day. She was grateful for having a job that she loved. A job that made so many demands on her time and attention that, eventually, it overpowered the emotions that sat so close to the surface of her consciousness. Her job actually made it possible to stop thinking about *him*. Her job enabled her to build that emotion-blocking wall and maintain it, without ever being fully aware of what she was doing. Until now. Until Jack.

Elaine marveled that memories and feelings she thought had been at last lost, were suddenly rising front and center. But in a good way. Because of Jack, those memories didn't seem to hurt anymore. Perhaps, now, she might finally let go of all she had been hiding deep inside, so that she could enjoy something good with Jack.

She placed her cup of tea on her desk, as she sat down at her computer and opened her work email account. As she perused new emails in the chronological order of their arrival, she deleted some, and clicked on a few others to see what they were about.

One received in the wee hours of the morning caught her attention. It was a Special Edition of Jack's blog, *The Seeker*. Although he normally published at the beginning of each week, he had said he was putting out a couple of extra editions this week because of the race to adjourn on Capitol Hill. He had already done a second edition yesterday. When he had found the time to issue a third edition less than 24 hours later, she wasn't sure, although he could have been working on it during the daytime yesterday, before he arrived at her house to help with the trick-or-treaters. But not a lot happened yesterday, legislatively, because the big push was scheduled for today. Maybe there's something major coming up that he knows about, Elaine mused.

Elaine opened the blog, and then all she could do was stare at her computer screen. Suddenly her whole world crashed right into her like a bulldozer, leaving her breathless, and unable to utter a sound. She sat perfectly still, while the window on her world shattered into millions of sharp, tiny shards of glass. She gasped, trying to suck in some air, as she felt herself suffocating. In an instant, her blood had turned to ice in her veins. She could feel nothing, not even whether she were still alive. The room was going dark, and darker...until she finally let out a screech that brought some air into her lungs. And she sucked it in hungrily, until her frozen nerves could begin to thaw.

This...this...just can't be..., her mind was racing, as she tried to convince herself that she must be dreaming—or having a nightmare. "This can't be," her mind kept repeating, over and over again, as her senses began to seep back into her consciousness—at least enough to let her recognize, somewhere in the deep recesses of her brain, that this was really, really, happening. Because there it still was, all over her computer screen, right in front of her eyes, in blazing color.

Three photos of Representative Blanchard in bed, with three different men. The photos. THE photos! It hit her in the gut. As if someone competing in the discus throw at the Olympics had hurled one right into her, obliterating her senses, her perceptions, her ability to feel. Betrayal!

Instinctively, her hands closed around her abdomen. She felt like a dried up raisin inside. All she wanted to do was curl up in the fetal position and hide. The betrayal—BETRAYAL! All over again! Just as she was thinking it would be safe to open up to someone romantically. Just when she was beginning to trust a man again. A nuclear bomb, dropped on her home, would have been more humane.

Is that why he tried to seduce me last night?! Was he planning this release all along?! Why did he bother trying to charm me? Why didn't he just publish the photos in the first place, if that's what he was going to do all along? Why did he PRETEND to be honorable?! Why did he pretend to be attracted to me? Why? Why? she kept asking herself. How can anyone be so monstrously cruel?

Elaine's world was in chaos. The realization of his duplicity overwhelmed her more than the release of the photos. She had actually, finally, believed that the interest this man had shown in her was genuine. She had actually let him into her private world. She had TRUSTED him! Of all the monstrous things a person could do, Elaine thought, none was more horrific than to pretend to be attracted to someone, to cultivate that interest, to pursue that person—when, in fact, it was all a *lie*! Everything he said was a lie! Just to achieve some ulterior objective! To *use* her! A lie!

How could she have been so stupid as to respond so readily to him? After being so careful, guarding her emotions for so many years, how could she have been so duped? So easily duped? How could she not have seen through the deceitfulness of his manipulation?

Her mind was racing! He had been attentive from the first, really. He had paid special attention to her as a person—remember that trip to the Smithsonian's Planetarium? He had been catering to her needs. He cared about helping! Or so he made her believe.

He had been so good about accepting Diggie's findings, and about killing a story that would have hugely expanded his blog's readership and visibility, even if it turned out to be untrue!

Is that what he was hoping? Did he think he could still gain the notoriety that publishing these photos would bring, even though Blanchard had proof they were phony—even if it came out that *he* knew they were phony before he published them? Was he that cynical? Was he so self-centered that he did not care how his actions would affect anyone else, let alone an election? Politics was his life—his blog was evidence of that. How could he be so destructive of the political process? And not care one iota? Because if he really cared about political principles, as his blog implies, he couldn't possibly have done something that would so destroy the integrity of an election. Not to mention the unfairness to both candidates.

None of this makes sense, Elaine thought. None of it! I can't believe he is that crude. He just can't be! And yet, there they were—the photos were staring at her from her computer screen, in a special edition of *The Seeker*, with today's date on it.

As some semblance of rationality started to seep back into her brain, Elaine hurriedly threw on a pair of jeans and a sweater, and headed back to the kitchen, where she donned shoes and her jacket, and headed out the door.

Chapter 28

She could have taken her car, but she preferred to walk. She could get there in ten minutes on foot, walking with determination and purpose. That would give her a few minutes, at least, to collect herself and her thoughts. Not that it did much good.

She rang Jack's doorbell. And when he didn't open the door right away, she started pounding on it with her fist. And she kept at it until she heard a groggy sounding voice shout, "Ok! Ok! I'm coming! Hold your horses!"

He was still tying the belt of his bathrobe when he finally opened the door. She felt her resolve shake, just a little, when she saw, first surprise, and then joy, flood his face, when he recognized his visitor. And in spite of everything, the one thought that filled her mind was how adorable he looked all disheveled and sleepy. And then she hated herself for thinking that after the incorrigible thing he had done.

"Really, Elaine, don't you think we should wait for the wedding before we wake up together so early in the morning?" he started lightly. And then the joy that had initially brightened his expression, was wiped from his face, to make way for an expression of shock, as Elaine hurled a tirade at him.

"YOU...You...You...hypocrite!" Elaine shouted, and she could have wakened his neighbors with her ringing voice in the quiet of the morning.

At first, Jack just stood there a moment, blinking his eyes. "What did I do?" he asked innocently, when he could muster a response. And then he thought out loud, "Are you just now reacting to the fact that I kissed you last night? And that you obviously liked it?" he added with a satisfied grin. "Is that what you're so upset about?"

"You...you...you...," Elaine was so enraged she couldn't get any other words out.

"Yes, we've established that it's me you're talking to," Jack chided.

"You...you...how COULD you?" she shouted again.

"How could I what? Kiss you? Well, you are a very attractive woman, Elaine, in case you hadn't noticed lately, hiding behind your wall, as you were. And I readily admit to being a full-blooded male. And you obviously think so, too, or you wouldn't have responded to my embrace as fully as you did," and Jack couldn't prevent a small smile of conquest from flitting across his face as he recalled their encounter.

"Why you *egomaniacal idiot!*" Elaine finally relayed a rational comment.

"Excuse me? Because I can look reality in the face and accept it?" he was a little perturbed at her hostility, but he squelched his instinctive reaction. "Is your emotional wall so thick that you can't see the world for what it is?" he chided again, though he took care to keep his banter light. And then he added, only half jokingly, as he looked down at her standing near the top of his front steps, "Don't you think we should take this discussion inside, so that I don't offend my neighbors, who've never seen me in my robe and pajamas before? I wouldn't want my image to upset their breakfasts!"

Elaine stood there, staring up at him with a blank face, her arms hanging limply by her sides. She couldn't believe what she was hearing. How could he be so blithe about what he had done? And there he was making jokes! Does he have no conscience at all, her internal voice shouted at her!

But the sense of his words did sink slowly into her brain, so that, after a moment, she did climb the stairs, somewhat like a zombie, and walk through the door.

Chapter 29

The sound of the door clicking closed behind her snapped Elaine into some semblance of rationality. To her surprise, her voice was low and reasonably steady as she confronted him.

"You abominable bastard. You rotten specimen of a human being. You scum of the earth. How can anyone be *so* wretched a human being as to do what you've done? Do you have *no* honor or integrity or...or...or simple *decency*?" Elaine opened, as she finally lifted her head to face him.

Jack stood there in the tiny space of his entryway and stared at her, trying to fathom what in hell she was talking about. She couldn't possibly be so very upset because he kissed her—could she? His mind just wouldn't accept that explanation. She had been fully responsive, returning his overture with a full embrace that seemed to hold nothing back. He was fully cognizant of the gift she had given him, opening her heart to his invitation. No. Something else was behind this tirade, this blizzard of abuse. But what?

"Look, Elaine," Jack said quietly, and deliberately, "spit it out. Just spit it out. What on earth are you talking about? How did I go from knight in shining armor, to "*Despicable Me*"? And in just a few short hours?"

Elaine looked up at him, the teensiest flicker of hope rising from somewhere deep inside. But her mind squelched it mercilessly, as she noted that no one else worked for his blog, only him. So it could only have been him.

"You're a bastard, that's what you are!" she explained, with a speck more energy. "You published those photos! As if you didn't know! How *could* you?! How *could* you do that? You claim to have integrity and decency, and yet you do something so abominable, because it can give you national attention!" As she spoke she moved toward him, reaching him in a single step; then she raised her arms, and beat her fists on his chest, harder and harder, until she collapsed against him, sobbing uncontrollably into his chest.

Jack's arms automatically closed around her shoulders as soon as she got close to him. He stood there stoically, holding her gently but firmly, as she pummeled him with her fists. And when she collapsed, he quietly held her close, closing his arms around her shoulders, as the sound of her sobs filled his home.

Now it was his turn to be stunned. The photos? The photos? Could she possibly mean the Blanchard photos? But that's incredible! He hasn't published them. Has someone finally gone public with them? But she said I did it, Jack recalled. That's crazy, he argued with himself. How could she think *I* did it?

To Elaine, who was still sobbing in his arms, he gently asked, "Elaine, have the Blanchard pictures been put into the public arena?"

Her head shot up. She looked him squarely in the face and said, with only mildly suppressed vehemence, "How *can* you? How can you *pretend*?! *Yes*, they've been published! You know they've been published! YOU published them! All the while you were cooing and charming me, you were plotting this surprise attack! You were just trying to keep me off my guard about you! So I wouldn't suspect what you were planning! So you could get inside information! And time your release to do the most damage! Oh, you must have had a terrific laugh at how *stupid* I was...how easily fooled I was! Your cruelty knows no bounds! Your selfishness is beyond credibility! Your...your..." Elaine pulled away from Jack as she searched for more crucifying epithets to hurl at him.

Jack stood there in front of her, arms hanging down by his sides now, just barely able to suppress his anger at her attack. She had accused him of something he didn't do. Without giving him a chance to defend himself against whatever caused her to accuse him. He's the one who's been stupid. Stupid to think this woman was someone special. Stupid to think they might have some kind of special connection that he had never felt with anyone else. Stupid to think that maybe he had finally met a woman who might turn out to be his soul mate. Stupid to think...what? That he might have actually found a woman he could love?

Well, she might not have given him the courtesy of explaining why she thought he was a traitor before brutally accusing him, but he would at least give her time to explain what was behind her accusation before he trashed his feelings for her.

"Ok, Elaine," Jack commented as calmly as he could, folding his arms across his chest and looking down at her, with one raised eyebrow questioning her. "Why don't you tell me why you think I published those photos of Blanchard?"

Elaine looked at him, astounded by his nonchalance. "You mean to stand there and try to pretend you don't know?"

"That's exactly what I'm telling you, Elaine. What is it I don't know?" and the constrained evenness of his tone, the quiet flexing of his jaw muscles, belied the emotional volcano that was building inside of him.

"You really think I'm that much of a fool to believe you don't know what I'm talking about?"

"No, Elaine. I do not think you are a fool," Jack replied, holding his voice as steady as possible. "But I truly do not know what you are talking about."

"*How* could you not know, when *you* published those photos in YOUR OWN BLOG!"

Jack's eyes opened wide in shock. For a moment, he was stunned into silence. All he could do was stare at Elaine, standing there, accusing him of publishing the photos in his blog.

"I don't know where you get your information from, Elaine, but I assure you I have *not* published those photos in my blog." It took all of his energy to keep the anger from exploding out of his voice.

"Oh, yes, you have, Mr. Amory!"

"I have not!" and the fury that was building inside was close to overflowing.

"Oh, yeah?" Elaine queried. "Well, let's go to your computer, and I will *show* you that you are *lying*!"

"Lying, Ms. Kent?" And the volcano erupted. "You are calling me a *liar*, Ms. Kent?" She had turned to go looking for his home office, but something in the quiet, controlled, tone of Jack's anger made Elaine stop in her tracks, and turn to face him.

"No one," Jack started, "not even you...*especially you*...has any valid basis for calling me a liar! I am *not* a liar, Ms. Kent! I am an honorable man. I don't go around lying for any reason, particularly not as a tool to manipulate people. I despise deception, and the people who use it to make puppets out of others. I don't *use* others for my own personal gain. When I give my word, I keep it. *I have not released those photos!*"

And in a steely voice, his anger not fully spent, he added, "Now, are you going to tell me exactly what has happened?"

"No, I will not *tell* you," Elaine's voice was as coldly angry as his, "I will *show* you. Where's your computer?"

Taken aback by this request, Jack nevertheless led Elaine to a second floor room he used as his office, and the home base for work on his blog. When they entered the room, Elaine went quickly to the computer, sat down in front of it, and logged in to her own work email account. Then she clicked on the email for the Special Edition of Jack's blog.

Jack stood behind her, watching every click of the keyboard. When the email opened up, he saw his blog banner at the top, with the label for a "special edition". Under the banner there was a brief narrative lead-in that merely said, "A picture is worth a thousand words. Here are three thousand 'words' for your reading pleasure. This should make the heretofore boring Blanchard/Billingsley Senate race a little bit more interesting! Don't you think?"

And, then, there were the photos. All three of them. In their full, prurient glory.

It was Jack's turn to be speechless. He stood there, looking down at his computer screen, not wanting to believe what he saw in front of him with his own eyes. But there it all was. But how?

"Look, Elaine," Jack finally started speaking slowly, when he could collect his senses enough to speak at all, "I don't know how this happened. I didn't do it. You have to believe me. I didn't do it," he repeated, his eyes still glued to the screen.

"How can you stand there saying that?!" Elaine swiveled around in her chair to look up at him. She had to suppress a powerful urge to shake him by the shoulders into admitting the truth. "It's *your* blog, and you have no one working for you! How can you still try to pretend you didn't do this?"

"I told you," he replied, looking down intensely into her face, "I don't lie. I don't manipulate. I don't engage in grand schemes, or pull puppet strings to make everything come out a certain way. I didn't do this," and he waved his right arm at the computer. And then he had a thought that made him panic inside, so he instructed her, "Get up, so I can check my blog distribution."

She rose without a word. He sank into the chair, and somewhere in the far recesses of his mind, he noted that the seat was warm from her body heat. He pushed the sensation aside, and started clicking away at the keyboard.

"Well, as I feared," he reported, dejectedly, "it's been sent through my distribution list to about 6,700 recipients."

"Oh. My. God." Elaine was incredulous. "You have 6,700 subscribers to your blog?"

"Last time I checked, somewhere thereabouts, yes. There are many people, Ms. Kent, all across the country, who appreciate truly objective, in-depth, thorough political reporting and analyses about Congressional activities! That is why Representative Blanchard just subscribed, is it not?" Jack queried, with the rise of one eyebrow. "Worse, though," he continued, when Elaine ignored his question, "is that I distribute gratis to all main stream media, and other media outlets. Everyone is on the master mailing list," he finished, with chagrin. "Maybe the lesson learned for me is to separate media recipients from the general subscriber list."

"Oh, dear. This is it. This is the end," Elaine slumped down into another chair.

"Now wait a minute," Jack kicked into gear. "There was always the chance—even the expectation—that someone else would be sent the photos to publish, and that whoever got them would end up publishing them, because any basic techie was going to label them as authentic. And when that

145

happened, we would *all* address the problem," he stated, emphasizing that he would be part of the solution, not the problem.

"But these came out on *your* blog, not through some other outlet," Elaine pointed out to him, as she looked him squarely in the eyes, with an expression that seemed to be pleading with him to convince her he was innocent.

"Look, Elaine," Jack returned her direct stare, "I did not do this. Listen to me. I—did—not—do—this." And with that final denial, his journalistic curiosity seemed to kick start. "Is your brother at your house?"

And the light bulb, a very low wattage light bulb, made some progress through the fog that had been shrouding her brain since she had first opened her email at home. "Yes! He is! I'll have him over here in a jiffy!" As she reached for her phone, she realized she had left her house so quickly she had forgotten her phone. "Do you have a phone?" she asked Jack.

He handed her his office landline phone, and she quickly dialed Diggie, waking him up, it seemed, from the sound of his groggy voice.

"You want me to what?!" she heard Diggie ask.

"Diggie, you need to get up *now,* and get over here right away! I'm at Jack's house, the Littleton Spite House, on B St. NE. What we feared would happen with the photos, has happened. And in a grotesque way. So, *please*, just get over here asap!"

"Do you know what time it is, Sis? And that it's barely a few hours since I got home, and crawled into bed?" Diggie retorted.

"Diggie! Please! This isn't a joking matter."

"Ok! Ok, Sis. I'll be there in a jif," and he hung up the phone.

"He's on his way," Elaine reported to Jack.

Chapter 30

"Well, someone definitely accessed your computer in the wee hours of this morning," Diggie informed Jack.

"You're sure?" Jack wanted confirmation. "Absolutely sure?"

Diggie turned to look up at Jack, who was looking over Diggie's right shoulder as he sat in front of Jack's computer screen. Diggie didn't say a word. He just stared at him with wide open eyes, and a pursed mouth, that dared Jack to challenge his conclusions.

As he turned back to the computer screen, Diggie stated, matter-of-factly, "You don't have any security software —no anti-virus or anti-malware programs. No firewall."

"True," Jack admitted.

"How can someone, whose business relies on sophisticated computer operations, be so derelict?"

It was a simple question, asked in a completely noncommittal tone, which somehow made Jack really feel like a schoolboy getting scolded in front of the class. Clearing his throat, he defended himself with, "I am not derelict in maintaining my computer. I deliberately did not install security software because I deal with, literally, thousands of communications every week. Security programs can be cumbersome, and can take up a lot of space, so they can slow down computer operations. I especially didn't want anything interfering with, and maybe randomly blocking, incoming emails, especially from someone who might be trying to send me a tip about possible political shenanigans. So, yes," Jack finished, with a little more of his confidence restored, "I don't have any security programs installed."

"Well, in protecting your 'sources', one of the emails you received carried a trojan—when you opened the email, it replaced an operating system file with its own version, which carried an additional extension that isn't normally part of that system file. That addition makes it possible for someone to access your computer remotely, and use it at will. Which someone did. I downloaded a software application that let me analyze your network connections, and I found that last night there was a new remote connection that occurred at exactly 12:37 a.m."

"Can you identify who, or what, that connection was with, Diggie?" Elaine asked in a soft, but shaky, voice that revealed the state of her nerves.

"I can give you the IP address of the computer it came directly from, but it's not usually the address of whoever is doing the actual hacking. But this instance is very curious," Diggie noted.

"How so?" Elaine asked.

"Well, usually hackers route their contact through lots of different computers that may be located anywhere in the world. It's how they disguise their identity. I traced the geographic location of the access address, and it's...," and here Diggie paused.

"It's *what,* Diggie?" Elaine pressed him.

"Well, the general geographic area of that address is somewhere nearby...here...in D.C.," he stated. "And possibly, as close as someplace here on Capitol Hill, Sis."

Chapter 31

Jack broke the spell of silence that had taken hold at Diggie's announcement. "That's strange, isn't it? Is the location nearby?"

"Yes, actually. It came from an Internet cafe at 9th and C, NE."

"Why is that strange, Diggie?" Elaine asked, still daunted by Diggie's discovery.

"Well, it's unusual for the apparent source, and the destination, computers to be so close geographically, Sis. To obscure the real source, the last location prior to accessing the target computer is usually thousands of miles away, typically in another country."

And then Jack had an idea. "Do you suppose, I mean, is it possible, that the hacker didn't bother to route through other computers? I mean,..."

"I know what you're getting at," Diggie cut in, not waiting for Jack to finish. "You think that the hacker may have accessed your computer directly, in a careless moment, or whatever?"

"Yeah, that's what I mean. Do you think it's possible? I mean, I'm not exactly a platform that would attract interest on a broad enough spectrum to warrant interest from entities sophisticated enough to hack from afar. It makes more sense to me if the person who sent me the photos, and who hacked into my computer, was the same person and was local. Someone who had interest in Congress, politics, and perhaps the Blanchard Senate race, in particular."

"Logically," Elaine noted, "that would make sense. Maybe the computer source is, indeed, the actual hacker. But it seems too simple an explanation, don't you think? Anyone going to the trouble of doing this can't be stupid enough not to cover their tracks."

"I think you're both on the right track," Diggie agreed, "but not from the logical standpoint—rather from the fact that the IP address that the connection came from was not the IP address of the computer associated with the Internet Cafe. That suggests it was someone who visited there, using their wifi connection. I checked out the cafe. It's advertising says that it stays open for wifi access 24-hours a day, even when the cafe itself is not open to customers. That service gets the cafe a pretty loyal following, I would think.

"What intrigues me even more," Diggie continued, "is this: why you, Amory?"

"Huh?" Jack was taken aback. "What do you mean, 'why me'?"

"Well, look at what's been happening. *You* received the photos originally. Not the main stream media. You. Whoever sent you those photos at least knows who you are."

"Wait a minute!" Jack interjected. "I have over sixty-seven hundred subscribers! A lot of people *know* me! Or know about my blog!"

"But when you didn't publish the photos in a timely fashion," Diggie continued as if Jack had never interrupted, "*you* were the one hacked to make the photos go public. Why you? Why not just send them to another news outlet?" At this point, Diggie had turned his chair so that he was facing both Elaine and Jack, who had remained standing behind him.

Elaine turned toward Jack, looking squarely at him, adding, "That's a really good question."

"Well, I don't have the answer, folks!" Jack shrugged his shoulders as he let out some of the pent up anxiety he had been feeling at this turn of events.

"Wait, don't get excited," Diggie appeased. "I'm asking because the photo leak may very likely be coming from someone who actually knows you. And that means you know this person, too!"

"Whether the person knows me or not, they sure are trying to hurt me—maybe even discredit me and my blog. It could be anyone. There are lots of people who know *of* me. There are several other key political bloggers that I compete with for readership. Maybe someone thought I would make a good patsy, that perhaps I wasn't clever enough to see through their scam. Someone who both wanted to kill Blanchard's career, and bring me down as an added bonus. Wean out alternative news sources. Maybe some political person, or lobbyist, doesn't like my in depth analyses that uncover hidden truths that other journalists are too superficial to notice. Maybe I'm as much a target as Blanchard..." Jack's voice trailed off as these ideas started to surface.

"Whoa!" Elaine exclaimed, as she remembered some of the broader implications. "The lobbyists! The ones in the photos! We'd better meet with Kate Blanchard pronto," and as much as she was still confused about whether she could trust Jack, she added pointedly, "all of us."

"Oh, so you believe me now?" Jack asked, a bit peevishly.

"Look, if Diggie says your computer was hacked, it was hacked. As much as I am always looking for deviousness in parties involved in political decisions, even I don't believe you would go to the trouble of going to an Internet cafe in the middle of the night to hack your own computer!" and she had to smile a little because the notion was too ridiculous. "No," she added more thoughtfully, "if you were going to publish those photos, I do believe you would have just gone and done it directly. None of this beating around the bush, so to speak," and the smile broadened, infusing her face with light. Or at least Jack thought so.

For a moment, he was mesmerized by the beauty her smile revealed. He had seen her smile before. Why hadn't he noticed earlier how smiling made her eyes sparkle with glitter? Then, with a voice that held all the warmth he could possibly manage, he said, "Thank you for that vote of confidence, Ms. Kent."

Diggie had been watching and listening, first with a question mark on his face, and then with the dawn of discovery, as he looked back and forth between Elaine and Jack. Well, well, he thought. What do you know? And if someone had held a mirror for him to look into at that moment, Diggie would have seen a very satisfied smile creep across his face.

"Ok, ok, you two..." Diggie interjected, firmly but not harshly, since it seemed to him that someone needed to take charge. "While you're getting dressed, Amory, I want to check a few more things on your computer. Then I'll be ready to face Mrs. Blanchard. Hurry up, now!" and he shooed Jack away.

Diggie watched as his sister plopped down in a nearby chair, drained from the emotional roller coaster ride she'd been on since opening her email that morning. He saw the relief that flooded her face as she finally accepted the reality that Jack hadn't been the one who released the photos after all. The notion that his sister had an emotional interest in some guy made him feel very protective towards her. He understood, only too well, the horrific torture she must have been feeling when she believed Jack had betrayed her. Diggie had been fourteen when Elaine moved to Washington, D.C. to work for Kate Blanchard; that was just eight years ago. He couldn't recall her ever having had a boyfriend in that whole time. Everything was about work. It cheered him to think she had met someone who awakened a part of her that seemed to have been buried for so long. In spite of his apparent youth, Diggie knew firsthand, how loving someone made you feel alive in ways you never dreamed of, even if that love had not yet been shared. Just loving someone could make you float on air. And as he, himself, was finally discovering with Caroline, when love is mutual, it is the greatest experience—and gift—that life has to offer.

"Don't worry, Sis," Diggie said, in a low voice, "everything will turn out ok. You'll see." And he wasn't just talking about the political scandal that was about to break wide open.

"I'm so glad you are here, Diggie," Elaine finally replied. "I don't know what we'd do without your genius skills, and with your stolid level-headedness in a crisis," she acknowledged.

Jack returned to his office at that moment, wearing a sharp navy blue suit, with a blue and wine striped tie. "Well, do I meet with your approval?" Jack directed the question generally, but he was looking at Elaine.

"Goodness! Do you have a meeting with the President today?" she asked.

"No. And neither do either of you. But I suggest we swing by your place so that the two of you can dress accordingly, as well. It's going to be a long day. And, I expect we will all be in the public eye as this story unfolds. It's best to look your best—professional appearances go a long way in generating credibility."

"Well, someone has gotten his stride in all of this now," Elaine observed wryly.

"Yes. And I suggest you both get yours, too! Come on, let's go!" Jack ushered them down the stairs and out his door.

Chapter 32

They were all there, in Kate Blanchard's living room, sitting around digesting the results of the video conference with Blanchard's campaign leadership back in her home state. Everyone seemed lost in the depths of their own thoughts. Everyone was so quiet, they could each hear the cat purring in the next room, where she had curled up on a dining room chair after having been coaxed, (read 'pushed'!), from the living room sofa to make room for the humans. It was barely 8:00 in the morning, so the barrage of media inquiries hadn't started yet, fortunately, but that gave them little pleasure, since they expected the onslaught to begin at any moment.

"Now that we have a game plan, and are all on the same track, we can move forward," Kate Blanchard stated. "I do believe we are right to keep our response to the photos here in Washington, since publication originated here, and not back home. Especially, too, since Congress is still in session, and I am here. I'm not sure it will give us any benefit in terms of minimizing coverage back home, but we can always hope."

Turning to Jack, she added, "I do appreciate your working with us on this, and all the cooperation you've given us already. I apologize, in advance, for any harm or discredit this whole episode may bring to your reputation as a journalist, or to respect for your blog. I do believe, however, that being honest and forthright will also redeem, or even enhance, acknowledgement of the integrity of your work in the future. I can't help feeling you are an unwitting pawn in this rather brutal onslaught on my Senate race—and I apologize for that." As she sighed in resignation, she added, "But that seems to be the political tactic of preference lately."

"Please, Representative Blanchard," Jack responded, with respect, "I will be fine. I've always believed that truth will out—eventually, anyway, if not in the most beneficial timeframe. I stand on the quality of my work, and I'm not afraid to speak bluntly to publish the truth. I feel that my blog is as much a target, now, as your campaign for the Senate. Why anyone went to the trouble to hack into my blog, rather than just send the photos to another outlet, I don't understand.

But I am going to do everything I can to find out who is behind all of this. My reputation is as much at stake now, as yours."

"Thank you, Mr. Amory. We'll fight this together, then. It's not going to be pretty, that's for sure!" Turning to Elaine, she added, "This isn't a campaign event, so I want you to oversee the media inquiries. Let our press assistant here help in any way you find possible, but you will be the one person interfacing directly with media requests that come to my office here. Barrett will forward all inquiries at campaign headquarters to the office here, so that we have only one communication point handle the inquiries. Hopefully, that will prevent any conflicting responses to the media. If there's even one conflicting story, or statement, coming out of my office, you know the media will fashion a conspiracy theory around it, and our efforts to get the truth out will be overshadowed by the sexier story, enabling them to keep it alive long after it should be dead and buried."

"Yes, Ma'am," Elaine accepted.

Then Blanchard continued her strategy directions with, "I guess we will start getting media requests soon, once they've had enough time to run the photos by an expert, who is likely to give them verification. In case anyone has gotten the phone number for the house, we won't answer any calls coming here. That should direct inquiries to the office. Also, if media camp outside the house, then we'll just tell them to contact the office, that no one will speak with them from here."

"Sounds good," Elaine noted.

"Ok," Blanchard sighed. "Elaine, Diggie, and I will work on my statement for a press conference, assuming all goes as we expect. Diggie, you need to be prepared to respond to questions, as much in English, please, as you can muster! Remember, we'll be talking to reporters with 30 second sound bites, not computer experts!"

"Yes, Mrs. Blanchard! I'll do my best," Diggie readily replied.

"Jack, you are probably going to get the initial onslaught of queries, since the photos came out in your blog.

Thank you for agreeing to hold your public response for the press conference, so that we can address this fully, together, and all at once. You might want to go home now, and get your real 'special edition' ready, and scheduled for distribution one hour before the press conference. Also, you might want to work on any statement you want to make at the press conference. I'm sure the media will direct lots of questions your way.

"There will probably be a media frenzy outside the office shortly, so be ready to defend yourselves as you come and go! Make sure you all get some breakfast, too! You might even want to bring some lunch or snacks into the office with you, because it's going to be a long day," Blanchard said, with a shrug of her shoulders that recognized there would be no avoiding the coming circus. And it would be a circus.

"Will do, Representative Blanchard," Jack agreed. As he stood up and headed towards the door, Elaine followed him. He had been thoroughly cooperative with Blanchard, as he had from the beginning. And yet, he seemed distant. At least, to her.

She touched his sleeve lightly, to get his attention when they reached the door. She hesitated a moment, as he looked at her without speaking.

"Jack, I want to apologize for my behavior this morning."

"No need," Jack stated, though the slight curtness in his voice belied his words.

"Yes, there is a need. To me, at least. But you have to admit, what was I supposed to think when I saw the email from your blog?" Elaine looked up at him imploringly, eyes wide with innocence.

His stance softened, but only a little, as he looked down at her and spoke, "Look, Elaine, I can understand that you would have simply reacted when you first opened the email. But you didn't even give me a fighting chance! You didn't *ask* me if I had done it. You *accused* me! You were *certain* that I had done such a horrid thing. You believed that I *could,* and *would,* do something so unethical, and so unprofessional. Somehow, it didn't even occur to you that maybe there was another explanation...that I might actually be innocent. You tried, convicted, and hanged me, without so much as the opportunity to pose a defense!"

"I know," Elaine said in a small voice. "And I am truly so sorry."

Somewhat ameliorated, Jack invited, "I'm going to swing by Craig's house again, would you like to come? I keep stopping by his house whenever I get a chance, but he's never been home. I still want to talk to him about his validation of the photos."

"Yes! Yes, I would like very much to come with you," Elaine readily agreed, as she read the invitation as an acceptance of her apology. The thought lifted her spirits surprisingly high. "But I have to get back quickly, to work on Kate's statement," she added.

In spite of the pressure of time, they walked rather slowly, each deep in thought. It was a clear, sunny, day, and the air was cool and crisp—the proverbial moment of peace that prefaced a pending storm. It was as if they both had silently hoped that by taking their time they could forestall the expected mania. Or maybe they were just enjoying a quiet moment alone, as each experienced a quiet sense of sharing with the other, a sharing that required trust.

As they rounded the corner onto the street where Craig Bittiford lived, Jack put his hand on Elaine's arm to stop her progress.

"Uh-oh," he groaned, "it looks like a couple of media vans in front of his house. They must want him to review the photos, although it looks like no one is home. Maybe we'd better get on with our other tasks before any of those media folks see us."

"Ok," Elaine agreed, as they both quickly turned back around the corner, and out of site of Craig's house.

"I'll check back with him before I head up to Blanchard's office. I've been trying to call him the last couple of days, too, but I guess he's just not answering his phone. I can't imagine why not. Or maybe he's just blocking my calls!" Jack laughed, a little nervously.

"Do you suppose," Elaine was tentative in her suggestion, "that he, somehow, might have realized—after the fact, of course—that maybe he made a mistake? And he's too embarrassed to face you?"

"I don't think so. He would have contacted me to tell me. There's no shame in making a mistake. If he suddenly figured out that he did, I think he would have told me."

Elaine looked up at him with as much warmth, and apology, as she could muster, as she humbly stated, "It's very difficult to admit it when you've made a mistake, Jack. I truly am so sorry."

Chapter 33

"Wow!" Jack exclaimed, as he squeezed his way through the entrance into Blanchard's office shortly before 1:00 P.M., after pushing his way through the dozen or more reporters and cameramen camping outside of her office door, in spite of the announcement that the press conference would be held on the steps of the Capitol. "Why do I feel like I just went through one of those old laundry wringers?"

"What? You're a journalist. You never camped outside some official's office for a story?" Elaine chided Jack about his own profession.

"I am one of those *rare* journalists who conducts in-depth research and analysis, to bring the true story to my readers," Jack beat his chest with his forefinger. "I don't just sit on someone's doorstep waiting for a story to drop in my lap!"

"Oh, *excuse me,* Mr. Blogger. Let me see. I seem to have a vague memory of you filling my car with the odors of burgers and fries, while we *sat* for more than two hours outside someone's house, waiting for something—anything—to happen, to give us a clue as to what was going on?" Elaine teased.

"*That* was research!" Jack gave back to her, tit for tat.

"Oh, that's right! I forgot! Graduate school rules for research, rule #6: 'learn to sit quietly in parked cars for hours at a time, to gather esoteric insights into your topic.'"

"Very funny, Ms. Know-it-all," and Jack sent a crumpled up piece of paper flying across the office in the direction of Elaine's desk.

"Now, isn't that just like a man! When you're losing the debate, throw things!" Elaine jeered.

"Now, children," Diggie interjected, "time to get serious here. We're on in fifteen minutes."

"Yes, Dad," Jack replied, in a gentle tease, as Representative Blanchard exited her private office, and said it was time to head over to the Capitol Building.

Both Blanchard, and Jack had agreed that an official press conference was essential to respond to the slanderous accusations of the photos, and to quell some wild speculation indicated by the barrage of questions that were being hurled their way. There was much concern that merely issuing a written statement from Blanchard, and even a separate one from Jack as well, would probably generate more questions. If Blanchard did not make herself available for direct questions from the press, then too many news reports might have used that 'refusal' to undermine the truth in her response.

The Press Conference had been called for 1:00 p.m. on the Capitol Building steps that face East. Before heading over to Blanchard's Hill office for the press conference, Jack had returned home to program distribution of a genuine Special Edition of his blog, one that included both a disclaimer for the bogus mailing that had gone out in the wee hours of the morning, and an explanation of what had occurred with regard to the photos. With the press conference scheduled for one o'clock, he scheduled distribution to begin at noon. He had stayed around for a little after distribution started, to make sure it was working as it was supposed to. Whoever had hacked into his computer might have tried to mess up his operation to prevent exactly what he was now trying to do— send out a followup message disclaiming the previous edition. Diggie had, though, cleaned up his computer files and added a security wall.

Blanchard had vetoed attendance at the press conference by either her husband or her daughter. She argued there was no reason for her family to attend what was really a 'business' event. The photos were using personal conduct to challenge her career. It was all about her career, so she believed that the presence of family would not only personalize the scandal, it might legitimize the scandal by making it appear there was something real to address—or hide.

And so, at 12:50 pm, the Congresswoman, Elaine, Jack, and Diggie, headed out of the office to walk over to the East steps of the Capitol. Of course, it wasn't that simple. The medley of reporters outside her office closed in on them as they emerged, shoved microphones in their faces, and shouted questions at them all the way over to the Capitol steps. Each was hoping to get something 'first'—something that they could use to set their story apart from all the others. It didn't matter what it was—as long as it was something they could run with now, while the other reporters attended the press conference.

Chapter 34

As Kate Blanchard stepped up to the microphones, Elaine surveyed the bevy of reporters and cameramen who were eagerly waiting for the show to start. Their numbers were increased by the reporters who had followed them from her office. This wasn't the first public controversy Representative Blanchard had faced, but it was the first dealing with a personal attack, and one that was built on a lie. Sensational stories, especially ones about politicians' personal lives, generated front page coverage and lots of time on camera. They were like manna from heaven for journalists.

If only we could get so much media attention for the critical issues that affect people's lives everyday, Elaine thought, with dismay. And to Jack, she whispered, with more than a touch of angry sarcasm, "We've *never* had this much media interest in any of the really important issues we've fought for in the eight years she's been in Congress!"

"Sshhh!" he cautioned, raising a finger to his pursed lips. Then close to her ear he added, "The microphones are on. One of them might pick up what you are saying."

At that moment, Representative Blanchard began to speak.

"How lovely of you all to come here just to hear me speak!" she began lightly. "I don't think in my eight years in office, I've attracted so much interest in the issues I care deeply about!" Nervous chuckles rippled through the reporters. "I see a few familiar faces, but if I knew I'd see so many new faces I would have brought copies of my many other press releases, to acquaint you with my actual legislative agenda!" The more seasoned journalists tried to suppress expressions of guilt that threatened to spread across their faces, while some of the reporters for outlets that focus on scandal "news" looked down at their feet, or suddenly developed great interest in cleaning their nails, while others turned to colleagues on their left or right, anywhere to hide from the comeuppance Representative Blanchard had just thrown at them.

And then she spoke from her heart. "I am here to address a truly serious issue. *You* are here because you are aware of some photos that were publicized today—unbeknownst, I might add, to the owner of the political blog, *TheSeeker*—photos which allege sexual liaisons between me and—not one!—but three men! And not just *any* men! Three Washington lobbyists! And not just any lobbyists! But three that I have consistently found myself in opposition to on various pieces of proposed legislation! Like the saying goes, it doesn't rain, it pours." Some nervous laughter rippled through the bevy of reporters.

"I can categorically say," Blanchard continued, "that there are no such liaisons—and there never have been such liaisons—with those men, or anyone else.

"And I can categorically state that the photos are not genuine!" A few rumblings of both surprise and sarcasm reached Blanchard's ears, but it didn't stop her.

"Last Friday, Jack Amory—the owner, Editor, and soul employee of *TheSeeker* political blog—received copies of these photos anonymously. As a good journalist should, he made an effort to have the photos validated. Although a computer expert told Mr. Amory that he believed the photos were genuine, Mr. Amory compared the message of those photos with my record and reputation in Congress, and realized there was a disconnect. So he came to me to get my side of the story, before going public with the photos.

"In addition to explaining that there were no such liaisons, I was able to have one of the leading experts in the country examine the photos to determine how they were made, since I knew they told a false story. That expert, Gregory Kent, discovered a very clever and sophisticated manufacturing process which produced photos that *your* computer specialists will likely pass as genuine, as did the expert Mr. Amory used. Mr. Kent is here with me now, and will be happy to answer questions shortly.

"As a result of Mr. Kent's discovery, Mr. Amory—as any journalist with integrity would do," and she pointedly scanned the full range of reporters collected in front of her, "chose not to publicize those photos, even though the

163

scandalous nature of the photos could have brought him national recognition had he gone ahead and published them—in spite of the fact that they were not genuine, and eventually would have been shown to be phony.

"What's more, Mr. Amory is here with me today to confirm that he did not send out the edition of his blog that was distributed a little before one a.m. this morning. Someone hacked into his computer, uploaded the phony special edition file of his blog, and distributed it through his subscription list to about 6700 recipients.

"So, I repeat, these photos are not genuine, and no such liaisons exist, or existed. It's as simple as that. We'll take questions now."

A wave of hands went up like a tsunami, amidst lots of shouting. Several reporters asked how the photos were manufactured, if in fact they were. Blanchard noted first that "the simplest proof that the photos were phony was that no such liaisons ever occurred," and then she motioned to Diggie to come to the microphones and explain the technicalities.

"Hi, I'm Gregory Kent. The photos are definitely manufactured, not true original photographs. The technician who created these photos was very skillful, but he—or she—apparently didn't have access to a computer powerful enough to really cinch the phony construction. Fortunately, I have access to an incredibly powerful computer at my alma mater. With that capability, I discovered that these photos were made, largely, by re-photographing the original computer-generated picture—about nineteen times, to be precise. That made the differences in pixels from the different photos that were combined to make these pictures, appear to disappear, to an analyst using generally available technology—which apparently the expert Mr. Amory approached, had been using. The photos are not genuine. Period."

"Mr. Kent," a more familiar reporter called out, "are you related to Rep. Blanchard's Chief of Staff, Elaine Kent?"

"Yes. I'm her brother."

Murmurs and mumbles spread through the group of reporters, and then a hand went up, and someone shouted, "Mr. Amory!" Jack nodded to the reporter, who asked, "How could you have trusted the conclusions on this matter from someone who is the brother of Blanchard's Chief of Staff? I mean, his sister not only works for Blanchard, but she runs Blanchard's Congressional office. If Blanchard doesn't win the Senate race, Elaine Kent is out of a job. It seems obvious that his loyalty would be to his sister's employer."

Diggie started to move forward, but Elaine grabbed his arm to hold him back. It was better that Jack answer this question, and then later, if necessary, Diggie could put forth his credentials.

"You are correct," Jack stated, "in principle, in thinking that normally there could, or would, be a conflict of interest in this case. But there are some people who are so highly skilled, and professional, that they literally cannot veer from the truth. I have every confidence that Gregory Kent is one of those people. You can check his academic and teaching record at MIT, where he is held in the highest esteem. In spite of his youth, he is already a highly accomplished computer engineer. The U.S. Department of Defense has such a high regard for his skills, and integrity, that they have given him a security clearance *above* the level of Top Secret, and have awarded him a consultant's contract to work on weapons programs for some of the most sensitive national defense systems."

Another hand went up, and Jack nodded. "Mr. Amory. How can you expect us to trust in your pronouncements, when you are reportedly involved in a romantic relationship with Blanchard's Chief of Staff? Here you are, claiming that the Chief of Staff's brother is a reliable expert, and you say that he has no conflict of interest, and yet what about you? It all sounds rather contrived to me. What about outside evaluation of the photos? We had an expert check them, and he said they were legitimate."

To save Jack from having to publicly discuss his private life, Diggie stepped forward to reply to this question, and this time Elaine did not hold him back.

"Sir, if you are determined to promulgate a false scandal, then there is nothing anyone can say that will stop you from putting forth the kind of story you want to publish.

We all know that sensational news draws a wider audience than every day news, and that makes it possible for your media outlet to charge more for advertising. Isn't that your real goal? To sensationalize the news, to create a scandal where there is none, just so you can charge more for advertising? Not to mention the visibility it gives to each of you in more on-camera time." A few reporters had the semblance to look a little ashamed at having this truth thrown in their faces.

"The real scandalous story here," Diggie continued, "is not Representative Blanchard's alleged liaisons, but whoever manufactured those photos—and I assure you they are not genuine—and who then hacked into Mr. Amory's computer to spread them around, when he failed to publish them, because he learned they were not genuine. I have no doubt that many computer analysts will pronounce the photos to be genuine, but they will be doing so on the basis of a superficial analysis. Whoever created those photos was quite skilled, because he, or she, was familiar enough with standard analytical procedures to be able to devise a concoction that would fool 99% of analysts.

"It took a dozen hours, and use of one of the most powerful computer capabilities in the world, to discover, and confirm, that these photos were manufactured, and how. As a faculty member at MIT, I have access to powerful computers at the University. How many *minutes* did your analyst spend reviewing the photos? Thirty? Ten? Either of those times would be impressive, because the standard analysis takes about five minutes. But, of course, if your first goal is a sensational news story, rather than accurate reporting, then you will probably choose to ignore the truth—because the truth kills your scandal story. And if there is no scandal to report, then you're not going to be interested in the true story. Because all too often, the truth won't generate higher advertising rates." And with that, Diggie stepped away from the microphone.

For a moment there was complete silence, a truly unusual occurrence at any press conference, let alone one about a politically explosive issue.

The moment didn't last long. Soon, hands were flying high again, amidst more shouts. Diggie pointed to one at random, not knowing any of the reporters himself.

"Are you saying that someone took photos of Mrs. Blanchard, and other photos of the three men, and put them together, and then photographed *that* picture nineteen times to produce the photos that were distributed?"

"Yes."

Another random selection.

"Why should we believe *you*, Mr. Kent, and *not* our own experts who are telling us these photos are genuine, as did the expert Mr. Amory asked?"

"I can give you my academic credentials, which include Bachelor's Degree, Master's, and Ph.D. from M.I.T. in Massachusetts. I went from high school graduate to Doctor in three years, start to finish. DOD trusts me to work on the most sensitive and advanced defense systems, so I think it's fair to expect that you can trust my conclusions on this issue."

Go, Diggie! Elaine cheered in her head. And she whispered again to Jack, "That should put them in their place!"

"Sshhh!" Jack repeated his last comment to her.

And then he heard, "Mr. Amory!" and he stepped up to the microphones as Diggie took a step back.

It was the same reporter who had alleged Jack's decision to hold off on publishing the photos was influenced by a 'personal' relationship between him and Blanchard's Chief of Staff. "You held off publishing the photos, at the determination by Elaine Kent's brother that they were phony pictures. Is it really because you have a *personal* relationship with Blanchard's Chief of Staff? The two of you were seen together at the Smithsonian's Planetarium on Sunday," and the attack on Jack's integrity was clear.

"Certainly not. I met Ms. Kent for the first time this past Saturday." And then in a lighter tone, hopefully to deflect some of the tension, he added, "Though I fancy myself a Casanova of sorts, whom women find irresistible, even I need more time than a few days to close a deal! And I'm not a fan of speed dating, either!" Chuckles all around, as he had hoped, which went a long way toward distracting the reporters from a sensitive question.

"Representative Blanchard," another reporter called out, "if these photos are phony, are you accusing the men in these photos of manufacturing them?"

Jack stepped back to let Blanchard move forward again. "Certainly not," she stated. "We do not know who created these photos. Only that someone did."

"But all three of these men," the same reporter continued, "have found themselves on the opposite side of your positions on several major pieces of legislation over the years. Is it possible, even probable, that one or more of them may be trying to set you up for failure in your Senate bid? You see, some of us have done our homework, Mrs. Blanchard, and we know that your opponent in the Senate race will likely be more sympathetic to their legislative agenda than you have been. As a matter of fact, probably any other candidate would at least be less of an opponent of their goals."

"You are right that my opponent *will* be more sympathetic to their agenda. But as I stated, we don't know who is behind this attempt, not just to destroy my Senate campaign, but to completely destroy my political career."

"Mrs. Blanchard. Why is Mr. Blanchard not here with you?" a reporter shot out.

"Is there any reason why he *should* be?" she countered. "Look, these photos are an attack on my career. And since the alleged liaisons are false, there is nothing my husband needs to protect me, or defend me, from. I can address any issue that arises in my professional life. I don't need family to prop me up emotionally against false allegations. And I will not subject my family to these kinds of circuses. The professionals who need to be here, are here," and she waved an arm to indicate Elaine, Diggie, and Jack.

"Mrs. Blanchard," hollered another reporter, "could it possibly be that you have contrived this whole event to *secure* your election to the Senate by creating some innuendo to discredit your opponent, by making it appear that he might have engaged in a 'dirty trick'?"

"Sigh. I would never do anything underhanded to skew any election race. And if I may quote Gregory, 'Period'." Then she underscored the idiocy of such an attack with, "And why would anyone with an eleven point lead over their opponent do something as stupid as that, and risk the entire election, if discovered?"

Then a reporter near the back, who had appeared to be very intent, spoke up with, "Mrs. Blanchard, I spoke with all three of these men, and they all replied 'No comment'. And I understand that all three of them attended your fundraiser two days ago. We have a picture of you talking with the three of them in the reception line, and everyone was looking very happy, or pleased. If these photos are indeed phony, why would any of them have attended a political function of yours, and why wouldn't each of them just flat-out deny the liaisons?" And suddenly you could hear a pin drop.

"Well," Blanchard started with a light note, "you're a man, Mr. Charrington. What man wants to admit they are not the stud they are made out to be, by owning up to *not* having liaisons they are publicly believed to have had? Especially the men in *this* town. What man wouldn't want people to believe he is candy to women—that women are just falling all over themselves to get their attention? And they did say 'no comment' which means they are not confirming the alleged liaisons."

"But they didn't deny it, either!" the reporter noted.

"And that lets them leave it to *you,* and any other reporter with the same thought, to do their dirty work for them! They never lied—because they never said it was true! They just refused to say it wasn't true, so that any journalist with shallow skills would assume what you are implying, and go with that story. That would let them succeed in helping to smear me, without ever having to take the blame for it. The spurious story would not be *their* fault, but the media's fault! Now, I am sure *you* are not so shallow as to go with a story that isn't confirmed true, just because someone wouldn't deny it's true. Are you, Mr. Charrington?"

And it was quiet. But again, only for a moment. Blanchard knew the reporter was trying to get her to accuse someone, especially the men in the photos, because then they could lead with the accusation, and set up a back-forth-argument between the parties, which would make a longer running sensational storyline. She wasn't going to let anyone goad her into accusations that she had no basis for making. So she dropped the bomb on them.

"Before you go writing stories that imply any of these men are responsible for creating the photos, in order to prevent my election to the Senate, you should be aware that, not only was my face photo-shopped into the photos, but *their* faces were as well. That doesn't mean they didn't create the photos, but it raises a lot of questions about the theory that they did. So I would advise you all to tread carefully if you are leaning in the direction of a storyline that accuses any one of them, however indirectly.

"By the way," she added, as a footnote, "the attendance of each of these men at my fundraiser was a complete surprise, and we returned their contributions, in full."

"Mr. Amory!" again. "You said you didn't publicize these photos. But it *was* your blog that they were published in."

"Yes," Jack again moved up to the microphones. "Someone hacked into my business computer, which is located at my home, where I have my business office. They hacked in a little before one a.m. this morning."

"Do you know who did the hacking?"

"No. But we did identify the IP address of the computer. And it turns out, it may be someone local. As Mr. Kent explained to us, normally a hacker routes their access through foreign countries, especially the last location right before accessing the hacked computer. We were able to identify the geographic location from which the hacking was done, and it was local—which may indicate the person was not a professional hacker, or that they just didn't have enough time to route through a bunch of locations, or was just in a hurry and got careless."

"How local was it?"

"*Very* local. Actually, it was done from a location just about a dozen blocks, or so, from where you are standing right now! Care to share the IP address of *your* computer, Mr. Harcourt?" Nervous laughs.

"Have you reported this to the police?"

Blanchard moved forward to answer this one. "No, we have not yet reported this. We just figured this out a few hours ago, so we are sorting through all of these events, trying to make sense out of them, if that's at all possible, before we decide how best to move forward."

And with a forceful "Thank you, everyone", Blanchard closed the press conference.

Chapter 35

As Blanchard headed straight for the House of Representatives chamber in the Capitol Building at the close of her press conference, she hoped that by the evening news cycle the story would be "old" news. Since there was no substance behind the photos' allegations, she thought—rather optimistically—that the story might just die a natural death. One can always hope, she murmured to herself. But all too often, hopes, like dreams, don't come to fruition.

Jack walked back to Blanchard's office with Elaine and Diggie. A few eager reporters tried to join them in their trek, and ask more questions, but Jack finally stopped the entourage and told the reporters, politely but in no uncertain terms, that the press conference was over. When they reached Blanchard's office, they just charged, in silence, through the reporters who had remained behind, and those who had returned to their vigils outside her office.

Once she closed the office door, Elaine let out a sigh of relief. "Whew! You two guys were just great out there! You didn't let anyone ride herd over you, or keep you from telling the truth! Although, from the questions that were asked, I'm not sure anyone was really looking for the truth, because it could only kill their visions of grandeur at reporting on a juicy political scandal. C'mon, let's see what the TV media are saying."

Diggie and Jack followed Elaine into Blanchard's private office, where she turned on the TV. She flipped through the stations, looking for any stories on the photos, but didn't hit on any coverage of the press conference.

"It could be," Jack commented, "that the stations are researching the story for the moment, trying to figure out what really is going on—or what kind of angle they can take to cover the story. After all, right now it's a 'he said/she said' argument, even about the authenticity of the photos. They're going to have to look for someone who can verify, or debunk, Diggie's analysis."

"Hey!" Diggie cut in. "No one can debunk my analysis, because it's the correct analysis!"

"Calm down, Diggie!" Elaine soothed. "Jack's only exploring what might have caused the delay in news coverage. You have to admit we dropped a bomb on them with your analysis, Diggie. Where are they going to find someone with your skills to validate or debunk your conclusions?"

"Well," Diggie was thinking, "there are a couple of folks at the Defense Department who have the computer capability and skills to do that in-depth analysis, but I don't know of any private sector folks locally who could do that. Advanced Aerospace Technologies in Northern Virginia might have the capacity, but I don't know for sure."

"The reporters at least have to do more digging on the story, beyond what they did before the press conference," Jack chimed in. Then he added, "I keep trying to get hold of Craig, but I still haven't been able to catch him at home." And to Elaine, he asked, "Want to go over to his house now with me, and check on him again?"

"Maybe he doesn't want to talk with you, Jack! Especially after today's breaking news. Surely, he must know the photos have been released to the public?"

"Well, yes! He's one of my subscribers! He would have received both special editions."

"So that means he would have seen your retraction issue."

"If he's reading his emails! But that doesn't explain any reluctance to talk to me prior to today, if that's what's going on."

"Then, yes, let's go and visit him now. But we should probably take a taxi. If we try to walk from here, there might be some reporters hounding us all the way. Besides, I don't think we want reporters following us to his house."

"Aren't you afraid someone will 'see' us getting into a taxi together?" Jack asked, a little mischievously. "What if one of them takes a photo of us getting into a taxi together, and then publishes it as 'evidence' that we are having an affair?" and again, that challenging twinkle in his eye.

"Well, if you are afraid, or embarrassed, to be associated with me socially, Mr. Amory, then we can go in separate cabs!" Elaine countered playfully, throwing Jack off

173

of his equilibrium at the hint that she didn't mind being associated with him socially.

"Oh, no, I don't mind at all, Ms. Kent, if *you* don't!" and he stared directly into her beautiful eyes. "I don't mind, at all," he added softly, and with such warmth that Elaine could feel a wave of heat moving through her, from the tips of her toes, all the way up to her cheeks, which she was sure were in the process of turning beet red.

"Then we should be on our way, I guess," she replied softly, never wavering her glance from his for an instant.

"Oh, *really*! Will you two lovebirds either get a room, or better yet, go do something constructive, and check out what your so-called 'expert' has to say about his validation of the photos last Friday?" This was Caroline, who had just come back from covering a hearing on the Hill for her mother, and had been standing there long enough, unnoticed, to hear—and see—the fullness of the exchange between Elaine and Jack. Of course, part of her motivation for getting rid of them was self-serving—that would give her and Diggie time together without the 'adults'!

"Ok! Ok!" Elaine laughed, a little nervously, as she and Jack were startled out of the lock on each other's eyes. It's a good thing, Jack was thinking, as the connection he felt with Elaine was becoming overwhelming. He couldn't afford overwhelming, not right now. He needed to be able to focus on finding out who was trying to destroy his credibility as a journalist, and the integrity of his political blog, which he had been working so hard to develop in the seven years since its inaugural issue.

Elaine, too, was glad the spell had been broken, because she had more important things to take care of just then. It was almost a perfunctory process—subordinating her own personal interests to her professional responsibilities. She had not realized how natural, or automatic, it had become for her to do that. Maybe her consummate professional manner scared men off, or simply prevented her from realizing when anyone might show a personal interest in her. She wondered if there would ever come a time when she would feel free to let a personal—ok, *romantic*—interest subordinate her professional

174

responsibilities, at least enough to let a romance bloom. Could Jack be the opportunity for exactly that? Or would any burgeoning affection between them be buried under their mutual professional pursuits?

An interesting conundrum, she thought.

"You are right, Caroline—about doing something useful, not about getting a room! Would you stay here with Diggie," and Elaine winked at Caroline, "and keep an eye on the TV news coverage in case anything needs our attention? I would really appreciate that. Otherwise Diggie might get bored here on his own!"

Diggie just grunted in his sister's direction at the suggestion he would be bored, but Caroline responded gleefully with a "Yes, Boss!"

"C'mon," Elaine ordered as she grasped Jack's hand, and led him through Blanchard's office and into her private bathroom. "There's a secret exit we can use, so that we don't have to run the gauntlet of the reporters outside the main entrance to the office."

In mock shock, Jack asked, "What? Are you going to flush us both down the toilet?" But he held tightly onto Elaine's hand, and all he could think about was how soft and silky and cool her skin felt.

"Don't be silly! Look here!" Once they were both in the bathroom, Elaine directed their steps to the left, toward what looked like a full length cabinet door with a mirror mounted on it. Elaine slowly opened the cabinet door as it swung inward, and then poked her head through it, looking from side to side to make sure no one was about. Then she flung the door wide open, and coaxed Jack in a whisper, "Quickly! Before anyone comes and sees us!" She raced through the door, pulling Jack behind her, where he found himself in the corridor of the office building, but around the corner from the main entrance to Blanchard's office. Once Elaine shut the door, it looked like just another part of the corridor wall, except for a small square button that opened the door when pressed. But you pretty much had to know the button was there to actually see it.

"Well!" Jack gasped in surprise. "In all my years working on the Hill, I had no idea such things existed!"

"They don't, normally," Elaine explained, as they headed down the corridor, and out a side exit. "This one is an anomaly, introduced by one of the previous occupants of that particular office suite. And it only works if you have an office that sits at the intersection of two corridors."

"I wonder what the motivation was?" Jack asked, lifting a single eyebrow as he posited the question to Elaine.

"I really don't know. I only know the scuttlebutt," Elaine explained, with a sly smile. "Supposedly, it was aimed at letting people *into* the office without being seen, more than about being able to *leave* without being seen."

"That's pretty boring!"

"That depends on who the member was letting in, doesn't it?" and she laughed, as they hopped into the nearest taxi on Independence Avenue.

On the short ride, Elaine wondered out loud who had seen them at the Planetarium on Sunday, and why that news was delivered to a reporter.

"Your guess is as good as mine," Jack stated, rather flatly. He, too, couldn't understand how, or why, anyone would have been paying attention to notice either of them, or remark that they were together, and at the Smithsonian's Air and Space Museum. Who would have cared?

They exited the cab at the corner of Craig's street, so that they could backtrack if there was still a bevy of reporters outside Craig's house. But with a powerful sense of relief, they saw that the street was clear. For whatever reason, the reporters had left. I wonder if they got what they had come for, Elaine mused.

"It looks like we're clear to go forth," Jack commented, as they headed towards Craig's house. As they got closer, Jack noted that "there's no buildup of newspapers in sight, so he can't have skipped town."

"*Au contraire*," Elaine contradicted him. "He might have someone who collects his newspapers when he's away. Or, he might even have put a temporary stop on delivery," she suggested.

Jack just looked at her without saying a word, but his expression spoke volumes.

They climbed the front steps and Jack rang the doorbell, which played a few bars of "Yankee Doodle Dandy". They waited a moment, and when no one opened the door, Jack rang the bell again. While they stood there, he looked up and down the street in search of Craig's car, as evidence that he was at home. But there was no sign of Craig's antique 1964 red Chevrolet Chevelle convertible on the street. It was true that he might have had to park further away, but with parking on many of these streets restricted to residents, even in daytime, Craig should have been able to park nearby.

"Well," Jack commented, in mock disappointment, as he and Elaine descended the front steps of Craig's house, "we could take Caroline's other advice, and get a room. Or, better yet, my house, if you recall, is only a few blocks away." There was that mischievous expression on his face again, that might have included a leering glance, as Elaine turned toward him to see if he was being serious.

He wasn't, of course. Or so Elaine told herself. She was really having trouble reading him. Was he joking, or serious? So she decided to keep things light. She looked up at him in mock horror, pressing her hand to her chest in disbelief. "Are you propositioning me, Mr. Amory?"

"Who, *me*?" he mimicked her tone, placing *his* hand on *his* chest to emphasize his words. Though the thought did cross his mind that he would rather be placing his hand on *her* chest. But he had to squelch the impulse quickly, as he felt it send his blood rushing toward a nascent arousal, much to his own surprise.

"Didn't you just say an hour or so ago—and to the *world*, I might add—that even *you* need more than a few days to close a deal?!" Elaine queried.

"Well, I didn't want to brag in public," he demurred. "But I've noticed how you stare at me when you think I'm not noticing," he teased, feeling more in control of himself now.

"Well, you can just deflate that immense ego of yours, because it would take a humongous effort on your part to close the deal with me!" she retorted. The words were scarcely out of her mouth, however, before she regretted every one of them. And as for the imminent rise in Jack's balloon, her words completely deflated it—in what seemed to Jack like record time.

Chapter 36

"Boy, am I glad you called!" he exhaled, relief flooding his voice. "I didn't want to risk trying to reach you in case other people were hanging around you."

"You did right. It's been a tough twenty-four hours, but oh, so glorious! You sound upset about something. What's going on?"

"I'm still concerned. Maybe even more so now."

"About what?" and the voice on the other end of the phone sounded somewhat leery of the response.

"Look, I just don't want any more direct involvement. I want to stay off the grid now."

"That should be fine. We've accomplished everything we needed to. The photos are out there now, and no one can undo *that*! And so much for Mr. Goody Two-Shoes. We fixed him for not publishing the photos, didn't we?! I wish I could have seen his face when he discovered what 'he' had done! So what's the problem?"

"I didn't know Blanchard's Chief of Staff's *brother* was a genius computer engineer! If I had known that to begin with, I would never have gone along with this caper. There's barely half a dozen experts in this country who could have figured out what I did, and he's one of them! Who'd have thought they would have access to one of those rarified figures? I assumed they wouldn't have anyone to go to with skills even as good as mine, let alone better!"

"But how did you find out about her brother's skills? The story hasn't hit the TV news yet. I expect it will be on the evening news programs in a couple of hours. The media outlets need time to do some of their own checking."

"I was at Blanchard's press conference this afternoon."

Tense silence filled the airwaves.

"What on earth possessed you to do that?" and he could hear the controlled anger in the question.

"Don't worry! I disguised myself! I stood way in the back to one side, wore sunglasses, a heavy coat, and a hat. And I held a notebook, and recorder, so that I just blended into

179

the melee of reporters. No one could recognize me. We're safe. For now. I just don't know how long that will last."

"What do you mean? What are you worried about, then, if you're sure no one recognized you?"

"Look, they already figured out Amory's computer was hacked into. They have the IP address of the computer that did the hacking—*my computer*! They have also discovered that the hacking was done from a Hill Internet cafe. It won't be long before they will identify me! I can't stay hidden for the rest of my life! At some point, I will need to venture out into the world again—as me. As the story unfolds, I might even get stuck having to give some news outlet an evaluation of the photos. There were a couple of media folks ringing my bell this morning, but I didn't answer. I don't know how much longer I can stay hidden."

"But what are you worried about? So what if you are grouped as one of the minions who could not see through the clever construction of the perpetrator. You just said there are barely half a dozen people across the country who could see through it."

"Oh, that's easy for you to say! It's my professional life on the line, not yours! You may not realize it, but I'm a highly respected computer engineer! How can I concur with Kent's analysis when I told Amory that the photos were genuine? And if I publicly cannot report that the photos were phony after Kent has determined they were, who's going to trust me enough to hire me when they need computer stuff? But worse, what if they figure out it was me who did the hacking? We're in *trouble*! Can't you see that?"

He might be in trouble, she knew, but she wasn't. But she didn't voice that knowledge. "I know you are an extremely competent computer engineer," her voice caressed. "That's why I knew you could pull this off. Why do you think I asked you, and not someone else?"

Somewhat mollified, he acknowledged the compliment, and tried to steady himself. "I'm sorry. I guess the tension is getting to me."

"Just try to relax. The election is only six days away. Once it is over, this will all wash away, and everything will be the way it was. No one will care anymore who created the photos, or who hacked into Amory's computer to publish them. Here today, gone tomorrow. You know the pattern, especially with the news. Once the election is over, this won't even make the back page, or a subtitle running across the bottom of the TV news."

"You're right," he sounded mollified. "I know it. I'm glad you called, because I really needed to talk with you. I'll be OK now."

"Are you sure?"

"Yeah. I'm good. Talk to you later," and he clicked off his phone.

But the person on the other end of the line wasn't so sure everything would be OK. Far from it.

Chapter 37

He was crossing Independence Avenue from the Longworth House Office Building, and heading towards the Capitol for the mid-afternoon session of the House, when Kevin Lowell approached him.

"Hey, Arthur!" Lowell greeted him. "Have you been following the brouhaha over the sex photos of Kate Blanchard in bed with you, me, and Barker Phillips!? Isn't it great?! She may have an eleven point lead in her Senate race today, but by tomorrow, I'm willing to bet money that she'll be lucky to be running neck and neck with Billingsley!"

"Beware of Greeks bearing gifts, or have you forgotten, Kevin?" Arthur replied, skeptical that they would, in the end, benefit from this scandal. He'd be happy if they could just avoid any negative effects from it.

"Hey, this is a bonus dropped in our laps, Arthur! What's not to like? We all stuck to our commitment to make no comment, and you know reporters will use that non-denial as an affirmation of trysts between Blanchard and each one of us! And that photographer who took a picture of the three of us at Blanchard's fundraiser now has a gold mine. That picture will imply even more support for those scandalous photos! What's your problem? This is a win-win for us! Or should I say, win-win-win?!"

"Look, Kevin, I went along with the decision to give a no-comment response, but we all know the photos aren't genuine photographs—because we all know that none of us is having an affair with Blanchard. Once that gets proven, what are we going to look like? Probably just like what we are. Powerful lobbyists trying to aid in the departure of a dreaded member of Congress who successfully fights us at every turn. If we don't come forward and deny this before the media acknowledges the photos are phony, the reporters may come back to us, and accuse us of conspiring to undermine an election. By then, no one will ever believe we had nothing to do with the photos. And where will that leave us here on the Hill? No one is going to trust us. And that means they might be afraid to work with us."

"You're worrying about nothing, Arthur! This will all be history after the election. There will be a new Congress in January, and a new session. Besides, no one on the Hill cares about anything except the money we funnel to their re-election campaigns. Believe me, and you know I am right, that's why members work with us. It has nothing to do with trust, Arthur. And everything to do with money. Money that they need to get re-elected. So relax! We're riding the crest of the wave!" And he patted Arthur on the shoulder, then took off across the Capitol grounds towards the Russell Senate Office Building.

Chapter 38

"Well, it sounds like the you-know-what has finally hit the fan," Jack muttered under his breath, as he and Elaine returned to Blanchard's office through the hidden door. Elaine had peaked around the corner to see if there were still reporters at the entrance to Blanchard's office, and not only were they still there, but they numbered at least three times as many as when she and Jack had left to go to Craig's. As they entered Blanchard's private bathroom, they could hear some heated exchanges coming from her office. Blanchard had returned from the House chamber, and was engaged in a video conference with her campaign headquarters. Caroline and Diggie were ensconced on one of the soft leather sofas in Kate's inner office.

"Krystal," Blanchard was imploring, "*please* do not respond directly again, in any way, to press inquiries, or any other inquiries about the photos. Please refer them all to Elaine here in Washington. And make sure Tony Esperanza doesn't make any remarks to his press contacts, either. We all agreed that the best strategy was to keep the focus on the issue here in Washington, to try to minimize any connection with the campaign!"

"I know what we agreed to do," Krystal replied, a little heatedly, "but it just isn't a realistic approach! I've gotten nearly two dozen calls from reporters, and who knows who else, and they don't like my telling them to call your Washington office. A few local reporters sarcastically commented about the local press 'not being good enough' to acknowledge! And that's one of the polite responses! Another reporter asked what you were trying to hide!" Krystal observed. "Telling them to call your Washington office was, to them, a non-answer, and that just stirred the pot and made it boil over, rather than cooling it down!"

Kate took a deep breath to calm her voice. She didn't want to antagonize her campaign manager less than a week before election day. Especially in view of a brewing crisis in the campaign. But Kate was getting frustrated with Krystal, who did not seem to understand the damage she had wrought because she had not kept to the play book. Flashing across the TV screen in Blanchard's office were multiple reports about Blanchard's campaign manager impugning the character of the three lobbyists by accusing them of creating the photos to hurt Blanchard's election chances.

"Do you not understand that your comment about the lobbyists has inflamed the story?" Kate asked, in as steady a voice as she could muster. "I think we had the story under control for what it is—a great big lie. The media here had been quiet, until you suddenly gave them a huge gift! Do you not see that?" How could anyone have such a political tin ear? Kate wondered.

"But who else could have done this?" and now it was Krystal who was getting frustrated. "I just asked that simple question to a reporter for the local paper, *The Star*, on what I thought was an off the record discussion, and instead he ran with it, and blew it all out of proportion! I know Billingsley has tried some unethical stuff during the campaign, but really, I don't think he would approve of this kind of attack. And I don't think he or anyone on his staff is clever enough to have thought of it, let alone actually produced something that is obviously so sophisticated!"

"You shouldn't have been making *any* comments to any reporters, Krystal! It was precisely to prevent what's happening now, because of your remark, that we all agreed to keep the center of communications on this issue here, in D.C. So that we didn't give the press anything that would sensationalize the story even more. We don't know that any of the lobbyists are behind this," Blanchard observed, in as even a voice as possible. "They could use your comment to accuse my campaign of slander. And if they are not behind this attack on me, they could very well take their concerns to court. And that would be just as bad for my campaign, *and* my political reputation, as those photos being true!"

"But I often have off the record chats with reporters about the campaign. It's never been a problem before, so I had no reason to think I couldn't trust *The Star* on this."

There was anger in Krystal's response, and it made Elaine wonder if Krystal had spoken to the reporter deliberately. Perhaps she resented being excluded from the center of the action, Elaine thought. Keeping the information flow restricted to Blanchard's Washington office, however, was the approach which they all agreed had the best chance of keeping the lid on the sensationalism of the released photos.

But Krystal's naivete, if that's what it was, had unleashed a media storm, whose winds were now ripping through the Capitol, *and* Blanchard's home state.

Chapter 39

Elaine and Jack quietly slid into the cushioned leather chairs, and joined Caroline and Diggie in listening to the video conference. Kate acknowledged them with a nod, and returned to her conversation with her campaign manager.

"Look, Krystal. The damage has been done. We will figure out how to address this new crisis here. Please, you should focus on the campaign, and—no matter how unrealistic you may think it is—do not answer, *or comment,* on or off the record, to the media about this issue. Is that clear?

"Also," Blanchard noted, "it looks like we will still be in session, at least through Friday, so you will need to cancel any personal appearances you have scheduled for me, at least through Friday. I apologize for upsetting your scheduling. Please extend my sincerest apologies to the folks or organizations involved in any of the schedule changes, and explain to them how important it is for me to be here at the end of the session."

There was a slight pause before Krystal replied, "Yes, ma'am." And then the connection went blank.

"Well," observed Diggie, "looks like she didn't like what you said, Mrs. Blanchard, because she cut off the video conference, not me."

"I'm sure she's feeling a little peeved, at the moment. And maybe we should have let her be involved in dealing with the media. We could have probably developed some kind of response for her to use, like 'the photos are not genuine, and you can contact the Washington office for more information'. Maybe it's my fault, then. As upset and frustrated as I am, I can't pin all of the blame on Krystal," Blanchard finished.

And then Elaine had a thought. "Caroline, have you seen or heard from that Spencer guy who we think might have planted the bugs?"

Caroline had been floating between pure joy at getting to spend so much time with Diggie, and abject misery over the political storm exploding over her mother's election bid. Maybe she could help in some way. "Well, he's been avoiding me. I thought it might be because I bruised his ego when I sent him off alone Saturday evening. But today, since the pictures were released, I feel like he's actually shunning me, like he doesn't want to have anything to do with me, or be seen with me. It doesn't bother me, but I thought I could try to unobtrusively discover if he knew anything about bugs, etc. But I haven't been able to talk with him."

"Now that's interesting," Elaine took note. "I wonder if he could avoid a direct request from your Mom to meet with her here?"

Caroline perked up. "He's an intern, and no intern can afford to offend any member of Congress! Not if he, or she," and she pointed to herself, "ever wants a permanent staff job on the Hill!"

"What are you thinking, Elaine?" Kate Blanchard asked.

"He's young. Just starting out professionally. He's obviously interested in a political career, or at least a professional career here on the Hill, at least for the immediate future."

"Oh," Caroline cut in, "he really does want to work here! Maybe Mom can frighten him into telling the truth!"

And here Jack interjected, "But if he is the one who planted the bugs, why would he own up to it, *especially* to Representative Blanchard? Especially right now! I would think that admitting he planted bugs in the office and home of a member of Congress would doom any chance of a career on the Hill!"

"You're right, Jack. But maybe Kate could agree to keep silent about the bugs if he just 'fesses up. I mean, she could tell him that we've narrowed the options down to just him. Make it clear to him that no one else had access to both locations, and that logically it could only be him. She could explain that she really would like to know who put him up to it, and why, and then agree not to tell anyone about the bugs, if he just answers her questions. And if I sit in on the meeting, I could hint that otherwise his professional reputation might find it has an unresolved issue of trust, which would doom his chances of getting hired by anyone here."

"Wow, you are a fox, Ms. Kent," and Jack leaned away from her as if to distance himself from her planned chicanery. "Remind me never to get on your bad side!"

"I don't have a bad side, Mr. Amory!" Elaine was quick to note. "Besides, it isn't trickery at all. Look, our worst nightmare has just come true. Not only are the photos out there, but we've failed...I know, I know," Elaine put her hand up to Jack's face, to quell the obvious comment that it was their own campaign manager's fault. "We've failed," she repeated, "to prevent the incident from producing a firestorm.

"So," Elaine continued, "if we can figure out who is behind the bugs, we might come closer to a solution to our problem. In order to prevent this firestorm from destroying Kate's election bid, we have to find out who's behind the bugs, and then maybe we'll find out who is behind the photo scandal!" she explained.

"And so I say again," Elaine continued, "I think Kate should invite Spencer to meet with her here, in her office—because a little intimidation might help—and ask him about the bugs. All she needs to do is assure him that we will, in time, find out who is behind the bugs, and that if we later discover that he did have any involvement which he failed to admit, any dreams he has of working on the Hill will be dead!" she finished with a flourish. But then she noted, "I don't think that's unethical. If he's straight with us, he'll be ok. But if we find out he lied to us, and on such an important matter, then he doesn't deserve to work here. Who knows, if he's fundamentally honest, he may learn a really good life lesson!"

"Are you saying that it's OK for staff to bug the office, and home, of a member of Congress? And if they only admit it when challenged, they can still have a career on the Hill?" Jack teased, with that single raised eyebrow.

"Don't raise your eyebrow to me, Mr. Amory! You don't frighten me!" she laughed back at him.

It was Representative Blanchard's turn to interject. "You are right, Elaine, that the only way we can survive this storm is to find out who is actually responsible for the photos, and the bugs. Logic would tell us that the two are related, but, you know, they may not be. I'm just not sure what is the best of way of discovering who's responsible. Let me think a while about inviting Spencer to meet with me." Having worked for Kate Blanchard for eight years, Elaine could recognize the signs that she was getting tired, and needed a break. But before she could get that respite, Jack gave her more to think about.

"May I make a suggestion, Representative Blanchard?" Jack asked.

"Of course," Kate accommodated him.

"Whether we discover the perpetrators or not, I suggest you plan maybe a three-minute political ad, that would air on TV on Sunday evening. In the ad, you should level with the voters in your state about what's been happening. If we know who did it, you can announce that then, if not before. But if we don't find out who is doing all of this, you should, nevertheless, give a frank statement to the voters, and why you hope they will look beyond this trick and vote for you."

Blanchard was quiet for a moment, and then noted, "I can see value in your suggestion. But if we find the truth, that will be news carried to the public by the media. And if we don't, that's the story that will probably dominate the media right into the election, no matter what kind of evidence we provide to prove the photos aren't genuine. Why should I make a statement in either case?"

"Because the voters need to hear from you directly, personally. And in a context that doesn't include shouting reporters, or reporters who interrupt your responses with insinuating comments or questions. If we don't find out who is doing this, the voters need to hear your story from you. The media isn't going to carry *your* story—they're going to play the storyline in the way that most helps them get viewers, or readers. That means keeping the sensational aspect alive, not resolving it. If we do learn who did this, the voters still need to hear directly from you what has happened. A press conference is not the ideal venue for you to connect with your voters, especially if that press conference is held here, in the District. You need to talk to your voters yourself."

After a moment, Blanchard replied, "Your suggestion and arguments are compelling, Mr. Amory. My inclination is to believe it is a very good idea, and, sitting here thinking about it, it is a suggestion that I will probably implement. But let's leave everything where it is just now. Nothing can be done tonight to quash the firestorm Krystal ignited, so everyone should go home and get a good night's sleep. Tomorrow we can review afresh, and plan our steps forward. I'd like my staff to be here at eight in the morning, and I would appreciate it very much if you would join us, Mr. Amory. I'll ask my office press agent to have ready for us an overview of what the news coverage has been. We can assess the situation then, and figure out the best way to move forward."

Chapter 40

"Can I interest you in one more check on whether Craig is home or not?" Jack asked Elaine. They were putting their coats on as they walked through Blanchard's private bathroom toward the hidden exit, as they headed home at the end of a difficult day. He hurriedly continued, "After all, we all live so close to each other, it's only a few blocks out of the way." He was getting so used to spending lots of time with her, that he was reluctant to just go home alone, and clunk around with pots and pans for the rest of the evening, to make it sound like his home was full. Funny, he thought, he never minded being home alone before. And his tiny house had never felt empty before. He actually liked that he was free to do and go, whatever and wherever, just as he pleased, without having to explain, or answer, to anyone. I guess it's just that these last few days have been so crazy, he thought. And it wasn't over yet. Not only was the situation unresolved, it was a veritable mess at the moment. Thanks to Blanchard's campaign manager.

"Sure," Elaine replied. "It can't hurt to try again. It really would be good to get to talk with him directly. I suspect, though, now that the story has really exploded, he may not want to speak to you."

"Yeah, maybe you're right. Maybe that's why I haven't been able to reach him. But I have to try. Not that it really will make much difference. Your brother did say that most analysts will miss the construction of the photos, and that's probably just what happened with Craig. But, you know, what still keeps nagging in the back of my mind, is what was he doing visiting with Kevin Lowell late on a Saturday night —*the* Saturday night after I received the photos."

"Well, you are right there. It could be a little fishy. But it could also just be that Lowell is a client. You did say that he freelances, didn't you?"

"Yeah. But on a *Saturday* night?" Jack's eyebrows were not raised, but they were knit—and closely.

"I know. It doesn't make sense. To us, at least. But maybe there is a simple explanation," Elaine smiled in an

192

attempt to spread some optimism. Jack was obviously upset at the prospect that his friend might have deliberately misled him.

"You may be right. I sure would feel a lot better if that were the case. I don't like thinking he's lied to me, especially when that lie could cost me my livelihood," and Jack rubbed his chin as he spoke.

They had reached A Street, NE and were heading east. It wasn't long before they reached the corner of Craig's street, at which point Jack put up his hand to stop Elaine.

"Let's look, first, and make sure there aren't any reporters there."

"They were gone this afternoon. Why would they come back now?" Elaine asked.

"Just because no one was there earlier, doesn't mean there won't be any reporters there now," Jack cautioned.

"True. Sorry. I guess I was just trying to wish all of this away," Elaine sighed, and shrugged her shoulders. She was caught unaware as Jack turned to her unexpectedly, and placed his hands gently on her shoulders, nudging her to move closer to him as he slowly wrapped his arms around her.

"But then, Ms. Kent, we would never have met," he whispered in her ear. Standing there in his arms, she could feel the overpowering sense of his masculinity. Some men, she believed, had a powerful essence of maleness—she didn't know what else to call it. Most men hovered around 40 to 80 percent of male essence, but Jack's sense of maleness was more like 150 percent. The electricity he projected was just so *male*! It wasn't charisma, it was something different. Charisma may ooze from charming manners, but the maleness of a man poured out of him naturally, unrestrained, from every cell, like powerful energy waves traveling through the air in every direction, without any letup.

With great effort, Elaine slowly, but deliberately, turned her face to look up at him. When her eyes locked onto his, she realized how very much she liked being wrapped in his arms, and she wished he would hold her in a slow, deliberate, embrace. She didn't care that he might read her desire. Actually, she hoped he would. It wasn't easy for her to openly express such wants. She hadn't allowed herself to feel anything like that for a very, very long time. Maybe that's changing, she thought. And if she wanted something to happen with this man, then she had to take some of the risk as well. She couldn't just expect someone else to make all of the overtures, and take all of the risk, especially without any encouragement. If she were going to have a relationship with any man, she was going to have to assume her share of the responsibility, and her share of the emotional exposure.

And so she stood there, looking into Jack's eyes with the warmest, and most inviting, expression she could reach out to him with, on this cold and blustery night. Without saying a word. She didn't have to.

Jack felt the appeal of her glance fan out through his whole body, like a blustery desert wind storm that poured wave upon wave of heat into his heart, which just pumped it out through every vein, to the tips of his fingers and the ends of his toes. And with that intense heat pulsating through him, he felt an overwhelming sense of joy and excitement. He was mesmerized by the unveiling of her desire, the unlocking of her heart. By her willingness to risk emotional exposure—for him. The realization left him feeling helpless and giddy, powerless to resist her invitation, unable to do anything but surrender.

His hands slowly moved across the back of her shoulders and down her spine, as he gently pulled Elaine closer, and lowered his face until their lips locked in a molten embrace. There was no hurry as he slowly teased her lips open until he could taste the sweetness of her soul. He could feel himself becoming aroused. And he knew that he wanted this woman. Like he had never wanted any other woman he'd ever known. Just being in the same room with her had turned him on like a motion sensor lamp that lights up when someone enters its sphere. And in a very short time, she had invaded his senses until, at this moment, he felt like he wouldn't be able to breathe if she walked away from him.

He lifted his lips from hers reluctantly, pulling lightly on her lower lip as they parted. "You know, I live just a few blocks from here. Maybe we should forget about Craig and go to my place, where we would be alone—just the two of us, and no one else in the world—not even any ghosts."

Elaine stared into his richly blue eyes as she felt joy flowing out of every cell in her body. She wanted to go with him. She wanted to be alone—really alone—with him. But something nagged at the back of her mind, and it made her pause. What if this wasn't real? What if they had met under no unusual circumstances? If all of the adrenaline flowing events of the past few days had never occurred, and they had met under normal social circumstances, would this connection still have developed? Maybe they were just turning to each other to help calm the stormy seas they had been sailing since the end of last week.

She didn't try to hide the joy he had brought her, but she didn't think she was ready for more—yet. She placed her hands on his chest, as he held her, and quietly asked, "What if we are just reacting to the pressures of the moment, Jack? What if this is just adrenaline? Maybe we shouldn't move too quickly. Maybe, when all of this is resolved, we'll discover we really can't stand one another," and though she laughed gently, there was nothing hostile in her expression.

Jack didn't believe that what they were feeling at this moment had anything to do with the heightened excitement of the last few days. Yes, this photo fiasco is what had brought them together. Yes, it had placed them in more intimate exposure to each other more quickly than would likely have been the case had they met under other circumstances. But that intimacy had made it possible for him to learn so much more about Elaine, in just a few days, than he would ever have learned about her, or anyone else, under more typical, uneventful, situations. Given the way she made him feel, though, made him sure that when everything quiets down, as it would in time, he was going to feel every bit as enamored with Elaine as he did that very moment. But he understood her concern, and her hesitation, so he didn't want to push her.

"Ok, I can wait," he replied softly, "because I know that I can wait for you forever, Ms. Kent."

Chapter 41

Elaine had never felt so humbled in her entire life. If for no other reason, she would be eternally grateful to Jack for the precious gift he had just given her. But she knew there was so much more to make her appreciate any regard he had for her.

"Look," she said, still enclosed in his arms, "let's go check on Craig, and then maybe we can hop over to Union Station for some supper. I don't know about you, but I am definitely starving!"

"Boy, you sure know how to deflate a guy!" Jack laughed, teasing, but not at all offended. "Ok, let's make another try for Craig, and then I will spirit you off in my car to Union Station, where we can stuff our faces to fill our cravings, *all* of our cravings, since no other options appear available at the moment," and he looked meaningfully at Elaine, who just smiled back at him.

They stood for a moment on the corner of Craig's street, to check whether anyone was hanging around outside his front door. The street was quiet, so they both strolled down to Craig's house and rang his doorbell, for the second time that day. The house was dark and still, with no signs of movement, or life, coming from the building. And no sign of his car anywhere nearby.

"Well," Jack observed, "wherever he is, I hope he's having fun. Come on," he said, grabbing Elaine's hand, "let's go get my car, and drive down to the Station."

She tugged at him, laughing, with a, "But we can walk there from here! Have you suddenly gone lazy?"

"I know we can walk—*now*, but it is already dark, and I'd rather drive home later, than walk back that late at night with a tummy full of food."

"Do I detect...?"

"No!" Jack shouted back before she could finish her question. "I just believe in being sensible. And it makes sense to me that we should drive there so when we are ready to come home, we can drive home."

"But where are you going to park over there?"

"In the parking garage, where else?" he queried, as if stating the obvious.

"Ok! Ok! I concede. We take your car," and Elaine squeezed his hand to show her agreement.

"That's what I like about you, Ms. Kent. You are so sensible!"

As Elaine contorted her face in a grimace, she noted, "Hhmmmm. That isn't exactly the most flattering of compliments, but it works for me—for now, at least. But you'll have to do better in the future, Mr. Amory," and she looked up at him with a challenge.

"I promise," he whispered in her ear, squeezing her hand back as they arrived at his car, jubilant at the thought she referenced a 'future' that he would be part of.

It took them about twenty minutes to go the few blocks to Union Station in the evening traffic. They were riding around the garage, looking for a parking place, when Jack suddenly became alert and stopped the car where there was no space in sight.

"Ummm, do I dare ask why we are stopping here?" Elaine queried.

"You certainly may dare. Look. Over there. See it?" he answered.

"Ummmm, see what, exactly?"

"Over there. That antique 1964 red Chevrolet Chevelle convertible. That's Craig's car!" he finished.

Chapter 42

"Are you sure it's his?" Elaine asked.

"Yes, absolutely sure! His car is an antique, and he keeps it in pristine condition. And see that D.C. license plate that says 'MYCHEVY'? There's not likely to be two cars like that registered in the District, and only one can have that license plate," Jack observed.

"Well, I'll be. So maybe he's gone somewhere by train. That must be why you haven't been able to get hold of him," Elaine suggested hopefully.

"Or maybe it means he's home, but hiding. You can't miss his car on the street, if you know that it's his car."

Checking out the fire red of the Chevelle, Elaine noted, "You're right. If you know which car is his, you couldn't miss it. And seeing it on the street would make you think he was home. Hmmm... He still could just be out of town. Isn't this the long term parking area for the station?"

"Yeah. But maybe we should check his house again on the way back. You never know."

"I'm good with that," she remarked. "But before we head home, could we possibly get something to eat?" she added, as she looked up at him with exaggeratedly pleading eyes.

Jack glanced quickly at Elaine, sitting beside him in his car, and he wondered if he could ever deny Elaine anything she requested. But he kept those thoughts to himself as he replied aloud, and hopefully with equivalent levity, "Well, I do recall suggesting we come here for some supper," and he smiled enigmatically at her as he shut off the engine in a parking spot not far from where Craig's car sat. "So, I guess I should follow through on that suggestion?"

"Yes," Elaine returned, with a laugh, "you should definitely follow through, or I am going to faint from hunger! I don't recall either one of us actually getting to have any lunch! And my stomach is grumbling like a thunderstorm just at the thought of food!"

"Does that mean if I feed you, I will have rescued a damsel in distress?" Jack looked expectantly at Elaine, as they walked toward the entrance to the train station.

Elaine hesitated, then answered slowly, as if she were trying to discover a hidden agenda in his question, "If I say 'yes', does that mean you will be looking for some kind of reward for your gallantry?"

Jack stopped, turned to look down at Elaine's upturned face as she halted along side him, and then enigmatically observed in quiet, even tones, "Just knowing that I could satisfy any one of your desires, Ms. Kent, is all the reward I need." Then he reached for her hand, placed it in the crook of his arm, and added, "Shall we head for the food court on the lower level? Or would you rather we have a sit-down at a real restaurant?"

* * * * *

Having satiated their hunger from the many options at the food court, they slowly meandered back to Jack's car. As they both observed that Craig's car was still there in the garage, Jack suggested they stop by Craig's house again anyway, "just in case."

"Even if he were there, and awake, do you think he would answer the door at this hour?" Elaine asked. "It's *nearly* eleven o'clock, you know."

"Nearly eleven?!" Jack was startled. "Did we just spend over three hours eating?"

"Well, not exactly, you know. We did walk around, and check out every vendor in the food court—*twice!*" Elaine pointed out. "Sampling, as available, too, remember," she added. "And then you *would* choose the longest line to wait in for a main meal!" she chuckled. "Not to mention the fifteen minutes or so we waited for dessert!"

"Is that a complaint, Ms. Kent?" Jack asked wryly, twisting his head to look at her in the dim lighting of the garage. Then he unexpectedly leaned towards her to add softly, "And what if I just wanted to spend as much time with you as possible?"

Her breath caught in her throat when he leaned toward her. While her voice may have sounded a little hoarse, her words were a caress, as she looked straight into his eyes, and replied invitingly, "Mr. Amory, please feel free to spend as much time with me as you would like—*after* we get this problem resolved!" she finished, before Jack could raise even a single expectation.

"There you go again, building me up just to tear me down! Heartless woman!" But the laughter in Jack's voice, and the broad smile on his face, belied the sting those words might otherwise have carried. "So, is that a promise, then, Ms. Kent?" he asked, as they continued their stroll back to his car.

"I guess we'll have to see, won't we? Who knows, by the time this election nightmare ends, you and I may have scratched each other's eyes out!" and this time it was Elaine who was laughing.

They climbed into Jack's car and rode the few blocks to Capitol Hill. Jack slowed down as they turned onto Craig's street, in case there were any news outlets around, but the street was dark and quiet. All seemed quite still as they reached Craig's house. There was nowhere to pull over, so Jack put his car in park right in front of Craig's, turned on his blinking lights, and jumped out of his car. He ran up the front steps to Craig's door and rang the bell. Nothing. He rang it again. And again, nothing.

Back in his car, Jack turned to Elaine to ask, but with only a smidgeon of hope, "I don't suppose you'd like to stop at my place for a good night...whatever?"

"Well," and Elaine tried to let him down as sweetly as she could, "I think we've both had a really long day, and it *is* late, and remember that Kate would like us all at her office by eight in the morning. So, what do you think?"

"Your house, it is!" he replied smartly. But they both sat contentedly during the few short blocks to Elaine's house.

As they pulled up in front of Elaine's, Jack observed that there were lights on. He saw a figure briefly pull a curtain aside in a first floor window, and then the curtain closed as the figure withdrew.

"Hhmmm," Jack remarked. "Looks like Diggie has been waiting up for you."

"Ummm, I suspect it's more a case of he's just gotten home from Caroline's!" Elaine chuckled.

As Elaine started to exit Jack's car, she turned back to him with a solemn tone, "Thank you, Jack. Not just for a fun supper. But for being so very...honorable...about all of this. If you are not careful, I might actually change my mind about *some* of the media types!"

"Well, don't get too gooey eyed, Elaine," Jack cautioned, to hide his embarrassment, as he indulged in some self-effacing humility. "Remember, it's *my* credibility and *my* reputation at stake, too. So don't go giving me too much credit! What I'm doing is as much for my benefit as for Representative Blanchard's." And as soon as the words escaped him, he wanted to kick himself in the butt, because that's just what he had done, only verbally. But Elaine was out of the car now, and climbing her front steps. He decided the better part of valor would be to just drive on back to his own abode.

Diggie was inside the door, arms akimbo, waiting to greet Elaine with "Ssoooooo." Pause. "Do you realize what time it is, Missy? And this a school night?" But Diggie was grinning from ear to ear.

"Oh, come on, Diggie! We just went to get something to eat! Neither one of us had eaten since breakfast!"

And with eyes wide with innocence, Diggie added, "Oh, I just asked a simple question!"

"Yeah, right!" as Elaine walked passed him towards the stairs.

"I hope my presence didn't scare him off!" Diggie's voice followed her ascent.

From halfway up the flight, Elaine turned to reply, "Look, you need your beauty sleep, so why don't you get on up to bed, and I will do the same. Kate wants us in at eight." And with that expression of authority, Elaine ran up the rest of the stairs to her own room, and quickly shut the door.

Diggie's teasing was right on the mark, and it was very unsettling. Now that Jack wasn't physically present, the conflicts between her feelings and her thoughts could rage unrestrained. As Elaine leaned her back against the door she had just closed, waves of varying emotions were pulsating through her body. Her heart was sending signals of joy and excitement, while her head was countering with caution and fear. Somewhere, in the dark recesses of her mind, she wondered which would prevail.

Chapter 43

As Elaine rolled around in bed in the early hours of the morning, her emotions were still battling it out inside her. She was certain that worry about the impact of the photo scandal on Kate Blanchard's Senate race was elevating her blood pressure off the charts, casting a dark shadow over her mood. But nascent romantic feelings for Jack lifted her spirits high in the air, making her want to run to a mountaintop and shout for joy like Julie Andrews does in "*The Sound of Music*". Instead of lying there, ruminating about these conflicting tugs on her emotions, she finally rolled out of bed. It was, after all, a little after six, so she should have been up and about already.

As she was putting a pot of water on the stove for tea, the phone rang.

"Hello?" she inquired, in a thick voice still groggy with sleep.

"Good morning, yourself," she recognized Jack's voice.

"Oh, it's you," she observed, noncommittally.

"Well, that's a fine good morning! I don't think I've ever known anyone who could rob me of my self esteem the way you do, Ms. Kent!" he replied, but in a tone that held a smile.

"Oh, I'm sorry. Really I am! I'm just not fully awake yet."

"Are you still in bed? Because that would be a stimulating image," Jack opined, his voice ripe with seduction.

"No! No!" Elaine quickly retorted, then added, "but I did just get up."

"Hhmmm...do you have any clothes on? I mean, do you wear pajamas, or perhaps a neglige´or do you sleep *au naturel,* in which case are you wondering around your house naked?" he asked expectantly, as all kinds of images were flashing through Jack's mind.

"That, Sir, is none of your business!" Elaine laughed back. "Just what are you calling about, anyway? Aren't we all supposed to be in Kate's office by eight?"

"Well, I think I told you once before, that when I say 'good night' to a lady, I like to say 'good morning' as well," Jack crooned.

With a chuckle full of delight, Elaine responded softly, "Good morning, Mr. Amory."

And then suddenly Elaine heard Diggie's booming voice from the other end of the kitchen bemoaning, "Oh, come on, Sis! Caroline was right! Why don't the two of you just get a room somewhere!"

"Diggie!" Elaine remonstrated.

But on the other end of the phone, Jack was remarking that he "liked the way Diggie's mind worked."

"Oh, honestly! The two of you must be in league together! Enough!" And to Jack, she instructed, "I'll see you at Kate's office at eight," then quickly ended the call.

Twenty minutes later, Elaine's door bell rang. In the kitchen munching on an English muffin, Diggie heard a gasp of "Oh my God!" that sounded a lot like Elaine's voice.

"Really, Jack!" was all Elaine could add as she exhaled her earlier intake of air.

"Well, I thought you might have something more interesting for breakfast than my usual plain cereal," Jack remarked hopefully.

As she stepped back to let him in, Elaine only chuckled and invited, "C'mon—this way."

Following Elaine to the kitchen, Jack noted, "Besides, I know you walk to work, so why shouldn't we all walk together? We'd probably run into each other anyway, so why not just start out together?" and his eyes were wide with feigned innocence.

"I guess you're right," Elaine conceded. "Can't be anything wrong with that, especially since we are all on the same mission."

"And since we've all become such good friends," Jack beamed collegially at the two of them, as he spied Diggie upon entering the kitchen. "Sharing the miseries can lighten the load for all of us. Right?"

"Here," Diggie offered Jack an English muffin that just popped out of the toaster. "I'm not sure this is tastier than your cereal, but it's what's on the menu this morning—and I'm afraid it's the only thing on the menu today. But we do have some delicious pecan apple butter from a farmers' market over the border in Virginia, if that runs to your tastes."

"It most definitely does!" Jack's voice leaped a notch or two.

"OK," Elaine took the lead as she poured orange juice all around, while they munched away seated at her kitchen's center island, "does anyone have any idea where we are on this horror show?"

"Look," Jack replied first, as he hastened to swallow a bit of muffin, "let's pool our thoughts after we get an overall picture of what kind of news coverage, if any, the photos have received. What's front page news here in D.C. may not be front page news in Blanchard's district."

"You're right, of course, we need the full picture," Elaine agreed. "We need to know how this is playing in the media back home, not just here, before we can figure out how to go forward."

"Sounds like we should get over to Mrs. Blanchard's office," Diggie observed.

"And, yes, you are right, too, Diggie. Ok, last one out the door buys the rest of us lunch," Elaine hollered as she ran out the front door.

Jack and Diggie just rolled their eyes at each other as both started towards the front door. Then Diggie stopped, as if he remembered something, and turning, said, "You two go on ahead. I need to check something before I leave. I'll catch up with you."

"What could you possibly have to check on, Diggie?" Elaine called out from her front steps.

"Well, I won't know unless I check to see if there's something there!" he exclaimed enigmatically.

"You aren't just playing fairy godmother, are you?" Elaine asked suspiciously.

"Don't you mean fairy god*father,* Ellie?" Diggie teased in reply.

"Oh, just go do what you need to do. We'll see you when we see you. But don't you dare be late!" Elaine called back, as she hastened down to the sidewalk where Jack joined her.

"What was that about a fairy godmother...or is it godfather?" Jack asked.

"Oh, I don't know!" Elaine exclaimed, in a voice that was a little high pitched. "I think Diggie sometimes likes to play big brother, even though I'm eight years older than he is."

"That speaks of a deep affection for you, I think," Jack suggested in a quiet voice. Then, to lighten the mood, he added, "Besides, that means he's the last one out the door, so he pays for lunch!"

"You're right again! Goodness, that's twice in one day, and it's only morning! You're on a roll, Mr. Amory! Hey!" Elaine added, as she grabbed hold of Jack's hand, and started to pull him into a trot, "let's run, so we can be sure to get there before him, and claim that he was late. He hates being late for meetings!"

She had grabbed his hand and was holding onto it. There was no way Jack was going to object to her suggestion. He liked holding her hand too much. Anyone else out and about that morning, who saw them, could only laugh as they watched two apparent adults running hand-in-hand toward the Cannon House Office Building, laughing like children who had just sprung a surprise on someone, and were running away to escape being chastised.

Chapter 44

They were gathered around the infamous coffee table in Kate Blanchard's congressional office. Elaine and Jack were there, along with Caroline and Blanchard's Washington press coordinator. Centered on the table was a speaker phone designed to accommodate conference calls involving lots of people, rather than individual phone calls. Kate had just opened the line to her campaign headquarters for a discussion of any fallout from the release of the photos, and how they might best address it. Just minutes after the conversation began, Diggie trotted into the office, a little out of breath.

"Well, folks, it looks like Gregory has deigned to join us after all," Blanchard teased, as she let her campaign staff on the other end of the call know he had arrived.

"I'm sorry I'm late. Please, go on," Diggie apologized, as he sat down on the sofa next to his sister.

Elaine leaned close to Diggie to ask him in a whisper, "Everything ok?"

"I'll tell you all later. After this call," he whispered back enigmatically. With the conference call in progress, Elaine had to be content with that for the moment, though she found his nonresponse puzzling—and, hence, a bit concerning.

From the other end of the conference call, the campaign manager was relaying a cautiously upbeat assessment of the coverage of the photos in the local media. "We've received about a half dozen calls from both print and TV media, which we forwarded to your Washington office as you directed," Krystal was explaining. "The story is being presented with a lot of caveats by the more responsible outlets, but, of course, outlets that are supporting Billingsley have provided more robust coverage, almost gleeful in tone."

"Well, just what are the outlets *saying* about the photos?" Kate was a little frustrated at Krystal's muddled assessment.

"Two of the three print outlets, and some of the TV news coverage," interjected the campaign's press agent, "seem to be hedging their bets. They are saying that there are some compromising photos circulating about you, but they did not reproduce the photos, and they did acknowledge that there was credible—and I emphasize that notion of 'credible'—indications that the referenced photos are not genuine. So their story line is more about the validity of the photos rather than the scandal they indicate." And the sighs of relief in Kate's office were audible. "But," Tony Esperanza added, "the third print outlet, which endorsed Billingsley remember, along with a couple of the local TV news options which slant their coverage in favor of Billingsley, reported more details about the photos and what they imply, but again, did not reproduce them."

And here Jack jumped in with, "It would seem that the news outlets, all of them, checked out Gregory's credentials, and perhaps were intimidated enough by them to hedge their bets rather than come out, full speed ahead, on the side of there being a real scandal here. They're not ignoring the story, but they don't want to knowingly stick their heads in a guillotine—especially if the blade is already in motion, which is what Gregory's findings imply."

"Yeah," Tony agreed, "that's a reasonable assessment. Which is good news for us—so far."

"I feel like I'm holding my breath, waiting for the other shoe to drop," Kate shared, in a somber voice. Then her D.C. office press coordinator let the campaign staff know that the coverage in D.C., so far, was also muted. "I think the press conference, along with Gregory's analysis, is making everyone be a little more careful, or cautious, than they normally would be. Reporting his findings may just have nipped the scandal part of the story in the bud. Or at least, it's keeping them from rushing to judgment like they usually do."

"I've got a polling survey ready to go, Representative Blanchard. Just tell me when," her campaign pollster reported.

"Thank you, Troy. I really appreciate that," Kate replied. "I think we should wait at least another day, or maybe two, so that the story can either explode, or play itself out. We still don't know how well the scandal storyline will take flight. Waiting a bit longer would give us a better readout of voters' reactions, and whether or not the photos are affecting support for my candidacy," Kate finished, without relish, but trying to prevent any sense of defeatism from surfacing in her voice.

"Will do, Ma'am," Troy acknowledged the directive. "I'll check with you again tomorrow."

"Thank you, Troy," and here Kate tried, unsuccessfully, to put a smile in her voice.

It was Elaine's turn to chime in. She was anxious to hear what made Diggie late so she noted, "Unless anyone has anything else to add, I guess we're on hold for a bit."

"Nothing more from this end," Krystal reported.

"Anything else from this end?" Elaine asked the group in Kate's office. All heads were shaking left to right for a 'no', including Kate's.

"Ok, Folks, that's it for now. Let us know immediately if this status changes, and we will do likewise." After the "OK" from Krystal, Elaine closed the call with, "Signing off from this end. Bye now."

Then without skipping a beat, or taking a breath, Elaine whirled to face Diggie and demanded, "Now! What's going on?"

Before the others had time to process Elaine's sudden change of tone, Diggie lowered his head a moment to stare at his folded hands. Then raising his head, and in a very quiet voice, he explained, "I asked my friend who teaches Forensics at the University to do some additional checking for me, since he has connections, and access, to several law enforcement organizations," and here Diggie paused.

"Don't stop now!" Elaine demanded again.

"I asked him if he could do a background check," and the pained expression on his face indicated he was dreading a possible hostile reaction from Caroline, but he continued, "on Spencer Ainsworth," and Diggie paused again.

This time it was Caroline demanding, "Well, go on, Diggie! What did you learn?"

Encouraged by Caroline's non-hostile interest, Diggie blurted out all that he had learned. "Well, he's from—guess where?—Omaha, Nebraska! He grew up there. Remember, the bugs were bought in Omaha. And it turns out, his mother's maiden name is—are you ready for this?—Billingsley!"

The astonishment in the room was pervasive. "Oh my goodness!" Elaine exclaimed. "So he did it!" Caroline chimed in. "I never," was all Kate could muster.

It was Jack who maintained a reasoned response. "So, he's related to Billingsley. How close?" he asked Diggie.

"His mother is a first cousin to candidate Billingsley. Their fathers are brothers."

"So," Jack analyzed, "that means it's highly likely that Spencer planted the bugs. And that he did it to gather intelligence for Billingsley." Then he added, "But, that doesn't mean he was involved with the photos, or even that Billingsley is either."

"Caroline," Kate turned to her daughter as she directed, "please contact Spencer right away, and request that he meet with me at ten o'clock this morning, in my office. Tell him, it's about his future on the Hill."

"Yes, Ma'am," Caroline agreed, and immediately left the office to call Spencer.

"What are you thinking, Kate?" Elaine asked.

"While it's highly likely that Spencer did this, it's still not conclusive evidence. I want to give him a chance to tell us just what, if any, involvement he has in this. We'll just have to take it from there."

Chapter 45

"Mr. Ainsworth, how good of you to come on such short notice," Kate Blanchard greeted the intern formally as he entered her inner office, followed by her daughter Caroline. "Please, join us around the coffee table for a chat," she extended that greeting, aware of the irony of where everyone was seated. "I'm not sure if you met my Chief of Staff, Elaine Kent, when you visited here with Caroline a few weeks ago," Kate extended her arm towards Elaine, as Spencer Ainsworth nodded acknowledgement to her.

As Kate continued the introductions for Jack and Diggie, Elaine noticed the slightest hint of stiffness emerge in his physical stance. Does he sense this is not going to be a pleasant meeting, Elaine wondered, as Ainsworth chose a chair to sit in, rather than the sofa where he could have sat beside Caroline, though it would have meant sharing it with Diggie, as well.

"Caroline said you wanted to talk with me," Ainsworth began, crossing his legs as if that would stabilize the nerves that were starting to unsettle him.

"Yes, Spencer, I do. And I will come right to the point. Look," Kate decided to be blunt, "we believe you are the person who secretly planted listening devices—bugs—not only in my office, but also in my home. So, did you do that?"

Ainsworth just sat there staring at Kate Blanchard for a moment, stunned by the brutal onslaught of the accusation, all kinds of questions running through his mind. Whatever he thought the request carried by Caroline was about, he never imagined the topic would be the bugs. How could they possibly have associated them with him?

"What?!" was all he could initially vocalize, straightening up in his seat as if a more formal posture could offer him some protection. It could not.

"I said, did you bug my office and my home?" Kate persisted, without the slightest intent of backing down.

"Representative Blanchard," Ainsworth proffered, as he formally addressed Kate to give himself a few more seconds to regroup his shattered senses, "why on earth would I do something like that to *any*one, let alone to you? I don't even know you."

"You haven't answered my question. Did you plant bugs in my office and home?"

"Representative Blanchard," Ainsworth was breathing in and out slowly, to help regain his composure, "how can you ask me something like that out of the blue? As if I go around doing that kind of thing as a matter of course."

"Well," and Kate leaned back in her seat, "I was hoping you would be honest about it, but I see you have little or no integrity. Look, we know the bugs were purchased in Omaha, Nebraska, which just happens to be your home town. We know your mother is the first cousin of my opponent in the Senate race back in my home state, and that makes you and Billingsley second cousins. You are the only stranger who had access to all of the locations where the bugs were planted. If I may sound like one of those TV detectives, you have motive, means, and opportunity, Mr. Ainsworth. Now, what's your response?" Kate asked, as she leaned forward toward Ainsworth to emphasize her point.

Ainsworth could feel his face heating up. His mind was racing to figure out how he should address the accusations.

"Mr. Ainsworth," Kate broke the silence, "let me put it to you this way. You are an intern here on the Hill, which presumably means you would like to pursue a career with Congress at some time. If you are honest with me, I will not publicize what you have done. But if you are not frank with me, I will make sure you will never be offered a position with any member of the House or Senate, now, or in the future," Kate laid out the options to him.

His initial reaction did not display a trait that would enhance his resume. "Really? How would you be able to do that if you are no longer a member of Congress, Representative Blanchard?" he challenged, with a slight hint of defiance.

"It's clear that you have not yet appreciated the bonds that congressional colleagues have with each other, whichever party they identify with, and whatever their positions on the

212

issues. Trust me, Mr. Ainsworth. If you are not honest with me today, your professional reputation on the Hill will suffer a fatal blemish. End of story."

Ainsworth recoiled at this direct attack, but acknowledged the possibility that Representative Blanchard could, in fact, black ball him on the Hill when he applied for staff positions in the future, which he had had every intention of doing. If he came clean, would she really keep quiet about it? Should he take that risk, or try to deflect again? The evidence was circumstantial, apparently, or coincidental, at best. If his cousin won the race, would his cousin hire him? Even in the face of whatever Blanchard could do to destroy his professional reputation? Maybe he would become too toxic even for his cousin to hire him. What would he do then? But the big question was: is his cousin's political career more important to him than his own future? The answer to that was obvious, at least to him.

"Representative Blanchard," Ainsworth began again, only this time he was more respectful, almost a little contrite, "I did a favor for a favorite cousin of my mom's. That's all I did."

Blanchard relaxed now, leaning back comfortably in her chair. "That's all you did," Kate repeated quietly. Then she added emphatically, "No, Mr. Ainsworth, that is *not* all you did. You violated my work and my home. You invaded my privacy. And all so that someone could maybe find something awful to discredit my candidacy for the U.S. Senate! I could probably have you arrested as a spy, Mr. Ainsworth. This is, after all, a Congressional office. Those bugs could have relayed government secrets. Tell me, who received whatever information those bugs transmitted?"

"I...I don't...know," Ainsworth stammered. And as Kate's eyes widened in disbelief, he added, "Really! I don't know!"

"You don't know?" Kate spoke so quietly and evenly that it sounded like a threat. "Do you really expect us to believe that?"

"Listen, all I know is that the bugs were linked to recording devices in my cousin's campaign headquarters...who monitored the bugs, I don't know," he faltered, looking a little deflated.

Kate lowered her glance, lifting her right hand to rub her forehead as if she could erase the thoughts that were running rampant. Everyone else in the office seemed to be holding their breath, scarcely willing to breathe so as not to interrupt the dialog.

"Mr. Ainsworth," Kate began ominously, "you call your cousin, and you tell him to get on the next flight to D.C., and to be in my office this evening at seven p.m. sharp. And you come with him. I will have my campaign manager meet him at the airport and accompany him here. Do you understand?"

"Yes, Ma'am."

"But before you go, there is something you must do," Kate admonished.

Chapter 46

Once Ainsworth had departed Blanchard's office, there was a collective sigh of relief, followed immediately by expressions of astonishment, as Kate sat there quietly with her hands folded in her lap, looking like she could not believe what she had just learned.

"Wow, Mom," Caroline was the first to react, forgetting she was not supposed to address her mother so familiarly in her Congressional office, "you were *awesome*! Boy, did he squirm!"

"First rate, Mrs. Blanchard," was Diggie's comment.

"Well done!" and "Congratulations" came from Elaine and Jack, respectively. But it was Elaine who brought the conversation back to the business at hand.

"Well, we now know who planted the bugs, but does that mean Billingsley is behind the photos, too?" Elaine asked, sobering the moment of elation brought on by their partial discovery.

"I don't think Ainsworth knows anything about them," Jack chimed in.

"I think you're right, Jack," Kate observed, "which is why I asked him to get Billingsley here today, so we can address that question directly to him. Besides, he's just a boy. Intimidating him into telling the truth wasn't really difficult. His life is ahead of him. And he put his own interests ahead of his cousin's, which he could be expected to do."

"I think you were very wise to request a face-to-face with Billingsley," Jack commented. "I think it gives you a better chance of finding out what he may, or may not, be involved in. After all, you could blow him out of the water if this went public."

"But that's just what I don't want to do," Kate lamented. "First of all, I don't want to win this election because of something scurrilous, even though he deserves to be blown out of the water, as you say. Imagine what kind of a Senator he would be if he's willing to do something like that in a campaign! No one's privacy would be safe! And the public's interests would be up for sale, I'm sure." She paused as she let out a big sigh, before adding, "I want to win because I've been a good representative of my constituents' interests, and of the public good. Because I've worked hard to improve people's lives, and because I revere our Constitution and our democracy. I doubt that Billingsley would work for the same things I have worked for if he were elected to the Senate," she concluded.

"He hasn't worked for anything but himself his entire life," Elaine noted.

"Yes, and I think our voters are generally aware of that, or I wouldn't have been eleven points ahead in the polls. If I went public with this, though, some—many—might question *my* character, because it could look like I was trying to beat a dead horse. That's not a good public image. So, I am constrained in what I can do. Nobody really knows what will happen," Kate observed.

"Well, if they don't know you couldn't do what those photos are claiming, Mom, then they don't deserve you!" Caroline was.

Kate smiled wanly, "Thank you, Dear, but I'm afraid I'm not everyone's Mom."

"But in a way you are, Representative Blanchard," Jack said. "As an elected public official, your job is to pursue, and support, the well-being of our nation and the communities you represent. Isn't that what a parent tries to do for their children? Secure their well-being? Make it possible for them to pursue their lives as they would like? Isn't the role of government in a democracy, to make it possible for all of us to pursue our lives to our best ability? Parents make rules to protect their children and to teach them how to live a healthy, happy life. And to keep peace in the family—little Tommy can't take Janey's doll and throw it in the lake! Government makes laws so that everyone can pursue their dreams in a healthy, peaceful, and safe environment. What does the Declaration of Independence say? 'Life, Liberty, and the Pursuit of Happiness'?"

"My goodness! Aren't you the Idealist!" Elaine exclaimed. But she wasn't making fun of him. No. Jack's words filled her with admiration and—delight?

216

"Hi, Honey," the voice caressed, "I just wanted to let you know that I'm planning to stop by your place late this evening."

"Oh, hi," his response was languid, rather than excited. There was no indication of the happiness she expected her visit to generate. Especially a late night visit.

"Ok," she exhaled through her teeth with exasperation, "what is it now?"

"Look, don't patronize *me!* You're not the one on the hook! You didn't actually *do* anything. I did. So don't go getting all high and mighty with me!"

"I didn't mean it like that. I just think you're fear is interfering with your rational thinking. I keep telling you, there is nothing to be afraid of. The election is just five days away. I told you, after next Tuesday, no one is going to care about the photos and whether they are real or not." After a moment's silence, she added, "Anyway, the media seem to be holding back significantly, which is so out of character for them. Even the media supporting Billingsley. Although, I think one of them tonight is starting to beat the scandal drum."

"Well, that's completely understandable if they are holding back," his own frustration escaping now. "They're spooked. Just like me. By Kent's reported findings. In spite of their appetite for political scandal, no one really wants to wake up and find they've got egg all over their faces—at least most of the media outlets don't want that," he replied flatly. "Blanchard has succeeded in stanching the normal flood of sensationalism that blows up stories all out of proportion. The media can't just throw the photos out there. They have to be able to counter Kent's results, because those results are already out there, ahead of the storm."

"You should have thought of this possibility before we got started on this."

"Oh, that's well and good for you to say!" he noted, aroused by this assault.

"Ok! Ok! I was only teasing! Look, I'll be by in a few hours, and we can talk about our options then. Can you wait a few hours?"

Ameliorated, he said he could. "But, if I go down, you'll go down with me! Just remember that!"

"But, you said yourself, darling, that I haven't done anything!" And into the silence on the other end of the call, she added, "I'm sorry! I was only teasing again! Get a grip! We'll both be just fine. You wait and see. See you soon, love!" Click.

Chapter 48

At Kate's request, Elaine and Jack were already ensconced in Kate's office when Krystal and Billingsley arrived a little before seven. Diggie and Caroline were only too happy to miss the pending fireworks.

For Ainsworth, getting Billingsley to come to D.C. had been a tough sell. Billingsley had finally seen the wisdom of a direct discussion after Ainsworth had related how much Blanchard's office had uncovered regarding the bugs, and the implication that Billingsley may also be behind the scandalous photos. Meeting with Blanchard might make it possible to blunt any impact from either issue, especially if he could convince her not to go public about the bugs. Since Blanchard had accommodated Ainsworth's professional concerns, she might be equally accommodating with regard to this election. After all, any public accusations could just as easily backfire on her, and cause her to throw away part, or all, of her lead.

He'd heard about the photos, but they were not yet front page headlines at home, so no one could even guess right now if they would have any kind of impact on voters, or what that impact might be. If the photos are proved to be phony, he was the logical one to blame. No one else would be credible as a culprit, since he would be the primary beneficiary of any scandal that hurt Blanchard's candidacy, even if it didn't actually change the expected outcome of the election. It would not be easy to reverse an eleven point lead. You'd have a better chance of winning the lottery! But understanding that wouldn't exonerate him of blame. Some might say he had nothing to lose, and everything to gain.

To say tensions were high on both sides, would be putting it mildly. But politicians, in general, know how to hide their true feelings in public. This meeting was a test of, and a testament to, the political skills of both candidates. And for Elaine, it was a challenge to her own self confidence and poise. Not in relation to Billingsley & Co., but with regard to Krystal.

Meeting someone across a computer screen in a live video conference was one thing. Meeting them in person was another. This was the first time Jack would actually be in the physical presence of Krystal, and fears about Krystal's appeal to men were revealing to Elaine some of her own hidden personality traits. Elaine was suddenly fully aware that no matter how chaotic Krystal's life as campaign manager for a U.S. Senate race was, she always managed to look like she had just walked off of a magazine cover. And in person, she exuded an aura that seemed to make men turn to blithering like fools.

Unlike me, Elaine thought. No matter how hard she tried, or how professionally she dressed, her unruly curls often made her feel she appeared slightly off-key, or a bit askew. While it had never bothered her before, she was suddenly very aware of what she saw as an unflattering contrast between herself and Krystal.

Could it be that her own attraction to Jack had triggered the birth of an ugly green monster inside herself, Elaine wondered? Was she being envious of Krystal, or jealous? There was a difference. And she was honest enough with herself to admit she was, indeed, at least fearful. After all, Jack was a very attractive man. And in response to her own personal insecurities, her fears were beginning to rumble through her nerves, like a train with one wheel off the track.

This is so silly, Elaine tried to reason away her qualms. I don't have any hold on Jack. We're not even dating! We are not a couple! He is a perfectly free man socially! He can see anyone he wants to see! And when this election is resolved, *I* probably won't even ever see him again anyway, she continued her lecture to herself. But when Krystal entered Blanchard's office, Elaine couldn't completely prevent a violent shudder from shattering her resolve to appear cool and collected.

Kate rose as Billingsley and the others entered, but she let Billingsley come to her rather than approach to usher him in. Krystal quickly sat down in a chair opposite the sofa where Elaine and Jack were both uncomfortably on edge from the palpable tension that filled the room in anticipation of a touchy exchange. Billingsley and Ainsworth were invited to seat themselves opposite Kate. When Billingsley descended into a sumptuous cushy leather chair, you could hear the air escaping, as if running in fright from the weight of his somewhat bulky frame. As the *swoosh!* from the crushed seat escaped, Elaine could hardly contain a soft chuckle. And she suddenly found herself unexpectedly relaxed. Now she, too, could let out a sigh of relief.

"Thank you for coming, Mr. Billingsley," Kate graciously opened the conversation. "I know this is highly unusual, but these are unusual circumstances. And I need to be here in Washington for several votes that are on the schedule this evening."

"I think we both know I didn't have much choice, Mrs. Blanchard. So let's get to the point of this meeting."

"Yes, let's," Kate bristled at his brusqueness. After all, *he* was the one in the wrong on this, not her. "We discovered several listening devices illegally hidden around my office— right here where we're sitting," she gestured towards the coffee table in front of them all, "and in my home. We were able to trace the sale of the items, *unequivocally*," she emphasized, "to a shop in Omaha, Nebraska, where, *coincidentally*, your cousin Spencer grew up. His mother, again coincidentally, is your first cousin, and, we understand, you are a favorite of hers. Spencer had access to all the locations where the bugs were planted, both here and in my home," she continued brutally, "and there is no one else that we can recall who had that same access in the relevant timeframe." Kate paused, to let all of that sink in.

"Sounds circumstantial to me, Mrs. Blanchard. Hundreds of thousands of people live in, and pass through, Omaha. I'm sure many of them also travel to Washington. And how can you possibly be so sure that only Spencer's visits overlap with the locations of these bugs you talk of?" Billingsley huffed.

So, Elaine thought, he's going to try to play hardball. Why am I not surprised? But Billingsley underestimates Kate, Elaine mused, with some satisfaction, as an enigmatic half smile found its way to her face.

"Mr. Billingsley," Kate began in a quiet voice that belied the approaching onslaught, "are you, or are you not, responsible for asking your cousin Spencer to secretly hide those bugs in my office and home?"

"Well,...why would I do that?" Billingsley wasn't going to give up easily. "You have more than enough weaknesses as a candidate that I would not need to do something like that! I assume the purpose of the bugs would be to obtain some damaging information that could be used to discredit your candidacy, but I don't need to secretly search for scurrilous conduct on your part! Your whole tenure in office is full of corrupt conduct! And your votes have consistently opposed the best interests of your district! I don't need to bug your life to successfully challenge your election!" Billingsley declared, his face turning deep red from the heat of his tirade. He surreptitiously glanced at Spencer beside him, hoping for some support, but Spencer was obsessed with staring at his nails.

In the distraction, Jack leaned over to whisper in Elaine's ear, "I hope he doesn't have a stroke!" Elaine nodded in agreement, as Kate replied to Billingsley's vitriolic attack.

Keeping her voice as even-keeled as she could, Kate observed, "I had hoped you would behave honorably, even though that has not been a professional trait of yours," Kate stuck the knife in him.

And then she twisted it. "I was prepared to overlook this gross travesty completely. I wasn't going to ask you to remove yourself from this election because of the total lack of respect you have shown for our governing principles, let alone our laws, by illegally planting bugs in my office and home. But you don't respond to principles of fairness and honesty. So let me give you something to respond to that you do respect." And she slid a sheet of paper from the folder in front of her, and tossed it toward him across the coffee table.

Billingsley picked up the sheet and quickly scanned the single piece of paper. If his face had been red before, it was now drained of all color. The pale pasty tone of his skin became even more disgusting, as patches of sweat seeped sporadically from his pores. His fury overwhelmed him. He had no regrets about what he did, but he hated that he had been caught.

In response to his silence, Kate decided to continue. "I have not yet reported the bugs to the Capitol Police, or," and she let this sink in, "to the FBI. Since this is a Congressional office, I should report this to both." Billingsley couldn't lift his eyes from the paper. "Because the bugs were in for a very short time, and I feel confident it was a fruitless effort," and again Kate paused, then inhaled deeply and continued, "I am willing to overlook your *zealousness* in this matter—if you answer me honestly about another matter." At this, Billingsley raised his head suddenly, then waited expectantly for the question he knew was inevitable.

"Mr. Billingsley," Kate plunged, "are you responsible for these phony, and fowl, photos of me?" and she threw copies onto the coffee table in his direction.

For a moment he just looked at the photos as they lay on the coffee table. Then slowly, he stretched out his right arm to reach for them, but decided against it. He then looked up straight into Kate Blanchard's eyes and stated emphatically, "No! I had nothing to do with those photos! I know *nothing* about them! And that's the truth!" He could say that with confidence because he knew it was, indeed, the truth. There would be no affidavit to throw at him to contradict his statement, because his statement was genuine.

And with the astuteness that many politicians develop when it comes to reading people, Kate was confident Billingsley wasn't lying.

Chapter 49

"I'll have someone drive you back to the airport, Mr. Billingsley," Kate offered, as she stood up, indicating the meeting was over. And to Krystal, she suggested, "I assume you are going back on the same flight, so the two of you can share a ride to the airport." She wanted to add, 'if you can stand to be alone with him for 45 minutes,' but she pursed her lips tightly so that the words would not escape her.

"Oh...uh...no, I'm not going back just yet," Krystal replied. "I'm booked on the red eye. I was hoping to meet up with a friend for dinner,... as long as I was here in the District," she explained. "I hope that's ok? I didn't think it would matter since I'd be getting back late anyway."

"Oh, yes, of course! It *is* late, I know, so I just assumed you'd want to get back as quickly as possible. No problem. I'm sure dinner with a friend will be a pleasant distraction from all this crazy stuff," Kate acknowledged.

Elaine had remained seated as the others were leaving, and she indicated to Jack that he, too, should remain where he was. She was sure Kate would want to talk with them once the others were gone. She was right. Closing her office door, Kate sat down again with Elaine and Jack.

"Well," she sighed as she finally felt free to let out the long breath she had been holding back, "that was fun...*not!*" After a pause, she continued, "It looks like we've got one problem solved, but not the other. I'm really surprised. I was sure the perpetrators would be the same person. But I am convinced Billingsley was telling the truth about not being behind the photo scandal. What do you two think?"

Jack let Elaine respond first, since it was her boss. "I agree, Kate. I can perfectly accept that he would do something like bugging your office and home, but I never quite could credit him with enough cleverness to develop the photo attack," and she turned to Jack for his input.

"Me, too. The construct of the photo issue is pretty sophisticated. Not just creating the photos themselves, which was no simple concept. But the nature of the attack—multiple photos rather than just one, and the choice of men was particularly cutting, and forcing a distribution by hacking my computer—and other aspects, all make me think someone smarter than Billingsley, or his chums, is probably behind the photo attack."

They sat there quietly for a moment, each one digesting this notion that someone other than Billingsley was after Kate's candidacy, and her career. But who?

Kate cut through their thoughts first. "Well, the bugging incident is resolved. We can close the books on that one."

"Are you just going to let him off the hook?" Elaine wanted to know.

Kate shrugged, then nodded. "I told you before, I don't want to win because of a scandal."

"But you don't want to *lose* either, do you, because of a manufactured scandal?" Elaine pointed out.

"No! Of course not! But I think we caught the bugs before they could be used to cause harm to my campaign. And at this point, I don't think Billingsley would try something like that again. He knows I've got the goods on him. He couldn't escape full blame for any kind of trumped up accusations that he tries to sell to the electorate about anything. And he's so far behind in the polls—at least, he was before the photos were released—that it's probably not worth risking any political future he may have at other governing levels. No. I think he's done with his dirty tricks in this campaign, after this."

"I think you are again giving him too much credit for strategizing," Elaine laughed nervously.

And Kate's responding chuckle helped lift a bit of the gloom for all of them. "I think you're right, as usual, Elaine!" Pause. "Let's not report the bugs to the police, or the FBI. Injecting that issue into the campaign would just complicate an already complicated terrain, without providing any relief from, or resolution to, what is now the real threat—the photos. We don't need to create any more threads of accusations, responses, and scandal than are already racing about."

Jack brought them to the logical next question. "So, how do you want to proceed about the photos? I know the media shouts have so far been somewhat muted. Fortunately, there are a lot of blockbuster stories about the major bills that are working their way through the Congress, to deflect attention from a story that is, not only a scandal rather than news, but a questionable scandal at that, thanks to Diggie's analysis. But there is no guarantee that distraction will last. It's Thursday evening, and the election is next Tuesday. I would strongly encourage you to tape a personal ad, to air Sunday evening, which is just you talking directly to your voters, about what you believe are the issues dominating this election, including the story about the photos."

"You don't think the photo issue will just die, then?" it was Elaine asking.

"Those outlets that support Billingsley will not let it die. Even if they accept that the photos aren't genuine, those outlets won't care that the scandal is based on a big lie. All they will care about is garnering a few more votes for Billingsley, any way they can. Even if it seems like the story might die, I believe that remaining silent would leave a negative image about Representative Blanchard's leadership capability. When you fail to give a direct response to such a brazen attack, you can appear to be weak in the eyes of the voters—even if the voters recognize the spuriousness of the attack. Americans like fighters! They want their public officials to fight for them! To defend them against the hostile forces that inhabit the world. So if a candidate doesn't fight attacks on themselves, how can voters be sure that candidate will fight for their interests if elected?"

It was a sobering moment. Finally, Kate acknowledged, "You are right, Jack. And thank you for the idea. I would prefer to handle this, again, here in Washington, since the photos are not a campaign event. Will you look into setting up the recording session, Elaine? Make sure the timing is outside of our legislative work day, remember."

"Of course," Elaine agreed.

"And, Jack, will you work with Elaine to draft the kind of statement I would make, and which you would like to hear? Before you agree, I should note that I would like the draft to review by eight tomorrow morning, before the legislative day gets started," Kate challenged with a knowing smile, then added, "I hope that won't be a problem, but I will understand fully if you would prefer not to do it."

He was a bit surprised at the request, but readily agreed. After all, he wanted the photo issue resolved, and his own reputation exonerated. And, it would mean spending more time with Elaine. And an eight a.m. deadline meant they would likely have to work late into the night. *Very* late into the night. Hhmmmm, he thought, there can't be a down side to *that,* as he turned to Elaine to ask, with conspiratorial glee and a half smile on his face, or perhaps it was a leer, "Your place, or mine?"

Chapter 50

They set up shop in the living room because Jack suggested they would be more comfortable there than in his tiny office. Actually, he just wanted to be able to sit beside Elaine on the sofa, rather than in two separate office chairs that really weren't meant for the kind of close collaborative effort he had in mind. He had finally won the drawn out debate about 'your place or mine' by observing that at his place they could be certain that Emily's ghost would not be interrupting them in the middle of their work. After all, Jack had astutely noted, the ghost might be angry at Elaine for having a male visitor, or she might go after Jack because he wasn't Emily's husband. And then, of course, at his place they would be alone. No Diggie.

As Jack brought his laptop computer into the living room, and set it on the coffee table, Elaine spread out the 'gourmet' feast they had picked up at the nearby Billie's Gourmet Burgers.

"Well, this reminds me of something," Elaine remarked, with only a touch of sarcasm, as she recalled their evening stakeout less than a week earlier.

"Doesn't it though?" Jack replied, with a smile in his voice as well as on his face, as he placed a couple of sodas on the table in front of them. "Can you believe how far we have come? Barely five or six days ago we were complete strangers, and now look at us! Sharing *another* intimate dinner!" he teased.

"Is this what you call 'intimate'?" Elaine laughed. "I'd hate to see what you call a working dinner, or even a casual one!"

Having joined Elaine on the sofa, he was sitting so close to her that the sensual warmth of his breath sent shivers through her as he whispered in her ear, "I can easily make it more romantic, if you like. We can turn out the lights, and put some quiet background music on, and..."

"Wait a minute!" she shot back, trying to regain her equilibrium and put a little emotional, and physical, distance between them. "We have a speech to write!"

"Well, *you* were the one complaining that the setting wasn't intimate enough!" he reminded her.

"No, I wasn't complaining! I was just commenting on what *you* described as 'intimate'!" she countered.

He donned a wounded puppy expression, placing a hand over his heart, and saying, "And here I was, thinking you were *intimating* that you wanted to enjoy a more *intimate* setting with me. I'm crushed," he observed, lowering his head.

"Oh, yeah! I'm sure you are," Elaine scoffed at him.

"I'm so glad you are sure," he ignored her ridicule, and added in a very somber tone, "because I sure would like to share a more intimate setting with *you*."

She was startled at his change of tone, and at the sensation of heat that rushed through her with a whooshing speed at his words. He wasn't joking with her this time. He was making a genuine overture—the fulfillment of the promise his embrace had offered just two nights ago. His words seemed to unlock a hunger inside of her. Her defenses were rapidly slipping away as she sat there, gripped by his unwavering gaze, unable to pull herself away. She felt a hunger inside of her that was reaching out to him to set it free. Only he could set it free. All the doubts that made her skittish about her attraction to him were struggling to suppress the desires he aroused in her. Her mind was saying "run!" while her heart was saying "let him in." She wanted to stretch her arms out to him, slip them around his neck, and draw him to her. She wanted to relive the passion that had suffused her body during his embrace on Tuesday evening. She wanted...she wanted...what?

Sensing her emotional struggle raised Jack's expectations. He was certain there was a genuine connection between the two of them, but that she was fighting it. He could see she wanted to succumb to her own natural inclinations, but the war going on inside her was immobilizing her. He decided to take sides in that battle, but that meant risking frightening her off. But anything worth fighting for involves risk, he told himself. If he didn't take the risk, and he lost her in this moment, he would never forgive himself.

As he held her in his gaze, he slowly leaned his body towards her. He slid one arm along the back of the sofa. With the other arm, he reached out to her, and gently drew her closer to him, as he closed the remaining distance between them.

When his lips closed gently on hers, the dam inside her broke, and a flood of emotions rippled through her body, in wave after wave, as she sank into his arms in a complete surrender. The indescribable joy from setting her emotions free filled every cell in her body. She was flying. She was shouting. She was laughing. And she was at peace. For the first time in a very long time, she was at peace, because now she was whole.

As their lips parted, and their eyes met, they shared a common understanding that something wonderful had just happened. And without saying a word, they both knew their lives had just changed forever.

It was a sobering realization. Elaine slipped her head onto Jack's shoulder, as he held her close to his heart. They sat quietly for a moment, neither saying a word, as if they both wanted to permanently burnish this wonder in their memories, and were not yet ready to break the spell it had cast.

Finally, Elaine quietly observed that if they didn't eat their burgers soon, they would be mushy and cold. Thoroughly content, Jack chuckled and released Elaine.

"Ok, my dear. We eat. And then we write. And then...," he looked at her with his own hunger completely exposed.

"And then," Elaine said, smiling, and looking up at him with softened eyes that conveyed all of the love she was feeling, "we call it a night."

"Yes," Jack replied, searing her with his glance, "and when we call it a night, I will lend you a pair of my pajamas so you can warm the other side of my bed. And tomorrow morning we will have breakfast together. Here."

Elaine returned his compelling gaze, smiled slowly, and replied with her love shining brightly through her glowing eyes, "Yes."

Chapter 51

She opened the door with her own key, knowing he would be skulking about on the lower level. Careful not to turn on a light, she announced her arrival with a bright "Hey, Honey! It's just me! I'm here! And I brought your favorite Chinese takeout! Moo Goo Guy Pan and pork fried rice!" Then she wended her way carefully in the dark towards the stairs that led down, to where he had been holed up for several days, hiding from visitors, especially inquiries from anyone in the media. She had to feel her way slowly because the only light coming from below was a very low glow from one of his computer screens.

She followed the direction of the glow, stopping in front of a low coffee table, where she unburdened the containers of food, and sat down beside the dark figure seated on the sofa in front of the table. The figure was quiet, with shoulders slightly slumped, and eyes focused on the computer screen in front of him. Divesting herself of her coat, she sat down gently beside the figure and consolingly stated, "Hey. Everything is going to be fine. You'll see."

For a moment, the figure remained still and silent. Then suddenly, as if jolted by a bolt of lightening, it came to life, jumping off the sofa with his arms gesturing as if to shake her off of him. He began pacing the floor as he countered, "How can you say that! Everything is *not* fine!" he hissed. "*Nothing* is fine! Everything is all a mess! I am going crazy down here! I can't even do my regular work for fear someone will realize I am actually here, even though I never let anyone in, or answer my phone!

"And how am I going to re-enter my life again when the election is over? What am I going to tell people who ask where I was, or why they couldn't reach me? That I was spirited away unexpectedly by an alien?!" he posited, as the pitch of his voice rose.

"And all of this is for what?" he continued. "Your plan isn't even working!"

"Of course it is!" was her rejoinder. "Just watch. When the next poll comes out on Saturday, it's bound to show

231

a big drop in Blanchard's lead! And in a couple of days, Billingsley will pull ahead! I'm sure of it! You just have to give it time!"

"Time? Time?" he nearly shouted back. "Time isn't on our side!"

"Yes it is! There's more than enough time for this to all come together! Time is actually on our side! It's Blanchard who doesn't have the time to escape the scandal, whatever she may think right now. The impact of the scandal will hit big just before election day. There won't be enough time for Blanchard to recover, even if the photos get proven to be fakes."

She had stood up, and now she approached him slowly, and with a voice that was both calm and caressing.

"C'mon," she encouraged, "let's eat. And I can fill you in on the latest."

Somewhat ameliorated, he returned to the sofa, and started opening the food containers. She returned to sit beside him, talking in a low voice, evenly and soothingly. But her suspicions were now confirmed. And she knew she had made the right decision.

Chapter 52

The sensuous aroma of bacon cooking finally seeped through to Elaine's sleep-fogged mind. Mmmmm, that smells so good, she thought, as she roused herself enough to roll over and open her eyes. For a moment the unfamiliar surroundings startled her, bringing to life even more of her brain cells. Within a few seconds, however, she remembered where she was, and how she—and Jack—had spent the night together, after they had finished writing the draft of a statement for Representative Blanchard to make in a recorded political ad.

She smiled to herself, as she let her eyes close again, and remembered how joyous and amazing the night had been. It had been so long since she had felt loved that she was surprised she could even recognize the sensation. Jack's tenderness, and her unbridled response, were both surprising and overpowering. She had been enveloped in rapture, and elevated to the heights of an ecstasy she had never experienced before. And it had been glorious!

But she was not allowed to enjoy this new discovery unfettered. That nagging voice in the back of her mind reared its ugly head, asking her "but what will happen when the election is over?" She tried to shove the question back into it's hiding place, in the deep recesses of her brain. Instead, with every push she made, it just got louder and louder, until she felt it was shouting in her ears. The only way to stop it was to get up, and face the reality of the day.

As she tried to chase the sleep away with soap and water, she heard an endearing voice call up to her. "I hear pattering about up there! About time, too!" Jack tried to sound threatening, but his voice was too full of smiles to scare anyone. "So," he continued, having had no reply, "has Sleeping Beauty decided to emerge from her trance, and actually do something useful today, like the rest of us nose-to-the-grinders?" In response to his needling, Elaine hastily donned the business suit and sweater she had let fall on the floor the evening before, and ran down the stairs. She entered the kitchen, and without hesitation, or even a pause, she threw her arms around his neck as she planted a warm embrace on his startled face.

"That," she explained, as she drew away, "should teach you *never* to denigrate my beauty sleep!"

Holding her in place with his arms around her waist, he disclaimed, "Au contraire, ma cher! That only serves to encourage me to go on the attack all the more!"

They stood there for a moment, face-to-face, arms around each other, their souls exposed through eyes that were no longer shrouded by veils, as they reveled in the new world they had discovered together. Without saying a word, they acknowledged with their eyes, their smiles, and their hearts, the bountiful treasure they had unearthed in each other.

Conversation over breakfast was low key, as they sorted through possible scenarios that might unfold before election day, and the potential consequences, or outcomes, that could occur. Neither could find much to be optimistic about.

"I'd better be off," Elaine finally said, as she finished her mug of tea, "I need to make a quick stop at home to change. I don't want to have to deflect all the questioning glances if I walk into the office in the same suit I was wearing yesterday!" After placing her breakfast dishes in the sink, she turned to him a little hesitantly, because he hadn't mentioned his plans for the day, "Will you be coming to the office, too?"

Jack joined her at the sink with his own dirty dishes, put an arm around her shoulder, and replied, "I've got some work to do for a weekend special edition of my blog, since Congress is still in session. I'd better concentrate on that first, and get it out of the way. So I'll probably stop by your office late afternoon, to find out what's happening."

"Are you sure? I mean, I don't want to take all the credit for this draft we did together."

"I'm not concerned about who gets credit for what on that," he laughed. "What I care about is finding out who is behind those photos, and trying to set me up to fail, as well. So, go, get going, and I'll see you later," and he gave her a peck on the forehead as he gently pushed her toward the front door.

"Ok! Ok! I'm going!" Elaine laughed, too. "Wow! Last night must have been so awful you can't wait to push me out the door!" she joked, only part of her really laughing.

At that wisecrack, Jack grabbed hold of her arm, quickly twirled her around, and wrapped her in his arms as he enveloped her in an embrace that left her breathless.

"Now! Go!" And Elaine grabbed her coat, a printed copy of the draft political statement, and, too overwhelmed with joy to speak, quickly closed the door behind her.

She hummed to herself as she ran down his front steps, marveling at how, in just a few days, her whole perspective on life could change so dramatically. She was filled with the sensation that she was finally coming alive, after a very long sleep. Just like Sleeping Beauty, after all, she smiled as she reached the sidewalk. Everything around her was bright and fresh, like the first spring day, in spite of the fact that the trees were bare of leaves, and she could see her breath whenever she exhaled.

As she turned in the direction of her house, something brought her to a full stop. For a split second, she wasn't sure what it was. Then her mind exploded. That color! Red! Bright red! She turned to look back behind her and she saw the model name. Chevelle. And that license plate! There couldn't possibly be two registered in the District, Jack had said. But...but...what was Craig Bittiford's car doing in front of Jack's home?

She was vaguely aware of her pulse speeding up, and her hands losing any sense of warmth under her gloves. It was not yet fully light, with a morning sky that was still gray, not blue. As she slowly crept back toward the vehicle, almost on tiptoe, she could scarcely make out if anyone was in the vehicle. It looked like someone might be sitting in the front, in the driver's seat, to be exact. If it was Craig's car, as she was certain it was, why would he just sit there, parked, at Jack's? Is he afraid of something? He must know Jack had been trying to reach him for days because of all the phone calls which Craig never answered. Had he been away, and just returned? Was he trying to return Jack's overtures? Why would he just be sitting there, and not get out? It's not so early in the morning that he could be worried about waking Jack. So, why wouldn't he get out?

She detected no movement as she approached the car, so she knocked on the closed front seat passenger window from the sidewalk. No response. Maybe he was asleep.

She bent over to look inside the car, and for a moment her body went rigid, frozen in place, in sharp contrast to the casual appearance of the person who was slumped back in the driver's seat of the car, with head hanging to one side. She couldn't move. She noticed that a dark reddish stain had spread out from a black hole near the right side of his t-shirt. The sight of that stain jolted her from the initial shock, letting her regain enough of her wits to run up the steps and start banging on Jack's front door, forgetting about the doorbell on the side of the doorframe. Though she was excitedly calling Jack's name, over and over, her voice was barely a whisper.

At the sound of fists pounding on his door, Jack came running, fearing that something had happened to Elaine. There was a split second of relief when he saw it was actually her standing there in front of him. But the twisted expression of fear on her face, her eyes wide with horror, and her inability to speak, told him something was wrong—very wrong.

He quickly seized her by the arm and tried to escort her into the house to calm her down, so she could explain to him what had spooked her, but she pulled back from him, pointing to the red car parked in front of his steps. He looked up, and it was clear that recognition instantly flooded his face. Finally, he thought, he would have this out with Craig.

"Ok! Ok, Elaine!" he tried to soothe her excited nerves, "I see! It's Craig!"

As he started to bolt down the stairs, Elaine grabbed his arm, this time to stop him. "No," she whispered. "It's not Craig," she could barely get the words out. "I mean...it's...it's...he's been shot, Jack! At least, I think so. And I..I think...I think...he might be dead," she heaved out a deep breath.

Jack stopped in motion, halfway down his front steps, and turned back to look up at Elaine with disbelief written all over his face. "Dead?" he quietly asked. "Did you say...dead?" he repeated, as if he had no idea what 'dead' meant.

He didn't move, but he glanced back again at the car and repeated, "Dead?" It was one thing to scan police radio messages, but another to actually encounter a dead body.

"I...I think so," Elaine confirmed. Regaining a little more composure, she added, "I think we need to call the police. Immediately."

"Maybe we need to call an ambulance!" Jack whispered nervously as he bolted down the rest of the stairs and headed to the driver's side of the car. "What if he's alive? Hurry, Elaine! Call 911!" As Elaine pulled out her cell phone and dialed '911', Jack opened the car door, checking Craig's wrist for a pulse, and putting his hand in front of Craig's face as he checked for breathing. As he slowly lowered his hand, having felt nothing, he could also see that there was no motion from Craig's chest to indicate he was breathing at all.

Elaine was talking to someone on the other end of the emergency call, giving them Jack's address, when Jack suggested she also ask for the police, because the man appeared to be already dead.

Chapter 53

"Police and medics are both coming," Elaine announced somberly, as she clicked off her cell phone. "Oh, Jack," she sighed heavily, "what on earth is going on?"

As he reached her midway up his front steps, he put his arm around her shoulders, and they both stood there, staring at the car. "I have no idea, Elaine," he admitted. "This just is so surreal! What on earth could have been so terrible that Craig would have to die?"

"You don't think it was suicide, do you?"

"Oh, no. I mean, the location of the gun shot could technically have been inflicted by himself. But, I just can't believe he would do something like that. Did you see the weapon on the front passenger seat?"

"No, I didn't really notice. I guess I had just been fixated on the fact that there was a person in there who didn't look like he could move anymore." Elaine rested her head on Jack's shoulder, to give her tired neck a rest.

"Well, it was a gun—and get this—it had a silencer on it, too!" he noted, as he leaned his cheek on her hair.

"How could I have missed that?" her head shot up again with the question.

"Well, it isn't a typical gun. It was printed out by a 3D printer! Both pieces, apparently. That's probably why it was left there."

"You can make a gun from a 3D printer?" Elaine asked, disbelief infused in every word.

And as Jack replied, "Oh, yeah," police and ambulance sirens came hurtling around the corner, and stopped in front of Craig's red Chevelle.

* * * * *

"Well, I emailed the file for the statement to Kate, and explained why I would not be in for a while," Elaine told Jack as she plopped herself down beside him on his living room sofa, where they waited while the police were examining the scene outside, knowing someone would want to talk to them in more depth at some point. "She was pretty shaken, I would say, when I told her someone was lying dead in a car in front of your house, and that we had discovered him. Then I think she nearly went into shock when I explained to her who it was."

Feeling a little more anchored, with the help of very strong coffee, Jack slipped his arm around Elaine's shoulders and held her close for a moment, not saying a word—just holding her, before relaxing his grip and leaning back into the sofa. He could tell she was still unnerved by the discovery. The urge to enclose her in his arms, and protect her from the horrors of the world, spread through him like a wildfire. But he held back for fear of scaring her off. They had shared so much these last 24 hours, with all kinds of barriers falling down like the proverbial "walls of Jericho" in Frank Capra's 1936 Oscar winning move "It Happened One Night". So he used whatever strength he could muster to restrain his impulse to wrap her in a protective shell. You can't protect anyone from the realities of life, he told himself. Efforts to shelter anyone from harm often backfire, and do nothing to help people cope and grow.

"I still can't get over feeling like we are in a time bubble, or a dream, and at any moment now, the bubble will burst," he finally observed. "What could possibly be so important that someone would actually kill another person over it?" By discussing an abstract concept, he tried to depersonalize the morning's event.

"But it happens every day, Jack," Elaine offered. "All over the world. People killing people. It can only make sense in self defense, I think, and if people weren't trying to harm other people in some way, there would be no need for self defense. I've never understood it. And especially now, I don't understand it. And I can't even begin to fathom how this might affect Kate's campaign for the Senate," Elaine's voice was acquiring a gloomy tone. "Goodness! If the idea of a sex scandal weren't enough, imagine how a *murder* added to the story will explode across the news outlets! No advance press conference is going to nip this story in the bud!"

Jack heaved a sigh, and then shrugged his shoulders. "I think you are right. Representative Blanchard is really in for a rough ride between now and the election on Tuesday—*if* they find a link. I mean, even we don't know that Craig's death is in any way linked to the photo scandal afflicting Blanchard."

"Oh, come on, Jack!" Elaine couldn't believe he was being so naive. "Craig is the person you went to for validation of the photos."

"But, remember, that is not public knowledge," a light bulb was struggling to go on in Jack's brain. "Only a few people know that he's the one I went to."

"Then he was killed, and left at your doorstep," Elaine continued, as if she had not been interrupted. "You can't tell me that the police won't think there is at least a link to you," Elaine eyeballed him, and then continued, "and what have you been working on this whole past week? The photo scandal!" she finished, with a flourish of her hands. "Voila!"

"Well," Jack smiled at her expansiveness, "not quite Voila!" After a moment of thought, he added, "There may not be an obvious link to the photo scandal. "There could be lots of reasons why someone snuffed out Craig's life. I just can't think of any. But then, I don't know what else he was working on, let alone if it would lend credence to any other reason for someone to want him dead. He was a computer geek, for goodness sake!" His exasperation was evident in his words.

"What makes this worse," Elaine observed, "is that, once the police do—*if* they do—find a link to the photo scandal story, none of this will touch Billingsley. It will all be linked to Kate because the photo scandal is about her. No matter how untrue it all is, it's *her* name in the stories. And that means that now, more than ever, we couldn't possibly release information about Billingsley bugging Kate's office and home, because it would sound like sour grapes. Like we're just trying to find something—*anything*—that could deflect attention away from this double scandal. It's like 'damned if you do, and damned if you don't'.

"This is so awful," Elaine continued, "because she has worked *so hard* to serve her constituents, to pursue the public good. These lies could bring down a true public servant, and elevate someone who never did a thing in his life for anyone else!"

"You don't know that putting the photo scandal story together with a murder will completely turn the tide in favor of Billingsley," Jack tried to relieve the pressure building in Elaine's heart and mind, even if he didn't quite believe what he was saying. "After all, he is—or was—eleven points behind. And obviously there is no proof, and never will be, that the photos are real. I would hope it would take a lot more than a trumped up scandal, and, perhaps, hints of a linked murder, to change a voter's mind."

It was Elaine's turn to sigh. "You may be right. But it's all about perceptions, isn't it? And while the voters in her House district may be familiar enough with her career to give her the benefit of the doubt, voters throughout the rest of the state don't really have experience with her as their elected representative. Maybe I'm not giving voters enough credit to see through the crap, and make their own judgments. Maybe the impact won't be as dire as I fear. Maybe." She looked at Jack, then, and tried to give him a smile that was a little bit hopeful, even though she didn't feel that hope.

Always looking for concrete evidence that might resolve the issue, Jack noted, "Isn't her campaign planning a poll tomorrow? That should give us some indication of how voters are understanding the stories."

"Yes, Krystal has one scheduled. And we should have the results by tomorrow afternoon." As she thought about the timing, however, she observed, "But, while polling tomorrow morning should reflect any impact of the photos, it won't indicate the potential hit her campaign could take if a murder is ever connected to the photos.

"We do plan to do a poll Monday morning, as well, though. But by the time we get those results," Elaine was clenching and unclenching her fists as she thought through the timeline, "it will be too late to mitigate any negative feelings among the electorate about anything. It will just, sort of, forewarn us about what to expect on election day." Elaine couldn't bear to think of the pain that Kate Blanchard would be enduring between now and then. The prospect that Kate could lose her lead, and the election, filled Elaine with a consummate grief that no palliative could alleviate.

Jack tried to change their focus. "I just can't fathom why anyone would want to actually kill Craig. I mean, I get enraged at the thought he might have been using me, or setting me up for failure, but it never made me want to kill him," Jack declared. "He's unique. We all are. And when someone dies, there's no bringing them back. They are gone."

Then, realizing this topic may not be the best to lighten the mood, he added with a wink and a small smile to Elaine, "Except for Emily, of course!

"As for Blanchard's Senate race," he could not escape returning to the main concern at hand, "who would suspect there was even any remote connection? Because there isn't, really. I'm the only one who had any contact with him, and all I did was ask him to verify the photos. So how could that small act have anything to do with someone wanting to kill him?" he puzzled. "I talk with lots of people every day. And not one has ever turned up on my doorstep dead—until today, that is. And besides, lots of folks must have been asked to look over those photos these last few days. I doubt, very much, that we'll find that any of them have been murdered," he finished, with a flourish of his arms.

"Oh, my goodness!" Elaine suddenly exclaimed, her hands flying up to her face as Jack's comment raised a completely unexpected potential. "Do you think Diggie is in any danger?" she implored him, with eyes round and wide. "Not only is he publicly associated with the photos, but he invalidated them in public, so whoever created them knows that Diggie has debunked them. Craig validated them! And he was killed! I better call Diggie and let him know what's going on. Maybe he shouldn't be alone at home. Maybe he should go hang out at Kate's office, or something, where he could be around people." Without waiting for a comment from Jack, Elaine jumped up to get her phone and make the call.

Some moments later, she settled back again on the sofa, feeling a little comforted after chatting with Diggie. He promised her that he would hang out at Kate's office for the day. It wasn't too hard of a sell, since Caroline would be there, too, he had joked. But the somberness in his voice after Elaine explained what had happened that morning, and his failure to give Elaine any pushback at all, told her that Diggie had been rattled, too, by the news of Craig's death.

"So," Jack opened, with a sly grin, "did Diggie say anything about your not returning home last night?" He was wondering if Elaine would own up to their growing intimacy, or if she would try to hide it from those close to her.

He was expecting her to blush, or maybe show some other indication of embarrassment, but he wasn't expecting her to laugh and look him in the eyes, as she explained that "Diggie got home so late last night, he arrived to a dark house and just assumed I was already sound asleep! So he just crawled upstairs and went straight to bed! He had no idea I hadn't been home so I let him believe I had gotten up early, and came over here to give a final polish to the speech! I saw no reason to enlighten him just now," Elaine finished, with her own version of a sly smile.

Not sure what her response meant, Jack decided not to pursue the issue just then, choosing, instead, to continue their earlier conversation as if there had been no break for a phone call. "Ok. Anyway, we don't know that Craig's death has anything at all to do with the photos. It could be something entirely unrelated going on in his life. But," he admitted reluctantly, "it really looks strange that he was found right in front of my house. I can't begin to figure out why—unless it does have something to do with the photos," he shrugged.

Surprised at Jack's quick surrender, Elaine at first only heard half of what Jack had been saying. When the words finally sank in, though, Elaine was again horror-struck. She sat up straight on the sofa, and turned to ask Jack, "What if someone is punishing you for not publishing the photos?"

"But I did publish them. Remember?" he noted, referring to the phony edition of his blog that had been sent by a hacker.

"But you publicly disavowed that transmission, through your followup email to your subscribers, and at the press conference," Elaine pointed out. "By disavowing ownership, and by standing with us at the press conference where Diggie declared the photos were phony, you made it possible for Kate to significantly downgrade their potential negative impact."

Here Elaine looked at him with admiration and respect as she noted, "Because you are honorable. And ethical. Because you did not want to be the cause of undue, or unfair, harm. To anyone. Especially in terms of the impact on an election. Because of your commitment to professional conduct," she emphasized, "we were able to prevent this monstrous attack from ruling the public discourse in the Senate race—at least until now, that is," and she sank back down into the sofa.

"But why would someone kill Craig to punish *me*?" Jack almost shouted. "Why wouldn't they just kill me?"

As if Jack hadn't spoken, Elaine observed, ruefully, "But, of course, all of that means you could be seen as a threat to whoever is behind this." And then, her voice becoming quiet and apprehensive, she noted, "And that could mean you are in danger, Jack."

In that moment of understanding, the knock on the door startled them both.

Chapter 54

"Mr. Amory," Detective Marsh began in a very dry, matter-of-fact, tone, "I understand that you and your friend," he nodded towards Elaine, "found the body? And that you knew Mr. Bittiford?"

"Yes, Detective. Elaine and I discovered him this morning. And, yes, I've known Craig for many years."

"When was the last time you saw him?"

Wide-eyed, and taking a risk that the Detective had a sense of humor, Jack replied with a blank face, "Why, this morning, of course."

"You mean, you saw him alive before you found him dead?" the Detective ignored Jack's lame attempt at humor as he searched for precision.

Failing to tickle Detective Marsh's funny bone, Jack quickly corrected the Detective's understanding. "No. No. I'm sorry. The last time I saw him *alive* was last Friday evening." But a split second later, as his mind rummaged through the past week on speed dial, he corrected himself, adding, "No. Wait. That's the last time I actually *spoke* with him. But I did see him after that—without speaking to him. Saturday night I saw him arriving at an acquaintance's house. That's the last time I saw him alive."

"And what did you speak with him about?" the Detective wanted all the details.

"Well, I had sent him a project to review late Friday afternoon, and met with him at his home Friday evening, to get his comments on the project."

"Sounds like an awfully short turn-around time. Was it an emergency?"

"Well...yes. And no. It is a short turn-around time, but I'm in the current news business, and there are no long-term projects when you are dealing with current news," Jack tried to explain, without actually explaining.

"Couldn't it have waited until Monday, Mr. Amory?"

"Certainly not!" Jack sounded aghast, but it was more of a show, for the Detective. "Congress was in session Friday, and was scheduled to be in session right through the weekend.

Events move quickly when Congress is trying to rush through legislation at the last minute, you see, before adjourning. You have to stay on top of what's happening. You know the old saying, Detective, about 'no rest for the weary'," Jack tried to fluff off the situation with a chuckle, followed by rocking back on his heels for a moment.

"Just what kind of project did you ask him to review?"

"Just to validate some computer files. He's a really smart computer engineer, and a talented Graphics Artist, too, who, like me, is self-employed," Jack hedged, forgetting that Craig was now past tense.

"And just what is it that you do, Mr. Amory?"

"I'm a journalist. I write a political blog about legislative proposals and politics in Congress."

Elaine was listening to all of this with a mixed mind. She realized Jack was trying not to tell the Detective anything that might link Craig to the photo scandal they were dealing with. Because any public hint of a link at all would blow the photo scandal story sky high, destroying all their hopes that it would peter out as old, unverifiable, news. With only four days left before election day, there could scarcely be enough time to rescue Kate's campaign from utter collapse, in the eyes of the voters, if a murder now became linked to the photo scandal. As Elaine tried to estimate a news cycle timeframe, however, she was roused from her calculations, when the Detective addressed a question directly to her.

"I'm afraid I never met the man, Detective," Elaine said, matter-of-factly. It was a true statement. For all of her pursuit of him with Jack, she had never actually met Craig.

"Which one of you actually found him? Or were you both leaving the house at the same time?" The Detective had the grace to try to keep his voice nonjudgmental, and free of innuendo.

Elaine and Jack both tried to respond, but it was Elaine who persisted. "I saw the car, and that someone was sitting in it, as I was leaving this morning, so I came back in to tell Jack." And after a moment, she added, "I recognized the car instantly, you see, but I only noticed that someone was in the car," her voice lowered, as she ended the story there.

"I'm sorry," the Detective squinted his eyes as he tried to understand what was not making sense to him, "what do you mean, you recognized him? If you've never met the man, how could you recognize him, Miss Kent?" the Detective finished innocently, his face full of wide-eyed question marks.

Jack was itching to answer for Elaine, but the Detective had pointedly directed his question at her, and not him. He had to let her speak for herself. She was, after all, a very skilled manager working in a sensitive, volatile, political environment. She had to be constantly alert to the moving, and changing, political currents on the Hill to be effective in her job. And she had to be able to deal with all kinds of people looking for all kinds of things. Just like she had dealt with him when he first brought the photos to Blanchard's office for a response. Recalling that made him relax as he listened to her response to the Detective's inquiry.

"It's the car I recognized, Detective, not the man," Elaine began. "It's a very unusual car." And then she brightened as she tried to explain, "Surely you've noticed that it's an antique car, Detective Marsh? And it has a vanity license plate. There couldn't be two such registered in the District," she affirmed with confidence.

"Please, Ms. Kent," Detective Marsh mildly rebuked Elaine, "do you take me for a fool?"

"No! Of course not!" Elaine replied, both eyebrows raised in surprise. Or was it fear? "No," she added more calmly, "I just knew that Jack knew someone with that kind of car...because when we went to Union Station for supper last Wednesday evening, he pointed it out to me as we drove through the parking garage, and mentioned that it belonged to a friend of his...and that there couldn't be two like it registered here, because the car's an antique and has an easily recognizable license plate," she finished with a smile, feeling a little pleased with herself for being as uninformative as she thought Jack had been.

Detective Marsh flipped through a few pages of notes in his small notebook, then looking at Elaine he observed, "I see you don't live here, Miss Kent."

"That's true," Elaine acknowledged, wondering what the Detective might be thinking in connection with that piece of information.

"Where did you say you worked?"

"Um...I work on the Hill...for a member of Congress," Elaine demurred.

Back to Jack. "Why do you think Mr. Bittiford's body was found outside of your home, Mr. Amory?"

"I honestly have absolutely no idea," Jack said, as he let out a breath so deep his shoulders slumped, and his head sank slightly forward as he folded his arms across his chest. And that was the truth, Jack reminded himself. Then he had a thought. "You know, Craig lives only a few blocks from here, Detective. Maybe he just couldn't find a parking place closer to his home?" he looked inquisitively at the Detective, without the slightest trace, he hoped, of avoidance showing through.

The Detective was no dummy. He didn't think they were lying to him, but he was sure they were holding back information. Why, and what it was, he didn't know. But he was certain he would find out in time. He had no reason to believe there was any hurry. After all, Mr. Bittiford was dead. He wouldn't be going anywhere.

"Do you know who his next of kin might be?"

Jack thought for a moment, looking down at the floor while his arms were still folded across his chest, then he replied as he lifted his head to address Detective Marsh directly, "Not really. He's not married,... and his parents are both deceased."

"Was he engaged, or dating anyone?"

"I'm pretty sure he wasn't engaged. I mean, I think I would have known something like that. And I don't believe he was dating anyone at the moment,...but I couldn't say for sure that he wasn't," Jack rubbed his chin as he tried to recall any relevant situations, while his other arm slid down his side. "He wasn't a social butterfly, Detective...more like a turtle. He could deal with people just fine in a business context, but socially he was more likely to pull inside a shell like a turtle, and hide there until the coast was clear, so to speak," Jack folded his arms across his chest again as he finished.

"Then you wouldn't know why he was carrying a diamond engagement ring in his pocket, would you?"

If the Detective was looking for a reaction, he got it. Jack was genuinely shocked by this news, his head shooting backwards as if someone had thrown a punch straight into his face. He opened his mouth in an effort to reply, but, not knowing what to say, just closed it again. His mind raced through his encounters with Craig over the last several months, and nothing indicated to him that Craig was even dating, let alone involved with one woman seriously enough to propose marriage.

"Can you think of any reason why he might want to kill himself, then?" the Detective took Jack's silence about the ring as a 'no'.

"Kill himself?!" Jack's eyes opened round and wide, even more stunned by what he obviously considered a ludicrous notion. After another moment of staring at the floor, however, he admitted, quite seriously, "No. I really can't, Detective. I would never have thought Craig was the suicidal type. I mean, he always seemed to be on an even keel. He wasn't a moody person. He didn't ride an emotional roller coaster. And he wasn't someone who would easily get depressed, which I would expect someone who commits suicide would be."

"Not always," Detective Marsh explained, as he showed the first signs of being a living human being. "Sometimes it's the very ones who never show emotional ups and downs that are really just hiding, or suppressing, those kinds of feelings. And then one day the dam bursts. And it can be the tiniest thing that breaks it. You said he was a loner, socially."

"Oh," Jack replied quietly, "yes, I did." Nevertheless, after some thought, he persisted, "But I still don't see Craig as someone who would commit suicide."

As the Detective turned to leave, he stopped to ask Jack one more question. "Oh, by the way, who was the acquaintance you saw Mr. Bittiford visiting last Saturday evening?"

Uh-oh, thought Elaine. Here it comes. This will open the door to the story of the photos.

But Elaine didn't give Jack enough credit for his skills at obfuscation. "It was Kevin Lowell's house that he was visiting. I believe he is one of Craig's clients."

"And just how was it," the Detective followed through with what he considered an obvious, but simple, question, "that you happened to see, but not talk to, Craig when he visited this Mr. Lowell?"

Elaine's heart leapt into her throat, as the saying goes. She froze in place, hoping her face masked the ice cold horror that filled her every limb. But again, she had underestimated Jack's skills.

"Well, I had stopped to pick up a burger at Billie's Gourmet Burgers, which is around the corner. The best parking space I could find was a few doors down from Mr. Lowell's house, and I noticed Craig arriving just as I returned to my car from getting my take home supper," Jack demurred.

Not leaving any stone unturned, the Detective asked one more question, as he looked directly at Jack, and gave him a smile that did not reach his eyes. "How do you know Mr. Lowell, and where he lives?"

"Well, Detective," and here Jack strutted his ego a bit as he inhaled deeply, lifting his chest high, "I do publish a political blog, as I said. It's my business to know Hill players, be they members of Congress, or lobbyists, or whoever."

"Or Hill staff," the Detective stated matter-of-factly as he nodded again, but didn't look, toward Elaine. He was not really looking for a response, and he got no more than a blank stare from Jack. "We can't forget the toilers on the Hill. Right, Mr. Amory?" he noted, with an enigmatic half smile. "How long have the two of you been a couple?" he asked, eyebrows squinting as if he could ferret out the truth by shear force of will.

Jack was amazingly cool, as Elaine told him later. "Oh, not very long at all, Detective," and Jack slipped an arm around Elaine's shoulders. "So short a time, as a matter of fact, that she actually still finds me irresistibly attractive," and he looked down at Elaine with a genuinely adoring, and somewhat conceited, expression. Elaine looked up at Jack with her own expression of adoration, and there was nothing phony about it.

Detective Marsh just looked at the two for a moment. He believed the mutual admiration society they had formed was genuine. He was also sure, however, that there was much more to this story, but he decided to bide his time. There was a lot of basic information that the police needed to collect before he could construct the full story behind the crime, and then seriously grill the both of them. But one thing was certain. He knew it wasn't suicide. It was definitely murder. And these two were holding back big time.

Chapter 55

After closing the door when the Detective finally departed, Jack exhaled forcefully. "Whew! An engagement ring! Wow! I would never have guessed he had it in him," he exclaimed, turning towards Elaine as they stood together behind that closed door.

"Well," Elaine was thoughtful, "he obviously did. But does that mean anything to us about the photos?"

"No. I can't imagine. It's just a surprise, that's all."

They stood there a moment, quiet and contemplative, both trying to digest the discussion with the Detective. Finally, Elaine observed, "I don't think anything that's happened today, or anything either of us said to the Detective, would indicate any kind of link with the photos, or Kate's campaign. I mean, all you did was show the photos to Craig and ask his opinion. It's not as if he created them. And who knows how many projects he has, finished or ongoing, that could generate enough hostility to want to end his life? I mean," and here Elaine started letting some of her shock at the morning's events rise to the surface, "my brain still can't fully register the fact that we found a man—someone you *know*—*dead*! Right in front of your house!" she looked up at Jack, her face full of astonishment, as well as questioning concern.

He carefully, but rapidly, went over in his mind the happenings of the day. "I know! I know! It's pretty shattering, I agree!" as he, too, tried to come to terms with what happened, running his fingers through his hair like a comb. "But, noooooo...," he dragged out his conclusion, "...I don't think there is any obvious link with the photos. But once the Detective does some digging, I don't see how he will avoid learning about the photos, one way or another, especially once he finds out who you work for. But I also don't see how that knowledge would create any link between Blanchard and Craig. Diggie is her publicly acknowledged computer expert, not Craig. Besides, since I didn't kill him, the fact that he was found in front of my house does not tie me to his death in any way."

"Did you leave copies of the photos with Craig on Friday?" Elaine asked, her nerves on edge as new fears started to grip her.

"No. I deliberately did not." Then it occurred to him, "But, you know, he never asked to keep a copy, and I just assumed he hadn't made any for himself. I mean, why would he? What would he have wanted with copies of those photos?"

"Then I don't see how the Detective would find anything to link the two events. I mean, we can't even link the two events, and *we* know all that anyone who was not involved in creating the photos, knows," Elaine said, almost out of breath.

"I'm not sure how, but my gut is telling me he will put the two together at some point, or try to, if only circumstantially. He's no dummy. He'll learn about the photos, and the scandal they threaten, if only because you work for Blanchard, and the photos have been in the realm of public discussion recently. He'll likely find out about Wednesday's press conference. And though you and I don't see a link, or any relation at all between the two events, the Detective might conclude otherwise. After all, the issue at the press conference was that the photos were not genuine photos. I spoke at that press conference. And I doubt it will take the Detective long to figure out that Craig was, as a computer geek, at least, one person who would be sought out to examine the photos for their authenticity. And I did say I met with Craig Friday to validate some computer files. And I am a journalist. Two and two equals...?"

Elaine shrugged in acknowledgement.

"On a completely different note," Jack went over to his jacket and pulled a small package out of the pocket, "I have something for you...or, at least, for your roommate, Emily Waring."

"You aren't making fun of me, are you Jack Amory?" Elaine was wary.

"Oh, no!" he hurriedly assured her. "Here. Put this beside the photo of Emily's husband. She'll understand."

Elaine opened the paper wrapping and for a moment was stunned, not in shock but by the beautiful surprise. The package was a framed photograph of a tombstone at United States Soldiers' and Airmen's Home National Cemetery, in Washington, D.C.. The name on the stone was 'Josiah Waring, Major, United States Army'.

"Oh, Jack," Elaine's breath caught in her throat. In a voice she could scarcely get above a whisper, she exclaimed in awe, "You found her husband!" That Jack had even bothered to follow up on Elaine's imaginings, amazed her. It was an incredibly magnanimous gesture that spoke louder than anything else could have of a profound empathy on Jack's part, not just for her, but also for Emily. The discovery that he hadn't just dismissed her story as a woman's hysterical fantasies overwhelmed her with a quiet joy. And to have gone to the trouble to go there and photograph the grave, to bring proof back to Emily, filled Elaine with warmth and gratitude, as a single tear rolled down her right cheek.

To hide his embarrassment, as if he were standing there naked, he quickly shifted his focus. "Look," he continued after hastily checking his watch, "it's almost 2:00, and I've got a special edition to get out, and you must have a lot of other work to do, since it looks like Congress will still be in session most, if not all, of the weekend."

"You are right, of course," Elaine acknowledged, with a swift wipe of her fingers across her cheek. Then more quietly, she asked, as she looked up at him, "Will you be stopping by my office later, or will you be working late into the night on your special edition?"

Jack looked longingly into Elaine's hungry eyes, thrilled by her open appeal, and in a moment of weakness he almost succumbed to the invitation so clearly written in her glance. It was a difficult time for them both, under the best of circumstances. Their romance was in the discovery stage, and it could go either way with the slightest misstep. To say nothing of the effect of a murder on his doorstep. He wanted to throw caution to the winds, and follow both of their longings. But he instinctively knew that the magnetism between them was more than just hormones gone wild. Their developing bond was something very special, and it had to be protected so that it could thrive. So he mustered his strength in support of common sense. There would be time later for impulsive orgies, and other flights of fancy.

"More than anything, I want to be with you," his voice caressed her heart as his eyes held hers with their magnetic draw, "but I think we are all in for some difficult days until the election is over, especially after today's horrific happenings. We don't want to do anything that would send the police sniffing around Blanchard's Senate race. I don't think I should be seen right now anywhere near Blanchard's office, that's for sure. And I believe it would be best if we did not get together this evening, at least."

Then he cushioned that blow with, "Who knows how long the police will be hanging around out front while they work on the car, before taking it wherever they take such things. If we stick to getting together outside of work, it would bolster the notion that our relationship is personal, social, and has nothing to do with any political goings on concerning Blanchard or her campaign."

After a slight pause, he added in a somber tone, "I just feel like we've seen only the tip of the Detective's knife, so to speak, and that he'll be watching the both of us. After all, I can't think of any other live players, so the Detective may be looking at us, or at least me, for a motive. Who else is there?"

"Well, Craig must have lots and lots of clients! Any one of them could have done it! And one of them must have done it! Because you and I know that neither one of us did it!" the pitch of Elaine's voice rose, becoming shrill, as she spoke.

"The question is," Jack noted, as he tried to calm her thoughts, "who really did kill Craig? And why? I think we've got to figure that out, and quickly, or we'll all be in hot water."

Chapter 56

Elaine hurried back to her house to change before heading to work. Everything was so mixed up inside of her. The joy she and Jack had found had to be pushed into a closet in her brain, almost suppressed, so that she could concentrate on what she needed to do for Kate before the Congressional session adjourned, which could happen any time this weekend.

Oh, I can't wait for next Tuesday to be over, Elaine muttered to herself as she headed out the door of her home, having brushed her teeth, and donned a fresh business suit. Elections created lots of additional pressures under normal circumstances, but first the photos, and now this shocking death, were blowing the lid off of this election cycle. At least for her, and possibly for Kate Blanchard. And if Kate loses, of course, Elaine will be looking for a new job.

Poor Kate, Elaine mused. She's worked so hard. And she's tried so tirelessly to be conscientious. Here I am moaning because these events are interfering with my personal life, which, she reminded herself, she wouldn't have if the photo threat had never occurred. While Kate, on the other hand, is facing a block of lies that could permanently destroy her exemplary reputation and professional life. Because Elaine was, inherently, not a selfish person, she admonished herself to just put whatever she felt about Jack on the back burner, for now. If there is anything real there, she told herself, it will still be there after Tuesday. The problem now was to save Kate from the heinous attack on her campaign. And with that reminder, Elaine put her qualms, her fears, her insecurities, her romantic notions, aside—for now, at least.

Her efforts, however, did not prevent her heart from racing when Jack called her a few hours later. He told himself it was just to find out if any current events had occurred that he should be aware of, but in the far recesses of his mind he knew the truth. He just wanted to hear the melodic sound of her voice.

"Jack!" Elaine exclaimed in a stage whisper when she picked up the phone. "Should you be calling me at work?"

"Well, don't lovers talk to each other at their workplaces?" Jack crooned.

"Lovers, is it?" Elaine's voice took on a sultry tone, even as she lowered it so that no one else in the office might hear what she was saying.

"Yes," Jack affirmed. "Lovers," he responded firmly.

"I like the sound of that, Mr. Amory," Elaine's voice smiled into the phone.

"Me, too, Ms. Kent," Jack agreed softly. "Me, too."

Chapter 57

It wasn't good news. But it wasn't really *bad* news, either. What it was, though, was a bit depressing. But not lethally so. At least, not yet.

It was Saturday afternoon, and Elaine had not even stopped for some lunch since arriving at work early in the morning. She read the report over several times before setting it down on her desk. She leaned back in her chair and closed her eyes, to absorb the portent of the results of the morning's public opinion poll on Kate Blanchard's Senate race.

Her eleven point lead had fallen to six points. That was still a good lead. And so close to election day, it was typical that a race would get closer, as more and more people finally decided who they were going to vote for. And, she reminded herself, that the six point lead was outside the margin of error, which meant the lead had substance—you could take it to the bank. Anything within the range of the margin of error would mean the race was a toss-up. But it was only a couple of points above the margin of error—a bit close for comfort.

Some of that drop, of course, had to be due to the photo scandal, but fortunately, the story had not yet overwhelmed the news cycle or Blanchard's credibility and record in Congress. Many voters were accepting her explanation, but clearly not all. I wonder what it takes to get the truth out there, Elaine mused. I wonder how people judge what they see, read, and learn, about any politician or elected official. I guess, she concluded, it really depends on the individual voter. Those who want to believe the worst will probably believe it, no matter what Blanchard says, or what evidence she provides to the contrary. But I guess there are also those who will never question the veracity of whatever she says, because they know or like her, or support her politically. What do those who are unfamiliar with her career believe, and how do they decide whether to vote for her, or her opponent? Elaine couldn't answer that question. Do they choose her for her political stands, no matter what? Do they oppose her because of some personally scandalous behavior, in spite of supporting her political views? How do they decide whether to believe her story about the photos, or the allegations hurled about by the photos? Elaine couldn't answer those questions, either. At that impasse, her ringing phone rescued her from puzzling over the unfathomable.

This time her heart literally skipped a beat when she saw from Caller ID that it was Jack rescuing her. They had not seen each other the night before, as agreed, and it was just as well, because they were both inundated with the work that had piled up while they dealt with the police. That made Friday evening the first evening, since the preceding Saturday, that they had not spent together in some fashion or other. Elaine marveled at how quickly her world had changed since she had met Jack. She embraced that change wholeheartedly now, with joy and excitement—and a little bit of fear. But not much fear, she reminded herself, with some astonishment, anxious to suppress any scary demons that might try to emerge to shatter her happiness. Not enough fear to negate the wonder at how lovely the world could be when you are filled with the glow of love for another human being, and the indescribable joy at the discovery of that love.

"I thought we were trying to play things cool," she scolded him thinly, unable to hide the smile in her voice, and in her heart, at the mere thought of him. Not only was she not prepared for his abruptness, but her upbeat mood suddenly went kaput. Her free hand instantly clutched at her waist, in a feeble attempt to keep her insides from completely sinking to the floor.

"Elaine," Jack's voice was flat, and his appeal was direct, "we need to talk. Please. The police were here, at my house, for a couple of hours this morning. I'm pretty sure they think I killed Craig. At least they sounded like they were trying to build a case against me. I need your clear thinking to help me work through this. I can't do it alone," he admitted, to himself as much as to Elaine. "When can you leave work?"

As hard as Jack had tried, he couldn't hide the tension that had been building in him since shortly after the police had arrived, and he had figured out what they seemed to be trying to do. Not that he thought they were constructing a false case.

Detective Marsh just seemed to seriously believe that somehow Jack was involved in Craig's death, and he was trying to figure out just how. His instinctive understanding that Elaine's company would help settle him enough so that he could think more clearly made Jack realize how much he had let Elaine into his world, in spite of the short time they had known each other. He was discovering that he didn't feel really whole when she wasn't around.

The night before had been a very long, and very lonely, evening, despite all the work he had to do, and had actually accomplished. Somehow those accomplishments were no longer enough to ground him. When he had finished the special edition of his blog, he found himself wishing Elaine had been there to share in his revels. Somehow, knowing within himself what he had accomplished, was no longer enough.

Relief flooded through Elaine when she realized that Jack's shortness with her had nothing to do with any diminished feelings for her. Her attraction to Jack had made her world quite fragile. She discovered that her equilibrium could be shattered in an instant. Then a rush of guilt ran through her as she recognized that her relief had come at Jack's expense. She had to put her own concerns aside, so she could help him in whatever way he needed, regardless of his feelings for her, or any changes in them. She owed him that much for being so fair—actually, way more than just fair—in his quest about the photos.

"I'll be right over, Jack! Don't worry! We'll figure this out together...see you in a few minutes," Elaine consoled. And in a flash, she had grabbed her coat and bag, and flew out the door.

Though she had taken a taxi to Jack's, Elaine was breathless when she arrived. Every nerve in her body was on fire. How could Detective Marsh *possibly* think Jack could do anything like kill someone, her mind was raging. Honestly! Obviously, it did not occur to Elaine that, having known Jack for barely one week, how could *she* be so positive about what he might, or might not, be capable of?

As she ran up Jack's front steps, his door opened. He had been watching for her from his front parlor window.

"Oh, Jack!" was all she could muster before she flung herself into his open arms. Clearly, it had felt the natural thing to do. For both of them. For a long moment they just stood there clinging to each other in the open doorway, savoring this moment of bonding, even though it had been triggered by a dangerous threat. Their very acquaintance, however, had been triggered by a dangerous threat. In this moment, they were acknowledging where they were, and where they had come from. And now, where they were likely going.

Jack gently released Elaine, then turned so they could both go inside. Once the door was closed, they hugged again for a moment, and then Elaine asked the critical question, "What on earth happened this morning?!" She was relieved when Jack's first reaction was a soft chuckle.

"Well, I guess I'm not the only one who gets right to the point when needed!" he remarked, alluding to his awareness of his own earlier bluntness. But he had been right to call her, and to ask her to come over. His unease following the Detective's departure was already dissipating. He could feel his 'normal' self regaining the upper hand.

He gestured her toward the kitchen with, "I've got hot water boiling. Want some tea?"

"Yes, please," Elaine smiled, as she doffed her coat and hung it over the back of one of the chairs. "And if you have anything to munch on, I would be most appreciative...I haven't eaten since breakfast, and it's almost 4 pm."

"How about a grilled cheese with tomato?" Jack smiled.

"Perfect!" Elaine beamed back at him. "And while you are making one for each of us...I don't like eating alone...you can fill me in on this morning's visit from the police. I want to know every detail, and every word."

"Yes, Ma'am!" and Jack saluted. But he wasn't mocking her, just trying to lighten the moment. The story would get heavy enough, and quickly enough.

"Well," he started, "I guess the first indication that I was...am...in trouble, was the warrant the Detective brought so that he could search my home and office."

"What?!" Elaine was genuinely shocked. "A warrant?! Oh my goodness! Why would he think he needed to search your place, and that he would need a warrant to do so?"

"Well, I guess he brought it so that there could be no problems or delays. I'm not sure what he was looking for, but...here's the rub...he wanted the files I asked Craig last Friday to verify."

There was a moment of silence that hung so heavily neither of them could move, let alone speak. They just stared at each other, Elaine looking up at Jack, Jack stopping in mid-air as he started to pour tea into a mug to give Elaine. When the import of what he said had sunk in, Jack continued.

"Naturally, Detective Marsh asked me why I needed to take the files to Craig for verification, and so I had to tell him the story of how I got these files anonymously, how they purported to represent a political scandal, and how I couldn't publish them until I had determined if they were valid."

As Jack placed a full mug in front of Elaine, and poured one for himself, he, too, sat down at the table, and then continued. "Even when they do figure out you work for Blanchard, there is still nothing to connect Craig's death with her," he affirmed. "I've thought about this very carefully. I just don't see a reason for the police to link the two. It's just a project I was working on, and I asked him to verify some of the information files. And since Craig was murdered *after* the photos went public, what would anyone associated with Blanchard gain by Craig's death?"

"But when they check into the story, learn that Craig validated the photos, and then find a record of the press conference where the photos were discredited," Elaine posited, "the police may construe that you were, maybe, angry with him for what you thought was falsification of his evaluation, which would have eventually destroyed your own credibility, and, hence, your livelihood, had you gone ahead and published them based on his validation."

"Exactly," Jack's response was somber, as he leaned back in his chair. "Only, they've already, apparently, figured out that angle. They've been working very fast on this, even though they are coming to the wrong conclusion," Jack shrugged. "I guess I'm the only one with a credible motive, so far."

"But you didn't have opportunity, Jack! I was with you all night! I'm your alibi!" Elaine was emphatic.

Her words flooded Jack's heart to overflowing. Looking into her eyes, he saw his soulmate. Looking into her eyes, he felt complete. Knowing that, understanding that, relaxed most of the nerves that had been shaken by the Detective's morning visit. But he knew that, right now, he had to focus on the possibility that he could be arrested for murder, so that he—they—could figure out how to prove he was not the culprit.

"You know that, and I know that," he told Elaine, "but, unfortunately, I suspect the police could shoot lots of holes into that alibi. Neither one of us could confirm what the other did, or did not do, when we were asleep," he noted. "I could have left the house, and then returned without you ever knowing, no matter what you say you are certain of.

"Besides, I can't get past the fact that Craig was found in front of my house. I have this nagging notion that someone was trying to set me up for the blame. But I honestly haven't the slightest idea *who* would do that, or *why*. Just like I haven't the slightest prospect for who would kill Craig, to begin with. If I can't think of anyone, I can almost understand why the police are so interested in me as a candidate for the murderer."

That last sentence transfused Elaine's veins with ice water, instead of blood. In her response, she acknowledged the credibility of what Jack had said. "Then we will just have to discover the truth—who *did* kill Craig. That's the only sure fire way, I guess, to convince the police that you are not the murderer. As for Craig being left in front of your house, do you think the person who sent you the photos in the first place could be the person who killed Craig?"

"I am wondering that myself, too, but I'm not sure how we can figure that out. But I have to try."

"You are *not* going to do this alone, Mr. Amory!" Elaine admonished. "We are in this together. After all, once the police figure out the photo issue, Kate will be at risk. Not only her Senate campaign, but her entire professional life could be besmirched beyond rescue."

Chapter 58

"We won't be breaking in...I know where he hides the emergency key!" he coaxed in hushed, but excited, tones. "And the police have removed their crime scene tape, so the building is no longer off limits. I know...I already checked," he tried to hide a somewhat triumphal grin. "Look, if you don't want to go in with me, that's perfectly fine. As a matter of fact, I would prefer you not get involved in this. But I do think you might pick up on something that I wouldn't notice, and vice versa. Between the two of us, we might find something that the police missed,... because they wouldn't have realized it might be important,... because they don't know all that we know."

"Oh, don't worry, I am going in with you, Mr. Detective!" Elaine bluntly informed him. "Besides, you are right. One of us might see something the other would never think was relevant. That's why I insisted that Diggie come with us. He's more likely to pick up on stuff that neither you nor I would. After all, Craig was a computer expert, and Diggie is the best!"

"You what?!" Jack nearly shouted into the dark, forgetting they were outside and how much more readily sound travels in the quiet of night.

"Sshhhhh!" Elaine admonished. "They'll be here in just a minute."

"*They*?!" Jack could not believe what he was hearing. "What do you think this is?!" he asked, his voice reminiscent of terror-filled sound effects from a Stephen King movie. "We're not going to an amusement park, you know! It's not a case of 'the more, the merrier'! It's more like, 'the more, the greater the risk of getting caught'," Jack tried to discourage her.

"But you said we're not breaking the law, because you have a key," Elaine pointed out, her eyes wide and round. "Besides, Caroline was with Diggie when I told him about our plans, and she insisted on coming, too. She argued that it's her mother's career that's at stake." Half smiling, Elaine added with a knowing, and pleased, chuckle, "You know, I think she and Diggie have just become inseparable these past few days." In her mind, she added to herself, 'Just like you and I.' Out loud again, she commented, "I'm so happy for them both. Goodness! It's taken them long enough to discover their mutual attraction!"

"Oh, fiddlesticks!" Jack was exasperated at having been caught by his own words, as he noticed Diggie and Caroline strolling purposefully towards them.

Elaine had returned to her office to close out her work for the day, when Jack had called her with his "brilliant" idea. By the time she met him back at his house again, it was dark outside. Elaine and Jack had walked to the corner of Craig's street, where he could only relent to the additional companions, knowing that he would never win the argument to leave Diggie and Caroline behind once they had arrived. On that note, the four headed down the street to Craig's house.

True to his words, Jack moved aside the proverbial pot at the bottom of the steps, and picked up a rather large old-fashioned key that had been comfortably ensconced underneath. As he started to straighten up, he suddenly stopped. He noticed another object under the pot, and discovered that the key he already grabbed had had company in its bungalow. He quickly bent down again to seize the other object. Holding it up so that some light from the nearby street lamp could reflect off of it, Jack found he had retrieved a second key, about a third of the size of the larger one, and more rounded in form.

He beamed at Elaine to flaunt his success. But in the dark, his triumphal grin remained hidden.

"Did you drop the key?" Elaine asked when she saw Jack bend over a second time. "I didn't hear anything fall."

"No," he replied slowly, as he turned to show her the two keys.

"Two of them?" Elaine asked, with wonder.

"Yes. Two keys. I know the black iron one is the front door key. I can't imagine any front door lock having a key as small as this other one, though," Jack observed.

Then Caroline chimed in with, "That looks just like my cash box key! When I do craft shows to sell my handmade

266

jewelry, I bring a small, metal, cash box with me. That key you have looks just like the one for my cash box."

And when Jack replied excitedly with "You're a genius, Caroline!", it was Diggie who was beaming then.

"That means," Elaine emphasized, "that there must be something important hidden in the house. But, what?"

"You are exactly right!" Jack was becoming hopeful. "Maybe there is something important that the police missed, something that could explain Craig's murder, and reveal his murderer. The police obviously didn't know there was a spare house key under this pot, or I'm sure they would have seized it —along with this other key."

"Are we just going to stand here, and analyze, all night?" Diggie asked, getting a little nervous that a neighbor might see them outside Craig's and call the police. "Or are we going to go inside, and search for this important piece of information?"

"Wait a minute," Elaine insisted, in a forceful whisper. She pulled out a handful of loose pieces that seemed soft and flappy from her jacket pocket, and started handing them around to everyone. "Here, put these plastic gloves on. We don't want to contaminate anything in case the police decide to return, and we don't want to leave any of our own fingerprints, either, I would expect."

"Oh, so clever, Elaine, to think of that," gushed Caroline.

As they all started to tiptoe up the front steps, Diggie couldn't help asking "Why do I feel like I'm in a *Scooby Doo* cartoon?"

"Because you are!" Caroline giggled, as she closed the front door behind them.

"Now, don't turn on any lights," Jack whispered, as they moved from the foyer into the living room, which sat to the left of the entrance.

"How are we supposed to see anything if we don't turn a light on?" Elaine asked the obvious.

"Do you have your cell phones with you?" Jack inquired. "In case you've never used it, there should be a flashlight app on your cell phone. Keep the light aimed down, though, so no one outside will notice any movement of light," Jack admonished.

"You know," and there was a laugh in Elaine's voice, even as she shivered a little, "you're right about the Scooby Doo cartoon, Diggie!"

"Sshhhhh...!" it was Jack's turn to give a warning hush, raising a finger to his lips, but he could not fully stifle the chuckle her analogy brought to mind. "I actually love Scooby Doo," he whispered. "Maybe, when this is over, we can binge watch a bunch of them," he suggested in a whisper, close to Elaine's ear, hoping only she could hear his invitation.

"Well, I just learned something new about you, Mr. Amory! How interesting. Hhmmmm."

He stopped, then, in the middle of the living room, and, looking straight into her eyes, which reflected the moonlight that was shining through the window, he said with a determined single-mindedness, "There are a lot of things you don't know about me, Ms. Kent. And I intend to make sure that you learn every last one of them," he threatened.

"*Every* one?" she countered, with another low chuckle. "And just how long would that take, Mr. Amory?" she challenged him.

"Ok," he paused. "Maybe not *every* one...but *most* of them!" he shot back, with a half smile. "C'mon, let's do our search," he then instructed. Before I stick my other foot in my mouth, he warned himself.

Diggie and Caroline just looked at each other and rolled their eyes, as if acknowledging that wayward children were in the vicinity, as they all spread out to get a closer look at the life Craig had lost. The foursome roamed around the ground floor and the two upstairs floors at will, looking for anything that might explain Craig's death. They each also kept a keen eye out for anything that the small key might fit.

"Hey, Jack," Diggie whispered as they all regrouped in the living room, full of disappointment at nothing jumping out at them to explain the previous day's event, "do you know where this fellow kept his computers? I didn't notice any, not even a laptop, on this floor or upstairs. Didn't you say he worked from home?"

"Yes, I did, and yes, he did. Well, the only other option would be the basement," Jack suggested. "Check in the kitchen for a stairway down. I've never been down there myself."

About one whole minute later, Diggie came racing back up the stairs, and through the kitchen, whispering excitedly, "Hey, All, you've gotta come and see what's downstairs! C'mon!"

It was, indeed, a classic scene from a *Scooby Doo*, with the four of them in single file, tiptoeing down the stairs to the lower level. "Oh, my goodness!" came from Elaine. "What on earth...?" was Caroline's unfinished question...unfinished because everyone understood just what she was alluding to. While "Wow!" accompanied a low whistle from Jack.

"Yeah! Exactly!" Diggie acknowledged, in a quietly audible whisper. "This is one powerful setup! Even I don't have all this stuff in my own home! Look over here! A 3D printer—state of the art!" And after a moment, Diggie remembered, "Jack. Didn't you say the weapon was a handgun printed out on a 3D printer?"

"Yup. Do you suppose it was printed here?" Then Jack wrinkled his nose in uncertainty, as he wondered out loud, "Would Craig print out the very weapon used to kill him? That doesn't make much sense. Unless he used it to commit suicide —which I don't believe for a nano second. Hhmmmm," he drifted off into deeper thought, as he slowly walked around the lower level. With all this equipment down here, he reasoned, maybe the secret box this key belongs to is here, too.

Then came a surprising observation from Diggie. "Hey, there are no hard drives in the five desk tops. That's weird."

But Jack explained that "maybe the police removed them during their search...so they can examine them later."

"Wouldn't they just take all the computers?" Diggie was skeptical.

"Not if they were in a hurry," Jack reasoned.

Then another revelation from Diggie. "There's no laptop down here, either, or at least I can't find one. Anyone else see one?"

"Not me," Jack admitted, as did Elaine and Caroline.

"That's crummy! We can't check for a matching IP address on a laptop if we can't find the laptop," Diggie exhaled with exasperation.

"Oh, crap!" Caroline suddenly shrieked, a little too loudly, becoming the center of attention. "Oh, don't you all look at me like that!" she commanded, in a more subdued tone. "I just stubbed my toe on something, that's all." In a split second, three cell phones lit the floor near Caroline, who had one leg bent so she could bring her foot up to her other knee and massage her injured toe.

"What are you doing wearing open-toed shoes in the winter, anyway, Caroline?" only Elaine could get away with asking. The two men exchanged a fleeting glance that might have said "Women!" Then, as Elaine looked more closely at the floor she noticed a slight bump in the woven carpet. She moved slowly, almost transfixed by her discovery, but leery that it could be a small snake, or something equally nasty, hiding under the carpet. They were, after all, in the basement, however sophisticated and polished Craig had made it.

Elaine bent down to examine the protuberation more closely, reaching for it with her hand.

"What are you doing?" Jack asked.

"Look at this," Elaine instructed. "It's hard. And I can put my fingers around it, but I can't quite grab hold of it," she lamented.

"Ok, let's lift the carpet and see what it is. I wouldn't be surprised if it's just a stray cat toy that got pushed under there, and never got found."

"Does he have a cat?" Caroline was instantly compassionate.

"He did. Not any more. It passed away about a year ago. Craig was crushed. That cat had been his companion for over ten years. It was roaming the streets around here, apparently, and decided he wanted to live with Craig. I guess the cat could see through Craig's standoffishness, to the human being that he was."

"Then he can't have been all bad," Caroline observed. "Cats have uncanny instincts when it comes to reading people."

Jack and Diggie had cleared away the few objects that anchored that end of the carpet to the floor, and with a "Heave ho!" from Jack, they lifted one side of the floor covering, and threw it over the other half of it, revealing...

"Oh my!" Elaine exclaimed.

"Bingo!" Diggie was excited. "It's a lid! There must be some kind of secret chamber under this level!"

"Look! There's a lock on the lid!" Jack could hardly contain himself. "I wonder..." and he took the small key from his jacket pocket, bent down, and...click. He looked up with surprise, and expectation, at his compatriots, who stood there wide-eyed and essentially speechless, as they stared down at him. Then he hooked his fingers around the stubby metal knob that had lain hidden beneath the carpet, and lifted.

There was a hissing sound as they all sucked in so much air at once that the basement became almost devoid of oxygen.

"Oh, my goodness! Look at that! I can't believe it!" Elaine scrunched down with her knees, and stretched her hand to reach into the chasm.

"Don't touch it!" Jack ordered. "Don't touch anything!" Elaine stopped her hand in mid-air, suspended about an inch above the top photo, and looked questioningly up at Jack. "It could be evidence," Jack's voice had grown serious.

"But I've got my surgical gloves on," Elaine appealed to him.

"I don't care. We shouldn't alter anything. It's obvious this could be really important, so I suggest we call Detective Marsh, and let him and his folks unravel whatever is in there. How could they have missed this? I can't imagine they would have left it if they had found this cache."

"I guess none of the police were wearing open-toed shoes!" Caroline giggled nervously as she tried to lighten the mood, and regain some of the composure she had lost after their devastating discovery.

271

"Look underneath!" Diggie directed, stretching out his arm and pointing his finger, without touching anything. "You can see the edge of a laptop under the spread of photos. I'm not a betting person, but I would bet lots and lots of money, that that computer will show the construction of the photos of Mrs. Blanchard that Anonymous sent you, Jack."

"Don't touch it, Diggie," Jack said ominously.

"Couldn't we just check the IP address? What if it's also the computer that hacked into your system, and sent out that phony special edition of your blog? Can't we just check that?" Diggie pleaded. "We've got our gloves on," he cajoled.

Jack let out a long, deep breath. It would be so easy to just dive into all the goodies Craig had stored in this hidden locker below his basement floor. It could answer so many questions. Maybe all of them. But this was deadly serious, no pun intended, he told himself.

"No, we shouldn't touch anything," he finally said aloud.

"But..." Elaine and Caroline started in unison.

"No 'buts'. Look, I know this could be devastating for your mom, Caroline. But we are dealing with murder here. Not to mention that yours truly appears to be a prime suspect." And at the sign of more efforts to protest, Jack held up his hand. "No, I know what you are going to say, believe me. But this isn't about just political skulduggery to win an election. It's about someone who has lost his life. And whatever this stuff says about what he did in that life, I had always known him as a decent person who, like all of us, was just trying to build the best life for himself that he was capable of. If he strayed from the straight and narrow, he's obviously paid dearly for it. No. It's time to call Detective Marsh. Or do I have to remind you all that, if this is relevant evidence, we could be charged with tampering with evidence, or obstructing a criminal investigation, if we somehow mess this stuff up?" Then it was his turn to try to lighten the mood with, "Haven't any of you learned anything from *NCIS,* or whatever police procedure TV series you gobble up?"

The others were all silent, humbled by Jack's words, even in the face of the possibility that Craig had done something horrific to another human being. And who, it now became plausible, may have lost his life because of what he did. It was no longer just about political chicanery. It was about a serious crime. It was about someone's life. It was about murder.

Suddenly the basement in Craig's house was flooded with light. Still enthralled by Jack's words, and too startled to be frightened, they looked toward the top of the stairs that led to the first floor, and found themselves staring into the stern and disapproving face of Detective Marsh. In a coldly calm, but raspy, voice, as if his mouth were as dry as sandpaper, Detective Marsh asked what they were doing, breaking into Craig's house, as he slowly descended the stairs, followed by two uniformed police officers.

"Oh, but we didn't break in, Detective Marsh," Jack contradicted. "You forget, I'm...was...a friend of Craig's," and then smiling brightly, added, "so I know where he kept his spare key!"

"But you are not here at Mr. Bittiford's invitation," Detective Marsh pushed his charge of breaking in.

"Oh, but yes we are," Jack insisted. "The fact that Craig told me where his spare key is constitutes an open invitation."

"Hhmmmm," the Detective muttered. "We'll let that hang in the air for a moment. Why don't you tell me why you decided to 'visit' Craig this evening, of all evenings?" And then, acknowledging the gloves they were wearing, "Did you come to make sure the police had cleaned up any mess they might have made in their search of the premises?"

The others were all only too willing to let Jack take the lead in answering Detective Marsh's questions.

"Really, Detective," Jack sounded a little sardonic. "No," came out in a more respectful tone, "we just thought we might find something that the police may not have noticed. I mean, I knew Craig, and Diggie, here, shares the computer profession with him, so we thought we might pick up on things the police may have just not noticed."

"It looks like you have, indeed, found something, at any rate," the Detective indicated their discovery under the floorboards.

"Yes!" Caroline chimed in, her voice reflecting that she was feeling a bit nervous. "Isn't it lucky that I wear open-toed shoes?"

Elaine decided she had better make the introductions. "This is Caroline Blanchard, Detective Marsh. She is my boss's daughter. And Diggie—Gregory Kent—is my brother. He, too, is a computer engineer, and a rather brilliant one, if I do say so myself. Perhaps he can help the police evaluate whatever is on the computer in that storage space?" Elaine queried.

"I guess we need to explain to you what that stuff appears to mean," Jack added.

"Maybe we should take this down to the station," Detective Marsh stated.

"Please, Detective. Some of this is politically very sensitive, if the stuff in that hole is what we all think it is. Can we just go to my house, since it's just a few blocks away, and discuss all this there?" Jack requested politely.

Chapter 59

They were all huddled around the coffee table in Jack's living room, drinking their beverages of choice. Given the atypically small size of Jack's house, it was a cozy grouping, even though the two uniformed officers had returned to the police station. Before leaving Craig's, however, the Detective had recalled the forensics team to Craig's, to deal with the basement discovery, including copying everything on the computer to a flash drive, which the Detective took with him to Jack's in case they could enlighten him about any of the data it contained.

A neighbor of Craig's had called the police because, upon arriving home, he had seen flashes, or dashes, of light through various windows as the visitors explored Craig's house. Knowing that Craig had been murdered made those light sparks suspicious. The officer who had taken the call about possible intruders, alerted Detective Marsh when he heard the address involved. So Detective Marsh had arrived in time to overhear the discussion in Craig's basement, after the foursome had discovered the underground stash. His instincts, after listening in, told him that, perhaps, or maybe even probably, Jack was not the murderer. But clearly, these four knew a lot that could be quite pertinent, and he wanted to know everything they knew. They had, after all, made an astounding discovery of information.

"Ok," Detective Marsh opened the discussion, "I want you to tell me everything that you have withheld from me, and what the stuff in Bittiford's basement means to you. And then we'll go from there...wherever 'there' is. We've confirmed now that the hidden laptop has the IP address of a computer you were all interested in finding. So, let's have the full story, please."

Jack led the response, telling the Detective about the anonymous photos, and his pursuit of the truth about them. The others piped in with comments, as appropriate, but they were more than happy to let Jack be the lead storyteller. After all, it was his receipt of the photos that started the events of the past week, and the only link that might hint at an explanation for why Craig was found in front of his home.

"I'm as perplexed as you all are about why Bittiford was killed, and why he ended up where he did," the Detective observed.

Diggie saw an opening and jumped in with, "Detective, if you would let me examine what was on the computer we found, that might help figure things out. It looks like Craig is the one who developed the scandal photos, and that he is the one who hacked into Jack's computer and sent out that bogus edition of his blog. I don't know why he tried to use Jack as the vehicle for publicizing the photos, but if we could confirm that it was, or wasn't him, behind this scam, that would help a lot in figuring out what came after."

Detective Marsh reached into his pocket and held up the flash drive with the download from the laptop they had found at Craig's. "Ok, genius. Can we take a look at this content right now, here?"

"Oh, yes!" Diggie was excited as he reached into his backpack and pulled out one of his own laptops. He reached for the flash drive, and in a tease, the Detective pulled it out of Diggie's reach, but just for a second, before he handed it over to him.

Diggie's nerves were on edge as he plugged the flash drive into his computer. His knees were bouncing up and down, as if he had an agitated tick, while his fingers were zipping across his keyboard. An abnormal silence permeated Jack's living room, with everyone almost afraid to breathe while they all sat there expectantly, waiting for who knew what. Finally, after what felt like hours, but in reality was only about ten minutes, Diggie looked up and around the room, then sank back into the sofa where he was seated.

Then he began. "Craig definitely is the one who created those photos. Or, at least, whoever that computer belongs to, is the one who created the photos."

For a moment, the strained silence returned. Then Elaine posed the obvious question, in a very soft voice, "Why?" and all eyes aimed at Diggie.

"Well, I can't tell you why!" he exclaimed. "I can only tell you that the files from that computer contain the construction files for creation of the photos." Then, a little sheepishly, he admitted, "But I was off on the actual number of times he reproduced the photos to dull the evidence of their construction. I thought it was nineteen, but based on these files, it was actually twenty."

"Oh, my goodness!" Caroline finally recovered from her stupor, to tease Diggie, and in the process bring everyone else back to life, or reality. "Fire the man! He made a mistake! He can't count right!" Though her laughter brought a full blush to Diggie's cheeks, he had become confident enough about their mutual attraction, that he laughed along with her instead of withdrawing into a shell at being the brunt of her joke. Elaine was amazed, but also so proud and happy for both of them.

Jack sat there shaking his head. "I can't believe he would do something like that. I just can't." And more head shaking, then, "Why? Why did he care about Kate Blanchard's campaign? And why would he try to palm the story off on *me?* He could have ruined me professionally if I had published the photos after he told me they were genuine." After a pause, and with still more head shaking, "I just can't believe it. I don't understand it."

"Well, you better believe it," Diggie admonished him, "because I'm not lying about this. I *am* assuming this is his computer, since we not only found it at his house, but found it locked up and hidden. And he was certainly clever enough to have concocted these kinds of phony photos."

The room was quiet for a moment, until the sound of the Detective's deep and somber voice broke that silence.

"You realize, don't you, Mr. Amory, that you now have a singularly monumental motive for killing Craig?"

Chapter 60

Jack could feel the blood rushing through his veins up to his face. And he could feel the heat turning his face a deep red. He opened his mouth to respond to the Detective's allegation, but his voice was trapped in his throat. The only sound that escaped was the sound someone might make when they are being strangled.

Elaine recovered from the shock of the Detective's words before Jack did. "You've got to be *crazy*!" were the first words out of her mouth, as she stared at Detective Marsh with horror written all over her face. Her shriek, however, was enough to break through Jack's momentary stupor.

"I didn't kill Craig!" Jack burst out. "I would never...I couldn't! Besides, until this moment I had no idea Craig was the one who created those photos, or had any other part in this fiasco!" And, as if the outburst helped settle Jack's nerves, he was able to add, "You'll have to find someone else to pin this on because it wasn't me. Clearly, he obviously had a grudge, or he wouldn't have tried to make me the patsy. But I have no idea what that grudge was, or might be. And it would never have occurred to me that he would do anything as unethical as what he has apparently done!"

As Jack started to think more clearly again, he added, "There must be someone else involved in this photo scheme. And, for some reason, turned on Craig. But I can't even begin to think who might be in cahoots with him, let alone who, for whatever reason, would have killed Craig." As he exhaled after this stream of thought, Jack sank back into his sofa, his face still revealing the evening's shocks.

"Most other detectives," Detective Marsh began, "at this point, would call this an open and shut case, and arrest you, Mr. Amory. Fortunately, I overheard your discussion when you opened that basement hideaway, and somehow I'm not convinced you are the murderer—at least, not yet." The momentary sense of relief that pervaded the room was eclipsed by that last phrase.

"But," the Detective continued, "he was found in front of your home. And I am at a loss for any other person who might have a motive for killing Bittiford. Not to imply we won't find one once we have gone through his other computer files. The problem is, the hard drives for the other computers down there were missing, so..."

"What?" Diggie interrupted, not sure he heard correctly. "You mean, the police weren't the ones who removed the hard drives from the desk tops?"

"That's right. There were no hard drives in those computers when we went through his house late Friday. It's possible, then, that something on those other computers might indicate another motive for killing him, and, hence, another killer."

"Then who has the hard drives?" Diggie wondered. "Did the police specifically look through the house for the hard drives, Detective? Were they in the hideaway under the floorboards?"

"There is no sign of them anywhere in the house," Detective Marsh sighed again.

"Tell me, did your people check already to see if Bittiford's 3D printer printed out a handgun?" Diggie asked.

"Yes. And yes. The memory bank of the printer indicates one was printed out on Thursday evening, late, sometime around midnight. Also, a silencer. The software files, though, were not retained. Maybe that's why the hard drives are missing from the desk tops, and the killer just didn't think to clear the memory of the printer."

"Wow!" Jack whistled. "Was he shot in his car after he parked in front of my house? Or was he just moved here after he was shot? A silencer would explain why he could have been killed after he got in his car, and even, after he parked in front of my house..."

"But didn't you say he was in the driver's seat?" Caroline asked. "How could someone convince him to drive here, only so they could shoot him? Maybe his location really was serendipity. Maybe it has nothing to do with Jack. Yet, how could someone else drive the car here, and then get him to move to the driver's seat, and then shoot him?"

"Those are very good questions, Miss Blanchard," Detective Marsh observed. "Unfortunately, we don't have the answers yet."

"Detective Marsh," Elaine interjected, "what if...I mean,...suppose...just suppose, that someone who opposed Congresswoman Blanchard was somehow linked up with Craig in all of this business? Could someone else have hired Craig, or maybe cajoled him into helping with this project? I mean, why would Craig want to hurt Kate Blanchard? What could he possibly have against her? I don't think he even knew her. Was someone paying him to hurt Kate? I can't believe he had any personal animosity towards her. I mean, he's never crossed our radar,...so why would he have done this?"

"More good questions, for which I have yet no answers," Detective Marsh sighed.

"You don't know this yet, but Kate's opponent in the election bugged her Capitol Hill Office and her Capitol Hill home," Elaine revealed to Marsh.

"Excuse me?"

Elaine hurried to explain. "We didn't report it to the police because we were able to resolve the intrusions quietly. He admitted to being behind it. His nephew, who is interning on the Hill right now, like Caroline, actually placed the bugs. Kate preferred to confront Billingsley directly about stopping his surveillance, once we had proof positive he was behind it."

"When was this?" the Detective asked.

"Just this past week, actually. He met with Kate on Thursday evening here in D.C., and when she placed the evidence before him, he caved. He said he would stop. But he was emphatic about not being behind the photo scandal effort." Then, in a flat voice, Elaine added, "We believed him. Maybe we were wrong to accept his disclaimer?" she looked at the Detective questioningly.

But before Detective Marsh could process and respond to this thunderbolt of information, Jack commented thoughtfully, "You know, maybe there is more to Craig's meeting with Lowell last Saturday evening than we realized."

"What do you mean?" the Detective wanted elaboration.

"Well, Lowell is one of the three men pictured in bed with Representative Blanchard in those scandal photos," he explained.

"Maybe he is just a victim in this, as well," Detective Marsh suggested.

"It's possible," Jack agreed. "But he and the other two lobbyists in the photos found a powerful opponent in Blanchard, practically from day one of her arrival in Congress. She does her homework, so she has very successfully thwarted most of the proposals on their collective legislative agendas. They don't necessarily work together, but they are often on the same side of an issue—the side which Blanchard just happens to oppose. As a Senator, she'd have much greater impact on legislation, so perhaps they were making their contribution to her election failure, for their own benefits."

"Well, now, that's a thought," Marsh noted. "Maybe Bittiford got cold feet after the photos failed to cause the kind of political damage expected. So maybe they thought they needed to silence him before he spilled the beans about their own involvement. And trying to throw the blame on you was just a way of deflecting attention from themselves."

To reinforce the storyline, Jack added that "they did not deny the alleged affairs when the photos went public. Why wouldn't they, if they really had nothing to do with it? Their non-denial lent some credibility to the existence of the affairs. They expressed no shock, or even surprise, at the allegations. It's almost as if they welcomed the scandal."

"And that might explain why they showed up en masse at last Monday's fundraiser! What if they already knew about the photos?!" A light bulb was flaring in Elaine's head. "They know she doesn't accept contributions from lobbyists on any side of an issue, yet they showed up, and paid $1000 a piece to be there! And they posed for a journalist's photo when they were talking with her in the reception line!"

"Well, now we may be getting somewhere. That's two lines of inquiry worth pursuing. They both would seem to check a lot of the boxes," Detective Marsh noted. Then he added, with a rueful chuckle, "Maybe even more boxes than you check as a suspect," and he almost half-smiled at Jack.

"Who knows," Elaine observed hopefully, "maybe those two lines of inquiry, as you call them, will turn out to be actually two parts of the same line."

Chapter 61

It was nearly 2 a.m. Sunday morning when the party finally broke up. Diggie left with Caroline to make sure she got home safely. Jack offered to drive them all, but Diggie and Caroline wanted to walk. "More time alone, and together," Elaine quietly observed to him.

"And that, my dear, also means more time for you and me—alone, and together," he spoke softly, hoping he sounded at least a little bit seductive, so that she would read the invitation in his heart and his words.

"Yes," she shrugged, "if only it weren't already early Sunday morning, and Congress didn't have a vote scheduled for 11 a.m." The smile on her face, and in her eyes, belied the rejection.

"Ever the pragmatic," Jack teased, as they headed out the door.

"Well, I do have to pay my mortgage, and my grocery bill, and my...well, you get the picture." Then, after a pause, "But if Kate loses this election, I'm going to have to find another way to pay all those bills." Before Jack could react, she grabbed her jacket, looped her arm through Jack's, and bid him "take me home, Sir Galahad! I have to get up in a couple of hours!"

"Any indication of whether Congress will adjourn tomorrow...uh...later today?"

"We can only hope. There's only three votes scheduled today, and I understand the intention is to adjourn, but you know as well as I do, that anything can happen until the gavel actually bangs adjournment.

"Anyway," Elaine continued, "with all this stuff going on about Craig, and not knowing what it means in terms of negative publicity, Kate has not yet taped that campaign message for tonight. And she's so busy today until they adjourn, assuming they do, that I can't see her taping anything that could be ready to air this evening."

"Well, that's quite understandable. It's probably a good idea to hold off in case something breaks later today, so that she can address whatever issues are in the public domain.

She might even consider doing it live...and possibly waiting until tomorrow evening. That way she could be sure of addressing whatever the most current and pressing issues are."

"I think you are right. As a matter of fact, I will suggest that to her as soon as I get into the office," Elaine declared.

Jack shut his car engine off in front of Elaine's home, and turned to her, slipping his arm across the back of her seat so that they could share an embrace, something he'd been wanting to do since they had met to go explore Craig's house. At the end of their kiss, he held her a moment longer in his gaze, just staring at her, so that he could memorize the loving expression on her face.

"Are you sure you wouldn't like me to come in?" he asked hopefully.

She replied gently, "There will be time for us when all this other crap is resolved. I think we're both riding on adrenalin until we get some answers. I'll let you know what Kate decides about the campaign message, and if we need to rewrite it, or whatever."

"You're the boss. But I want you to know now," he commented softly, "I could sit here looking at you forever. I've never understood before how a person could become so mesmerized by another that all they could think of was that other person. But with you, it's as if you have infused my entire being with your soul, and when we are not together, I am not whole. And that's not going to change, no matter what happens."

Elaine was so overwhelmed by this exposure of his feelings that, for a moment, she couldn't speak. Was her attraction to him as powerful as Jack had just declared his to be to her? Could she honestly make a similar declaration? Would she be true to her heart if she did? She had never felt the depth of attachment that she had developed for Jack. But they had come together so quickly that there was a nagging fear in the back of her mind that the feelings of one, or both, of them might not be solid enough to survive once the crises they were dealing with were resolved. In her heart, she believed their bond would more than survive—it would thrive.

But her head was sending shivers of doubt through her that she had not yet been able to squash.

Chapter 62

The phone in her office rang a little before noon. Her heart felt suddenly light when Caller ID indicated it was Jack. Nevertheless, she was surprised he was calling so early, because they had arranged to meet for supper that evening, after what Elaine hoped would be the vote to adjourn. They had thought they could have a special dinner, just the two of them, to at least celebrate the absence of one of the many distractions they were coping with.

"Hi!" Elaine's greeting was happy, but exposed her surprise.

"Hi, yourself," Jack replied. "Um, can you stop by my house right about now—um, just for a few minutes. I know you must be racing around just about now, but I think it best for you to come to my place," and he paused, before adding enigmatically, "rather than have the police come to your office for a visit."

"Ok," Elaine went into crisis mode, "what's going on, Jack?"

"Well, Detective Marsh is here right now, with another officer who takes finger prints. They found two sets of prints on the hidden laptop we found at Craig's. One set belongs to Craig, but the other set is unknown. Diggie's prints are on file because of his security clearance, but they couldn't find prints for me, you, or Caroline. So you need to bring Caroline with you, too."

"Does he still think you—or any of us, for that matter—had something to do with Craig's death?!" Elaine was exasperated.

"Well, I'm not sure what he thinks, but I do understand their need to cross all the t's and dot all the i's. They have prints that they cannot identify the owner of. We are players in this case, so I can see how they would want to at least eliminate us. None of us touched the laptop, so there shouldn't be a problem. I just thought—and the Detective was most cooperative about this—that it would be better to get your prints, and Caroline's, here at my house, rather than have the police visit you two at Blanchard's office."

Elaine sighed. "You are right, of course. We shall both be there in a few minutes. We'll hop a cab. See you." And she hung up the phone.

Jack opened his front door for them as they emerged from the taxi. As they got to the top step, Elaine heard someone call her name, so she and Caroline both turned back toward the sidewalk, and they were hit with the momentary blindness caused when someone aims a camera flash in your eyes. By the time the spots disappeared enough for all three of them, all anyone could see was a man in a dark jacket running down the street and turning the corner.

"What could that have been about?" Elaine asked in an agitated voice.

"I'm not sure," Jack answered, as his glance spread around to check out anything else that might be strange in the vicinity of his home. "One thing, for sure, someone just took a photograph of, apparently, all three of us. I wonder why."

They found Detective Marsh waiting for them inside, along with his colleague who would be recording their finger prints.

"Thank you both for coming here," Detective Marsh greeted them.

"No problem," Elaine assured him. "It was good of you to let us come here, rather than for you and your force to descend on Representative Blanchard's office," she added graciously.

The Detective acknowledged their appreciation, then introduced them to Officer Sanchez. "He'll take your prints, and then you can get back to your busy lives."

While their prints were being digitally scanned, Detective Marsh asked no one in particular what their beverage of choice was. "Coffee? Tea?" he inquired.

"Tea," Elaine and Jack replied, nearly in unison, though the expressions on both their faces showed they thought it was a weird question.

"Would you like some, Detective?" Jack graciously offered his guest.

"No. No, thanks. I was just wondering. What about you, Miss?" he aimed his question at Caroline, who had remained silent.

"Who? Me?" she seemed startled at being singled out. "Why, no. I mean, I'm not much of a coffee drinker. I guess my preferred beverage is a soda, preferably cold."

"What? No one here likes hot chocolate?" Marsh tried to make a joke of it.

"Well, yes," Elaine admitted, "especially in the winter. But only if it's made from scratch, and not an instant mix. Those mixes aren't any good. They don't really have any substance in them."

"When was the last time you had some?" Marsh inquired innocently.

Elaine kind of shook her head a little in wonderment. "Not for a while, I don't think. Certainly not since this scandal first broke. Who's had time to fix any?"

"Who, indeed?" the Detective observed.

"Wait a minute," Jack interjected. "What's all this interest in our favorite go-to beverages? What does that have to do with all this crap that's been going on?"

"It has a great deal to do with Craig's murder," the Detective elaborated. "Craig's body had a very high level of barbiturates in him. Phenobarbital, to be exact. Not enough to kill him, but enough to make him very drowsy. He ingested it with some hot cocoa."

"Wow!" Another near unison response, this time from all three of them.

Again, Jack was putting the pieces together, "Does that mean Craig couldn't have driven the car over here?"

"That's exactly what that means," Detective Marsh was emphatic. "It also means he must have been moved into the driver's seat, probably before he was shot but after the car was parked. Someone could have cajoled him into moving, which would be easier to accomplish than moving a dead weight."

"But that means," and Jack was all astonishment, his eyes big and round, "that someone else went to a great deal of trouble to plant Craig in front of my home! Who would do that? Who hates me so much that they wanted to frame me for murder?!"

And another "Who, indeed?" from Detective Marsh.

After Officer Sanchez finished recording Elaine's prints, and as she tried to absorb this new information, she observed that "None of us touched the laptop, you know, so the unknown prints can't be any of ours. But this makes me wonder, if you can share with us, if you've learned anything from any of the other prints you must have found in Craig's house." It had occurred to her that, while Jack's prints were unlikely to be on the hidden laptop, his prints may exist elsewhere in the house since he had visited Craig there many times over the years.

"Are you expecting to know who any of the other prints belong to, Miss Kent?" the Detective asked, understanding exactly what she was concerned about.

"Nnoooo...not really...no one in particular. I was just wondering if you had learned anything useful from them?"

"Well, what I will share with you all is that there were no prints on the desk top computers, or even the keyboards. Not even Craig's. And, of course, his should have been there, wouldn't you think?" he asked innocently.

Jack pounced on that. "What? None? Not even his own? Someone's gone to a lot of trouble on this. It had to be carefully planned, then. Not a spur of the moment kind of thing."

"That's right," Detective Marsh agreed.

Caroline put it all together, though, with "That means someone wiped down the computers! That means there must be an accomplice, who for some reason, decided it was necessary to kill him! That must be who took the hard drives! There must be something incriminating on those drives! Maybe that person was an accomplice, or the reason Craig created those horrible photos, to begin with. And that accomplice would be whoever it was that drove Craig over here to Jack's. It must be whoever's prints are on that laptop that we found under the floor, then."

"It's possible, Miss Blanchard. But that accomplice could be anyone, including any of you in this room."

Caroline really took offense at that suggestion. "You've got to be crazy! Why would any of us want to hurt my Mom?! And none of us is capable of killing! Not even a fly!"

"Really, Miss Blanchard," the Detective was skeptical —and sarcastic. "You've never killed a fly?"

"Well—you know what I mean!" she was irritated. "It's only an expression! But it's meaning is true! And since none of us touched that laptop, it can't be any of us!"

"Ok," the Detective placated Caroline, with a half smile. "I hear you. I was just teasing."

"Detective," Elaine interjected, as she and Caroline were putting their coats on to return to the Hill, "are you getting the prints of the three lobbyists in those photos, as well?"

"Yes, ma'am, we already have. And, yes, we have actually spoken with them all, as well. We've also already spoken to Mr. Ainsworth, and got his prints. And we're also coordinating with the local police in Blanchard's home state to get the finger prints of Mr. Billingsley."

"Oh, wonderful!" she replied. "Thank you! All this must have something to do with one or more of them. The more I think of the lobbyists' conduct, the more I am convinced that they, at least, knew about the photos and contrived how to benefit from them. That makes me believe they are behind the photos, because who else would gain from the scandal, besides Billingsley? And that means we could have been wrong to accept Billingsley's disclaimers. He could very well be in cahoots with them. It's the only thing that makes sense."

Jack asked anxiously—and hopefully, "Can you share with us what you learned from your talks with the lobbyists? Or at least, did you find out why Craig visited Lowell that Saturday evening?"

"Well," Detective Marsh interjected, "I suppose I can tell you that the three of them have an explanation for their conduct. One that doesn't seem to lend itself to murder, though. You won't like it."

"Please?!" Jack pleaded plaintively.

"Ok. Mr. Lowell said that Craig visited him to sell him some information. He said that Craig offered him information that could be very damaging to Rep. Blanchard's Senate campaign. He explained that the damaging information involved him and two other lobbyists, but it wouldn't hurt them at all. Only Blanchard. Lowell paid him $50,000 that night, by check. We confirmed with Craig's bank that Craig deposited a check from Lowell, for that amount, on last Monday morning. It would seem that was the money he used to pay for that engagement ring we found on him. He bought the ring on Tuesday, according to the Jeweler, for eleven thousand dollars." Detective Marsh went quiet for a moment, to let Jack and Elaine process that information.

"But what kind of damaging information?" Elaine finally pursued.

"He brought copies of the photos with him, showed them to Lowell...even leaving a copy of each with him...and told him they were about to be released to the media. He explained that he thought Lowell and his friends would be interested in knowing about them in advance, in case they wanted to somehow use the information for their own benefit."

"Good grief!" was all Elaine could say.

Jack was processing the implications of these revelations a little faster. "Are you saying, then, that you don't think they were involved in the murder? And not even in the initial perpetration of the photo scandal?"

"According to their story, that would be the case. They claim they only decided to use this opportunity that was handed to them on a silver platter, as the expression goes, to help discredit her campaign by simply not denying the affairs. A non-denial is not a lie. That would leave the media unable to confirm a denial from them, thereby causing the media to imply that a non-denial was a confirmation of the affairs. And that would leave the question of the legitimacy of the photos unresolved, perhaps thereby keeping the scandal alive in the media." Into the dumbstruck expressions on all of their faces, he noted, however, "But we are not closing any doors until we know for sure what the facts are," Detective Marsh assured them.

"What swine!" was all Elaine could muster, as she buttoned her coat. Caroline was too numb with horror at such treachery. And Jack could only shake his head in silence, as the Detective, Officer Sanchez, Elaine and Caroline all began their exit.

As she stepped through the door into the cold, Elaine turned to Jack to ask, "There's a vote in the House scheduled for 5:00 p.m., to concur on a bill passed by the Senate last night. Then the plan is for Congress to adjourn. Kate needs to decide what to do about that election message. Do you think you could stop by around 5:30 and help us think through our options? In case we need to rewrite her statement?"

Chapter 63

The Estate Attorney at Sturgiss & Sturgiss was really pissed off. Detective Marsh had commanded him to go into his law offices on a Sunday, the only day of the week that he really closed off to work so that he could have some little bit of a personal life. But he was there, waiting in the reception area of their suite of offices, when the Detective arrived.

Not even trying to hide his annoyance, the attorney greeted Detective Marsh with, "Now, can you tell me why you had to rouse me from my home on a Sunday, Detective? Couldn't it have waited until tomorrow, at least?"

"I'm really sorry," the Detective was all honey, "but, no, this couldn't wait. It has to do with the murder of Craig Bittiford, who I believe is a client of yours?"

"Well, I'll have to check our files. I can't remember the names of all of our clients. We have so many. And unless you are a multi-millionaire, requiring lots of legal work, I can't say that any of us remember all of our clients' names."

"I would appreciate it if you would check, then."

Detective Marsh followed the attorney through a door marked "Records Room". On one side of the room there was a row of about six computers, while on the opposite side of the room, the wall was lined with formal, highly polished, wood file cabinets. The attorney went over to one of the computers, turned it on, and started clicking away at drop down menus until a search window showed up.

"What was that name again, Detective?"

"Craig Bittiford. B-i-t-t-i-f-o-r-d."

When the attorney hit the return button, the screen was filled with a folder bearing Craig's name, and a particular file number. The attorney seemed surprised, but only mildly so.

He got up from the computer, and headed for the next to last file cabinet behind him, opened the second draw, and pulled out a file with Craig's name on it. He quickly glanced through the papers in it, and then slammed the folder closed. It was a very thin file.

"I hope you realize, Detective, that this is privileged information. You will need a warrant to see it."

"Well, first, can you tell me just what kind of legal services you provided to Mr. Bittiford?"

"Well, I really can't do even that."

"The man is dead, sir. Making me get a warrant will just cause unnecessary delay. And this is a case that has a major time-sensitive issue."

"Dead, you say?" and the attorney raised his eyebrows questioningly. When the Detective nodded, the attorney then offered, "Well, that's ironic. The only work Mr. Bittiford had us do for him was prepare his Last Will and Testament."

"A young fellow like that had a will drawn up?"

"Yes. As a matter of fact, it was completed and signed only a couple of weeks ago. I was not familiar with his name because, being a very simple will, his case was handled by one of our junior lawyers."

"What makes it a simple will?"

"Well, he just had one provision in it. He left all of his worldly possessions to one person. That was it. Nothing complicated about that."

"I need to know who that person is, and I need to know now," the Detective would brook no opposition to his request.

Chapter 64

When Jack arrived at Blanchard's office a little before 5:30 p.m., he slipped in through the hidden side door that Elaine had shown him. A few reporters had already collected outside the main entrance to Blanchard's office, in response to a breaking story in a hostile media blog, that featured the surprise photo taken as Elaine and Caroline had arrived at Jack's home to be fingerprinted by the police. The headline read: *"Rep. Blanchard's Chief of Staff and Daughter Meet Secretly with Police About a MURDER!"*

Jack knocked gently before opening the bathroom door leading to Representative Blanchard's inner office, knowing that Elaine and Blanchard were awaiting his arrival. The three just looked at each other for a moment, no one uttering a word as they each tried to digest the latest turn of events.

Elaine eventually broke the silence with, "Can you believe this?" referring to the blog article. "I mean, who told this blogger where we would be, and why? How did anyone else know?!"

"And what interest did this blogger have in this story?" Jack added a question of his own.

"Well, Mr. Blogger," Elaine looked at Jack with wide eyes, and obvious innuendo, but without any animosity, "can't you answer that question for us?"

Jack just looked at Elaine for a moment with raised eyebrows, before stating what was obvious to him, "No. I can't. What we need to know is how the author found out there was any connection between a murder and Representative Blanchard's staff. And how the author knew about the meeting at my house with the police. What I do know about this particular blogger is that his output is more like a scandal sheet, so his interest is probably, primarily, in increasing recognition of his blog. I don't think he particularly cares about any individual story, or any potential consequences of what he writes, only that he gain broader recognition. The more popular or recognizable his blog is, the more advertising revenue he can generate. Which, of course, means more money for him."

"So you think this guy has no personal grudge against me and my campaign, only that he saw an opportunity to spread a story that would generate publicity for his own blog?" Kate Blanchard summed up.

"Yes," Jack replied, "I think that's exactly what his interest is. So, whoever alerted him to this story is someone who is trying to derail your campaign."

"And that could be whoever it is that was behind the photos in the first place, and even who murdered Craig," Elaine contributed.

"I think you're right, Elaine," Jack agreed.

"So we are back to the original question," Kate Blanchard commented, "of who is behind those scandal photos."

"Yup," Jack said simply.

After a moment of quiet while each person scoured their minds to come up with a plausible suggestion for the culprit, or culprits, Kate Blanchard decided, "We had better do the campaign broadcast tomorrow evening, as you suggested, Jack, and do it live. We need time to decide what the lies are and how to respond to them, as clearly and directly as possible."

Elaine and Jack both nodded in agreement, as Elaine added, though not very convincingly, "Perhaps by tomorrow evening, the police will have figured out exactly what is going on."

"Perhaps," Kate mumbled.

Having known Kate Blanchard for so long, however, Elaine recognized a slight note of defeatism in Kate's voice. As she and Jack headed to her own desk in the outer office, Elaine released some of her anger with, "This is just so unfair! Kate's worked so hard, and she is so decent, and truly public spirited! And to have this crap thrown at her by totally unscrupulous people! I feel so helpless! What can we do?" She looked up at Jack with pleading eyes that also feared defeat. Jack wished he could right all the wrongs in the world for her, and assure her that good would win out in the end. But he couldn't. No one could. Not with even a scintilla of honesty.

Instead, he explained, "Look, somehow we all grow up believing that life is fair. That good wins out, just because it is good. But the reality is, life is *not* necessarily fair. There is no guarantee that life will be fair, or that right will topple wrong. So what we have to do is just keep on fighting. Fighting for what we believe in. Fighting for the kind of world that will let justice prevail, at least more often than it does now. Fighting for a world where there will be less pain and suffering than there is today, for everyone. And as long as we keep fighting, and others keep fighting, there will be hope. Hope that we will succeed. Hope that more and more will join the fight. And hope that, in the days and years to come, good *will* win out more and more. As long as we are fighting, that success will always be possible. Once we stop fighting, then we have lost. Because there will be no hope for a better future, if we stop fighting for it.

"And there will always be a need to defend and protect whatever progress we make, and to continue to fight for it, because there will always be those who will work to serve only their own greed and self-interests, to the detriment of others. There will always be people who care nothing for who they step on, or hurt, or trample, as long as they are achieving their own selfish goals." Here Jack let out a breath, as if he had been holding it in all of his life. He hadn't meant to lecture, but his exasperation seemed to gush uncontrollably, as if it had been held in chains, and something finally managed to break the chain.

Elaine stared up at him, as admiration and respect, and yes, love, filled her heart and her mind, and then escaped from her to envelop Jack in a cloud of emotional power, like the billows of lava from an exploding volcano. She didn't need to say anything...it was all there, in the glow on her face, in the shining stars in her eyes.

"I know you are right, Jack. But I just can't seem to wrap my head around the notion that anyone—just anyone—could so easily, and thoroughly, destroy another person's whole life with outright blatant lies, just because those lies keep getting repeated in the public discourse. I mean, it's as if nothing Kate has done up until now matters—only the disparaging and destructive stories, and the ugly innuendo triggered by these photos. And how can anyone be so absolutely cold, and immoral, as to engage in such an attack? I just can't comprehend it."

He could see the pain writ large all over her face. If only he could relieve her of her anguish. "Don't give up yet, Elaine. We are going to do everything we can to make sure the truth is discovered, and not only gets reported, but gets as much, if not more, publicity, than the lies. This time will be different—because you and I are going to make sure it is different. Look, anyone who knows Kate Blanchard, or has knowledge of her efforts as the elected Representative for her district, *knows* her character, her dedication, her integrity, and her professionalism. Some of that understanding may be temporarily clouded by these public allegations and innuendo, but they, and the truth, cannot stay hidden for long. Because you and I are not going to let the truth stay hidden." And as his eyes locked onto Elaine's with a compelling hold she could not turn away from, he added emphatically, "I promise you that."

The raw emotional energy they shared at that moment, as they stood there face to face, established a bond between them that made them feel they had transcended to another dimension. But they were quickly brought back to earth by the sound of someone trying to clear their throat. It was Caroline, who asked what the plan was, in face of the new blog bombshell.

Elaine re-grouped, answering, "We need to see how this plays out in the media, and what progress the police make, so we can figure out just what Kate needs to say in an address to voters. I expect this linking of the photos with a murder will prove a more daunting story to deal with, and one the media won't be able to ignore no matter what evidence Kate presents. The fact that this is all about an attack on Kate won't prevent her from being billed as the villain, and even gives the media a motive for Kate being behind the murder of the person who apparently produced the scandalous photos,"

Elaine shrugged her shoulders in acceptance of what a horrible situation they were in.

"O.M.G." Caroline remarked.

"Yes, Caroline, O.M.G." Elaine agreed. "I'm afraid we are going to have a full-blown media storm descend on us in the next few hours."

Chapter 65

Instead of leaving with Jack and joining him for dinner, Elaine had to send him on his way alone. The five p.m. vote had been postponed until nine p.m., so she had to remain at the office. But she agreed to meet him at his home as soon as Congress officially adjourned.

Jack found himself with some unexpected time on his hands. He was too restless to just go home and wait for Elaine. And he was eager to get the unanswered questions about the murder and the photos resolved. But how? he asked himself, as he meandered down the streets East of the Capitol.

Then a light bulb lit up! What a brilliant idea! He would go back to Craig's house. If he could find a way in, he would again search the house for anything that might help. After all, the police might never have found the evidence hidden under the floor of Craig's basement if he and the others hadn't gone snooping. There's no telling what he might discover that the police were too jaded to have noticed. Especially about the identity of the mystery woman that Craig apparently hoped to marry. The only problem would be getting into Craig's house. Jack was sure the police would not have returned that spare key to its hiding place under the pot out front.

But he needn't have worried. When Jack climbed the stairs to explore ways to get in, he found the door unlocked. It was closed, but it was unlocked. Perhaps the police just forgot to lock it up after they scoured the place the evening/morning before, he mused. At any rate, it solved one problem. And this time, he decided to lower the shades wherever he searched, so that he wouldn't arouse any curiosity from the neighbors.

He stepped into the foyer, and quietly closed the door behind him, leaving it unlocked as he had found it. After drawing the shades down in the front living room, he felt emboldened enough to turn on a small lamp. The shades were room-darkeners, so he felt comfortable that the light would go unnoticed.

He peered about the room, slowly swiveling his head left and right, letting his eyes pick out every detail. He had no idea what he was looking for, but was sure he would know if he saw anything useful. Last night they had focused on finding Craig's computers. Tonight he would focus on trying to determine if there was anything that might identify another person's presence. Given that the police, as well as he and Elaine and company, had trampled all through the house, he realized he was probably on a fool's errand. But he had nothing better to do for the next couple of hours.

As he examined every nook and cranny of the living room, behind every picture on the walls, under the cushions on the sofa, and every piece of memorabilia on the fireplace mantel, he began to wonder if he had been crazy to come. What could he find that the police had not already found in their own meticulous searches? But there was a restless nagging in him that drove him to try, egging him on whenever he harbored thoughts of giving up. He would have no peace of mind until the mysteries were completely solved. The big question is, would the resolution come in time, or too late, to save Kate Blanchard's campaign? So he continued his rounds, moving into the Dining Room, and then into the kitchen in the back of the first floor, always lowering the shades before turning on any lights.

I had no idea how domesticated Craig was, Jack noted, as he opened various kitchen cabinet doors that revealed a well-stocked culinary support assemblage of cooking utensils and foods. And then something struck him as strange. He was sure the police would have removed all kinds of items, even garbage, for analysis, especially once they discovered that Craig had consumed barbiturates. But would they have been so fastidious, then leave a lone wrapper in the waste bin, for none other than a packet of instant hot cocoa? Craig had ingested the barbiturates with cocoa. Certainly, the police wouldn't have missed a lone wrapper like that. Yet, there it was.

Suddenly, a chill swept through him in waves, but he brushed it aside. How ridiculous! Could the murderer have returned after the police had finished this morning? Would a murderer who had hidden his or her identity so well until now, be foolish enough to return to the scene of the crime, so to speak? What for? Let alone make a cup of hot cocoa! But that could explain the unlocked door. Jack was sure the police would not have left a door unlocked like that.

He had been in the house now for twenty minutes or more, and the only sounds he had heard were the ones he was making himself. So if anyone had returned, they must already be gone. A second shiver, less threatening than the first, however, sent him out of the kitchen and up the stairs to the bedrooms.

If there was a woman in his life, Jack reasoned, the most logical place for signs of her would be the bedroom, and perhaps the attached bathroom. The first bedroom he entered must have been the guest room, because it was as neat as a pin, in spite of the police's search. And there weren't any personal items lying about on the dresser, in the bathroom, or anywhere else. But the other bedroom on that floor was much larger, and obviously was the master bedroom. In it, Jack found a modicum of disarray, probably from the police search. The sheets had been removed from the bed, perhaps to test for DNA that did not belong to Craig, Jack mused. But if he was expecting to find, maybe, a stray piece of women's underwear, or a lost earring, or whatever, he was disappointed. If only this were a made for TV murder mystery, Jack amused himself, because by now I would have found some tell tale piece of obscure evidence that would answer all the questions, and solve the riddle, all by itself. Whoever the woman in Craig's life was, either the police had found whatever traces of her visits she might have left, or she never came to his house, or...she was really really good at hiding her identity.

He decided he had been foolish to come, after all, and that he should just leave, so he headed back down the stairs. But something, perhaps the trashed instant cocoa envelope, kept tugging at him.

He was almost out the front door when his own unease instinctively pulled him back inside. He closed the door again, and headed toward the stairs to the lower level. Though he was not as savvy as Diggie when it came to computers, he still might see something they hadn't seen before. Once they had found the hidden compartment under

302

the floor, they had stopped looking, because Detective Marsh had shown up. What Jack expected to find after the police had given the lower level not one, but two careful examinations, he didn't know. But he hated to leave any stone unturned, in case it could reveal some hidden secret, like the pot out front had revealed the second key.

He turned the light on at the top of the stairs that led down. As he deliberately descended the steps one at a time, he tried to glance around the main computer office to get a general sense of whether anything might be, or simply feel, amiss. That's when he saw it. The rest light on the 3D printer was on. When you turn a printer on, but leave it idle for a while, most of the lights go out, but one usually remains lit to remind you that, in fact, the printer is on, and not shut completely off. He tried to remember, as he arrived at the bottom of the stairs, if that printer had been on when they were there last night, but he could not recall. They had all been so excited and fascinated by the elaborate electronic setup, that he couldn't recall if the printer rest light was on or off.

Would the police have left the 3D printer on? Someone had checked the printer history, because that's how they knew it had been used to produce a pistol and silencer. He didn't think the police would have left it on unless it was just an oversight. After all, the front door had been unlocked. And then there was that cocoa wrapper sitting in the bottom of the kitchen waste bin.

As if an alarm had just gone off in his ears, Jack decided it would be best if he left. He should also probably call Detective Marsh and tell him about his visit, and the inconsistencies he had noted. Marsh might be really angry with me for coming here again, Jack realized, but it would be best to come clean on my own, than for Marsh to perhaps figure it out later, and decide it made Jack look suspicious again. He didn't like being a suspect in any kind of crime, let alone a murder.

He turned from the printer, and headed for the stairs. The shadow of a figure under the steps momentarily paralyzed him. And then—poof! The lights went out. Figuratively, that is. The actual lights on the lower level were still on, but Jack was out cold on the floor. Before he could rouse himself, his assailant had his hands tied tightly behind his back with a strong, waxed, packaging cord. As consciousness slowly returned, he tried to stand up, but found his feet were also tied tightly with the same kind of cord.

Chapter 66

Congress finally adjourned around seven-thirty p.m. All the business Congress was going to accomplish before actually adjourning had been completed earlier than expected. The nine o'clock vote had been moved up.

Kate Blanchard called her campaign office to get an update from her campaign manager on the media chaos that the blog article about the murder might be causing. The receptionist gave her call to her campaign press agent, Tony, since Krystal was not available. Tony told the Congresswoman that he had received numerous media inquiries looking for comments from her. He had assured them there was no truth to the accusations, and, beyond that, he had deflected requests by noting that "Congresswoman Blanchard was still in Washington, D.C. where Congress was close to adjourning," so they would have to wait until her return to her district the next day for her response. Tony also told her that their pollster, Troy, had a poll scheduled for first thing Monday morning, to identify public reaction to the latest news. Krystal, he explained, had gone home since there was nothing they could do but wait and see what the fallout would be.

Though Elaine had a lot of legislative clean up work to take care of, after Kate told her about her call to campaign headquarters, Elaine hurried out the door, promising herself she would be in the office very early the next morning.

She decided to surprise Jack by going straight to his home, because he wasn't expecting her until after nine p.m. But as she approached his place, she noticed that the windows were all dark. She walked up the stairs and rang his doorbell. After waiting what seemed like a long time, she turned around and slowly descended the steps again. Perhaps he thought she would go to her own home first, and wanted to surprise her. She pulled out her cell phone, and called him to let him know she was on her way, in case he had heard that Congress had indeed adjourned. Her call got switched to voice mail.

Then she called Diggie, and asked him if Jack was there, thinking Diggie was at her home. "He's not at his house, and he's not answering his cell phone," Elaine explained. "You don't suppose Detective Marsh decided to arrest him, do you?" she asked incredulously.

"I wouldn't know, Sis. I'm at Caroline's, and I haven't been home since around noon."

"Oh, I didn't realize. Sorry to bother you, Diggie."

"No bother. Do you want me to check your house to see if Jack is there?"

"No, no! I'll do that myself. I was supposed to meet him for dinner. I just got off work, so I might as well go home, and change into more comfortable clothes, anyway. Have fun! Talk to you later!"

As Elaine meandered in the direction of her home, she wondered if Jack might be out doing some errands. After all, he wasn't expecting her until after nine. It would feel good to have a few minutes to change into comfy clothes, she acknowledged. In the tiny recesses of her mind, though, she harbored a hope that Jack would be waiting for her with open arms when she arrived home, so she was more than a little chagrined to come home to an empty house.

Oh, well, she shrugged off her disappointment, I probably had better odds of winning the lottery than of finding Jack here, just now. She decided she had enough time to take a hot shower to wash off the day's events, and make a fresh start to the evening. After all, Congress had adjourned, finally.

Even though she would be back in work the next day, the session was over. Hhmmmm, she thought, as she let the hot water pour over her, one more day before election day. And what a mess everything was. The practical side of her doubted Kate's campaign for Senate could be salvaged after this evening's media circus. There didn't seem to be enough time to address the allegations and innuendos, even if the murder were somehow miraculously solved before Tuesday.

Well, Elaine realized, I will probably be looking for a new job, come January. What that would be, she wasn't sure. She could try to work for another member of Congress, or a Freshman newly elected on Tuesday. But, somehow, the prospect of working for a stranger, even another existing member, with the dedication you had to make to be effective in the legislative environment, did not terribly motivate her.

She was even more keenly aware now than ever before, that working for an elected official meant you were working for *their* career, not your own, not really. She wasn't a new college graduate anymore. She had worked on the Hill for eight years now. Even if Kate wins the Senate race, maybe this would still be the right time for her to reinvent her future. Perhaps it was time to figure out what *she* wanted to do for the rest of her life, instead of working to support another person's goals for their own life. Perhaps it was time to re-evaluate her own interests and professional goals. But what direction did she want to pursue?

She donned a casual sweater and corduroy slacks, then went downstairs to the kitchen, where she had left her phone. She redialed Jack's number, but again got no answer. It was just a little after nine. He should be waiting at his house for her by now, Elaine reasoned. Where could he be? Especially if he's not even answering his phone?

As she grabbed her jacket, and started out her front door, she suddenly stopped in mid-motion, just before clicking her door closed. He wouldn't have gone back to Craig's house...would he? For what? They had searched the whole house last night. And because of the new evidence they had discovered under the floor boards, the police had done a second thorough search, looking for finger prints, and whatever. What could he possibly have thought to accomplish by going back? How would he even get in? I'm pretty sure, she laughed to herself, that the police were not going to return that spare key to its usual resting place! That wouldn't make any sense! What a foolish thought!

She clicked her door closed, and started walking towards Jack's house. Perhaps by the time I get there, he will be home. As she turned the corner onto his street, this time she noticed that his car was sitting a few doors past his house. Her spirits lifted. It had been foolish of her to be worried. He must have been out doing errands. Maybe he was planning a lovely surprise for her, like whipping up a special dinner at home, for just the two of them.

The anticipation of seeing him in a moment or two, in spite of the volatility of the political storm that was probably brewing back home concerning Kate's campaign, made her walk a little faster. The firestorm would have to be faced tomorrow, but tonight would be theirs.

As she climbed his front steps, however, she could see no lights on anywhere in the house. How could that be? she wondered. She rang the doorbell. Again, no one opened the front door. Not Jack. Not anyone.

She stood at the top of his steps, and looked around the street. His car was here, so he couldn't be far. Would he be at a neighbor's? Without telling her? Then why wouldn't he answer his phone? Since she had met him just over a week ago, she couldn't recall any point in their activities that he had shut off his phone, or simply let a call pass without answering it. Why now?

She called her office, just to make sure he hadn't gone there looking for her. But everyone was gone by now. There was no one there to answer the office phone.

Finally, she succumbed to the notion that perhaps, just perhaps, he had indeed gone to Craig's house again, in spite of such a visit being a fool's errand. He would probably just have walked there, which would explain why his car remained on his own street. She reluctantly turned around, and started walking toward Craig's, to check. It's not like it's out of the way, or even very far, she reminded herself.

As she expected, his house, too, appeared dark. His house should be dark, she reminded herself. She climbed the steps anyway, and from the top step she caught sight of a narrow dull ray of light streaming out from the corner of the first floor front window to the left of the door. The shade apparently was down, but the side of the shade was a little ajar from the wall. Was someone in there, Elaine wondered, or did the police just forget to shut off all the lights?

Elaine's first instinct was to ring the bell. But her common sense instantly took over, and made her pause. It was so quiet on the street, and she felt no sense of movement inside the building. She decided to check the pot first, just in case the police had been silly enough to return the spare key to its original abode. She ran back down the stairs and gently moved the pot. Nothing was there. That could just mean that someone had taken it out of its hiding place, and used it to get into the house. But she dismissed that notion, because she really couldn't imagine the police leaving the spare key outside the house.

Before she tried the door, Elaine called Jack again on her phone. He still wasn't picking up. But a chill spread up her spine, and down her arms, as her ears registered the brief, but soft, sound of an excerpt from a Souza March. Jack's ring was an excerpt from a Souza March. But if that was his phone, he must be inside the house. Why wouldn't he answer? He would know it was her calling.

She felt her pulse pick up a little speed as she slowly ascended the front steps. She leaned her ear against the door, but found only silence. Instinctively, she placed her hand on the doorknob, and gently tried to turn it.

Warning bells suddenly exploded in her head! The door was unlocked! Elaine was startled, every nerve in her body tingled, alive and alert. The proverbial hairs on the back of her neck were standing on their proverbial ends.

Chapter 67

"Oh, come on, Mr. Amory," his assailant cajoled, mocking him as he rolled around on the floor, onto his side and off of his stomach. He was barely aware that there was someone else in the room, but his mind was foggy, and he couldn't at first see who. "I didn't hit you that hard, Mr. Super Sleuth. Just enough to momentarily disable you." He heard another chuckle, as his captor made fun of his incapacitation. "I wouldn't try to squirm out of that cord I've tied you with, because you might hurt yourself, and you'll never get it undone by pulling or twisting on it. It's powerful stuff, used to secure heavy-weight packages, and it's only about an eighth of an inch thick, so you could do some pretty painful damage if you twist it about. You might even start bleeding! You wouldn't want to just bleed out on the floor here, now would you?" This time the laugh was a bit more menacing.

Jack had turned the angle of his body so that he could see who had attacked him. His assailant was casually seated on a stool, half-smiling, watching him closely, almost taking a perverse pleasure at his shock. He was totally mystified as recognition took hold. "You?" he couldn't hide his surprise, and wonder. "What are *you* doing *here*?" Another laugh, but his head was starting to clear. "You...you're supposed to be back home, running the show. What are you doing *here*?" While he was still a little groggy, the implications were starting to creep in, as the fog continued to slowly dissipate.

"Why, Mr. Amory...can I call you Jack? After all, this is hardly a formal occasion! Why, Jack, I am really hurt that you think I am out of place here. I've spent a lot of time in this house. Shall I share some of the more, um, more intimate moments I've known here?" and the laugh echoed ominously through the basement level.

"How could you have spent very much time here? There's practically no trace of you anywhere. No finger prints around the house. Nothing." Suddenly he wondered if the empty packet of instant cocoa in the kitchen waste basket would have prints on it, so he decided to keep quiet about it.

"That was no accident," the woman bragged. "I very carefully covered the tips of my fingers in clear nail polish before I ever visited in here. That way, I wouldn't leave any prints."

"But what...why...were you ever here? How did you even know Craig?" Jack relayed genuine curiosity.

"Oh, I've known Craig for a long time. Actually, we were in graduate school together. He was such a nerd. And so shy with girls. But he was sweet, too. And brilliant! Wow, was he brilliant! I decided it was in my interest to have him as a friend...a regular, so to speak...someone to hang out with. And it paid off...handsomely. He helped me with a lot of independent research assignments, and helped me get through computer classes with flying colors! I was pretty sure he had a crush on me, though. While I was a good friend to him, nevertheless, I never let him pursue a romantic relationship. I stayed in touch with him, tantalizingly friendly, to keep him hopeful, in case I ever needed his help. But after we got our degrees, it was more useful to keep our connection hidden."

"You mean, you kept him baited...always letting him believe there just might be a chance, when in fact there wasn't a chance in hell...right?" Jack was angry.

"Why not? Men do it all the time with women! What, you don't like having the tables turned?"

The throbbing pain in his head was starting to ebb, letting him think a bit more clearly. "So, what are you doing here now? You know, this might be your fatal mistake. You might have gotten away with it if you hadn't returned here today."

"Gotten away with what, Jack?" and she laughed again. "I'm just here mourning the loss of a good friend," she claimed, with wide-eyed innocence.

"Somehow, I doubt you are mourning Craig's death. As a matter of fact, you are probably the one who murdered him, aren't you?"

"What?" she let out a fake gasp. "Why would I murder Craig? One of my dearest friends! I can prove we go back a long way! And I am mortified at his loss!" she pretended, as she patted her heart with her hand. But her deep-throated laugh belied the veracity of her claim.

"If you aren't his murderer, then why am I tied up?" Jack asked what he thought was an obvious question, the answer to which countered her cry of innocence.

"Oh, but you frightened me! I heard an intruder in the house, and I tried to protect myself in any way I could!"

"So, then why don't you untie me?" he challenged.

"Oh, poor Jack," she commiserated forebodingly, "don't you see? In your hurry to search the house, you forgot to turn the light on at the top of the stairs. In the dark, you fell down those very steep stairs and broke your neck...or some injury so horrible that you didn't survive that awful fall," she explained, her eyebrows raised and her face full of empathetic pity.

"So, you *did* kill Craig," Jack stated flatly.

"Well, of course I killed him," she finally admitted, with a huge sigh of exasperation.

It was a simple question, but he had to ask it. "Why?"

"Why? Why?" she was annoyed now. "Why did he get cold feet? Why did he want to back out of our deal? Why couldn't he just stick to the script and let it play out? Why did his cowardice threaten to wreck the entire plan...and ruin me in the process?" her anger building, and her voice rising, as she recited the litany of his failings.

Jack could only stare at her for a moment of silence as the realization of what she just admitted to sank in. "You," finally gurgled from deep in his throat. "It was you, wasn't it? You are the one behind the photo scandal to discredit Kate Blanchard's Senate campaign! Not Craig!" The shock of that realization still left him incredulous. Why would Kate Blanchard's Campaign Manager want to fatally sabotage Blanchard's Senate campaign? What on earth could be going on in her twisted mind to cause her to go to such lengths to destroy the campaign, and the career, of the candidate she was supposed to be getting elected? A loss for Kate Blanchard wouldn't harbor well for her skills as a campaign manager.

"Of course it wasn't his idea!" she declared, implying how could anyone think Craig could concoct such a plot.

"He's very very smart when it comes to computers, but, really, he doesn't have the killer instinct to plan something like the photo scandal," she elucidated, as she dismissed Craig's character with a disdainful "sheeesh!".

Suddenly, Jack realized that she must know the answer to one of the key questions that had been plaguing him since he learned that the photos were phony. "Why were the photos sent to me to release? Was that Craig's idea?"

"Craig's idea?" Krytal snickered. "Well, he suggested you, but only after I explained that we should try to get the photos released by someone who would come to him for verification, and would really trust his conclusion. Apparently, you were the only media type of outlet that he felt confident would come to him." And after a slight pause, as Jack was digesting this information, she added, with a smirk in her voice, "It was nothing personal, Mr. Amory. You just fit the bill for what we needed."

The answer was mostly disappointing. Craig may not have used him out of personal hostility, but he did throw him to the wolves. He was willing to completely destroy Jack's professional life, to secure his own personal goal, cementing his relationship with this woman.

"But when I didn't publish them right away, why didn't you just send them to a different outlet? I'm sure there were many who would have been only too happy for that kind of limelight."

"Well, I admit, I was the one who wanted to nail you, then, for not publishing them right away. Your delay was screwing up our scheme. We were losing time. So I insisted Craig find some way to get the photos out into the public domain, while giving you all the credit! I'm only sorry I wasn't a fly on the wall when you discovered your 'special edition'!" and she laughed rather heartily at her image of that moment.

And then another piece of the puzzle found its place. "Was it you who leaked the story about the possible link between the murder and Kate Blanchard?"

"Bingo, again! Give the man a cigar! Not everyone has your scruples. Honestly! You and your principles really screwed things up for us. It's a good thing that not everyone is as fuss budgety as you are about the truth. Thank goodness for those folks who just want to make a buck!"

Jack could scarcely believe what he was seeing and hearing, yet he knew it was all very real. Craig may not have had the killer instinct, but this woman had it in spades. Craig must have been blindly in love with her to risk his professional credentials, all that he had worked so hard for. No wonder he never mentioned Krystal Kincaid. He never really knew where he stood. He was probably afraid of making a public fool of himself if he told anyone how he felt in case he later got rejected.

"Did you know that Craig had bought a rather expensive diamond engagement ring, just last Tuesday?" Jack asked, when he could finally speak in spite of his inner rage.

"Did he really? I was afraid he might think I would be receptive to such an arrangement," she was not at all impressed. "Well, maybe I did the little weasel a favor then, by killing him. I saved him from a totally broken heart...that probably would have been much more painful, and unbearable, for him than losing his life! First, there would be the rejection to deal with. And then he would no longer have had any hope to keep him going. As long as I could prevent him from declaring himself, you see, he could always think that 'we' were a possibility. Once the election was over, however, our little escapade would have ended, too."

Horrors! Jack thought. What cold brutality!

"You see, I had to get sexually involved with him," Krystal continued, "to charm him, to mesmerize him to the point where he would do anything for me to keep me happy. It wasn't easy to convince him to create the scandalous photos that I wanted. Basically, he was an honest, decent person. So I needed to have enough power over him to influence him to do things that kind of violated his moral compass. He was so easy to fool, and to manipulate," she laughed heartily. "Having that kind of power over someone is quite heady stuff! I will miss that high. But, then, being the principal...the candidate...in an election, who then wins the election, and gets to enjoy all the benefits of being the one with the power, the one everyone else fawns over, the one everyone wants to please, the one lobbyists ass kiss as they virtually beg for your vote, the one who holds all the aces...now *that's* really heady stuff!" Her eyes rolled up in their sockets as she imagined herself having that special aura of power.

"If that's what you wanted, why didn't you just run for office yourself, instead of managing others' campaigns?" Jack asked.

"If 'Miss Goody Two-Shoes', Kate Blanchard, had won this Senate race, there wouldn't be much opportunity back home, if any, to run for a seat in either the House or the Senate. Someone else will be elected to her Congressional District this year, and if they do even just a decent job, they are likely to hold it for decades, as Blanchard would have if she had not had this opportunity to seek a Senate seat. After all, the person she would be replacing in the Senate had held that seat for 42 years. She would have done the same. She's young enough."

"But you could have run for her Congressional seat yourself, this year. Why did you sign on to be her campaign manager instead?"

"I didn't have the credentials yet to garner enough party support as a candidate, or the recognition to generate enough financing, to successfully run a race of my own this year. Nor did I have the recognition in her district. The Congressional race I managed last time around was in the neighboring House district. She actually did me a favor asking me to manage her Senate race," she explained.

"I've done a great job with her Senate campaign," Krystal continued, "and could now be a credible candidate for her Senate seat. I've established political, and financial, connections and relationships all across the state. I wouldn't be so scrupulous about not accepting interest group funding, but until now I wouldn't have generated that kind of financial backing. Now, everyone knows me! I could easily strike out on my own at this point. Which is exactly what I intend to do!" she asserted.

"But Billingsley will likely win this race, if your scandal-mongering succeeds, so where does that leave you?"

"Well, the photos were supposed to remove Kate in time for me to become the substitute candidate, at the last minute, you see. No time for anyone else to logically step in, but enough time for me to win in her place. But your integrity threw the whole schedule off," she grimaced as she contemplated him stretched out on the floor.

"So, Billingsley may win on Tuesday," she admitted. "But I know all about his attempts to eavesdrop on Kate's office and home, remember? Once I go public with that, he will be disgraced to the point he would have to relinquish his win under heavy public pressure, and there would then have to be a special election, in which I will announce my candidacy. I will become the standard-bearer for Kate's supporters. I would be bound to win, because there isn't currently another candidate within the party, or an opposition candidate, with enough standing or recognition to beat me. It's still all so simple!"

Again, he could only stare at her, momentarily speechless while his brain tried to comprehend such diabolical plotting. She had clearly thought through every detail of her scheme. Rather thoroughly, as a matter of fact, in spite of the curve balls he may have thrown her way. But there had to be a fly in her ointment, Jack thought, or she wouldn't have felt compelled to return to Craig's house. She was really on track to get away with her plotting and her crime. Something in the house, however, must be able to reveal her role, or at least her complicity, or her relationship with Craig, to motivate her to come looking for it. Something in the house was still a threat to her success.

He commented carefully, "Well, you seem to have thought of everything. Whatever made you come back here tonight, and risk the success of all of your planning?"

"I might ask you the same thing. That is, what were you looking for here tonight?"

"I was just fishing," he explained noncommittally. "I was just looking for anything that might help provide some answers. I am, apparently, the chief suspect," he said, wanting her to feel secure.

"Well, now, that's really interesting. Maybe we can find some way to convince the police that you are, in fact, the correct suspect. And since you will be too dead to contradict that conclusion...well, case closed!" she sounded very pleased with herself.

At that moment, Jack's phone rang again. But he didn't have it. She had relieved him of it before he recovered consciousness. "Oh, look, it's Elaine calling you again!" she teased. "I must say, you two have become pretty cozy in so short a time. And you have me to thank for you ever meeting!" Her smile didn't reach her eyes, as she rejected the call. "Ooooh, too bad. You aren't available to take her call," she chided.

"You didn't answer my question," Jack tried to bring her back to their discussion.

"Oh, you mean why did I come here tonight?" In response to his nod, she noted, "Well, maybe you can help me with this. You see, there was one occasion when I failed to cover my fingers with the nail polish. It was an impromptu get together. Unscheduled, you might say. I put my hand on the laptop that Craig brought to the Internet Cafe when he hacked into your computer to send out your very special Special Edition publicizing the photos. I thought I had picked up the laptop, when I also grabbed all the hard drives from his computers. But it turns out, I had the wrong laptop. So I came looking for the one he used for our adventures." She paused a moment before adding in a voice full of girlish innocence, "Do you, by any chance, know where that laptop is?"

Wow, Jack thought. So the prints on the computer they found under the floorboards are hers! Bingo! But aloud, he simply noted, "Sorry, I'm afraid I can't help you there."

She studied him carefully. Was he telling the truth...or not? Before she could inquire, however, they both heard footsteps above them, as someone entered the house on the first floor.

Chapter 68

It's been too long, Diggie sat there, thinking to himself. To Caroline he said aloud, "I should have heard from Ellie by now, don't you think?"

"Maybe she hooked up with Amory, and is too absorbed by his charms to think to call you," Caroline smiled at Diggie, aware of her own inner warmth at Diggie's finally opening up to her about how he feels, and had felt, for so long. "If you're worried," she added, "then call her and find out."

"But if she's in a clinch, or something more, with Jack, she will be less than thrilled at my interruption," Diggie shrugged his shoulders.

"Better to have her momentarily upset with you, than for there to be something wrong, where you could have helped her, but didn't, just because you were afraid she'd be angry with you," Caroline wisely counseled.

"Yeah, you're right," and he engulfed her in the joy of his admiring smile as he leaned close to her beside him on the sofa, and added, "as usual." He kissed her then, on the forehead, as he pulled out his phone, and instantly dialed his sister.

"Ummm...she's not picking up."

"Try Amory."

"Hhmmmm...he's not picking up, either."

"Well, maybe they *are* in a clinch," Caroline smiled suggestively at him.

"Or maybe there's something wrong."

"Try Detective Marsh. Maybe they are tied up with him for some reason."

"Marsh, here," the voice on the other end of Diggie's phone answered.

Diggie was so relieved that he let out a big sigh. "Yes, sir. Hi. This is Gregory Kent. Yes. Um, by any chance, are Elaine and/or Jack Amory with you, at the moment?"

"No. Why would you think they were?"

"Oh," his disappointment was palpable. "Have you, by any chance, heard from either one in the last hour or so?"

"Nope. Should I have?" the Detective was becoming a little apprehensive, but he tried to keep his concerns out of his voice.

"Oh," a little nervously, "no...no reason in particular. I was just trying to reach them, but neither one is picking up on their phone. I was just trying to locate them."

"Maybe they just don't want to be disturbed," the Detective suggested, with the obvious innuendo.

"Yeah, that could be. It's just that, well, about an hour ago, Elaine had called me looking for Jack, because he wasn't picking up on his phone. I think they were supposed to have dinner together, but she couldn't find him."

"Oh?" the Detective was suddenly fully alert. "When did you say you last spoke with your sister?"

"More than an hour ago."

"Well," the Detective tried to console Diggie, "I can't imagine they would be in any kind of trouble. I'm pretty sure they are just taking some time alone, together, if you know what I mean?" You could hear the Detective's raised eyebrows in his voice. "It's been a pretty tough couple of days for both of them, what with finding a dead body, and with Amory being a chief suspect...which he isn't anymore," he hastened to add.

"I guess you are right. Sorry to have bothered you," Diggie closed, somewhat discouraged.

"No problem, Mr. Kent."

Chapter 69

Neither, of course, was satisfied with the conclusion of their conversation. Not Diggie. Not the Detective. The latter was concerned about the inaccessibility of both Jack and Elaine. While he tried to dampen the unspoken fears in Diggie's voice, he himself did not believe one, let alone both, would be off the grid at the same time. Not with all the stuff going on that they were both trying to figure out. And not, he laughed to himself, given how determined they both seemed, to solve the murder themselves.

Detective Marsh had been avidly seeking the heir listed in Craig's will. He was stunned when he learned who the heir was—Congresswoman Kate Blanchard's campaign manager, Krystal Kincaid. It didn't make any sense. There was no doubt now that Craig was behind the photo scandal that could derail Blanchard's Senate bid. How could Blanchard's campaign manager be so tight with someone who was working to defeat what she was working so hard to achieve?

Unless? Unless, what exactly? She wasn't back home doing her job. His staff had traced her to the District, oddly enough, via a late afternoon flight. But they had lost her trail at the airport. Blanchard's Capitol Hill office was closed, had been for a couple of hours. Where else would she be in the District, and what else would she have come here for? She certainly hadn't come to visit Craig. Or had she?

An ugly thought started creeping into the Detective's mind. He had seen a lot during his career that he would have thought was unimaginable, but he now opened his mind to all kinds of possibilities. The unidentified fingerprints on the laptop the police had confiscated from Bittiford's basement were likely female. They were smaller in size, and narrower in shape, than most men's prints. Of course, that didn't eliminate the possibility they were another man's, but it was unlikely. It now seemed entirely possible that those prints might belong to Krystal Kincaid, the sole heir to Craig's house and belongings.

Kincaid had flown to the Metropolitan area that afternoon. Where would she go, with Blanchard's office closed, but either to Blanchard's house, if she was in town to see the candidate...or to Craig's? If she was close enough to him to be his sole heir, then she must be the woman he bought the engagement ring for. And that means she probably had a key to his house. Suddenly, the Detective had a frightening thought. He called Blanchard's home. No, Krystal was not there, she was back home.

He called Jack's number. No answer still. He tried Elaine. Again, no answer still. He rose from his desk, called loudly to his lieutenant and two of his sergeants, with a "C'mon! Quickly!" and led them out the door and to their cars.

Chapter 70

Nothing but silence greeted Elaine as she very slowly, and carefully, pushed the door open, just wide enough for her to slip through it. She could see that a small, low wattage table lamp was shining in the living room just to the left of the foyer, giving off a dull light, and sending that ray of light out the corner of the front window. The rest of the house seemed dark. She also sensed no motion on the floor. Does that mean Jack is not here, like she thought, and even hoped, given that he was not at home or answering his phone? It looks like the police just forgot that one lamp, Elaine concluded.

As she returned to the foyer to leave, Elaine noticed that the door to the lower level was ajar. It had been closed when they arrived at the house the evening before, so perhaps the police didn't close it all the way after they finished their work. But something stirred inside Elaine's nerves. She felt her body suddenly become shrouded with a prickling sensation.

'Oh, for heaven's sake, Elaine, get hold of yourself,' her inner voice commanded. Honestly! Jack's not here. You need to go find him. Something must be wrong if he has unexpectedly fallen off of the grid. It was not normal for him to be incommunicado. I mean, his professional life is dependent on him being accessible 24/7.

She headed towards the front door, mission bound. Then she heard a noise. Not a normal house creaking kind of noise. More like the muffled sound of someone trying to stifle a sneeze, and only partly succeeding. The noise had come from the direction of the stairs leading to the lower level. She froze in mid-motion, waiting to discover if she would hear the sound again.

Silence. Nothing but silence. And yet? "Jack?" she called gently. No answer. Nothing. Elaine had always trusted her instincts. And her instincts were telling her now that something was amiss. Should she explore by herself? Or should she call someone else? Diggie? Detective Marsh?

She decided to explore, but only after she turned on her phone, so that she could be traced through her phone's

GPS, just in case. With her finger on the direct dial key for Diggie, she dropped her phone into her jacket pocket and held it there, as she walked toward the door leading downstairs.

She flicked on the light switch on the wall just inside the doorway, and slowly descended the stairs. Not until she was nearly all the way down did her eyes land on the shadowy figure of a man, sprawled on the floor at the far end of the room, with what appeared to be tied hands and feet, and a strip of masking tape flung across his mouth. And when the light from the stairwell reflected off of those beautiful blue eyes, looking at her so apologetically, she froze again, her mind frantically trying to make sense of what she saw. It was Jack, of course. But what? And why? And *who*? In what was barely a split second, but which felt like an eternity, Elaine regained enough alertness to race down the last few steps to reach Jack and hopefully release him, when the lights went out, again. Figuratively speaking, of course, again.

As she slowly regained consciousness, Elaine found herself on the floor near Jack, hands and feet bound, just like his. A trickle of blood had rolled down her neck from where Elaine felt a hammer striking her relentlessly in the back of her head. Her mouth had not been taped into silence, and the tape on Jack's face had been removed. Nevertheless, their eyes met in silence, with Elaine's full of questions which she didn't need to voice for Jack to know what they were.

But nothing could have prepared her for the violence of the shock waves that spread over her like a tsunami when she turned towards the motion of another person, and discovered Krystal Kincaid standing above the two of them, grinning mischievously, like the cat that caught the canary. The whole room seemed to shake, as if the tremors of a major earthquake were rippling through the ground underneath them.

"Well, well, well. Look what the cats dragged in. If it isn't the pair of lovebirds! You two have really become glued together, haven't you?"

All Elaine could do was stare in disbelief. What on earth was Krystal doing here? In Craig's house? And looking so menacingly at them, incapacitated, on the floor? Why isn't she helping them get free? But she didn't have the wherewithal yet to get the questions out. Or to realize yet the full implications of what she was discovering.

"A little tongue-tied, are we, Ms. Kent?" Krystal cooed. "Let me help you, then. Yes, it's me, Krystal. And, yes, I am the reason you two are, literally," and she chuckled at her little joke, "all tied up!"

Jack was watching Elaine as she processed what she was discovering. "Elaine," was all he could say. Elaine looked at him, this time with more understanding, but still not fully cognizant of what the current circumstances meant.

"It's a lot to take in, I know," Jack explained softly, intensely searching her face to gauge her reaction, "but, if you're wondering if Krystal was in cahoots with Craig, and that actually she was behind the photo scandal scheme," and here he paused a moment, before adding gently, "and that she killed Craig, you would be right."

Elaine's eyes opened as wide as a football field, first full of disbelief, then slowly registering acceptance, as Jack kept a steady gaze fixed on her, confirming that what he was saying was the truth—the truth that had been so successfully hidden, until now. Finally, she turned to face Krystal and asked, simply, "Why?"

"Oh, been there, done that. I'll let lover boy explain it all to you!" Elaine raised her eyebrows at the nomenclature. "Oh, yeah," Krystal continued, "it's obvious you two were becoming enamored with each other. It was probably more obvious to others than to yourselves! Too bad. One, or even both, of you might not be here right now if it weren't for your so cozy mutual attraction! Isn't that a hoot?! If not for your hormones, you might never be in this predicament!"

"And just what kind of predicament are we in?" Jack asked, as he tried to keep his agitation from surfacing.

"Well, you're both smart people. You should be able to figure that out for yourselves."

"Are you going to kill us, too?" Elaine blurted out.

"Me?" Krystal asked innocently. "Oh, no, dear, I'm not going to kill you." But before either Jack or Elaine could let out a sigh of relief, Krystal continued, "You're obviously going to have some kind of accident. I'm not sure what yet,

324

but together we can come up with something credible." Then she walked over to a desk in the dark, back corner of the room, near her hiding place under the stairs, and she picked up an object that was sitting on the corner of the desk.

"Now, we could probably come up with a story line whereby one or the other of you—in checking out this pistol to see if it actually worked—accidentally, but fatally, shoots the other one." She held up in her hand another pistol printed out on Craig's 3D printer.

The object rekindled Jack's memory. "That's why the printer's rest light was on when I came down here, isn't it? You had printed out another gun, like the one you used to shoot Craig."

"Score one for the nose-to-the-grind reporter!" Krystal acknowledged.

"Why? What did you need another pistol for? You left the one you used on Craig in his car."

"Actually, I probably didn't *need* it. I expected this to be my last visit here, and just thought it might be a nice thing to have. But you arrived before I could print out the silencer, as well. After all, if you two weren't so nosy, you wouldn't be in your current predicament!"

"If you fire it, someone will hear the shot," Elaine warned, trying to discourage Krystal from using the gun.

"And you get only one shot with that weapon," Jack tried to reinforce Elaine's effort.

"Yes, most likely, but then since one of you will have shot the other, it's no skin off my back!" Krystal countered.

"What if the police were called, and they got here before you had time to escape?" Elaine pursued.

"Trust me. There'll be no gun shot sounds until I have everything figured out, including my escape without a trace," Krystal's menacing smile sent quivers down Elaine's spine. "Besides, I just may print out the silencer before I shoot one of you. Meanwhile, perhaps you two would like some hot cocoa, to maybe fend off any creeping hunger pains? I know I'm starving. They don't serve food on most flights anymore, and I've been here for a while. And my guess is, both of you have missed your dinner tonight, as well. Right? Unfortunately, I'm afraid all I can offer is hot cocoa."

To Elaine's surprise, Jack readily accepted the offer, claiming his innards were growling painfully. All Elaine could do was sit there in silence, stunned. She hadn't forgotten that Detective Marsh told them that the barbiturates that made Craig unable to defend himself had been ingested with hot cocoa. Had Jack forgotten?

"Wonderful!" Krystal sounded happy. "I will go upstairs and play domestic, and be back down with some cocoa for each of us in a few minutes." Then she turned and ran up the stairs, leaving the door at the top open.

"Are you crazy?" Elaine only mouthed the words, hoping Jack could lip read well enough to figure out what she was saying. He formed the shape of his own words in silence, as well, telling her "I know. But I wanted to get rid of her for a moment."

"Oh," was Elaine's silent reply, shaping her lips into a big round 'O', which caused Jack's heart to lurch into his throat with a desire to wrap his own lips around that tempting circle. But now was not the time to be thinking such thoughts, he told himself.

In as soft a whisper as he could muster, he asked Elaine if she would reach out to his hands and try to untie the knots on the string around his wrists. "Quickly as you can," he urged. He figured they only had as much time as it takes water to boil. The mugs would be ready and waiting with whatever drugs and ingredients Krystal was going to put in them, by the time the bubbles started boiling their way up to the surface.

Elaine slid along the floor a bit more, as soundlessly as she could, and stretched out her own tied hands to his, and started working on the knots. Luckily, she could move her fingers rather freely, so the task was not as daunting as it might at first have seemed. And Krystal's knot-tying skills did not hold enough strength in them to resist Elaine's efforts. In what seemed like hours, instead of the one or two minutes that had actually passed, Jack's hands were free. He untied his feet as quickly, and as stealthily as he could, then started working on Elaine's hands.

Before Jack could get Elaine's hands completely free, they heard footsteps start to descend the stairs. Jack hurried to hide in the corner blindspot under the stairs, where Krystal, herself, had hidden before attacking each of them. He crouched under the stairs breathlessly, waiting, each footfall causing his heart to pound away more loudly each time, so much so that he was sure Krystal must hear him. As her shoes came into view, and then her legs, and knees, he realized her steps were purposeful, and careful, because she was carrying a tray with three large mugs, each full of a steaming brew. His right hand lay instantly, instinctively, as if it knew what was there, on the bat that Krystal had used to level him, and then Elaine, as each of them had descended into the basement. When Krystal was just a few steps from the bottom, she suddenly stopped, as her mind registered a disturbing image—that Elaine was alone on the floor. As Krystal turned to see if Jack were hiding in wait for her, Jack swung the bat ferociously, hitting the tray from underneath.

As the scalding beverages drenched her face and torso, Krystal's piercing screams ricocheted off the walls, along with the sounds of the breaking mugs and clanging tray, as they smashed upon impact with the floor. Still a couple of steps up, Krystal came tumbling down the remainder of the flight, as the impetus from Jack's attack on her tray destroyed her balance.

Never one to dawdle, Krystal was up on all fours in seconds, then she rose to her standing height, steadfastly ignoring the burning pain and bruising that had battered her body. Her survival instincts overpowered everything else. Jack anticipated her quick recovery, so he stood there with the bat raised, ready to swing, as if he were at home plate waiting for the pitcher to hurl the ball at him. Across the room, having rid herself of the remaining ties around her wrists, Elaine was working intensely to free her feet.

Krystal's face was contorted in a wild grimace, as she assessed her chances of reaching the 3D printed pistol she had left on top of the printer before heading upstairs to make the cocoa. Jack was probably expecting her to lunge after him, but he stood to her right, Elaine was to her left, and the printer was

327

a b-line between the two of them. Could she reach the pistol before Jack grabbed at her and disabled her? She couldn't see any other option. She'd never make it up the stairs fast enough to evade Jack and escape the house.

"You might as well give up, Krystal. There's two of us, and only one of you," Jack tried to mentally disarm her.

"But it's not the fourth down yet," Krystal argued, thinking she could use a football play feint to the right to make Jack think she was going to make a run for the stairs, then she might have just the split second she needed to grab the pistol. She feinted. Jack swung the bat toward the stairs, the inertia of his swing precluding a break in that forward motion until the bat had hit an object.

Krystal lunged for the pistol. Her hands were inches away when she felt Elaine's grip pulling on her ankles. As Krystal fell forward, she thrust her arm toward the printer and grabbed, before the floor reached up to meet her. As Krystal fell, the gun went off.

Chapter 71

Detective Marsh and his fellow officers were racing up the front steps of Craig's house when they heard the gunshot. Marsh was ready with the key, only to find the front door was already unlocked. He and his colleagues ran into the house, guns drawn. A split-second assessment told them no one was on the first floor, but they could hear a bundle of loud exclamations and scuffling noise coming from the lower level.

With Detective Marsh in the lead, they headed down the stairs to the basement, where they found such a tangle of arms and legs flaying about on the floor that Detective Marsh wasn't sure how many people were entwined in the tussle, or who they were. In a booming voice, he ordered the scuffling to "STOP! Right NOW! Or I'll SHOOT!"

The bodies on the floor froze in place.

"Alright. Slowly—and I *mean slowly*—untangle yourselves, limb by limb, until you are all standing," Detective Marsh ordered, as his fellow officers stood around the clump on the floor with their weapons aimed right at them.

Krystal was the first to find her voice, before she was even standing tall. "Oh, Officer! Thank goodness you are here! I found these two rummaging around, probably trying to steal something!" she rapidly seized the high ground. "They must have broken in! They're not supposed to be here! They're trespassing!"

Detective Marsh stood quietly, ignoring Krystal's accusations as Jack and Elaine stood up, shaking the kinks out as they tried to regain some modicum of composure, before he commented, "And what are *you* doing here, Ms. Kincaid? You *are* Krystal Kincaid, are you not?" He had to admire how quickly this woman had collected her own composure, and produced a story line to legitimize her presence, but not Jack's and Elaine's. Thrown a little off kilter by the Detective's question, and his knowing her name, Krystal just nodded her head to admit she was who she was.

Chapter 72

It was about eleven o'clock Sunday evening, and they were all sitting around Kate Blanchard's living room, trying to understand, and digest, the events of the evening. Jack and Elaine still had a date with Detective Marsh, after this meeting, to give formal statements about what happened at Craig's earlier that evening. Right now, the group, which included Caroline and Diggie and Kate's husband, were trying to figure out if there was any chance, or hope, of putting enough pieces of this shattered campaign together to go forward. After all, election day was the day after tomorrow.

"If I withdraw," Kate was observing, "then Billingsley will win, by default. No matter how many millions of tiny pieces my race is broken into at the moment, I just can't accept the thought that someone supporting the policies that Billingsley supports, and with the lack of character—and lack of respect for the rule of law—that he has demonstrated by his bugging my office and home, could cake walk into the U.S. Senate because of the madness of someone else...something totally unrelated to the work and commitment that I have brought to my Congressional duties and responsibilities. I don't think I can live with that. *I* did not engage in the salacious affairs those photos allege. *I* did not murder anyone. Why should either, let alone both, of those occurrences cause people not to vote for me?" she finished. In spite of her words, her voice sounded full of defeat.

"The irony," Elaine added, "is that Krystal was driven to these wild actions because you have been so very effective. Your constituents know it, and they thank you with their solid support. Or at least, they have until now."

"May I make a suggestion, as an outsider?" Jack softly queried.

"Of course," Kate quickly encouraged. "You've been a rock in all of this, Jack, and I want to extend to you my deepest appreciation. I know! I know!" she put up her hands to quell Jack's reiteration that his reputation was as much at stake as the Congresswoman's election. "Just let me say that you are truly a remarkable agent of the media, nevertheless! Your integrity is impeccable. And I am grateful for that," she finished.

"Thank you, Congresswoman," Jack quietly accepted the compliment. "Here's my two cents worth: I don't think you should throw in the towel. Your conduct has been professional and impeccable. Your constituents, and the voters throughout the state, should be given enough credit to be able to judge this situation, and make their own decisions. But they need to hear directly from you what has happened, and what your commitment to them as a U. S. Senator would be. You cannot leave it to others to tell the story of this week's events.

"What I would suggest is that you make a public statement tomorrow, since the one that was planned for tonight had to be aborted. Make it about noon, after the news reports carry whatever they are going to carry on this story. Tape the statement, and run it as a political ad 3 or 4 more times during the afternoon and evening, with the last time about eight o'clock tomorrow night. You can gauge voters' reactions through a public opinion poll you conduct between 8:30 and 9:00 that evening. Granted, you'll need a lot of folks on the phones. But at least that will give you some idea of what you can expect the outcome to be after the polls close on Tuesday."

"You could always go public, too, with Billingsley's bugging your office and D.C. home," Caroline was trying to be helpful.

"No, Dear," Kate quashed that notion, "I don't want to stoop to his level. I don't want to win just by giving voters a reason *not* to vote for Billingsley because of conduct that has no relation to the policies he does or doesn't support. I want voters to not vote for him because of the horrific policies he would support in Congress. I want the voters to support me because I have worked hard to provide the best representation for my constituents, and for the public good, that I could. And because those new constituents state-wide whom I want to also represent, value the work that I have done for residents of my House district. I don't want to win because Billingsley bugged my office."

"And that's what sets you apart...from Billingsley, and most other elected officials," Kate's husband observed, as he put his arm around her, and kissed her cheek.

The others remained quiet while Kate mulled over Jack's suggestion and her own thoughts about whether, and how, to proceed. She finally looked around at all of the expectant faces surrounding her in the living room. She sensed nothing but encouragement, and support, from each one. "OK," she agreed, "I think your suggestion is a good one, Jack. I should not assume the people of my state would conclude they could not vote for me because of a falsified scandal."

Then she straightened up on the sofa where she was sitting, and went into work mode with, "I will call my pollster now, and ask him to set up a poll for tomorrow evening. And I will call my campaign press agent, and ask him to set up a time for a public statement back home with the local media outlets. And I'll have him reserve advertising time to replay the statement during the afternoon and early evening. I will fly back home in the morning, early, and I will write my own statement this time. That way, it will genuinely be my words, my thoughts, and my commitments that I will be communicating to voters. How's that for a plan?" she looked around the room, feeling somewhat uplifted, if only for having decided how to move forward.

"Whoopppeeee, Mom!" Caroline was first out the gate. "I knew you were a fighter!"

Elaine just smiled broadly, which told Kate all she needed to know. Her husband kissed her on the cheek again, and whispered in her ear, "I am so proud of you, dear. I love you very, very much." That was all Kate needed to hear.

Chapter 73

"Well, you sure know how to show a girl a good time, Mr. Amory," Elaine teased, as she and Jack walked out of the police station. It was a little after one a.m., Monday morning, and they had just spent nearly two hours being interviewed and giving formal statements about the events at Craig's house earlier that evening. As Jack pulled up in front of Elaine's house, he asked, hopefully, "Shall I shut the engine off, and we can make this an all-nighter? It is almost morning, anyway, and I'd bet you a gourmet breakfast that Diggie is still over at Caroline's," he encouraged.

"Ha-ha!" Elaine chided. "You'd lose that bet. I'm sure that he is already sound asleep and packed to fly home tomorr...I mean, later this morning, with Caroline and her family. You don't think he'll stay here in D.C. when Caroline's going to be home—not after they've become just about inseparable, do you? Besides," Elaine added, "he should be available in case Kate gets questions about the photos after her statement."

"We could always go to my place," Jack suggested.

Elaine leaned close to him, looking pointedly, and asked tenderly, "Hasn't your day been full enough, Mr. Amory?"

"Not full enough of you, Ms. Kent," he responded, close enough to her that she could feel the inviting warmth of his breath on her face, as she closed the remaining gap between them to accept the fulness of his embrace.

"If we spent all 24 hours of a day together, that still would not be a day full enough of you," Jack elaborated, as he looked deeply into her soft brown eyes.

Even in the dark, Elaine could see that Jack had, in that moment, bared his soul to her. She planted a kiss on the tips of her fingers, then transferred the kiss to Jack's lips with the touch of those same fingers, as she said very somberly, "Thank you for that, Jack Amory. Thank you for that."

As she exited Jack's car, Elaine suggested that he pick up some take out lunch and meet her at her office a little before noon, where they could watch Kate's public statement on TV together.

"Done!" Jack agreed. "Goodnight," he added, more softly. He waited until Elaine had closed her front door behind her, before driving on to his own abode.

Chapter 74

True to his word, Jack showed up at Elaine's office a little before noon, with lunch for two.

"Mmmmmm...something smells delicious," Elaine crooned, half-closing her eyes, as Jack's entry was preceded by the steaming aroma of melting cheese and tomato sauce emanating from two paper bags.

"Your favorite," Jack claimed.

Elaine sat upright at her desk in mock defiance, and asked, "How do you know what my favorite is? I don't recall ever saying."

"Well, if you want to eat what I brought, then whatever it is has to be your favorite!" Jack countered.

"Hmmmm...well I admit it certainly smells inviting. I smell Italian fragrances...tomato sauce, cheese,...garlic?"

"You're good! Meatball parmesan subs from Antonio's!"

"Antonio's?! Well, you couldn't do better for Italian take out, that's for sure!" Elaine was delighted. "C'mon, let's go into Kate's office, and watch on her TV. Otherwise," she laughed, "we might have to share our lunch with some of my colleagues!"

"I'm way too hungry to want to share," Jack moaned. "You may have forgotten, but we really didn't get anything to eat last night. I was so tired, I went right to bed, sans supper. And breakfast was one piece of toast."

"Oh, you poor baby! I agree, though, I'm really hungry, too." She got up and led the way into Kate's office. As she gestured to Jack to follow her, she tried to grab one of the bags he was carrying, but he pulled back playfully with, "Oh, no you don't!"

"Why not? I thought one of those lunches was for me!"

"It is!" he replied, enigmatically. "Just get in there, and let me spread the table, so to speak, so we can get all set up before your boss starts her statement."

While Jack unpacked their lunches on the very same coffee table that had hosted Billingsley's bug, Elaine switched on the TV to the station that the campaign pollster had told her would be carrying the full statement and press conference live. Then she joined Jack on the sofa, to find a paper tablecloth with a patriotic red, white, and blue design, laid out across the coffee table, and their lunches looking like a waiter in a tuxedo had just served them at a very expensive restaurant.

"Surprise!" Jack waived her to sit. She couldn't find the words to explain to him how sweet his gesture was, so she quietly sat very close to him on the sofa...very close...as she lifted the main course to her mouth.

"MMmmmm...that is *so* good!" Elaine exclaimed, as she bit into the sumptuous sandwich.

"You are so right!" Jack agreed, as he did the same, though his real attention was focused on the consciousness that Elaine's whole body was lined up touching his, from shoulder to ankle. They munched away in compatible silence until the station announced a break in its regular programming. "Oh, wait! There she is!" Jack alerted, as Kate Blanchard appeared front and center on the TV screen, standing outside her campaign headquarters. Elaine and Jack automatically relinquished their food as they leaned forward in unison on the sofa, to listen intently to what Kate Blanchard would say, standing there in front of at least a dozen microphones from a variety of news outlets.

"I wonder if some of those reporters are expecting Blanchard to withdraw from the Senate race," Jack said.

"Well, if they think that, they will be in for a whopping surprise!" Elaine responded forcefully. She was very proud of what Kate was about to do, and she was keenly aware of how incredibly difficult it was to do it.

Kate composed herself as she looked out at the sea of reporters. She knew she had nothing to be ashamed of, or defensive about, and that understanding gave her a calm confidence. She reminded herself that she was proud of the policies and programs she had pursued, and what she had accomplished in her eight years in Congress. She was comfortable in the knowledge that she had done nothing inappropriate, and committed no crime. This was just one more in a long list of press conferences she had held, or participated in, over the years. But she was sharply aware that this would be the most important press conference of her political career. And that it could be her last. She had decided to speak from her heart, with no written statement or teleprompter. And so she began.

"Thank you, Ladies and Gentlemen, for your interest in coming here today. I have a statement to make, so if you could hold your questions until after I've finished, I would appreciate it." The reporters were politely quiet, but you could hear rustling of papers, and restlessness in the crowd.

"I stand here today with a very, very heavy heart," Kate Blanchard began. "Just a few hours ago, I learned some truly devastating news. I learned that my very own campaign manager is the person who devised the slanderous attack on my candidacy that used phony photos to allege that I was having an illicit affair with not one, but three men...Washington lobbyists whose legislative goals I have consistently opposed as a member of Congress."

There were gasps among many of the reporters, because they were hearing this news for the first time. Kate paused a moment while her audience digested what she had said, and then grew silent, as if everyone listening wanted to make sure they didn't miss a word.

"I am told," Kate continued, "that the purpose of that effort was to derail my candidacy, with the expectation that my campaign manager would manage somehow to replace me, and be the person elected to represent this magnificent state in the U.S. Senate.

"If that wasn't traumatic enough, I learned at the same time that, again, my very own campaign manager...murdered her co-conspirator in that project," (more gasps) "the person who actually created the photos. She apparently feared that his weakness and cowardice threatened to sabotage the achievement of her malicious goal.

"I cannot comprehend how anyone...*anyone*...could engage in such destructive behavior to achieve elective office, at any level of government. I am horrified that someone associated with my election campaign could engage in such heinous conduct. But while she was *my* campaign manager in this election, I am convinced that she would have done what she did to whomever she thought was blocking her chance to achieve what she wanted. It just happened to be me, much to my regret and chagrin.

"Those of you whom I have had the honor to represent in Congress for these past eight years know...or I hope you all know by now...that I have worked diligently on your behalf, to protect what you value, and to fight for your interests against those who would diminish your ability to pursue your dreams and goals of 'life, liberty, and the pursuit of happiness' that is a cornerstone of our great nation. In Congress, I have supported those legislative measures that I believed would enhance your quality of life in so many ways, and would advance educational and economic opportunities for everyone.

"If you were wondering if I came here today to withdraw from this Senate race, you are very mistaken. I know there are lots of rumors, and false stories, swirling around the manufactured attack on my integrity and morality, and that my political opponents hope to capitalize on these false accusations. But I believe, as I have always believed, that the people of this wonderful state are better than to allow themselves to be swayed by blatant misrepresentation, and falsification, of the truth, in the face of what they know about me through my conduct and performance over the past eight years representing this District in Congress.

"I am here today to let you know that I remain a candidate for election to the U.S. Senate from this very special state in the Union. I have never engaged in inappropriate, or illegal, conduct. And I am proud of my record in Congress. I ask you, the voters, to examine my record closely, and if you believe I would best serve your needs and interests, then I ask you to vote for me tomorrow.

"Thank you. I will respond to questions now, if anyone has one." After which, just about every hand in the bevy of reporters went up, accompanied by a loud cry for attention.

Chapter 75

"I used to believe that all people were fundamentally good," Elaine was explaining, or maybe trying to just understand. It was election night, and Elaine and Jack were at her home, ensconced on her living room sofa, with their eyes glued to the nonstop news coverage of the election results across the country. Jack kept flipping among different channels, trying to track the results for Congress nationwide. He would publish another Special Edition tomorrow with all of the results collated and analyzed.

There was an open bottle of wine sitting on her coffee table, with two glasses that were still half full. A bowl of tortilla chips, and another of potato chips, with two or three options for dips, covered the remaining space on the table.

"I also used to believe that evil was an aberration," Elaine continued. "I know now that there are more people than I care to think, who are not good people at all. Who have much less good in them, than bad. I hate acknowledging that. But I still feel—I mean, I have to believe—that *most* folks are, indeed, basically good. That their hearts are mostly filled with decency and compassion. And that they want to leave this world a better place for their children than they found it. If I am right—then Kate will win. And I do believe I am right," Elaine bluntly concluded.

"In that case, I, too, believe that when all the votes are counted, your home state will have elected Kate Blanchard to the United States Senate," Jack proffered. But a bigger question in his mind was the elephant in the room, which he finally had to face up to. "And what about you?" he asked. "Will you follow her to the Senate?" Jack asked in a soft voice.

Elaine was quiet for a moment, collecting what had been a scattering of thoughts on the rest of her life, before she replied. "You know, ten days ago I would have said 'of course' without the least hesitation," Elaine observed. "I mean, it just wasn't an issue. If Kate won, as we all expected her to ten days ago, well, she had already promised me the Chief of Staff position in her new roll in the Senate. It was a given that I would go with her, as would anyone on her House staff who wanted to stay with her."

"And now?" Jack hesitantly inquired, wondering what, if anything, might have changed that certainty.

"And now? Well, now I think that when Kate becomes a U.S. Senator, that will be my cue to exit stage right. I'm not sure why this notion would, or should, have come up all of a sudden...or now...but I think it's time I strike out on my own. In what direction, I'm not sure. What I am sure about, though, is that I want to pursue *my* life...for me, not for someone else. I want to be the one standing on my own achievements, not someone else." Here Elaine half laughed, adding, "I just don't know what it is I want to do, or achieve! Does that make any sense?" she turned to Jack, her face full of brightness, but her nose scrunched up in uncertainty.

"It makes perfect sense," Jack assured her, almost beaming with joy—and relief? Knowing that Elaine had found herself, and on her own, without anything else to compromise her decision by trying to influence her in one direction or the other, made him very proud of her. "So much sense that I have a proposition for you," he then added.

Before he could continue, Elaine jumped in with, "A proposition, is it?" smiling enigmatically. Jack caught the clear innuendo, though.

"No! Not that kind of proposition—although," he backtracked suddenly, "the notion sounds very appealing, so let's not close the door on that idea yet—but, no, what I have in mind is, I hope, a tempting professional opportunity."

"Oh?" Elaine faked disappointment, before pursuing his dangling treat. "And what kind of professional opportunity can you tempt me with?"

"Look, Elaine," he donned his business demeanor, "you've worked on the Hill for eight years, in a very responsible position. You know the legislative process inside and out. You know how, and where, to find out the most obscure information about legislation and Congressional actions affecting that legislation. You know the players on the Hill, in both the House and the Senate. You have a gold mine of knowledge and skills for ferreting out the detailed steps, and understanding the implications, of the Congressional process and the politics driving it. You would be dynamite doing the kind of work I do. If you were interested in making a one-year commitment, to start, to work with me on my blog, I think you would really enjoy it, and together we could expand the features offered, and make the blog the premier source on Congressional activities."

And before she could turn him down, he urged, "I can pay you well. More than you're earning now."

Elaine's surprise overtook her, "With a blog? How could you even pay me at all? I think we paid about twenty-five dollars for the subscription I sent you this past week!"

"That's because subscriptions run from January to December. They cost one hundred and twenty dollars for the twelve month period. Any subscriptions that come in starting in April, I charge only a prorated amount for however many months are remaining in the calendar year." And to convince her of the truth in his offer of an increase in her income, he reminded her that, "I have over sixty-seven hundred annual subscribers now. That brings in a healthy annual income—you do the math!" he challenged her.

And when the dawn of light—or was it shock—spread across her face, he pushed his case, "And I now have only minimal overhead costs. So I am pretty comfortable, financially," and he couldn't quite hide the pride he felt being able to make that observation. "But it's no accident," he pursued his point. "My blog has a sterling reputation, that's why I've generated so many subscribers across the country. But with you working on it, too, we could expand the kinds of information, and special analyses, that the blog could provide, and really put ourselves on the map!" Jack was obviously excited about the possibilities that she would bring to his project.

Elaine searched his face to discover if he was serious, or just joking with her. But his expression was full of hope and anticipation, without a trace of humor. The whole idea was so amazing to her—and so appealing. She would be, like Jack, a political analyst and journalist. It would be her professional career, and she would establish her own credentials. Playfully, but also seriously, she asked, "Would I have my own by-line?"

"Of course!" Jack responded, without even a nanosecond of hesitation.

At this moment, Elaine's heart was overflowing with love for Jack, just because of who he was, and the kind of person that he was. She marveled at her good fortune that he had come into her life, and that he obviously held her in such high regard and esteem. Even without this 'proposition', Jack had been true to his impeccable principles, and true to his professional standards of integrity and honesty.

At the same time, he had been a consistently reliable partner in pursuit of the challenges to Kate's candidacy. He could have taken the easy way out, but he didn't. His blog would have survived. But survival wasn't what he wanted. Justice was a major motivator in all the work that Jack did. He firmly believed that 'the people' not only had a right to know, but needed to know, what policies and laws their political representatives were pursuing, and produced. Publishing phony photos, even though he could have credibly talked his way out of being blamed for promulgating false information, was against his ethical standards, and would not have provided justice. Not to the member of Congress affected, and not to her constituents. He chose the difficult path. And he stuck to it, under the most trying of conditions. No wonder I love him, Elaine told herself.

But her mind also registered a cautionary note. What would happen to the love that she believed they both shared, if they worked together, day after day? Jack was watching her, and he could read that concern spread across her face as clearly as if she had shouted it out loud.

"I know what you're thinking. We will be fine," he assured her. "No. Let me correct that. We will be better than fine. We will grow together. We will share more than most couples ever experience in their lifetimes. Because we will be sharing a commitment, not only to each other personally, but to work that we both passionately believe in. And I think there is nothing more fulfilling than being able to share *all* of life's pursuits with one very special person."

"Do you really think we can bridge that cavern, Jack?" Elaine asked anxiously.

"Yes!" he was firm. "You know why? Because we already have! What do you think we've been doing this past week or so? We started out working together. It didn't keep us from falling in love. And yet we continued to be able to work together on a common objective. As a matter of fact, I think our love made us better professional partners. It added an even more powerful bond. A deeper dimension of commitment—because it included a commitment to each other, not just to our quest.

"And who knows," Jack added softly...so softly that Elaine had to lean in really close to hear him, "that year-long professional partnership may even turn into a lifelong personal partnership."

"Stranger things have happened," Elaine beamed at him in agreement, and in anticipation.

"For the rest of our lives," he whispered, as he searched her face with imploring eyes, until their lips met with warmth and a promise full of a future together.

The End

"All good books are alike in that they are truer than if they had really happened and after you are finished reading one you will feel that all that happened to you and afterwards it all belongs to you: the good and the bad, the ecstasy, the remorse and sorrow, the people and the places and how the weather was. If you can get to that you can give that to people, then you are a writer."

Ernest Hemingway